CW01025040

Catesby's Ghost

A Mystery of Shakespeare

LEONARD TOURNEY

Catesby's Ghost

- A Mystery of Shakespeare -
Book Four

LUME BOOKS

LUME BOOKS

Published in 2021 by Lume Books

ISBN 978-1-83901-286-0

Typeset using Atomik ePublisher from Easypress Technologies

www.lumebooks.co.uk

For Judith, once again and always.

Prologue

The tongue is an unruly member, a flame of fire. It is a betrayer of truth to the shame of him who cannot keep his peace but ever must say what he thinks as soon as he thinks it. The apostle, James, speaks of this, which is sufficient warrant for its veracity, I suppose, being as it is from Holy Writ. Still, I know it be true for myself.

I speak from long and sad experience.

Yet, methinks Reverend Watts' sermon was more at fault than I. Our good vicar discoursed learnedly one Stratford Sabbath on Lazarus whom Christ delivered from the grave to the amazement of those witnessing the miracle. The vicar said it happened once but could not happen again, this miracle, until the Day of Judgement when all stand, a great army of hoary corpses rising from their graves. A grisly apocalypse, his vision of things.

I answered him to contradict, to stir the pot. I confess it freely, for I found the cleric's piety more annoying than exemplary. It has happened since, I declared, this rising from the dead, although now that I think upon it, the case whereof I spoke was perhaps a bit different.

"You mean to say, Master Shakespeare, that you knew one who was sick unto death and he recovered," the vicar said, charitably I think,

1

in an apparent effort to mitigate my audacity, or my ignorance of theology. His face beamed with a false benignity, for I think he liked me not, as I was one who had spent so many years in London, that sinkhole of vice and atheism, corrupted beyond redemption in his eyes.

"Something like unto that," I replied, though I had meant nothing of the kind. "Yes, something very near unto that."

The Reverend Watts smiled agreeably. No offence had been given, none taken.

But I spoke no more to him of resurrections.

The congregation filed out of Holy Trinity, my God-fearing neighbours, bless them. My wife, Anne, had come up behind me, tugged me on my arm, pressing me to hasten, not to linger in what she supposed was idle chatter with our vicar. We were having our daughter, Susanna, and her husband, the doctor, for supper, and the Reverend Watts, I believe, as well. Anne wanted to hurry home. Preparations needed to be made, and much was left undone. Hers was a timely interruption, benefitting all concerned.

Afterwards, at supper in New Place, my pleasant house on Chapel Lane, the vicar said nothing of resurrections. In days of yore or now. I was most glad of it. I had spoken a sad truth about a man I once knew, but it was a truth that would put me in great jeopardy of life and fortune were it to be conveyed to certain persons in high places.

And thereby hangs a tale.

But then you might have supposed as much. Tales, after all, have been my daily bread for years, as all in Stratford-upon-Avon know. Now, I no longer write plays. I sit at home or visit friends. I potter about in my garden. I read. I meditate upon my life, fast drawing to its close I fear, for I am past fifty years and that is no small thing in the ages of man. Yet an author gives up storytelling reluctantly, if at all. With his last breath he conceives a plot, even as he glimpses ahead his own tragic close and the gaping door, to heaven or to hell, as he has lived and Christ's grace affords.

Yet must I disclose it to someone before I die, this story. For all the danger it puts me in, I do avow 'tis too good a tale to go untold. After my death it will matter little, the part I played. Let them in high authority pull me from my grave, draw and quarter my bones, fix my skull upon a pole to frighten children and admonish the public against treason.

Powers that be, do your worst.

I shall be gone.

I shall sleep.

Public enmity shall not touch me, nor old guilt afflict me.

The truth be this and nothing less: I knew a man who suffered a traitor's fate and then rose from the dead. Reader, it is a strange, improbable tale, stranger than any the wily Persian queen, Shahrazad, ever spun to keep her own death at bay.

In telling my story I shall speak plainly, like one soul to another, not in jangling rhyme of the common folk, nor metered verse of the mighty and great. Who speaks so, but on the stage or in some sonnet? I avow I am a man, and a man's voice you shall have.

Whether you will or no.

Yes, it is a strange and improbable story I give you.

Still, what true story is not?

1

What manner of man was this Gabriel Catesby that I should write of him and be silent concerning so many greater ones I knew in my time? I cannot say I knew him well, or loved him well, or wept at his passing. Far from it. In the end I despised him as a traitor and villain devoid of natural affection and without scruples or any sense of filial obligation. Earlier, he had been a schoolfellow with whom, as a boy, I explored field and fen, woods and dale, and, when somewhat older, poached the odd rabbit or deer to my disgrace and peril of the law's long arm.

There were four or five of us, boys of good Stratford families. And then there was Gabriel. He was somewhat younger than we and poorer. He aped our ways as much as he could to be like us, was always smiling and jesting with a humour that disgusted rather than pleased. We suffered his companionship because, well, because I suppose we were gratified in being envied by him.

He was not from Stratford but from Lapworth, which, as you may know, is north of us, where he said he had lived with his mother and her two sisters, until there was some deal of trouble there. He never said what, though later I discovered the truth of it.

As I have related above, Gabriel was a schoolmate. I remember how he ever boasted of his family connections. He was, he claimed, a near cousin to a knight. His ancestors, he said, had been counsellors to kings. Still to us, he was but a poor boy, an outsider, living in Stratford with an old uncle. All of us found his boasting obnoxious. None of us believed a word of it.

That he once saved my life I allow, and my gratitude would have known no bounds had he not taken pains to remind me of it so often that I grew sick of it. All we boys did.

The event took place when I was fourteen or fifteen, I think. Gabriel and I and two or three boys of the neighbourhood spent a pleasant afternoon hunting in the woods. I remember not their names, save for Richard Fields, who became at length the first to publish my work in London.

Well, not hunting, we boys. After all these years, I give it its true name: poaching rabbits. Which we did more for sport than need.

Once at the end of our play, hot and sweat-drenched, we resorted to a sheltered pond and there, stripping bare until we stood beneath the trees like four young Adams on the sixth day of creation, we plunged from a dead stump into what we took to be the deeper part.

The water was cool beneath the trees and murky yet inviting. What boy could resist its allure? My friends leapt in before me, fearless, laughing. They swam about like dolphins, children of Proteus, their legs and arms unencumbered, the flesh of their bare backs and buttocks pale and shimmering beneath the surface.

I came last, timorous of deeper water, and had no sooner submerged when my leg caught upon a hidden branch. A sharp pain seized my calf and then, in my struggle to come up to air and sky, I quickly knew I was held fast.

How well I remember that dreadful moment, my head swelling, my chest aflame, and worse, I think, the sullen green water as murky as ditchwater and as foul tasting. And, yes, naught before my eyes but a Stygian darkness and the prospect of an untimely death.

Some say that in such extremities a man sees all that has gone before in his life, though he be sixty or seventy years or more and his few pathetic hairs be as white as bone. Every chapter and verse of his history, trivial or no, parades before his eyes on a stage in his mind.

I cannot attest to this. To speak truth, I remember no thought, but all my senses alight and sharp like a razor's edge and my gut by fear possessed.

I uttered no prayer for salvation. That must needs have required thought. Of heaven, of earth, and of me betwixt, my peril observed by a loving God powerful to save, of these weighty matters I had no thought at all.

Then my breath gone, my head about to burst, I felt the roots of my hair pulled upward and my body following meekly, my feet as suddenly detached from the grip of the submerged tree limb and in the next moment air, blissful air, filling my tortured lungs.

It was Gabriel who rescued me. He alone of my friends perceived my distress, swam to me, dove deep to free my leg from its cruel restraint, and pulled me to the grassy verge and my salvation.

How good is life at the best of times, but also at the worst, when one hangs on to mortality like a mere thread, a wretched petitioner to heaven above.

I remember my legs lingered in the water. I lay on my back, looking upward, enduring my humiliation as all stood around me, they peering down as though I were some strange, beached amphibian, a freak of nature on display to curious eyes. One friend laughed and made light

6

of my near brush with death. Another patted Gabriel on the back and commended him, saying that he was a brave fellow for leaping in after me and that now I owed Gabriel a debt.

"A debt?" I said.

"For your very life," he answered.

But how was I to pay so weighty a debt? In what coin? I never before had been saved by anyone. Nor had I known anyone saved so as to know what to do.

Later, limping home with the others, I even asked Gabriel, wanting to even the score. It was no simple effort. What was my life worth? I had no thought. I could not name a sum. Besides which, the situation was awkward. For I had joined in the mockery of Gabriel a thousand times, pointing the finger at his shabby garments, his pretention to affinity with a family far above his station.

Now I was his debtor.

"I pray you come home with me to Lapworth," Gabriel said.

"Where is that?" I said.

"Some miles distant. A good day's walk, perhaps a bit more. I want you to meet my family. My mother and her sisters. And, most especially my young cousin, who lives in the manor house."

This was Gabriel's request. After what he had done for me, how could I deny him? Besides which, I was curious. He had spoken of a manor house. Perhaps, I thought, these distinguished relatives of his were more than a youthful delusion.

It was but a small imposition. I passed my time in school, parsing Latin and enduring endless drills. When at home, my father, the prosperous glover, set me to work in his shop. Wherefore, the thought of an excursion out of Stratford to Lapworth, where Gabriel said his relations dwelt, was not without its appeal.

We boys were of the same age, or nearly so, Gabriel being slightly the younger though he was taller than I, broader in the shoulders with the square honest face of a ploughman. Still he was a boy. He had the promise of a beard at his chin and above the lip, the barest evidence of a moustache. His hair and brows were fair, his expression somewhat dull, yet he had an exuberance that seemed more forced than natural to him. He seemed ever so much to be one with his schoolfellows. He was an outsider amongst us, for we were Stratford boys and that he attended a Stratford school did not make him one of us.

Besides the which, he was a Papist although, since I long suspected my father of being likewise, this meant little to me who, as a youth, despite churchgoing, rarely had religion on my mind.

So it was that Gabriel and I set out for Lapworth and, wonder of wonders, with my father's blessing. How secured I this rare permission you might well ask?

My father had learned of how his son was saved by this lad and how Gabriel claimed high-born relations in the county. My father was impressed on both counts, perhaps more by the latter fact than the former. He said that he knew this Catesby knight, at least by reputation, and that he was a good man much abused by the old queen. He said Sir William Catesby was a man of deep religious feeling, and one whose present misfortunes were undeserved. Thus, where I sought mere permission for my journey and expected some resistance to my plan, I achieved a strong encouragement from my father that I should go.

"Take two days, three if needed. But do not dally along the way. Here, Will, go you to Sir William Catesby and take something with you."

My father went to a chest in his chamber and drew from it a pair of gloves of his own making. They were, I knew, of excellent sheepskin and cut and stitched most artfully, as was my father's skill. "Go you

8

to Lapworth, to Sir William. Commend me to His Honour and give him the gloves."

"Shall he pay well for them?" I asked, thinking that given their quality they should bring a handsome sum.

"By God's blood, William, he shall not give a penny. Be clear about that should he ask. Beseech him to accept the gloves as a token of my esteem."

"Your esteem?"

"You heard me, son."

I waited to hear more. What esteem did he mean? I had never before heard my father speak of any Sir William Catesby. But now here was a relationship that I was obliged to honour. Yet my father added nothing to what he had already said. He pointed to the door. "Go you, son. Remember my words and your errand."

The journey we took was not arduous. The weather was tolerable, the road north toward Lapworth dry and certain. We supposed it would take us all the day and into the next, at least in part. We would sleep by the road, for we had no means for an inn and little inclination to lodge there. We were boys, used to living rough. All was an adventure, which a modicum of hardship made the more delicious to us.

We talked along the way, sharing stories, some true, and spoke of persons in the town we thought worthy of our commendation or contempt. But Gabriel spoke most of his Catesby kin. He said his ancestor was Sir William Catesby.

"So my father's said. So, Gabriel, you have said, many times."

Gabriel looked at me seriously. "Not he who now bears the title, but he of famous memory. Sir William of whom I speak was a great lord in the time of King Richard, third of that name. He was counsellor to that mighty monarch. He was, as well, a good son of the Church."

By this phrase, I knew Gabriel meant a believer in the Old Religion, the great Bishop of Rome, whom many of my pious Stratford neighbours held to be the very Antichrist.

In those days, my father was a man of importance in the town, and in the countryside about. He was an alderman and knew everyone, even persons of some stature who dwelt in houses that dwarfed our own. But in matters of religion, he was most circumspect. All we Shakespeares worshipped in Holy Trinity Church as the law required, but I knew my father's heart was not in it. All he did was for form's sake, and perhaps for my mother's.

And so, Gabriel Catesby and I made our way.

Happy youth, fearless, innocent as angels, ignorant as savages.

2

As we came to our destination, Catesby Hall appeared to my youthful eyes less imposing than I expected, given the fame of the family whose seat it was. Gabriel steered us away from the courtyard and main entry and toward the side of the house to a more modest portal which I supposed was used by servants and tradesmen.

I said, "You are a kinsman of the lord of the manor and yet he would have you come in with the servants?"

"None uses the great doors," Gabriel explained, taking me by the arm and drawing me quickly to this lesser entrance, as though he feared someone spying upon us.

"None?" I asked, thinking it was an improbable answer to my question. For surely the master of the house would use the chief portal with its fine stone masonry, noble columns, and elegantly carved door, not to mention his gentlemen guests and their lady wives. And indeed, I later learned that this was a lie, this business about the door.

It was not the last or worst of many lies Gabriel's lips would utter in the years I knew him.

Before we were able to knock upon the postern door, it opened and there appeared a tall, severe-looking man of my father's age or older, very solemn and eyeing us disapprovingly as though we were vagrants come abegging or known malefactors for whom the constable should be presently fetched. "What will you?" he asked in a broader Warwickshire accent than my own.

"This is Stokes," Gabriel said, turning toward me. "He's Sir William's butler, his factotum."

I gave a little bow of acknowledgement. Stokes said nothing but kept a sharp eye upon us, lest we attempt to enter without his permission. Then he recognized Gabriel.

"You were not to come here again, Master Gabriel. Them was Sir William's orders. If he knew you was here, it would go very badly for you."

Then Stokes glowered at me. I felt his withering contempt as though my very association with Gabriel damned me in his eyes. "And who, pray, might you be, sirrah?"

I liked not his disrespectful tone. He was after all a servant, regardless of whose, and though I was not yet a man, like any youth I had a grown man's pride.

"I am Will Shakespeare. My father is alderman in Stratford-upon-Avon, a town you have surely heard of. I bring a gift for Sir William."

"He is not here," Stokes answered. "And, yes, I have heard of Stratford and that it is a town of neither merit nor distinction."

Before I could respond to this insult to my birthplace, he continued:

"Both my master and his lady have gone to London, not that that be any of your business." He glared at me with withering contempt.

"Is my cousin here?" Gabriel asked. "Perhaps he will accept the gift my friend intends for his father."

"He is here, but whether he will see you I cannot say."

"Tell him I—we—have come. With a gift for Sir William."

Stokes glared, tight-lipped. After a long pause, he said, "Very well. Wait here, the both of you."

Stokes shut the door. We were left alone.

"This is passing strange," I said.

"What?" Gabriel asked.

"This house," I said. "This is your family and they treat you no better than a beggar. This Stokes fellow is insufferable."

"Oh, that's the old man's way," Gabriel said, as though he had never been slighted. But I liked not the butler's way at all. Even as a youth I detested noxious servants who made themselves little tyrants over those beneath them while toadying to all above.

Presently, Stokes returned. I expected him now to thrust us out. I was beginning to suspect that all Gabriel's claims as to his family connections were as illusory as moonlight. But it proved otherwise.

"Master Robert is in the garden. With his tutor, Master Goodyear."

"Come, Will, I know the way," Gabriel said, guiding me by the shoulder around the other side of the house.

We came then upon a spacious garden, very well laid-out and tended, covering as much land as an acre or two. We walked along a gravel path between a tall stand of trees and shrubs until, in a little clearing, I saw two persons seated upon a stone bench conversing pleasantly. One held a book in his hand.

The boy was a pretty youth of seven or eight years, certainly not more than ten, well dressed in ruff collar and suit of light colours. His companion was a man of twenty-five or so with a round, smooth face and long, yellow hair that fell to his shoulders. I noticed he wore a crucifix about his neck, but on looking up to where Gabriel and I stood, he moved his hand to his throat, as though his intent were to conceal it from us.

13

Drawing nearer I could see the book on the man's lap was a small leather-bound volume like a prayer book or hymnal.

"Hello to you, cousin," called the boy, seeing Gabriel. Gabriel responded warmly. He seemed as relieved as I to see that we should not be treated as housebreakers.

Robert Catesby, whom Gabriel addressed as Robin, smiled in a friendly way, but the other man, whom I took to be the tutor Stokes had mentioned, continued to regard us with curiosity at least, if not mild annoyance that we had disturbed some private communication.

Gabriel walked forward to take the tutor's hand. The man had stood as we approached, placing his book on the bench. "I am Miles Goodyear," he said, making a curt bow.

I could see now that Goodyear had the look of a schoolmaster, which is to say that he had a somewhat solemn mien and his voice had the cultured sound of someone used to hearing himself speak and enjoying the experience. I suspected that while he might be Robin Catesby's tutor, he was also a priest, for it was not uncommon in those days, as now, for priests to take up residence in the country houses of Papist families such as the Catesbys, disguised as servants, sometimes as tutors and well-prepared to hide in holes and hallows within the house should the authorities come seeking them. The book, the crucifix, the effort to conceal them both, all bespoke this.

"My friend has brought a gift for your father," Gabriel said.

"A gift," the boy said, his eyes bright with expectation. "What manner of gift?"

Gabriel nodded to me and I took from inside my shirt the gloves, unwrapped the oilskin with a good deal of ceremony, and showed them to the young master and to his tutor.

"Artfully crafted," Master Goodyear said, fondling the gloves and smiling with approval. "Sir William will be pleased."

14

"They were made by my father," I said, unable to keep the pride out of my voice, for they were truly an excellent pair, as fine as my father had ever made. Indeed, they would, I believe, have done honour to a duke or prince in his wearing of them.

"And the occasion for the gift?" Goodyear asked.

"It is a gift, nothing more. My father asks for nothing in return, but Sir William's goodwill."

"Goodwill, you say. To what end?"

"That he should know of my father's esteem."

I would have spoken more eloquently had I known whereof I spoke. But all was a mystery to me, this tribute to a knight of whom I had never heard. Yet my father had given me what to say and I had said it, whereby I had some satisfaction in having done my duty.

Young Robert Catesby took the gloves and said he would deliver them to his father upon the knight's return, which he said would be within the week. Then he stood, took Gabriel by one hand and the gloves in the other, and the two walked toward the house, leaving me alone with the tutor.

"My father is John Shakespeare of Stratford-upon-Avon," I said after an awkward silence.

"Ah," Goodyear said, "Shakespeare. I think I know your father, or at least know of him. Shakespeare. It is a most unusual name."

This was not the first time in my young life that I had heard this, though we Shakespeares were not a few in Warwickshire and had inhabited the county for generations according to my father's account.

"My father's an alderman in Stratford," I said again, not sure the tutor had heard.

"That I know."

"For these three years," I said.

"A worthy man, indeed, your father," Goodyear said. "I have heard much good of him."

I moved to follow Gabriel into the house with Robin Catesby, but the tutor beseeched me to remain with him. He sat down again upon the bench and gestured to me to join him, smiling as though I were an old and dear friend and we should now pass a pleasant time conversing. I was not eager to do this. I had known the man but for a few minutes, and already I disliked him. From his behaviour thus far, I could see that he was arrogant and condescending, but I suspect my enmity was more deeply rooted than this. The young, rarely gifted with wisdom, are often endowed with sound instincts.

"You seem an intelligent lad," Goodyear said, examining me head to toe. "William, is it not?"

"I am William, usually just Will."

"A bright boy, one that I would gladly teach. I shall call you William. It is more dignified. You do not mind, do you?"

"No, sir," I said. "You may call me as you like. It is all one to me since I am who I am regardless of my name."

"Quite so," Goodyear said, smiling.

I confess I was flattered by this man's attention and his praise of me, despite my dislike of him.

He asked me then if I were in school and what I was being taught and how, for he being a schoolmaster of sorts himself he was eager to learn of other teachers' methods of instruction. Some were good he said, effectual in planting knowledge deep in the pupils' heads and hearts. Others wasted time of teacher and pupil both and were the recourse of idiots and fools.

Bristling a little at this seeming dismissal of my school, I told him that we read every day Cicero and sometimes Seneca, but that we also learn mathematics and other useful knowledge. Goodyear nodded approvingly and said this was excellent, that every boy should learn Latin and from the best authors of antiquity, which these indeed were.

"There are other things, of course, to be learned, Will."

"Other things, Master Goodyear?"

"I speak of matters of faith, of religion true and undefiled."

"I and my family attend Holy Trinity in Stratford," I said, eager to dispel the idea that we Shakespeares were heathens, for I rather suspected he thought that of us without knowing our family at all. And his easy assumption made me dislike him even more. "So we have done all of my life. We have a clergyman there, a learned man, whose sermons are full of matters of faith, as you have called them."

I felt put upon, I confess it, for although I spent little time in those years thinking of God and His commandments, I knew I was about to hear Goodyear's mighty arguments for his faith and against my own, such as it was.

Goodyear smiled thinly, then leaned toward me as though to whisper in my ear. His lips reached only within an inch of my cheeks. I remember his breath was moist and a little sour. I liked not such closeness to a stranger, which is what he was.

"Your father may kneel in Holy Trinity on each Sabbath day and so avoid the strictures of the law. Yet if I know of him at all, I know his heart, and it is with the Old Faith, the true faith."

I was about to deny this, to defend my father's good name as a follower of the Queen's religion, not Rome's, but somehow I knew that what this tutor had said was true. I had long sensed my father's reservations about the reforms that the bishops of England had undertaken with the queen's blessing. Then it occurred to me that it was best I say as little as possible to this man, who I suspected was a priest but might just as well have been a spy, determined to secure in me some damning admission that would prove the undoing of

17

my father and me both. For though I was young and inexperienced I knew this was the way of things in my country then. They are hardly better now, a web of deception and treachery, wherein a wrong word in the wrong ear could mean prison or even death.

"I know what I see my father do, and my mother," I said.

Goodyear the priest—for now I had little doubt that that was what he was—smiled his subtle, condescending smile. "Be it as you have said, young Master Shakespeare. Nonetheless, I have something to give your father in return. It is but a modest gift, yet I do think he will value it most highly."

I could not help asking him what manner of gift it was.

"Oh, it is a mere paper, a sort of testament, which he can read and affirm at his leisure if he finds it agreeable with his conscience. But it is for his eyes alone, not for yours. May I have your word on that?"

I shrugged and agreed. A paper, or testament, as he had called it, meant little to me. I was but a youth. Such matters as documents belonged to a quite different world than I was wont to inhabit.

Goodyear had a small bag beside him. From this he removed a sheaf of papers, selected one sheet, folded it neatly in quarters, and handed it to me.

"Remember," he said, "you have given me your word, young Master Shakespeare. This is for your father's eyes only. Not for yours, not for your young friend's."

I took the paper, which meant nothing to me and which I could not imagine meaning very much to my father and put it inside my shirt. I had no reason, after all, not to comply with the man's wishes.

Then he asked me what friends I had and if I liked pretty maids and if so what features made me admire some rather than others. He said that it was easy to fall in love for silly reasons when a boy was

18

young, but with maturity and wisdom, other qualities would appear the more desirable. "In men as well as in women."

I listened to him discourse on this topic for some time but felt very uncomfortable with it, for it all seemed very personal what he spoke of and really none of his business at all whom I might love or not and for what reason.

Presently Gabriel and his cousin rejoined us. I presumed the gloves had been placed where Sir William could find them upon his return, a supposition Gabriel confirmed. "The gloves are upon Sir William's desk with a note saying who they are from. Now we must go."

I was surprised at this, for Gabriel had assured me we would be welcome in his kinsman's house, and I had looked forward, after our two-day's journey, to a soft bed in one of the manor's guest chambers, of which Gabriel had said there were many. I was also much hungered, having eaten but a handful of nuts and an apple that morning.

"Farewell then, Master Shakespeare," Goodyear said. "I trust we shall meet again in God's good time."

"Perhaps," I replied, not really caring whether I met the tutor again or not. Then Gabriel shook his young cousin's hand, bid farewell to him and to Goodyear and we set off the way we had come.

"What happened to your great kinsman's hospitality?" I asked, not only disappointed but angered too, feeling I had been betrayed by Gabriel's stories. He told me Sir William was hospitable enough, and his good lady, but not Stokes, who in his master and mistresses' absence pretended he owned the house and had no love for Gabriel or his mother.

"For what cause?" I asked, thinking it strange that a servant's will could so usurp that of his employer's. It seemed an unlikely cause for our cold treatment, but then I was but a boy and as yet unacquainted with the devious turns of family ways.

"When I was younger, I lived in the manor," Gabriel said. "But then my mother and her sisters were cast out, falsely accused of corrupting my young cousin, which upon my oath they never did."

"You seemed friendly enough just now," I observed, remembering how warmly his young cousin had received him.

"Oh, Robin never blamed us for aught, nor Master Goodyear, his tutor. It was Stokes, and then Stokes persuaded Sir William. Stokes said my mother and my aunts practiced black arts. He said that I had given their son an amulet with certain magical properties within. I suppose thereby I offended Sir William's religion. It's certain I offended Stokes."

"Had you?" I asked.

"I gave him an amulet. It was an innocent thing."

"What was its purpose?"

"A healing instrument. It was some concoction of my mother's. We shall stay at my mother's cottage," Gabriel said, as the crenelated roofs of the manor disappeared behind us.

"And where would that be, this cottage you speak of?"

"Not far. Through the woods. Not more than a mile. An easy walk."

"Shall we be welcomed there?" I asked, not bothering to hide my annoyance and supposing he would surely discern the irony in my question.

He did not.

"Of course we shall," Gabriel said. "Trust me, Will Shakespeare, o ye of little faith."

3

It was near a mile through deep woods to the cottage where Gabriel's mother and her two sisters lived, yet it did seem ten or more, so footsore I was. Still Gabriel seemed all the stronger for the journey, singing as he walked, not seeming to care that I had fallen silent and become the worst sort of travelling companion. That is, one whose studied silence is no less than an implied rebuke. Truth was that I blamed Gabriel for the unpleasantness at the manor. He had told me he was well approved by his kinsmen, not that he and his mother had been cast out, despised and even feared.

Yet should I not have known? He was, as I have said, given to the lie. At least he had not lied about the relationship between himself and the family whose name he shared, though its peculiar nature was as yet undisclosed to me. That would come later.

But I must describe his mother's humble dwelling, or you might imagine it quite different from what it was. I said humble dwelling, and you suppose some rustic cottage, festooned with flowers or other greenery, impoverished but not devoid of appeal, a monument to the simple dignity of the rural poor, their pastoral joys and pleasures. But wait! Think you rather of a dismal cave, its roughly thatched roof no more than a foot or two above the forest floor, as though it were not so much rising from the earth as does a proper house, but descending into it.

A thin column of smoke rose into the late afternoon air and gave the woods around us a sweetish air. I remember it had no windows, the hovel, and the door was not of wood but heavy canvas, like a scrap of ship's sail much abused by wind and rain.

Entering—or descending, I should say—we found a smoky interior and an earthen floor and the crudest of furnishings. There was a square oak table, covered with knife marks and stains. Three stools sat about that table. In the dark corners of what appeared to be a low-ceilinged single chamber there was a wide bed, and against a wall, a rough stone hearth within which sat a cauldron. There was a manner of crude crucifix upon the wall, made of two sticks bound with string. What I remember most after all these years, was the odour—not an animal odour, but that of decayed fruit, sour and sweetish at the same time and enough to make one retch, or at the least yearn for the purer air of the woods.

"Your mother lives here?" I asked incredulously, praying that it was otherwise, for this horrid hovel was no better than a pig's sty in my youthful estimation. I had expected poverty since Gabriel's mother was but an outcast, perhaps poverty of the direst sort, but not this abject squalor.

"Only for the time being," Gabriel said, taking no note of my dismay and disdain, which must have been as evident in my voice as on my face. "She and her sisters, my aunts, we have lived much better in the past, helped by our kinsmen. But their fortunes will change. My mother is assured of that."

"By what assurance?" I said, taking a closer look at the single bed, which was a mere pad stuffed with straw and very wide, so that I suddenly had the vision of the three women sleeping there side by side, their bodies wrapped about each other for warmth, or perhaps some more godless purpose. I had heard of such women, unnatural in their practices. Were these dismal surroundings not a suitable habitation for such perversion?

"My mother has a gift," Gabriel said, as though informing me so made better the deplorable conditions of the place.

"A gift?"

"What is obscure to most is visible to her," Gabriel said. "She can tell the weather on Sunday when it is but midweek. She can foresee the fate of our neighbours. And what will transpire in the villages round about."

"Can she see your fate, then?"

Gabriel laughed. "Oh, of me she said I would die from hanging, and for that reason sent me to Stratford to live with her brother that I should be spared Sir William's enmity."

I wondered that Gabriel should treat so lightly this grim prediction. His faith in his mother seemed unfeigned. But I knew him well enough by then to know him to be cheerful to a fault. In the months I knew him as a youth, and the several years I knew him as a man, he was sanguine in any weather.

Yet I admit I was affected, remembering what Gabriel had called the false charge against him and his mother, the charmed amulet. Was this, in truth, a witch's den? Now, though weary from the day's journey, I wished nothing more than to be free of this cursed wood, free of Gabriel and his kinfolk, great and humble. I was about to make for the door when I heard voices without.

That they were female voices I took on faith, in the likelihood that Gabriel's mother and her sisters were returning, yet they were low and husky and might have been taken for men's voices otherwise.

23

"That will be my mother and her sisters," Gabriel said brightly, going to the doorway and beckoning me to follow. This I did readily, eager to take leave of this vile den.

But it was too late for that, for in the next moment the canvas parted and there appeared the denizens of the place, three women of forty or more years, garbed almost identically in dark, grey gowns that dragged upon the ground and were covered with a generous measure of dirt and leaves as though they had crawled home rather than walked.

They presented to me a frightening spectacle, given Gabriel's account of his mother's strange gifts. If I ever imagined in my heart how a true witch might appear, these three creatures were the very likeness thereof.

"Why, who is your young companion, my son?" the first one said, whereby I knew this to be Gabriel's mother and the leader of the three. "Nay, tell me not, but let me guess. He is some friend of thine, come with thee from Stratford town. Is it not so? And is he not the youth whom thou snatched from the jaws of death, from the bottomless pool, so that he might breathe still and live?"

How the mother learned of her son's heroic effort on my behalf, I had no thought, save he had written her of it. But, of course, he would have. As I have said, it was a story he told freely and with undisguised pleasure, often elaborating on the details such as that the pond in which I had nearly drowned was without bottom. Whoever told him that? Did not all ponds have bottoms? Surely even profundity had its limits.

"He is indeed, good mother, a worthy friend." Gabriel seized me by the arm and led me closer to the woman who had just spoken, so close that I could see every little wen and wart upon her face.

"Ah, I can see he is worthy," the woman said, taking me in from

24

head to toe as though I were a cow or pig she was about to purchase on market day.

"I am Will Shakespeare," I said, not waiting for Gabriel to give me a name.

"Welcome, then, young Master Will Shakespeare. You are most welcome in our home," she said, extending her bare, mottled arms as though she were presenting the place as a gift I would be ungracious to refuse. "We three live simply here, blessed by God and His Holy Mother. These are my sisters, Delia and Lucasta."

4

I should gladly give fuller account of these two women were my memory the sharper. Time has given them a similar countenance in my ageing brain. These curious creatures were pale, bony, sharp-chinned, with dark, piercing eyes. I do not know to this day whether these two other women had powers equal to their sister's but like Gabriel's mother they fit every trait of witchery all knew in those days. Moreover, I did not know whether they shared the same parents or merely the same disposition or curse and were therefore not related in blood, but merely his mother's confederates in whatever dark enterprise they practiced.

I mumbled some words of thanks for the expected hospitality, for Gabriel had given me to understand we were to spend the night beneath his mother's roof before returning to Stratford in the morning. As for me, I could not conceive, even as weary as I was, that I could sleep beneath such a roof, feed in so filthy a den, breathe such noxious air.

Did I regard myself too good in those days of youth to break bread with the humble of the earth? I am not too proud now in my maturity to confess that it was so. At home, my mother set an abundant table. We ate well and often. But these dreary woods were as much another world as was Catesby Hall with its stately towers and its arrogant, malicious manservant and supercilious priest. How I wished to be home, and at my own hearth now, listening to the familiar voices of my father, mother, my brothers and sisters.

We supped outside of the hovel, seated upon roughhewn logs, there not being sufficient space within to sit at the table. I remember we were served a sort of gruel with a few globs of grey meat within.

Wooden bowls we had. Long wooden spoons. What was this strange stuff? I could not tell by the taste and did not want to think what creature it might be. That it was neither fish, beef, or fowl I was sure, but rather some crawling thing I would have disdained to eat in happier circumstances. That there was neither wine nor other liquor to quench our thirst did not surprise. We were invited to drink from a bucket of water, drawn from a nearby spring. The water, I must admit, was fresh and sweet. I thanked God for that, for nothing else in those dismal environs was so.

As we ate, I observed my chief hostess more closely. She who claimed to be Gabriel's mother might have at one time been fair to look upon, God knows. Now she was hideous, her face marred. Her hair, what I could see beneath the hood, was grey, but on her pointed chin sprouted black hairs. Her complexion was as pale as a corpse's, and her voice, as I think I have already said, was deep and hoarse, as though something—perhaps some evil spirit—dwelt angrily within her bosom.

The two other women, Delia and Lucasta, ate in silence, from time to time looking up at me curiously. Their glances, whose intent I could not interpret, made my blood cold.

Having eaten as much of the gruel as I could stomach, I was the more ready for sleep, though I knew not where I would lay my head there being but a single bed within. Still Gabriel insisted that I should be entertained.

"Entertained!" I exclaimed, imagining a Morris dance or magic show, trained bears, or a band of musicians plucking lutes or beating tabors.

As for entertainment, it was no less than what a guest deserved, Gabriel said. He turned to his mother. "Good mother, my friend would like to know his future if it can be revealed to you."

"Would he?" she asked, looking up at me and smiling grimly. "Why, 'tis easy enough to ask—and for me to provide. Come, young men, come within."

Obediently we followed. What else was there to do? The night was falling fast; the wood about was dark and threatening. That we should now embark on the journey home was beyond thought.

Within, Gabriel and I were seated on two of the stools while the three hags stood before the iron cauldron in which our supper had been prepared earlier but was now to be a part of the ceremonies to follow. All of us sat, or stood, in silence for a while, the cottage becoming almost completely dark but for the fire beneath the cauldron.

The three women began to chant.

It was a strange and solemn sound that caused me to be much afraid, not only for my body's health but for my very soul. These curious ceremonies I knew to be the black arts, not lawful practice a Christian could approve, and though I might not be a pious youth, yet was I Christian born and bred. I had endured many a tedious sermon, partook of Christ's body and blood, could recite the creed by heart and I know not how many passages of Holy Writ which I could quote upon demand, locating them neatly by chapter and verse. I knew thereby that these obscure ceremonies were no hallowed practice, but some alien thing, some devilish thing.

I suspected now that Gabriel and his mother's expulsion from Catesby Hall was surely warranted. The amulet she had given young

Robert Catesby was no doubt a charm compounded by the same noxious stuff now brewing here. Though it undoubtedly had some benign purpose, at least in the eyes of Gabriel's mother, the good Christian inhabitants of Catesby Hall would have looked upon it with horror and disdain.

As the cauldron steamed, the three women took from little boxes each held, and sprinkled some substance, I know not what, into the boiling water which exuded now such a noxious odour that I began to feel sick. While I struggled to avoid emptying my stomach on the dirt floor, the witches—I call them such boldly, for such I now knew them to be—inhaled deeply of the stinking brew.

Finally, they ceased. Gabriel's mother turned to her son and said, "I am ready, son. Let me place my hand upon thy brow."

She was about to do this when Gabriel said, "Nay, mother, my friend William first. He's our guest."

The woman paused, gave her son a strange look that may have been reproof, or perhaps even gratitude. She approached me and placed her cold hand upon my forehead.

I shrunk from the touch. Who would not? It was as I supposed a serpent's skin would feel dared I caress its scaly side. But she pressed her palm the harder, bringing her long, slender fingers down to cover my eyes.

Now I was as if blind, the darkness absolute.

She took a deep breath. I could hear her lungs fill with the steam of the cauldron. She began to speak, in a different voice now, high and shrill, not the deep, huskiness of before. "You are a boy who shall grow to be a man, Will Shakespeare. You shall be great, greater than your father, yet your gifts shall not be the same. You shall leave this place and travel far, travel to a city of thousands upon thousands of souls who will commend thy gifts and take delight in thy works."

"What manner of works?" I heard myself whisper, for I wanted to know. What was I to become and what to do and was it for good or ill? Who would not be curious under such circumstances? Her prophetic utterances might well be a fraud. I suspected they were. Yet was I curious still. Would you not have been, had you been I?

The woman paused and pressed my forehead again. She continued in her shrill, unearthly voice. "You shall draw forth spirits from ancient times and make them live again. Kings and queens, bishops, and great nobles you shall summon from their graves. Heroes, too. I see men in battle, clashes of swords, the thunder of musket and cannon."

"Shall I be a soldier then?" I asked, interrupting her rapturous vision.

"Nay, no soldier," she returned.

I was right glad to hear this, for I did not suppose that I could ever wound, much less kill, another soul, though I be seized by anger or commanded of God. Nor had I desire that some arrow or blade pierce my bosom to my hurt and my mother's grief.

"Then a magistrate, like unto my father?"

"Neither," the woman said. "I see you renowned, both in your time and beyond, but from no famous victories or your possession of high office. I see you in no royal robes or fine garments."

"Yet still great?" I asked, beginning to doubt that the woman could see anything in the smoke but her own strange imaginings.

"You are like a tree from which many leaves fall. But for you there will be no winter. No winter. No end of leaves…"

Her voice drifted off. No end of leaves? So I was to become a tree. This made to my young mind no sense at all. She removed her hand from my forehead. She breathed deeply, and I opened my eyes. The fire had burned low beneath the cauldron. The stench was less. Or perhaps I was only becoming inured to it.

The ungodly ceremony ended. I was greatly relieved, but not

greatly edified. I was but a boy, yet I knew a fraud when I saw it. I did wonder that Gabriel was not disturbed by his mother's prophecy that he should die a malefactor's death, even if she had concocted the vision. Who would want to hear such a prophecy from his mother, or even imagine that it might be true? What mother would burden her son with such a curse?

5

That night I slept badly outside the cottage on the cold ground, not within, where the three women curled like cats in the same bed, their breathings a raucous chorus of snores and whimpers.

Gabriel slept beside me. His sleep was deep, untroubled, but mine a riot of horrid shapes. I dreamed of the three women and their dance about the cauldron, their moans and unintelligible chants, their sharp bloodless faces, corpse-like and grim.

In my dream, the few hairs at the chin of Gabriel's mother had become a beard, long and coarse like a horse's tail.

And what was I in this nocturnal vision? A boy, a child, younger than I was in my waking life. The three women of the dream loomed large above me. They thrust their faces into mine, mocking me with their prophecies, jabbing their sharp fingers into my face accusingly.

But what I had done to wrong them, to wrong anyone, I had no thought.

At dawn I awoke, relieved that the horrid night was done, my body racked with a thousand aches and pains from the hard ground. Gabriel lay beside me. He was still in deep repose, but I put an end to that with a sharp poke in his ribs, which brought him up smartly. My greatest desire now was that we should set out for Stratford.

And so we did, not bidding goodbye to the women who I supposed slept still in their hovel, save for the old woman's cat, who was wandering about the yard. After all these years, I remember its name, Graymalkin.

"My mother's familiar, Graymalkin," Gabriel said.

"Her what?"

"You know, her familiar, her familiar spirit. A familiar is—"

"I know what a familiar is," I said, bridling that he took me for a simpleton. "It's a forbidden practice. It is a dog, cat, owl, toad, some other creature. Or so it does appear in its outward parts. But in truth the familiar is the devil's tool, condemned in Holy Writ, forbidden by the Church."

"What church?" Gabriel asked.

"Why any church, the Roman pontiff's church, or the old queen's, or some Puritan brotherhood. It is all one with them all. It is witchcraft plain and simple."

"Then they misunderstand the workings of Nature's God," Gabriel said, surprising me with the vigour of his defence. "The cat comes to her in the night and whispers in her ear. She counsels. She protects. How could that be blameworthy? Consider the prophecy concerning yourself. Did it not please you to look forward to such greatness?"

"Consider the prophecy she made of you, that you should hang. Do you not believe it? If so, do you not quake with fear at so dire a prospect?"

Gabriel shrugged. He even laughed. "Oh Will, it matters not about me. We are talking about my mother's gift."

We quarrelled about this for an hour or more, whether witchcraft fell within or without the bounds of true religion. Neither of us made headway in our disputation, until each seeing the futility of persuading the other, we fell into another silence and contented ourselves with continuing our journey toward Stratford. But although I was convinced of the rightness of my view, I finally conceded, at least in a way, although not vocally. What did I know of these dark arts or their practitioners? Were there not things in heaven and earth beyond my own philosophy?

If I was certain of anything it was that.

Within the month, Gabriel left Stratford. Why he left or where he went I did not know. I cannot say I missed him. I never liked him that much, and I had grown more than weary of his constant boasting of how he saved me from a watery grave.

I put him quite out of mind, him and his wretched mother and her sisters.

6

Now has merciless Time plucked a score of years or more from my petty store of days, and I am well removed beyond my youthful joys and misdemeanours. I am husband, father, exile by choice from Stratford's little scene. I thrive in London, the very centre of the world. I, who was once young and lean as a reed, am now middle-aged, balding, paunchy, easily winded, plagued by numerous minor ailments including aching joints, dyspepsia, and flatulence.

It is a pretty picture, is it not? Yet it is what I am, and so no more of that, for even a flawed creature may still be honest.

As for London itself, the town is in arms and turmoil, for our ageing queen invites in her much-anticipated demise ever so many upstarts who would seize the throne and make it theirs by some claim of blood or pretence of care for the public good.

For prudence's sake, I remain aloof from all these broils in which several of my old patrons are up to their necks. I am neutral, walking a thin line of caution. I see what befalls traitors daily, their heads upon pikes, their families disgraced and driven into penury or exile or both.

Sadly, I think of Robert Devereux, the late Earl of Essex, and remember his many benisons to me, though his rebellion was foolhardy and tragic in its end. That tragedy is several years past.

Advance you then to the summer of 1604. The queen is dead. The new king reigns along with his buxom Danish wife and I know not how many of his Scottish countrymen, poor lords and sundry hangers-on who, like sun-loving fowl, have winged south to have joy of His Majesty's bounty. London is plague-stricken. The theatres are closed. A pall hangs over the city I have come to love, but sometimes fear and sometimes hate as well, for like so much in this life, it is a heady brew of vice and virtue, hope and despair.

We players spend much time in Mortlake, a village nigh unto London, where one of our company, Augustine Phillips, has built a fine new house.

Since arriving in London years before, I have gone from holding horses in Newington Butts, to apprentice actor at the Theatre, to shareholder and principal playwright in the Lord Chamberlain's Men, which was the company that was most favoured at the court, despite Edward Alleyn's protestations that his Admiral's Men were more deserving. Truth be told, they were not so by any credible measure, as our later royal appointment would prove. As the King's Men, we now wear royal livery and perform at court as oft as it pleases the King's Majesty, who for all his eccentricities and whims is not a bad fellow at all. He dotes upon us players, a happy disposition that for me hides a multitude of sins.

My progress pleases me and amazes those companions of my youth who live still in Stratford and learn of me from afar, or whom I visit on rarer occasions now. I write my wife once a quarter or more, send her money and my best wishes, ask her to remember me to my two daughters. I live a jolly bachelor here, yet with many friends, both men and not a few women, poets and playwrights, patrons who love my craft, fellow actors without whom my work is naught but an empty page, void and voiceless.

Of Gabriel Catesby, I had not heard a word since leaving Stratford. After our journey to Lapworth, our association, such as it was, ended.

But then he appeared again in my life, and in a strange, most unforeseen way.

On a day of that year, my good friend and colleague, Dick Burbage, came round to where I lived. My rooms were in Cripplegate, in the house of Christopher Mountjoy, who was a Frenchman, as any man could hear in his voice and see in his manner. *Chez* Mountjoy was a large, well-timbered house with a generous front and over-hanging upstairs so that it put the narrow street below, Silver Street, in perpetual shade.

Monsieur Mountjoy did a brisk business in his ground-floor shop there making woman's headpieces, which were in much demand in the city, sometimes even decking the heads of fair ladies of the court. My rooms there were modest but comfortable.

I came to know them all quite well, the Mountjoys, and some years after this I was called as a witness in a suit Mountjoy's son-in-law brought against the old bugger for withholding a promised dowry. The son-in-law won the suit. I do not think he ever collected the money, at least not all that was promised him.

But I digress.

So it happened thus. Dick Burbage came to me in a flurry of gestures, his face flushed, waving his arms in that way he had when he was in distress, troubled with his wife, or undone by some busi-ness gone bad at the theatre. He said, "Augustine Phillips is sick unto death. I have only now come from his house where he lies abed, hot to the touch. If he does not at this moment stand before his maker, he shall anon."

"So shall we all," I answered, then regretted my feeble quip, though it was true.

You may remember Augustine Phillips. Although he is dead these dozen years or more, he was proficient in his craft and did our company no little service when he appeared before the Privy Council to absolve us from any involvement in the rebellion of the Earl of Essex.

I remember asking if it was the plague Augustine suffered, praying it was not, for I loved the man and would not have seen him suffer so wretched a death. He was a good friend as well as a fellow sharer in our company's profits. As an actor he was insightful and subtle. I would have mourned his death a month or more had his illness proved fatal. Besides, his part in my current play of *Othello* was most important. Augustine played Iago, that devilish villain, and played it most convincingly.

"Shall he recover, think you?" I asked Burbage.

"The doctor says he may, God willing. But I warrant you he will not tread upon the boards this week or the next."

"I must go to him," I said. "It's the least I can do."

"God knows it is more than you should do," Burbage said, pressing my arm. "It may not be the plague that troubles him, yet it is a contagion, and while we will miss him in the company for the time being, we should miss you the more. Stay your charitable impulse, Will. Don't be foolhardy."

I recognized the truth in what he said but felt myself a coward nonetheless. Not visit a sick friend? It seemed most uncharitable indeed.

We had conversed thusly in my chamber, which was close and cluttered with my papers and books. "Let us go abroad," I said, taking

Burbage by the arm and steering him toward the door. "I promise to stand clear of disease, but we are still left with finding someone to fill Augustine's shoes as Iago."

"Ah," Burbage said. "Big shoes, I warrant you. But you remind me of another matter."

"Out with it," I said, pulling Burbage along with me. We were walking toward the Globe. I remember the day. It was overcast and gloomy. The street was crowded. Walkers, wagons heavily laden, much noise, but not more than the ordinary.

"A man came to me today, one of your countrymen," Burbage said.

"An Englishman? No novelty there. London is full of them."

"From Warwickshire. He speaks like unto you. Were I to hear his voice and not see his face, I would swear it be you who spoke."

Fled to London, I had never believed it important that I should shed my native speech, as though I were sloughing off an old self for a new. I liked the muscle of my Warwickshire tongue, its lilt and crack. Was I not understood by all and sundry? Wherefore should I change or be ashamed? Sir Walter Raleigh spoke broad Devon and never altered his tongue, even for the queen, who ever delighted in his speech, or so I heard.

"Well and good," I said. "That is a mark in his favour, his speech. But who is this worthy fellow and what does he want?"

"He says his name's Gabriel Catesby."

It took several beats of my heart and as many steps before I remembered the boy so called. But then I thought it might be another with the same name. Was it not possible? Gabriel was a common enough name, and there must have been dozens of Catesbys in England beyond the ones I had known.

But then Burbage said that which left no doubt of whom he spoke.

"Catesby said you owed your life to him. He said you had fallen into a bottomless pool and he had snatched you from the jaws of death. He said he revived you with his own breath."

So it was Gabriel.

Yet that business about reviving me with his own breath was invention pure and simple. I had no memory of his mouth upon mine, a repellent thought. I had come around by myself, thanks be to God. Gabriel had embellished the tale again, added drama to fact.

Why was I not surprised?

I remembered how I had once been entertained by his witch of a mother and her two sisters, as cursed as she. I supposed Gabriel had said nothing of that in tooting his own horn to Burbage about saving me from a watery grave.

"He wants to join the company," Burbage said.

"Does he?" I exclaimed. "Is he a carpenter then? An actor? If an actor, is he practiced or merely one who aspires, as do half the boys and men in London?"

"He says he is experienced. He says he has played many parts."

"Not here in London," I said.

I knew all the actors in the city. My old schoolfellow was not amongst them.

"In York and other parts north," Burbage said.

"We have no place for him, whoever he is. Even if he is as practiced in the craft as he claims," I said, still trying to imagine the boy I knew as a man nearly as old as I, as an actor. As I have said, I had heard nothing of him for years, had not thought of him. Yet here he was again, turning up like a bad penny.

"I wonder, Will, could he take Augustine's place? Perhaps his appearance is a godsend. We could let him read the part. If he stumbles, he shall fall. We will give him thanks for your salvation from an early

40

death and give him the boot. If he succeeds, the gain is his and ours. The play shall proceed as we have planned."

"We shall see. I will hear him speak the speech," I said, not hopeful, and not eager to let Burbage imagine that Gabriel was anything to me but a boyhood acquaintance who had, yes, saved my life once and who, perhaps, deserved a hearing on that account. Yet I was curious to see Gabriel Catesby again, if only to verify that it was indeed the boy I had known and not some imposter bearing his name and mimicking his speech.

"Tell him to come to the theatre, this afternoon."

"I think he's already there," Burbage said, pointing ahead of us to where I could see a solitary figure standing next to the theatre door.

Had I passed Gabriel Catesby in the street on any ordinary day, I should hardly have noticed him, for his manner and dress were not such as to impress or set forth any singularity in him. Certain I am that I would not have recognized him as my old playfellow from Stratford. He was a good deal taller, which was within reason, he being but thirteen or fourteen when I knew him, and thicker about the waist and shoulders. His face was lined with age and his chin and jaw fringed with a ruddy beard, his eyes cerulean blue. "Master Shakespeare," he said. "Will. I have much joy in seeing you again after all these years."

I do not remember my response. Perhaps I said, "Yes, and I have joy in seeing you again too, friend Gabriel." Or maybe I said, "I think I remember you, sir. Pray remind me how we knew each other." Or perhaps it was something in between. Whichever, it was no more than a few minutes later that we had entered the theatre, taken seats in the lower gallery, and watched, Dick Burbage and I, while Gabriel recited lines from an old play. I have long forgotten which. It was none of mine.

41

As it befell, Gabriel was not ill-suited for the stage. His voice was clear, full, confident. He did not mumble and squirm as some players do when nervous, as he must indeed have been with Burbage and me attending so closely. His gestures were manly, expressive, not frantic or unnatural. Could he play the devious and devilish Iago of my play? God only knew, but at that moment I could not think of another so ready at hand and hungry for the work, for he had confessed that he was in desperate straits, just come to London and eager to establish himself. He said he had sought me out because of our former friendship. He had no money, he said, and no ready means to secure it.

In my bag I carried a copy of the playbook, much marked and revised, for we had yet to perform the play. I let him spend an hour or more reading it, while Burbage and I busied ourselves elsewhere. When I returned, Gabriel leapt from the bench upon which he had been sitting and ran toward me, almost throwing himself upon me in his joy.

"Why it is marvellously done, Will," Gabriel cried, discarding the more formal mark of respect by which he addressed me earlier. He slapped me on the shoulder good-humouredly as though the years intervening were no more than a blink of the eye and he was as confident of having the part as he was of breathing or seeing.

I was not so sure.

I chose a scene in the third act, a favourite of mine, in which Iago tempts his general Othello into believing that his wife, the innocent and most virtuous Desdemona, has betrayed him with his lieutenant Cassio. It was not a bombastic scene of the sort Gabriel had chosen when first presenting his skills to me, but one, rather, that required subtlety. I told him I would read Othello's part and pointed out the passage. My own reading I downplayed, feeding him his cues and commenced so doing with, "*What dost thou mean?*"

42

Gabriel's eyes fell to the script, he took a deep breath before responding, then spoke the lines:

Good name in man and woman, dear my lord, is the immediate jewel of their souls.

He did tolerably with the lines following. You will remember them, I would hope. That business about filching a good name. How one's purse is but trash, but a good name lost leaves a man poor indeed.

When Gabriel came to the most important line, he lifted his eyes from the page and looked at me directly, imploringly I would say, as though he were not acting at all, but his counsel he drew from some deep well of his own sad and obscure history.

Oh beware, my lord, of jealousy. It is the green-eyed monster which doth mock the meat it feeds on.

He did not go onto the next line, but paused, looking at me now as though to ask if what he had read was not sufficient proof of his skill.

I had to admit to myself it was. I reckoned that if he could so deliver the exhortation he had pronounced, he might well do the rest. Was he as able in the craft as our Augustine? I thought not. Augustine's voice was the more resonant; it would carry farther in the theatre. His speech had the more variety and because Augustine was London born, his speech would undoubtedly be the more intelligible to the throngs in the theatre who when they did not understand a line would shout out their complaints, drowning out all to the detriment of any good order in the house. Nothing offended me more than such outbursts, yet there was little to be done to stop them, save the audience should be muzzled or there be no audience at all, a thing unthinkable.

I looked at Burbage. He nodded his approval. Our votes were those that counted.

"Gabriel, you have the part," I said. "If you can keep it. Augustine Phillips will recover. The part is his when he returns."

"But if I do well in it, as well as Phillips, may I continue in the company?"

What could I have said to this appeal? I said yes with my lips, but in truth not my full heart, for I had more than a dozen reservations about Gabriel, not the least my memory of him as one whose stories about himself were often false and self-serving. Yet that had been in his youth. Did not one change with years, grow the more prudent, more discerning, more measured in temper? I thought myself to have done so. Why not he? Besides, I owed him much. He had saved my life. Now I was saving him from destitution, a charitable act from which I myself might benefit should he prove as capable as his audition promised. Perhaps that was enough to even the score. A life for a life.

Of the plays I had written in those first years of the century, my tragedy of the Moor, *Othello*, was my favourite. Why? Because of all my characters he was the most deserving of compassion, the most evocative of what those old Greeks had believed moved the audience to pity and awe. And all of that in turn had heightened my dedication to this work.

I had found the story in an old book by an Italian named Cinthio. The tale was in choice Italian, and a friend who had been in Rome and knew that tongue read the story, translated it for me, whereby I had constructed my plot, devised my characters. Otherwise, the language was my own, for I needed no tutor, Italian or English, for my phrasing. My pen flowed in a mighty stream with only occasional eddies and backwaters, with which I still struggled in the manuscript.

The performance thereof was yet to come. Within the month I thought to stage it, perhaps before the king.

That day I returned home still thinking about Gabriel. He had not said where he lived but he had promised to return each day to the theatre. That was enough, at least for Burbage. For me, I desired more. His sudden reappearance in my life made me uneasy. I imagined him spreading the word among my friends that he had saved my life, even as he had already related this to Burbage. Would he also have regaled them with fantastical tales of his mother and her two sisters to my friends? Would he declare that I had consorted with witches? Should he do so it was unlikely my conduct would be dismissed as youthful folly but rather as some hitherto concealed and perverse credulity, subjecting me to ridicule and scorn.

Later that night I dreamed a dream. I was not surprised therein to find myself in Stratford again, asleep in the bed of my youth. I had the thought that my parents were below me in the large kitchen of our house. In this same dream, I heard my father's voice, though in life he had been dead for two years. Where were my brothers with whom I shared the chamber? Then I felt myself not alone. There was—how may I describe it?—a presence there. I looked about me. I had no lamp. The chamber was as black as pitch. Still, I was aware I was not alone. One feels such things, does one not?

And then I saw them, emerging from the gloom. Gabriel's mother and her sisters. The three witches, all staring down at me as I slept, their faces white, their mouths agape, their eyes luminous as starlit pools.

I expected from their lips some prophecy, some stern admonition or dire warning.

Their silence was more terrifying than their words could have been.

I awoke in a damp of sweat, my throat dry, my ears ringing with the sound of a cry that might have been my own and, if heard, would certainly alarm my landlord and his family.

But the cry too may have been a dream, for come morning I descended, and nothing was said at the breakfast table about alarms in the night.

I was much relieved. I liked the family with whom I lived, and I cared about what they thought of their theatrical lodger.

7

In the days to follow we rehearsed my play three times—not in the theatre where in the afternoons another play was being performed, but rather in a large chamber above a tavern on Fleet Street called the Whale. It was a space we rented regularly from a man named Hopkins, a ruddy-cheeked fellow who loved our art and charged us a pittance for the space. Eight of us were there, some of whom had not yet met our newest player. It fell to me to introduce him to the others, which I did hurriedly in hope he would not offer his account of my near-drowning and his heroic rescue. Of that exploit, I had heard enough. For one thing, I did not know how to respond to it. Whatever may be said otherwise, gratitude is a purse half-empty, its contents quickly spent.

"Friends, this is Gabriel Catesby, who will be our Iago."

I was surprised when several of the company declared that they already knew Gabriel. Two of the actors embraced him as though he were a brother. Another kissed him on the cheek. Yet another slapped him on the back. Gabriel had no time to relate our mutual history before he was engaged in conversation with the others, but since he was so well known there, I supposed he had already described how fate had joined us in an indissoluble bond.

We eight filled the low-ceilinged chamber. It was hot and the air filled with tobacco smoke, which I ever found an offence to my senses. Yet I forbore to upbraid them for fellowship's sake. All of us had been drinking and we were very merry for the theatre had been filled each afternoon that week and each day there were more who wanted to come in than we could allow. Besides the which, our patrons now included several powerful lords that I supposed would further our state in the commonwealth and strengthen us against the carping Puritans who were ever accusing us of corrupting youth and foolish women.

Burbage had charge of the rehearsal and played the Moor. I was to play Brabantio, Desdemona's outraged father. I played my scene and then was content to simply observe the others. It was my habit. I would imagine I was not the play's author but one of the audience, for whom the plot was yet to be revealed. I would attempt to pay less heed to the words, my dearest love, and more to the scene: how we filled the space, moved as bodies, might be observed.

I attended most to Gabriel's performance. He had learned each line by heart already, and his countenance assumed the deceitful mien of the devious tempter most excellently, as though he were to the manner born. I could see in the face of the others their approval of my choice of Gabriel as Augustine's substitute.

We did the whole of it, the play. I stopped our players once to change a phrase, and once or twice, like a zealous gardener, rooted out a word and planted another, pruned an overflowing phrase and left a bare but, to my mind, more effective remnant. Such was my practice too, for when was a play truly done? But the company was used to that. When we were finished, we all prepared to leave, wishing each other a goodnight, when one who had been amongst us a year before and had left for another company in the city came into the

48

chamber and said it was most urgent that he talk to me. His name was Samuel Rogers.

"I am for home and bed, Samuel," I said. "Tomorrow, if it please you?"

"Tomorrow if it please you, Will. Yet were you to know my news, you would want to hear it now, rather than later. And alone, Will, alone, I beseech you."

"*Beseech* me? Then are you indeed serious with this if you must beseech rather than merely ask," I said.

"I am, Will. I truly am."

Samuel looked about the room suspiciously.

"Come then," I said, thinking this might be no small matter and wanting to be free of listening ears too, especially those of Gabriel whom I suddenly saw was watching us intently as though what Samuel might say to me was of concern to him as well.

Samuel, I knew, was not given to sudden fears or anxieties, fantastical conspiracies or plots.

"We shall talk anon," I said. "Below stairs. You shall have all the privacy you desire to relate your news, whatever it may be, and I do pray it is worth my while."

"Never fear," Samuel said. "You shall know all and agree my story is worth my few minutes in telling it."

8

I led Samuel Rogers down Silver Street where we passed into St Olave's Church, a small edifice, yet happily suited in its solitude for my purpose. This venerable pile was empty, it being near midnight, for I soon after heard the chimes resound across the sleeping city. We two sat in the darkness on a bench by the entrance and the old baptistry. It was cold in the church, colder than out of doors, but at least it was a dry and private place, which was what Samuel seemed to require to disclose his mysterious news.

I said, "I pray you speak now and quickly. Wherefore this unwonted urgency, Samuel—and the need for secrecy?"

I heard my friend breathe deeply, as though grieved. Now was my impatience greater than my curiosity, for I considered how I might be better employed at such an hour, at my books or, perchance, sound asleep like any other decent man in Christendom.

"Speak, or I swear I'll leave you here to meditate by yourself."

"I was at the Talbot," he said. "Yesternight."

I knew the Talbot, a scurvy place, as much brothel as tavern, not usually patronized by us players, much less persons of quality.

"I hope you took nothing to eat there, or to drink. It is the very mouth of hell and mother of all temptations."

"It's not that bad, Will. I was meeting a friend."

I laughed. "A friend? Some pert doxy, I warrant."

"Not so, Will, but an old friend, although he never came. Besides, you're a right hypocrite to taunt me about women, with that French landlady of yours, who I hear has planted horns firmly on her husband's head more than once."

"She has," I said, laughing again. "But I have no hand in it. She already has a lover, and I suspect she is with child by him to hear her husband's complaints."

Again, I urged him to spell out his tale, determined that if this was a piece of idle gossip, I would strangle him, even if God's house were the scene of the crime.

"What did you overhear? Speak now or fare thee well and I am home to bed."

"Two men, nay three, sitting in a corner. Huddled like conspirators."

"Go on," I said. "Why conspirators? Only because they kept their voices low? More power to them, for the usual complaint is that such company speak too loudly, as though they were in a field calling out to each other. As for the huddling, who does not in company that they may keep their business to themselves? I see naught untoward in what you observed."

Annoyed, I stood, preparing to leave, eager to set course for home.

"Hear me out then," Samuel said, seizing my arm. "I walked by them. I swear I was as close as I to you now. I could smell the foul breath of one of them. I was on my way to the jakes out of doors, you see, my bladder full and about to burst."

"And?"

"They spoke of Othello."

The name caused me to gasp. I leaned toward him, until my face was but a hand's span from his. "What of Othello?"

"They told the story of the whole first act. Just as you wrote it, Will. They mentioned Desdemona, Brabantio, Cassio, Iago—all the characters of your play—and I do swear they recited more than one line, as though they were as familiar with the text as yourself."

"The whole play?" I exclaimed.

Now you must know that I was ever careful with my drafts. Especially when it was a play yet to be birthed, in this case not yet fully sprung from the womb of my imagination. To my knowledge, no one but the dozen players in our company had seen my *Othello*, and each had sworn to keep mum about it, our usual practice. More than careful, I was scrupulously so. For such thefts of another's work were not uncommon in those days. They still are, I believe.

"Did you hear how they came upon this knowledge? It was not you who disclosed it, was it?"

That my question had offended my friend was clear. I could see it in his eyes. I could hear his pain in the darkness.

"Never, Will. I took the same oath as the others to keep the play to ourselves, knowing that script thieves lurked. I had never before seen any of these men, nor have I seen the play but heard tell of it.

"What manner of men were they? Their ages, their faces, their speech? Tell me all you remember of them."

"One—he who spoke of the play so confidently—had a scraggly beard, hairs every which way. He was about fifty years or thereabouts. Tall, a big man, barrel chested. The kind who likes to push a smaller man around for the sheer joy of it."

"His speech?"

"Not London. From the north, maybe York, or even farther."

"Scotland?"

"Not that far north."

I leaned forward. Our knees almost touched. "And the other two?"

"Younger, one a mere boy. Fourteen or fifteen. The older of the twain had a long, narrow face and eyes crowding about his nose. Yellow hair beneath his cap, pushed back on his forehead. A mean fellow, if God ever created one. He looked like a shopkeeper who sells you a half-penny's worth for your penny without a blink in his eye and attends church regularly as though his greed were a cardinal virtue."

"How did you know the big man was tall if he was sitting at a table?" I asked.

"I could see his legs. I came near to tripping over them as I passed. They were long and thick legs, like the trunks of trees."

"And the boy?"

"As I have said, thirteen, fourteen, not more than fifteen I should say. Smooth skin, rosy cheeks, lips likewise, a handsome lad."

"Were any names spoken?"

"Well, as I said, Othello, Casio, Iago."

"No, no, I do mean their names, those you call conspirators."

"I don't remember."

"I pray you do make the effort," I said. "Your news is worth little otherwise."

Samuel paused. A man's thoughts are silent. But in this instance, I could almost hear Samuel's brain labour, recalling the scene, hearing again the whispered voices.

"I think one was called Phillip."

"Which?"

"The lad, I think."

"And you can remember no other names, facts, or circumstance by which you could say who these men were or how they came to know my play?"

Samuel shrugged, then said, "One quoted a line or two."

"Whose line?"

"Iago's. About stealing a purse."

"Jesus," I whispered.

And then it came to me who the narrow-faced man was.

Nicholas Morgan had been a young actor in the Admiral's Men when I first came to London. I remember he played the women's parts then. He was a competent actor. Later, when I too achieved that glory, to be an actor I mean, we performed together in a work by Thomas Dekker. I have forgotten its name, the character I played, or its very plot save to say it was a plodding tragedy, cribbed from some Spanish story and most ill-suited for transplantation to English soil.

We were not friends, this Nicholas Morgan and I, only acquaintances. I liked him well enough but not greatly, for he always seemed of too sour a temper for me. He was from Norfolk, I think, and like me had fled the outer regions of the land in hope of making something of himself in London. In those days, it seemed half the persons I met in London were from somewhere else.

He seemed honest to me then, at least as honest as any man about the city. Now it appeared by Samuel's report that Morgan had chosen a devious course aimed at undermining my authorship. Was it he who had stolen my play, concealing himself somewhere in the empty theatre while we rehearsed and writing down the lines in some moth-eaten journal, then concealing the same in his shirt?

Or was it one of the other two at the table?

After my long time in London, I believed I knew everyone in our craft. But these were two whom, by Samuel's description, I did not know. If they were indeed from the north, say Norwich or York, as Samuel had surmised by their speech, then this would follow.

Or was it one in my own company who betrayed me?

Did I think of Gabriel Catesby as the suspect in chief? He was new to us, had no long-nurtured loyalty to our common cause, had lied more than once during the years I had known him. Besides, the others in our company I would have trusted with my life. Given that the several weeks of his employ with us would have allowed him full exposure to the playbook and considering his quite competent memory, as demonstrated, I resolved to start with him, at least.

But even before that I thought I would visit the Talbot.

But not alone.

I prevailed upon Samuel to accompany me the night following. I wanted to see these men with my own eyes, confirm Samuel's report with my own ears.

9

I did not oft visit the Talbot although it was the public house nearest to the Mountjoys. I knew its host, Francis Wright, having met him more than once at the theatre, for he delighted in plays and rarely missed one from my pen. But the wine and ale were suspect, the company coarse and ill-mannered, and of nights there were often brawls and, once, a murder so gruesome that it had been spoken of in the city for a month's time until the event lost ground to some new enormity.

But this was London, not Stratford.

It was near eight of the evening when we came to the place, finding it full of custom, mostly labouring men by their dress, a few impoverished clerks and apprentices and a handful of women whose demeanour and dress left little doubt as to their profession. We were hard put to find a table to ourselves but at last were led by our host to a bench in a dark corner.

It was a seat not designed to accommodate anyone without complaint, but we made the best of it and were cheered to find it afforded a broad view of the larger chamber and its patrons. I ordered up something. I don't remember what, not intending to drink it but believing it was my host's due. Otherwise, we were merely taking up space, which out of courtesy I was loath to do.

We sat silently and watched.

It was near midnight when Samuel said, "Will, look you. There they are. At the door, even as we speak."

I looked up to see the very three men that Samuel had described and confirmed for myself that the second of these was in truth my erstwhile colleague Nicholas Morgan.

In the three hours of our sojourn in the Talbot the number of patrons had increased and then decreased, so now there were only a dozen or so men still there to partake of mine host's bounty, such as it was. Nicholas and the two others had found their place in the centre of the room.

"Come," I said. "Let's confront them."

I approached slowly, with Samuel at my back. Samuel was a timorous soul, disliking confrontation. I knew this of him and had not expected him to be by my side, his hand on the pommel of a sword or the haft of a knife. I was much of the same inclination but was driven by too much curiosity and outrage to be cautious.

He of the unkempt hair and beard looked up at me. I had not said a word but already I saw malice in his eyes, and it came to me that while I did not know him, he did know me and already anticipated my reason in approaching him.

"I am Will Shakespeare," I said and waited. Now all the men, including my former colleague, looked up from their drinks and stared. They seemed not to notice, or if they did, not to care that I was not alone but that Samuel was with me.

The hairy man spoke. "I know who you are, Master Shakespeare. How may I serve you? Do sit, sir, for we shall all be honoured by your company."

I declined with a stiff bow, determined to remain standing. He nodded to the man at his side, the one I knew from a dozen years before.

"This is Nicholas Morgan. And our young friend is Phillip." He paused for a moment as though he could not remember the young man's family name or perhaps never knew it, but then said, "Phillip Gilbert."

"I think I know Master Morgan," I said, looking down at him about whom we were speaking. "It has been some years, but if memory serves, we acted together once in Master Dekker's play."

Nicholas Morgan acknowledged this with a nod but said nothing. I think he hoped I had forgotten him, but the truth is that my memory is sharp, most especially for names, and from the wrinkles aside his eyes, the harder jaw, and the fuller beard peeked the younger version of himself I did well recall.

I presented Samuel to the men, who seemed not to recognize him as one who passed by them the night before and overheard their conversation.

Now was the tavern almost vacant but for us, the tables being cleared of pots and tankards, a suggestion of tobacco smoke left to remind us of the bustling hours.

Our host stood behind the bar watching us. Impatient for us to leave, I think. And it was late. Yet our business remained undone.

"As I said, Master Shakespeare, what can we do for you, being as you are so celebrated a maker of plays and I do believe often a player therein?"

"Tell me first, your name, sir," I said to the older man who was clearly their chief. "I like not conversing with strangers."

He smiled, assumed a false modesty as transparent as glass. "Oh, sir, I am a nobody, hardly worthy of your notice. My name is John Flynt."

I said, "Well, John Flynt, my friend here was in this very tavern this past night. He overheard, not by intention, a conversation of you three in which certain matters were discussed."

"Certain matters?"

"Certain matters that pertained to me, sir."

Flynt frowned and rubbed his forehead as though he were confused or his head ached. "With all due respect, Master Shakespeare, we three never spoke your name, nor did we say aught of you, either good or ill."

The other two, my old colleague and the boy, affirmed the same. No one had spoken of me, nor of my plays, nor of any matter that might be thought to pertain to me. They regarded me with blank stares.

"Not my name but my words," I said, more sternly.

"We know not your meaning, Master Shakespeare," Flynt said.

"You were quoting from something that I wrote. Those words were my words."

"Were they indeed?" Flynt exclaimed, his eyes widening in astonishment.

I detected amusement in his eyes. Now my anger came near to overflowing.

"It seems your friend here was mistaken," Flynt said, pointing an accusing finger at Samuel. "The tavern is a boisterous place of an evening. There are many voices, many things said that a man may overhear and misunderstand. As in this case, evidently."

Behind me still, Samuel protested, "I did not misunderstand. I heard you recite lines from Master Shakespeare's play, one that has yet to be seen in the city or at the court. The lines about Iago and Othello and Desdemona. You recited Master Shakespeare's very words."

Flynt laughed. "Iago? Othello? Never have I heard of these gentlemen, Italian or some other foreigners, I warrant. As for Desdemona, I think my friend Nicholas here had a whore of such

59

a name. Was that not so, Nicholas? Was she not some punk you lay with in Cripplegate?"

Nicholas Morgan did not answer. Flynt looked back to me with an insolent grin. "Besides the which, it is unthinkable that from my mouth should proceed words of Master Shakespeare's eloquence."

I was not so foolish to think Flynt's compliments anything but gross impudence. I looked down at his evil face with contempt, hoping that in my severe mien he might confess the truth. For I did not believe for a moment that Samuel had lied to me about what he heard, or in some way misinterpreted it. But Flynt had built a wall of denial and, given that there were three witnesses against one, I was at a loss to know how to penetrate it. I stood there frustrated and angry, wanting to give the lie to this wretch and at the same time not wishing to have the encounter turn even more ugly, perhaps violent.

I turned to Samuel. "Come," I said. "We waste our time with these fellows. We will not bother them more."

Flynt pushed his chair back and stood. He gave a low mocking bow, the final insult. I walked several feet toward the door and then turned back. I said to Flynt, "If it had been otherwise than you say, Master Flynt, that is, had you admitted to having knowledge of my play, even to the true lines, I should have warned you against such a theft. I should have told you that I have friends, friends in high places, friends more than eager to come to my aid and the aid of the King's Men, of whom I am honoured to be one."

"Why, do you threaten us, Master Shakespeare?" Flynt returned, leaping to his feet, his eyes filled with mockery and false indignation. "With the law? Why what law have we broken or statute violated? None, I think. I do hope I misunderstand your words, sir. For we too are not without friends in the city, sir. Besides, it's all about money is it not? You fear someone may steal your precious play and benefit therefrom. Remember, sir, he who steals my play steals trash. Even if it were otherwise, the play is no more than a silly trifle. We can hardly drive one as successful as you into penury."

Now he laughed a raucous, impudent laugh that left my face aflame, and I hated him to the depths of my soul. I freely confess it, both for his impudence and what he said about my play.

I turned on my heels to go, bidding Samuel to follow. Samuel was clearly shaken by this encounter, as was I. Neither of us had stomach for more confrontation that night.

In the street, I said, "The man's a devil, this John Flynt."

"I did tell you the truth, Will, about what I heard. His parting words, what he said of the purse, or your play, those were Iago's lines."

"I know them. I wrote them," I returned sharply. "This Flynt lies and, what is more, he knows I know he lies, which makes it all the worse. All three of them do. Yet now I know who they are and shall find out where they lodge. They must have been privy to my playbook somehow, which means there remains another villain to discover, one who delivered my play to them, for they stand on the periphery of this mischief, I warrant you. Not at the centre."

I bade Samuel goodnight and made haste through the dark street toward my lodgings where, amid the familiar surrounds of my books and papers, I would feel myself safe. My heart was pounding, my face moist with sweat, my fancy rife with images of gross assault and battery and even death, afflicted upon me by this Flynt, whose malice and villainy were so plainly writ upon his brow that they could not be denied.

I looked behind me, fearing that I would be followed by Flynt and his friends. In answer to my accusations, the man had offered no violence to me, not in so many words. Still, I was not so dull of mind as to miss his thinly veiled threat.

What powerful friends did Flynt have to threaten me?

I did not know and feared to discover.

No fool I. I knew what I had done. I had trod on dangerous ground in confronting these thieves so directly with only mild-mannered Samuel beside me. Yet I was resolute. I had not laboured over my play to see another have either credit or profit on it. By God, I would discover who had stolen it and given it to Flynt.

I would not rest until I did.

During the week that followed, no less than three missives, crudely lettered, were left for me at the Globe. Each threatened me with death, one with dismemberment.

All were unsigned, yet I knew full well what devil had written them.

10

Abed, I dream and live again my worst fears. I am alone in the narrow streets of some city. It is at once London and not, for I am searching for refuge in places I have never before seen. Not a house or shop or church steeple is familiar to my eye. No tree, sign or face. Behind me comes John Flynt and his vile companions in hot pursuit, bent on my destruction. I am their prey. I know I will not escape their talons. My sense of the inevitability of this fate is the worst of it.

I woke in a sweat, gasping for air, my heart pounding as though I had in truth run through those dreary streets and then, calming myself with the comforting reality of my chamber and its familiar furnishings, I wondered what the dream did mean. For I hold that man does not dream for naught, but that these visions of the night oft bespeak what is to come, or what mysteries by human reason unplumbed might mean. In times past God spoke in this nocturnal tongue to men wise enough to interpret its syllables. Who does not know this?

Yet my fear of the men had conjured it forth from my sleeping brain. Did they want more than my play's words? Did they also want my life, as the letters, anonymously writ and delivered, threatened?

Now though I forbear to boast and make myself more than I am, I protest that I am well loved by most with whom I pass my days, even those with whom I compete for acclaim. I do mean my rival playwrights of the city, the lords and ladies of the court who admire our work, the commoners who fawn upon us and would that we players be their special friends and so forth. Yet like any man, I cannot please all. My manner of speech, my gait, the shape of my nose, mouth, lips, chin, the cut of my beard or the colour of my eyes, my broad forehead and half-bald pate—any feature might offend, for all men and women too are different in their particular tastes as well as inclinations.

I must have enemies perforce. It follows as night follows the day.

But which enemy in this case? I did not believe that Flynt and his villainous friends acted alone, but that some larger conspiracy threatened to undo me.

I had risen at seven o'clock, later than my wonted time, to dress myself and begin the day's business. I had agreed to breakfast with Burbage in an inn on Market Street. I was eager to relate to him my experiences of the night and break the news that my play—our play since it was at last the company that owned it—had been stolen. But when I arrived at the meeting place my news was stale. Burbage already knew of the theft. But how?

As I soon learned, Samuel had disclosed all. I had sworn him to silence about the play's contents but not forbade him from telling about its theft. In securing the discretion of others, such nice distinctions are not unimportant.

"Who can the thief be? These three obtained the script from a fourth person surely," I said.

Good-hearted Burbage nodded sagely. Then his lips formed a

kind of snarl. His eyes blazed. "Some punk or whore I wager. They frequent the theatres as often as the gentry, plying their trade. They have wondrous memories. And some, they say, know our lines as well as our players do. Why, they could if need set foot upon the stage and play the requisite part most admirably."

"True," I said. "'Tis a curious thought, this cast of whores you imagine. Yet methinks this plot against us runs deeper still."

"More than the money or the honour?" Burbage asked.

"More than the money or the honour," I answered.

Although reluctant so to do, I told him about my suspicions of Gabriel Catesby.

"Your old friend and saviour, you mean? I'faith, he does to me seem a most amiable fellow, easy to entreat, respectful, and of prodigious memory as well."

I winced at these descriptions, embarrassed since I knew not how to counter them. It was true I owed Gabriel my life, and in suspecting him of fault I felt a twinge of guilt that Burbage must have seen in my face.

Burbage was very like that, perceptive I mean. His glance seemed to convey an unspoken accusation of disloyalty, a grievous offence to me, who thinks himself true to his friends and would not be called traitor for all the world.

Burbage began to praise Gabriel even more fulsomely.

"Confess it, Will. His Iago is not to be scorned. His voice most sweet and apt, when needed, harsh and pointed elsewhere. And now it seems we have lost our friend Augustine for the season, and what we can see in the future, his presence amongst us is even more to be valued and, if I may say it, preserved. Take care before you impugn the honour of this Gabriel Catesby, to whom both you and the rest of us owe so great a debt."

I admit Burbage's caution touched me. "I make no direct accusation against him," I said. "I note only that he is new among us, inexperienced in London. He is unaware perhaps of the dangers of the city, the unsavoury connections, the diverse temptations. Perhaps he simply talked, I mean to a friend, who then passed the same on to Flynt."

I knew this was a foolish notion as soon as it passed my lips. So did Burbage. He said, "That would have been much to remember, given your account of what these men knew. I think a more plausible explanation is in order."

We sat quietly for a while, then Burbage said, "I have a scheme whereby we can discover the thief. We shall find out the truth in such a way as to leave neither of us in doubt. And I do warrant you that Gabriel will not be found at fault."

"What do you mean?" I asked.

"You have heard of this Doctor Forman, Simon Forman?"

"I have," I said, "but do not know him well, more by reputation than aught else."

But in speaking thus, I was not entirely truthful. I did know Doctor Forman. Who had not heard of this man, and indeed, who has not heard of him since? Few in London save he that has slept these past dozen years. I forbear therefore to say more of this man lest some reader of this chronicle object that Doctor Forman, as he was wont to style himself, is one who needs neither introduction nor epitaph, for he is, as of this writing, food for worms.

Three years after his death, he was accused—and rightly I avow—as having been party to the murder of Sir Thomas Overby of infamous memory, that he did wilfully and maliciously supply poison to the furtherance of that evil enterprise. Lady Francis Howard, Overby's lover, had been accused of securing poison from Forman to carry out the murderous deed, since she held Overby to be her enemy.

66

It was all a messy business, talked of for months and months, but I spare you the tedious and salacious details.

"You know he is also well grounded in astrological lore," Burbage said, speaking of Doctor Forman. "He is a deep student thereof, having learned his art even in the great cities of Europe. He claims powers beyond those of mortal men and his claims go undisputed by many of those who have sought his services."

"I heard it, and do in part believe it, for it lies near unto the physician's art, this examination of the stars and planets," I said.

"Our friend, Heminges, has consulted him from time to time," Burbage said.

John Heminges was he who handled the company's business. He had been an actor in the old Admiral's Men but had found his place amongst us for his excellent head for figures and in negotiating with shopkeepers, costumers, and other tradesmen whose skills we required. He was a good friend to me, but one who did not always disclose his private affairs.

Heminges' visit to Forman was news to me. As for Doctor Forman, I knew more of him than I revealed to Burbage, for I knew Mistress Mountjoy, my landlord's wife, had consulted him several times whereby she had undoubtedly been, as so many women he had treated, one of the good doctor's conquests. Though he consorted with heavenly bodies, he did not disdain earthly ones. He was rumoured to have seduced a hundred or more virgins and married women as well, in his practice as a physician and astrologer and had written of it in his journals.

"Doctor Forman helps those who have lost things of value, finds persons who have disappeared from family and friends. His insights are said to be remarkable," Burbage said.

"I am sure they are remarkable," I answered. "You are suggesting that I consult Doctor Forman as to who among us is guilty? You think he possesses such powers of discernment?"

"I do not doubt it," he said.

I considered this. "I have heard Forman's services are not cheap," I said.

"You do want to know who has betrayed us, do you not?"

"Most certainly," I said. "I have promised the king a new work, a work from my pen. I have described to His Majesty the very plot and substance of *Othello.* Should it appear in any form but at court, I will be disgraced. The company will be disgraced. It might even be thought that we copied the play from the thieves."

"Then give the doctor what he asks," Burbage said. "Do pay his fee from our company's purse, not from your own. After all, the wrong is done to us all, not to you alone."

11

And so it was that later that very day I crossed the river to Lambeth where I had learned Forman resided in a house near marshy ground.

I remember a gravel path led to his front door and spared my shoes from the mud and filth. He lived there with a young woman he claimed to be his wife, though I understand she was but a lodger in his house before.

As for Forman himself, I knew him somewhat from his attendance at the Globe, for whatever his faults he was nonetheless a great playgoer and had more than once praised my work to my face, for which I was most grateful, not being so convinced of my genius that I could rest content without such commendations.

I had heard that Forman kept a book in which all who sought his counsel were named and their diverse complaints and conditions writ of. There, too, were the notes concerning the numerous women he had seduced. I marvelled not so much at his prodigious lust as at his success in gratifying it, for as I will presently record, his own mother would have not called him handsome. What did his quiet little wife think of her husband's infidelities? I suspect, like most husbands, he kept these matters to himself.

"Master Shakespeare. I am honoured," Forman declared, opening the door himself almost before I had chance to knock. "In truth, I have been expecting you since cockcrow."

"Since cockcrow!" I exclaimed. "How can that be when I only conceived of my visit at noon."

Forman smiled mysteriously, giving me no answer.

This peculiar gentleman was a man of about my years, pigeon-breasted with a wide forehead and a full head of hair as dark and curled as an Ethiope's. He had as well a thick black beard that gave him a ferocious mien even when he endeavoured to be pleasant, as now.

Within I found a small, cramped house with low ceiling and a strange array of odours which I took to proceed from his many medicines and nostrums. We passed from the entrance to a much larger room I took to be his inner sanctum, where I suppose from other furnishings he consulted with his clients. There I saw first a large oblong table piled high with books, papers, and various instruments of a nature and purpose quite unknown to me. Upon the walls, where one might have found in any ordinary house wall hangings or portraits, were an array of charts of stars and planets, a multitude of figures, a mathematician's paradise it seemed, all apparently useful in his obscure art.

For myself, I had no fear. I was no virgin or bored housewife in peril of seduction. I imagined that his respect for me was real and that I would suffer no personal danger in this place as strange as it was from any habitation I had known.

He invited me to sit at the table across from the chair that was obviously his scholar's seat, for its high back was carved with a fantastical design: creatures of the ancient world all tangled in a most monstrous and unnatural embrace. I did sit, and suddenly there appeared at his side the young woman of whom I had heard. His wife, I do mean.

By my reckoning, she was less than half his age. She had a small, oval face, grey eyes, and a thin hipless form. If she had a woman's breasts, they had been so tightly bound in her bodice that she might have been a boy in disguise. And she was speechless, or might have been, for she said not a word, nor did she regard me, but stared only at him as though he alone were in the chamber and I were not there at all. I was unaccustomed to being so invisible, yet I was uncomfortable in any case. Forman said, "Wine, I think, Jane. A Spanish grape, for Master William Shakespeare, our distinguished guest."

Forman looked at me to see if I approved. I did. The wife, Jane as he had called her, disappeared into an adjoining room and then returned almost at once with a flagon and two glasses. Further proof, were it wanted, that my visit was not unexpected.

We sipped the clear liquor, an excellent vintage, and then he spoke of my play of Prince Hamlet and his woes. Indeed, he spoke most glowingly until, my face hot with embarrassment, I prevailed upon him to cease. The play was good I knew, far better than the usual run of plays about wronged princes and their pursuit of vengeance. Still, I was no Sophocles or Euripides, by any measure. Those great men were to emulate, never equal, much less surpass.

Forman said he was most taken by certain lines spoken in the play, lines that he then quoted, even as I had written them, even as if he had the play book open before him. Hamlet's soliloquy. Polonius's tedious advice to his son. Horatio's remorse upon Hamlet's death. All these he rendered most expressively, though nothing like unto Burbage who was the more excellent. Then Forman said, "But you are not here for praise, sir, but for information, intelligence. Is that not so?"

I said it was true and was about to tell my tale when he admonished me to silence with a finger raised to his lips.

"Let me see now, Master Shakespeare, before you speak. Your question has something to do with the theatre," he said, rubbing his forehead slowly, as though I could afford to keep silent.

"Yes, something about the theatre," I said.

I related to him the events that had plagued me. I told him everything: Samuel's discovery, my encounter with the three men at the Talbot, their threats against me and even my own against them. The terrifying letters.

I even told him of my dream, and said I feared it might become truth.

I also told him about Gabriel Catesby. That I suspected it was he, being as he was new to our company, and one who had dissembled before, and yet one to whom I owed my life. I explained how I was conflicted thereby, how my gratitude warred with distrust.

"I can understand your dilemma," Forman said. "Do tell how he saved you. And do hold nothing back, for I must know all."

"He saved me from drowning," I said, drawing first a deep breath of resolve, for I had recited these facts too many times to count.

He nodded for me to go on, which of course I did.

"When we were boys in Stratford-upon-Avon, where I was born and reared. I jumped into a pond. My leg became tangled in branches beneath the water. I struggled for breath. Gabriel freed me, brought me up to the surface. That I sit before you today, that I lived to write the play you so much admire, I do owe to him."

"He played the hero's part, then?"

"You might call it that," I answered.

"Yet you suspect him of betrayal, of theft of your work. Do you have proof of his complicity?" Forman asked.

"No more than I have said," I admitted. "Only a feeling of unease around him. No trust or confidence where I would wish them."

Forman laughed, a mocking laugh I liked not at all, and leaned forward in his chair. He pointed his finger at me as though he were a schoolmaster and I a dull-witted pupil. So great was that impression I felt I was in Stratford school a second time, a boy of twelve, quaking beneath the master's ferule.

Forman said, "A magistrate would ridicule you for grounding your suspicion in a mere intuition, Master Shakespeare. But have no fear. I am no magistrate bound by rules of evidence. I myself prefer astral proof."

"Astral proof? What do you mean?" I asked, although in truth I knew where he was bound with this phrase.

Forman waved his hands toward his charts. "A man's fate, his very nature, is written in the stars, Master Shakespeare. All is predetermined. The man you seek is traitor as well as thief. He has stolen knowingly, and so to do requires that he seem a friend. Yet, trust me, he is a traitor to his core. It is the very essence of his being. It lies in his very nature, not in his circumstance. And yet, thereby, we have the means to find him out."

"Can you find him out, sir?"

"Most certainly," Forman said, smiling triumphantly.

I considered this. I allowed that the stars influenced us but had no faith that we were mere chess pieces in the universe, ordained to be what the stars directed. Were it so, why should man be praised or condemned for what he did or did not if all was beyond help, if his free will were a mere illusion? The thought did not set well with me. It never had.

Yet I chose not to dispute these matters with the astrologer before me. My interest was in knowing who among my compatriots had I to thank for the theft of my work.

I resolved not to quibble over method. Though it were madness or self-delusion or, as I suspect, the boldest chicanery in the world, yet would I stay judgement until Forman had worked his magic and produced a name, thereby clearing Gabriel Catesby of complicity or convicting him.

"Will you be ruled by me, Master Shakespeare?" Forman asked, casting upon me his schoolmasterly visage a second time.

"I will, sir. I will do what the law allows and whatever good conscience permits."

"Very good, then, do you this," Forman said, "go you and discover when this man, this Gabriel Catesby, was born, not only the year but the very hour, for though he be a hero, yet may he be a villain also. A man may be both in the same skin, if I may say so."

I agreed. Forman went on.

"Mark you his birthplace, even unto the very house wherein he uttered his first cry. But take heed in your questioning of him. Use indirection, even as your Prince Hamlet used the same to find his father's murderer out. This Catesby fellow must not learn the purpose of your questions. When you have the information I need, bring it to me straightway."

I told him I understood and would indeed do what he said.

"In the meantime, my advice is that you do not walk unescorted in the city," Forman continued. "These men you met have threatened you. These malicious missives you received are certainly theirs and bear clear mark of their evil intent. Regard your dream as prophecy, or at least a warning. Stand clear of them. If you are accompanied, they will be less likely to accost you. If they accost, accompanied you are less likely to suffer bodily injury or, heaven forfend, death. It is simple as that. But choose your guardian well. Let him be a brawny, bold fellow who would rather fight than eat, kill than sleep. One whose honour is in his fist or his knife or his sword."

Saying this, he paused and stared at me as if I might have such a fellow concealed beneath my cloak.

I searched my memory for whom I might choose for this service. I could think of no one who answered to Forman's description. At least no one among my closest friends. Nor anyone I knew from days of yore whom I might summon to do me present service came to mind. Nonetheless, I said I would follow his advice. I would look out for myself. I understood, I said, my danger.

Then I asked him how much he wanted for his services to me.

Forman smiled. It was as I saw it a true smile, a revelation of a generous nature, although it did little to mitigate the ugliness of his face. In a dozen years thereafter, men would call him a devil. The Devil Forman, as one of our learned judges said of him.

In hindsight, I could see how this might seem so, his devilishness I mean. The devil is said to have power to assume a pleasing shape, but yet the reality of his visage is most hideous, a perfect mirror of his internal nature—malicious, cunning, deceptive. Hence his mask of good will. Without it, who would not perceive the evil truly in his face and flee from it?

"For you, Master Shakespeare, who has given me so much pleasure in your works, I ask nothing but to continue to regard you as a friend. And even as I have done you a service in this instance, you may well return the favour on some future day."

He held his smile, waiting my response.

I bowed gracefully and mumbled some words of thanks, eager now to leave this place, but not to learn what favour Forman might have in mind.

Oddly, his words reminded me of Gabriel, to whom my debt

of life might never be paid, at least in his eyes. Nor, perhaps, in my own.

Then Forman reached toward me and put his hand on my shoulder. I shrank at the touch. His hands were gloved for it was cold in his house, but I do swear I could feel the ice of his naked fingers on my flesh.

It was like unto the claw of some rapacious bird.

12

Taking my leave of the astrologer, I could think of little but his counsel that I find a protector, a bodyguard. His admonition built upon what I had already feared, that the theft of my play was but the beginning of my troubles with Flynt and his friends. First my lines purloined, then my life? It did indeed seem to me a likely, if terrible, progression. I shuddered to think upon it and could not get Flynt's snarling visage and the threatening letters from my head. They occupied me quite, stealing from me all hope and joy of life.

All was more a reminder of my vulnerable mortality than a death's head.

But despite my fears, I began to plan how I might secure the information Doctor Forman needed to complete Gabriel's horoscope and settle my doubts concerning him. Forman had suggested indirection in securing what was needed so that Gabriel would not suspect my motives for questioning him. He even quoted my Hamlet, which much pleased me. But I thought, what more indirect than to contrive a way for Gabriel to provide the information directly to Forman?

When I returned to the theatre, I found Gabriel and told him with great excitement, how I had just come from the renowned astrologer and learned many marvellous things about my future.

"I thought you were sceptical of horoscopes and questioned whether men were governed by the stars." Gabriel said.

"And so I was until today," I answered, feigning a conversion to the astrologer's art.

I could see the envy in Gabriel's eyes. The desire to have some prediction about himself to feed his pride and vainglory. It was what he ever hungered for. I told Gabriel that Forman would need to know certain facts pertaining to his birth and the circumstances thereof.

"By God, he shall have them," Gabriel said, with an eagerness I had not seen in him before.

And with that he was out the door and my mission accomplished. Before the day was done, I had a message from Forman. He wrote that Gabriel visited him, provided information about his birth, and that Forman would have answers to my uncertainties soon.

It would in fact be some months before I heard from Forman again. By then I would need no starry horoscope to aid me. I would have confirmed Gabriel's true nature for myself. I would have looked into his dark and treacherous heart. I would have understood how deep the vein of evil ran within him.

It was now hard toward evening. The air had cooled and heavy clouds hung over the city so that it seemed later in the day than it truly was. Straightway I went to see Burbage at a nearby tavern he was wont to patronize this time of day. I thought that, since he had pointed me to the astrologer in the first place, he might well advise me on how I might find the protection Doctor Forman had recommended.

But Burbage was not alone. He sat with two other of our friends, drinking and laughing and talking of I do not know what, but surely something much more trivial than the concerns that lay heavily upon me.

I greeted all three, joined them at table, and then, after a decent interval in which I partook in the general talk, I signalled to Burbage, who knew my expressions well enough to mark them right, that we should talk privately. I did not want my business with these thieves to become common knowledge. I wanted neither pity nor ridicule that I made more of these dangers than they deserved.

Presently the two others left, each in goodly humour, unaware I think of the fear that ruled my heart and ruined my joy in friendly conversation. Then did I unfold to Burbage all that had transpired in my meeting with Forman. As it fell out, Burbage was as eager to ask me of the outcome of my visit as I was to report it. I did not, however, make mention of Forman's directions regarding Gabriel Catesby, only the doctor's concern for my safety from the threats of Flynt and his companions.

Nodding in agreement and obviously pleased with my report, Burbage said, "You must look to yourself first, Will. Your Moor's tragedy is not worth your life. It is but an idea on paper, a few weeks' labour of brain and passion. Easy enough for you. You could write a dozen such plays. But if your life is threatened then you need just the protection Forman recommends. He suggested one man or two, did he? Why not three or four if it keeps you the safer from assault or worse?"

"Great men employ such guards of their body," I said. "Not I."

"You are great enough, given the circumstances. I hold your life, Will, to be of greater value than that of any earl or duke I know."

"Many thanks for that," I said. "But you do give me too much credit."

"By God, I do not," he answered, pounding his fist on the table.

I said, "I need not an army but a good right arm. But whose? I am having enough trouble thinking of a single man, much less two or three. And I will not be served by a muscle-bound blockhead who does not know me from Adam. I have my work to do. I have my privacy to nurture. I am a writer who must have a healthy measure of solitude, not a courtier who without company cannot long endure."

"Well," said Burbage," I could name one who would serve your purpose if you would have him."

"And who might that be?" I asked.

"Ah, let me tell first his merits, his qualities, which I learned but this past hour from our friends here. Then tell me if he be not the very man you seek."

"Very well," I said. "Tell me about this paragon of virtue."

Burbage said, "Consider this. He of whom I speak is in height a good six feet if not more. In age, about yours or perhaps younger. He is of manly parts all, sturdy of limb. Best of all, he is experienced."

"How experienced?"

"Why, in truth, that experience most pertinent to your need. He has been a soldier in the wars."

"What wars?"

"In Holland. The Spanish against the Dutch."

"Which side?"

Burbage asked, "Does it matter if he is hardened in the wars, if he can wield a sword and hold his own with a club or his fists, if his nostrils have been filled with cannon smoke and scars boast of his courage? If he can fire a pistol and hit his mark at fifty paces?"

"It might make a difference, if he fought for the Spaniard or against him."

"For the Spaniard. Yes, he's a Papist. But do you really care what religion he professes if he serves your need?"

I said I supposed it did not, though my preference was for the other side in the conflict. While I had no great regard for the watery Dutch, I held the Spaniard in greater contempt.

"But he does not know me, or us. I won't be guarded by a stranger."

"Not even if he's one of us?"

"You mean an actor," I said.

"I do. And of our company."

"None of us is a soldier of any war that I know of, save wars of words, of which we are all veterans. Now Ben Jonson was a soldier once as all who know him are aware, but he has never been of our company."

"Well," Burbage said, beaming with pleasure at his imminent revelation. "I do speak of your erstwhile friend and saviour, Gabriel Catesby himself."

"Gabriel?" I exclaimed. "A soldier? Now you mock me for sure and make light of my misery. This is not the act of a friend, Dick."

"Nay, Will, I tell you what he told my friends."

"He never said aught to me about having been in any wars, save perhaps on some stage where he has played a boasting *miles gloriosus*, beating the air with a wooden sword and thrilling the groundlings who would not know a real battle from a tavern brawl."

Burbage laid a hand on mine. He leaned close. I could smell his winey breath and wondered if he were more besotted than he appeared. "Put Catesby to the test."

And so I did. Put Gabriel to the test, I mean. Next hour I drew him aside and told him all that had happened at the tavern and since. I said I wanted him to do me an added service if he would. But only if he would. "It is no thing you must do, Gabriel. You are free to decline, and for whatever reason. It matters not to me."

81

He did not decline, but instead seemed eager to take up his new commission. He asked me to tell him about the three men.

"The chief of them, a man named Flynt, spoke most deviously. He was subtle at first, pretending my accusations were a misunderstanding. Then more boldly he declared that they were false and I a liar for accusing him."

I took a breath, then continued. "This Flynt denied it all. At least at first. But then seemed to admit that it was so, that the lines from my play were uttered and he cared not that I knew it, or that I thought him a thief. He as much said that there was nothing I could do about his larceny. His friends seconded his innocence with the same impudence. I was faced with three shameless liars."

"Some witnesses, these villainous curs," Gabriel said with a dry laugh. "What else would his boon companions say but that their friend was honest. But tell me of these other two men. What manner of men were they?"

I described the two, beginning with John Flynt and then I described Nicholas Morgan, with whom, years before, I had shared the stage in Norwich.

"Nicholas?" he said, a look of astonishment on his face.

He asked me to describe this Nicholas again.

"A young man, younger than we, fair, light eyes, thin lipped, a hard, slender body, a narrow face. Nicholas Morgan."

Gabriel took a deep breath and said, "Good God, I do swear I know the man, not well but enough. He occupies the chamber next to my own. This is passing strange, Will, defying reason and belief, though true. Yet I do swear by Christ's wounds that he and I are not friends, but acquaintances only. I know his name. I greet him if we pass in the street. He returns the greeting. We have talked from time to time. Idle chatter, nothing more. And you say he was one of the men at the table?"

82

"The very man," I said. "He speaks like a Yorkshireman. He did not threaten me. That would have been Flynt. Yet he consented to my humiliation."

"More evidence that he is one and the same as my neighbour, his manner of speech."

My old schoolfellow paused, staring for a moment into his lap where his hands were folded as though he were at prayer. Then suddenly he looked up and into my face, half turning on the bench. "I pray, Will, you do not think that I told him of the play, that I betrayed you and the company, which thing I would never do, but would die first."

He looked at me passionately, as though the accusation cut him to the quick. For a moment, I thought he would fall to his knees, a supplicant to my mercy and understanding of his innocence. I confess I was moved by it. Quickly I assured him that I thought no such thing.

Looking back across the years, I surprise myself in the ease with which these assurances flowed from my lips. Truth was, his protest had taken me by surprise. I thought myself a good judge of men, and at that moment I judged Gabriel Catesby and found him free of blame. Yet that he and Nicholas were neighbours was the strangest of coincidences, and while such things happen, they always invite speculation as to how they possibly could.

"Come now," I said. "Take me to your lodgings. I want to see Morgan when he is not with his confederates. Perhaps he will be more open as to how he came to know my play. You with me, he may speak truth, if only for fear."

"Do I go as your protector, then, your bodyguard?" Gabriel asked, looking at me uncertainly.

"You do indeed," I answered. "Take up your office, sir. Arm yourself, for I am in your hands."

13

Does it seem strange that I should put my life in the hands of him whom I professed to distrust, my childhood friend Gabriel Catesby? Looking back, I find it strange myself, a kind of madness of which I was possessed, but true it was. Absurd or no, ill-fated or no, that decision, yet I cannot change the past, what I did. I may repent my decision, but I may not change it, if truth be told.

Gabriel Catesby lodged very poorly in a shabby neighbourhood in Aldgate. Here were only rude tenements in much need of repair and a narrow street down the middle of which coursed a foul-smelling sewer. There had been fires there, for several houses were the blackened skeletons of their former selves. The people there too were an unsavoury lot, prone to eke out their living with petty crimes and occasional murders. Many were foreigners speaking languages I did not recognize, although I did hear one speaking French. Another, Dutch.

In those years, it was often difficult to find affordable lodgings in the city that were free of rats and other noxious vermin. Gabriel said he had the lease of a mere hole in the wall but for a month. The tenement in which he lived he said was occupied by twenty or so men, mostly young, and some former soldiers like unto himself. A priest lived there too, he said, under a false name. No one believed it. Gabriel said it was a joke, such disguises, for he said that priests ever had a certain way of walking and holding themselves upright and they were ever making the sign of the cross to dispel evil spirits, of which there were many in the neighbourhood. Gabriel truly believed that, I think, but then I remembered his mother and her sisters. His belief made a kind of sense, at least to him.

I followed my new protector up two flights of narrow stairs until we came to a dark corridor from which there were several doors. "This is where I live," Gabriel announced, pointing to one of them. "And next unto me is Nicholas Morgan."

I gave three sharp raps on the door to which Gabriel had pointed.

No answer came. I rapped again, and then Gabriel called out Morgan's name. I tried the door to find it unbolted and went inside.

It was a very small chamber, hardly large enough for a bed. There was a small window that let in a little light, a bedstead without any coverings and an oblong chest in the corner, into which I supposed Morgan had placed his earthly goods. If there was anyone dwelling here, it was evident he had flown, for we examined the chest only to find it empty save for some old rat droppings at the bottom.

I should have foreseen it, the flight I mean.

"He's gone," Gabriel said helplessly and unnecessarily, for nothing was more obvious than that.

We went downstairs where the master of the house lived in more commodious rooms with his family. We found him in the midst of berating a serving girl who looked not above ten years of age, but he had the courtesy to cease when we appeared at his door.

"He moved himself and his things from the house just this morning, this Morgan fellow did, and at my behest, I should say, sir."

"Your behest?" I asked. "Did he offend you as a tenant?"

"Oh, he did, sir. And mightily, he did. He had his vices, you see, more vices than I could easily abide. I have a family, you see, and property to protect. But he did say he cared not that I evict him, for he said he was well enough off and would find better lodgings easy enough."

"That's curious," I said.

"He said he had found employment elsewhere."

"Did he say what employment?" Gabriel asked, before I could.

"This Morgan fellow is an actor. He told me that he has secured a place with one of the companies of players in the city. He boasted of it."

"Which company would that be?" I asked.

Morgan's landlord thought for a moment. He was a small man, fifty or thereabouts, with a ruddy, smooth-shaven face. When he was not beating servants, I imagined he made more of himself by playing the tyrant to his tenants. I knew the type well enough. I had had more than one landlord of the same ilk since first coming to the city.

"I think he said it was the King's Men, those who serve up Master Shakespeare's plays," the landlord continued. "He said he had been given a part in a new play called—By the mass, I cannot remember what it was called."

"*Othello*?" I asked, somehow knowing his answer before he gave it.

"Why, I do believe that was its name. Yes, sir, it was *Othello*. And Master Shakespeare, I do believe, was the writer of it. I don't doubt but you have heard of him, sir?"

Gabriel started to speak, but I bid him be silent with a warning look.

"Yes, we have heard of the man," I said. "An upstart know-it-all who thinks too much of himself."

The landlord laughed. "Aye, sir, there be not a few of that sort in the city nowadays."

"Alas, too true," I said.

Gabriel agreed it was true and winked at me when his landlord looked away.

"Why would you not tell my landlord who you were?" Gabriel asked when the little man had gone indoors and we were alone again.

"I did not want Morgan to know of my visit, should he return. It would seem Morgan knows too much of my business already." Whereupon a thought came to me. I said, "Tell me, Gabriel, do you talk in your sleep?"

Gabriel seemed amused by the question. Perhaps he was uncertain how it touched upon anything we had been speaking of. But he answered, I think forthrightly:

"Sometimes I do, or so they claim who have shared my bed."

He grinned and laughed a little at this, looking very cocky. Evidently his Papist piety did not restrict his libidinous urges. I had heard him boast of his conquests but knew not if they were true. So much of what he said was not.

We started to walk toward the Mountjoys. It was nearly dark now and the streets were emptying. The houses and shops beside us were beginning to show the pale lights of lamps and candles.

"What of your chamber? Does the door lock?"

"It does."

"You have a key?"

"I do."

He stuck his hand in his belt where there was a little purse, felt within, and said, "Yes, it is where I put it. Why do you ask?"

"I thought perhaps he broke into your chamber. You copied lines from the play, did you not?"

"I did. Was I wrong to do so?"

I paused before answering, remembering that the practice was not uncommon, especially in the early stages of rehearsal. Before I had trusted that nothing would befall the script parts by my companions' so doing, now it seemed reckless, an ill-considered practice likely to permit, if not promote, theft.

"You think Morgan might have found his way into my chamber and taken the script, copied it out perhaps whilst I slept and then returned it to me?"

"Was that possible?" I asked, for his thoughts matched my own to perfection.

We must have taken twenty more steps down the street before either of us spoke another word and then he said, "One night I came home late. I wanted to read over my lines before bed, my custom. In so doing the words seem to seethe within my brain while I do sleep and, thus, I learn them better and faster. I went to my chest where I kept the script. There I found it, but it lay atop a cloak I wore in the winter, whereas it is my custom to keep the script folded within the same garment. I remember thinking that this was strange, this untoward displacement. I learned long ago, Will, that one makes fewer mistakes in this life if one's ways are set. But then I thought no more about it, this strange thing, thinking that I might simply have mislaid it unawares. You see nothing else was taken in my room. Nor was aught else disturbed."

I said, "If Morgan found a way into your room and into your chest, he may have filched the script, copied it, and then returned it, failing to note the exact place from which he secured it. How did he know you had it in the first place?"

"My fault there, I think. When he found out the both of us were unemployed actors, we shared our misery, for it is true as they say, misery does love company. It did seem natural enough, harmless I mean, our sharing. Then when you took me on with the King's Men, he first celebrated my achievement, but then his countenance fell. Jealousy, I think. I had succeeded where he had not, not uncommon among those who compete for the same parts. He asked me what play it was I was to act in and I told him it was a play called by its tragic hero's name."

"*Othello*?"

"Yes."

"Tell me, who else might have a key to your chamber?"

"Well, our landlord, but I doubt he would give a key to Morgan."

"But not unlikely that Morgan could have stolen it. Your landlord did say he had sent Morgan away because of vices in him. He did not say which particular vice."

"God knows, Will, they are beyond counting in any mortal man."

"Many indeed, but I am thinking of one particular violation of the commandments. Perhaps the script was not the only thing Nicholas Morgan took. Your landlord spoke of protecting his property. That could mean theft, could it not? Tomorrow find out more from your landlord about Morgan's fault."

"I shall, Will. Trust me."

Gabriel was as good as his word, at least in this instance. Late the next day he came to me, his face alight with his news. "Small stuff and large, he steals. From others who live in the house—and from the landlord himself. He caught Morgan in the very act."

"What did he take?"

"A cloak, some silver spoons. I know not what else. Probably money. A thief is a thief. If he steals one thing, he'll steal another. All's his, if he can take it. It is in his very nature, thievery."

14

Our friend and colleague Augustine Phillips did not mend despite all prayers said for him. In the spring of that year he died, leaving his widow, Anne, and four daughters to mourn his loss.

His passing weighed heavily upon us all. To say he was loved by us is to say too little, for he was a most excellent actor and musician as well, good-natured and of so honest a heart that everyone who knew him commended him for it. He was indeed a prince amongst men, uncrowned 'tis true, but venerated notwithstanding. In the next world if he does not sit upon the right hand of Sophocles or Seneca, I shall miss my guess.

Augustine, who had profited as much as I in our common venture, had a goodly house in Mortlake, as I have said. It was a well-timbered house where we actors were wont to gather in the summer when we were not on the road in some country town or gentleman's manor because royal edict had closed the theatres. The air was purer, healthier in Mortlake than in London, a good six or seven miles distant, and Augustine's garden delighted us with its rich variety of trees and plants, some brought from remote lands and yet thriving wondrously despite our sodden climate.

There we would discuss our work, rehearse, quarrel over scenes, talk of books and plays, and assess the strengths and flaws of our rivals, the main one of which was the Admiral's Men. We were, I believe, more beloved of the populace than they. Our repertory was more varied; our spectacles beyond compare. And it is no little thing to mark how we enjoyed royal patronage as the King's Men.

We were at that time making plans for another excursion into the north country, and I was most glad of it. A week had passed without further menace from Flynt, yet the very thought of him gave me little rest. Flynt and his friends stalked my dreams, made sleep a curse. Fear ruled my days and nights.

Aware of my distress, Gabriel, now my constant companion, had brought a friend around, a man he had served with in Flanders. This was Guy Fawkes, who then was known to few in London but would become infamous before the year was done.

Guy Fawkes said he preferred to be called Guido. He said it was a name he had chosen for himself.

"Are you Italian, then?" I was tempted to ask, for why an Englishman should take an Italian name I could not fathom, the English having no great love for Italians whom they often thought of as a degenerate race of libertines and poisoners. I suppose he wanted to distinguish himself from the rabble of returning soldiers, many of whom were reduced to begging in the streets, a great disgrace considering their service to crown and country.

For me, I say a man may call himself what he will, though he must own the consequences of his choice.

We three retreated into the garden where Gabriel was pleased to introduce me to his friend, which he did with many fulsome commendations. "This is Master William Shakespeare. He is a celebrated playwright, the most famous in England. Indeed, in the whole world.

He is written God knows how many plays and has been good enough to let me join his company as an actor."

Gabriel did not reveal, at least in my presence, his role as my guardian. I supposed he had related this to Fawkes already as well as informing him just who I was and for what I was known and how he had once saved my life, doubtless with a plenty of new-coined, self-aggrandizing details. I thought this introduction was more for me than for Fawkes. Gabriel was nothing if not theatrical, yet I could hardly fault him for that. Was not theatricality the work and glory of us all, to be enjoined, not disdained?

Fawkes was of Gabriel's years, five and thirty or so, tall, broad-shouldered, with a long, narrow face and dark, piercing eyes that continually darted about as though he were a dutiful sentry. His beard and moustache were full and black. I thought he looked more Spanish than English. He dressed fashionably, with broad hat adorned with feathers, a crimson cape and black boots that rose to his knees and must have cost a pretty penny. He wore a rapier by his side and a dagger sheathed in his belt, and I had no doubt he could use both ably if need be. I noted his large, strong hands and his fingernails. They were uncut like talons and were fearful to look upon.

His speech was marked with a northern accent, York I think, or maybe Norwich. By his carriage and manner, I put him down as a gentleman, which he later confirmed by mention of an estate inherited from his father. When I asked him where he lived and how, he said he served presently in the house of Sir Gabriel Maury as his secretary. Fawkes had a wife, I think, and may have had a son, but these persons he mentioned but once and briefly while I knew him, and without any special affection for either.

Like Gabriel, Fawkes was a zealous Catholic, a truth I saw at once, for he was so bold as to ask me upon introduction which faith

I practiced, even though Gabriel must have told him that I was so lukewarm in such matters as to seem to have no religion at all.

I said, "I am of the king's religion since he employs me to entertain him and the court and because he is our anointed king. I venerate Christ, and thereby love nothing more than that there should be peace, Christ being the Prince thereof. I would rather the public come to the theatre than battle in the streets or in some foreign field."

I allow it was a terse response, yet no more than Fawkes deserved, since we had just met and I liked not being interrogated on personal matters by strangers.

Fawkes said, "Yet your plays, Master Shakespeare, are rife with war and death, the sound of alarms and cannon fire as frequent as the sweet plucking of a lover's lute."

"You know my plays? I thought you had been abroad these dozen years?"

"I have been, sir, but your reputation travels far."

I confess these words pleased me, for it is no small thing to be known beyond one's own land. Still, I defended the matter of my plays, supposing he spoke of my histories and tragedies which did, I allow, drip with blood and gore. Yet how could I candy o'er the truth of England's past, which was indeed a spectacle of violence and treachery, or depict tragedy without death, which is its very essence and signature?

I said, "I feed the public what it has a taste for. But as a private man I abhor the alarms of war. And of the body politic and its operations, I know little and understand less."

"Oh, surely you are too modest, Master Shakespeare," Fawkes said with a broad grin. "None writes as well as you and is ignorant of men and things."

93

We made our way along the garden path, Fawkes commenting on this tree or that shrub and expressing gratitude for being in England again. His knowledge of Flora's bounty impressed me. I wondered how he came to it, being as was a soldier, no university man or scholar that I could ever learn.

Fawkes smiled crookedly and said he well understood the need to be cautious in expressing religious opinions. "I do not blame a man for looking out for his own interests, Master Shakespeare. All do so in our earthly pilgrimage. Yet some of the gentlemen of the court are not of the king's persuasion. Why, sir, I could name a dozen lords and gentlemen who would be happy to see this country restored to true Christian faith and imagine thousands of common folk who would applaud their worthy efforts. And as for peace, was it not promised by King James when he came down from Scotland with his rout of Scots toadies? Then did we all cry God Save the King because we supposed him to be tolerant at least, supportive at best, of our righteous cause. A new day for us Catholics and our valiant priests. Or so thought we in our innocence."

Fawkes took a breath before continuing. I sensed this was a speech he had delivered before, whether in a great assembly or to private persons.

"Now is the case altered. The king has broken his promise. He has become a persecutor, as vengeful as Saul before seeing the light on that Damascus road. If he has his way, all of our faith will be driven from England, those he has not slain or imprisoned. Their lands will be forfeited to the crown. Does that seem right and just to you, Master Shakespeare?"

I said, "I doubt that His Majesty's position is so extreme or England's state so precarious, Master Fawkes. Look you now and consider well—there are persons of your faith in His Majesty's

94

councils. They walk freely and discourse with their friends and enjoy the king's bounty. It is said that the queen is well disposed to Rome and even has a priest in her confidence, who performs mass at her behest and hears her confessions. None of this is done in a dark corner, sir. And I have yet to hear gossip that His Majesty intends to send his buxom bride packing home to Denmark from whence she came."

"It is not the queen who counts in these matters," Fawkes said, "but her royal husband, and I assure you, Master Shakespeare, that the case is no less dire than I have said. There will be war, a civil war. Nations will rise to aid that effort. The true faith against heretics of every stripe whether they sit upon thrones or squat upon stools. Blood will flow. I assure you of that, sir. All this I predict without fear or shame."

"You are a prognosticator then as well as soldier?" I asked.

"I am a reasonable man who can discern the signs of the times, sir."

"You mean Spain," I said. "When you speak of help from abroad."

"Spain and other nations."

I said, "So Spain endeavoured in 1588 with their Armada, and God sent a mighty tempest to frustrate them. The bones of Spanish ships and Spanish men rest upon the ocean floor."

"Not God's work, but Nature's," Fawkes said.

"Is not God the god of Nature?" I replied. "Does anything happen save He cause or suffer it?"

"Perhaps God's anger was not at the full with English heresy then," Fawkes said. "Times are different now. Times are worse. Every man must stand and declare himself, for heaven or for hell, for freedom of religion or the tyranny of despots."

Fawkes' language had grown strong, his forehead shone with sweat. But I was becoming weary of this debate, which seemed beyond

95

resolve. Of my craft, I might have talked for hours. Not of religion. Not of politics.

I said, "Well, Master Fawkes, you asked me of my faith and I have said what it is and what it is not. I will not contend with you on matters theological. I am neither churchman nor politician. Besides which, I have other concerns more demanding of my attention than the doctrines and dogmas of either men or angels."

I had responded sharply to Fawkes. In truth, I liked not the man, as though in my dislike there was a prescient shadow of horrors to come. Upon his new born acquaintance of me, he seemed to presume over much, as though I were one of his troop and he were the commander. Later Gabriel told me that Fawkes had been an officer of great valour at the siege of Calais and while in Spain had even conversed with several Spanish generals and lords about matters neither he nor Fawkes was at liberty to disclose.

I took Gabriel aside while Fawkes walked ahead, examining some rare plant he had given a Latin name I had never heard. He said the plant thrived in Spain. Its seeds were used to stimulate amorous affection. He smiled as he said it, lasciviously I would say.

"All well and good," I said to Gabriel, taking him aside by the arm, and leaving Fawkes to his botanical meditation. "Your soldier friend, Guido Fawkes, pray tell me what does he want of me? I sense he wants something. Surely, you have not brought him by to pass the time of day or preach religion?"

"Guido has offered to serve you, as I am now."

"Serve me?" I said, much surprised at this since I understood him to be already employed to his satisfaction.

"As a guard of your person."

"Indeed," I said, turning to Fawkes, who had joined us again. "Master Fawkes, are you then so desperate for new employment that you should scorn the service of some high-born gentleman to save the skin of a poor playwright who takes crumbs from the king's table and who may but imagine the dangers he is in."

Fawkes said, "I am particular, Master Shakespeare. For whom I work, that is. I have offered my sword and my honour to a certain gentleman, but it would please me more to serve you."

"Though I love not the Roman pontiff?" I asked.

"Your religion, Master Shakespeare, or the lack of it, is a matter of indifference to me. I do have an open mind. Gabriel has told me of your troubles."

"My troubles?"

"I mean he has told me of your enemies, these men who harass you."

"More than harass. They have threatened my life," I said.

"Be at ease, sir, there is a remedy for that," Fawkes said. He laid a hand on the pommel of his rapier. His lips curled into a snarl.

"And I trust you can apply such a remedy?" I asked.

"Oh, I can, Master Shakespeare. I can in truth."

I looked at Gabriel, then at Fawkes, who was smiling agreeably as though our bargain had been already struck. He did seem sincere, and with his strong arms and shoulders, his ready blade, I could not deny he fit my purposes. I still did not like him but resolved to discount his arrogance and presumption if he doubled, and perhaps tripled, my safety.

"Very well, Master Fawkes. I will employ you."

"I pray you call me Guido, Master Shakespeare."

"As you please, sir. Guido let it be."

Gabriel said, "All's settled then. By the way, Will, I have news, good news I do think. I have seen Nicholas Morgan."

"Not at the Globe?"

"No, at the Bear and Bellows, in Southwark."

"With his friends?"

"Alone. But can the other two be far behind, being as they are such boon companions and co-conspirators in this mischief?"

"Did you accost him, question him, accuse him of the theft of which we now know Morgan is guilty?"

"I thought it the wiser to wait until I had Guido for help."

"Yes," I said, "that was wise. But come. I will go with you. It will be three against three, if he is accompanied by his friends. Equal enough odds since our cause is just."

15

We walked back to the city, it being as I have said not many miles, enjoying the midday warmth and several lengthy tales of martial hardihood from Guido Fawkes. He was a voluble man, inventive and precise in his detail, with a dry wit, and I found myself enjoying his stories even though I suspected some of them exaggerated his feats of daring. Could any one mortal withstand such a force as he claimed at Calais? Was there ever a soldier so afflicted with wounds that could march the whole day through mud and rain as he recounted?

Besides which I was glad that he spoke no more of religion. I liked not such disputations and especially the ardour of those most inclined to foretell the worst. What could be said to them but beseech them to temper their fears, for such fears were ever that poisonous milk whereon the untutored multitude sucked up discontent and spewed out disorder in the State.

Presently, by late afternoon, we came to the tavern where Gabriel had said he had seen Nicholas Morgan. He was not to be seen now. Disappointed, I told my companions we should leave, but Fawkes said, "Nay, sir. Stay, I pray you. It is still early in the day for those who wile away the hours in strong drink."

I soon saw that it was true. Slowly the tavern filled, a noisy congregation of merchants and tradesmen, apprentices, and former soldiers, in all a better class than at the Talbot.

Near seven o'clock, the man we sought appeared, but no sooner did he see us three but, like a wary fox who spots the hounds that seek to have him, bolted for the door and into the street without. Fawkes and Gabriel ran after. I trailed through the crowded neighbourhood at a distance, my companions being more fleet of foot than I. I was anxious that Morgan and the others be caught but not eager to be proximate to the conflict that was sure to follow.

My timidity shamed me, yet I yielded to it. I am a player, and a maker of plays, no warrior. Ahead of me I could see Fawkes. I recognized him by his feathered hat and scarlet cape, and next to him the man I thought to be Gabriel. Suddenly they turned into a narrow lane I knew well. I followed after but had no sooner done so when I beheld three persons ahead blocking my way. At first, I thought my two protectors had caught Morgan, for I could see him in the shadows.

Then I saw my mistake. It was neither Gabriel nor Fawkes, but the very persons I feared, John Flynt, Morgan, and the callow youth Gilbert.

My would-be murderers advanced toward me.

I stopped, breathless, and began backing up slowly, prepared to flee for my life. It was then I heard a cry, or cries, two voices, one I recognized instantly.

Behind my assailants came my rescuers. Fawkes had drawn his rapier and was waving it about his head. He made a howl I expected he had used in battle to terrify his enemies. My old schoolfellow had brandished a dagger. He stumbled, fell to the ground, and in a moment was up again, but limping forward. His face contorted in pain, his eyes full of resolve.

My enemies stopped in front of me, obviously alarmed by this counterattack, which I doubt any of them expected, for how could they have known about my doughty protectors?

My friends caught up with them, and I saw Fawkes point his rapier at Flynt's breast, his eyes ablaze, his mouth full of vicious curses, so that had his violence been directed at me I should have died from the very terror of his threats.

In an instant, Flynt fell to his knees. As quickly he was joined by Morgan and Gilbert, while Fawkes pointed his blade first to one and then the other as though he were trying to decide which of my enemies to kill first.

Fawkes turned to me with a fierce and triumphant expression. "See you, Master Shakespeare, the power of the sword, how quickly it does expose the coward's heart and the miscreant's perfidy. These men who would kill for a pittance now quake with fear before you."

Fawkes' words were not bad lines, I thought. Unscripted, heart-felt. But this was true life, not theatre.

Flynt was weeping. I could hear sobs coming from the man and his upper body was shaking as though he were as cold as death, though it was a warm night. Likewise, Morgan and Gilbert were in great distress and had begun pleading for their lives.

Regarding these events, I avow my memory is perfect. Never had I before or after witnessed such a reversal of fortune. They who had been exultant brutes with their murderous threats and strewn them in my path with impunity were now as abject as the slave before his master, humbled, subdued, as much a prisoner of their guilt as of Fawkes' sword.

Fawkes had accomplished this. And Gabriel, too, whose merit was enhanced in my eyes in that he had been wounded in my defence, at least by his stumbling in the street, which after all is a manner of wound, is it not?

"You have injured your foot, your ankle," I said.

"A little thing, Will. A small sacrifice for a friend."

He made a flourish with his hand and a little bow. He had saved me a second time from death.

Now surely my debt to him was greater than ever it had been.

We took the three men with us back to the tavern and begged of the host a private room at the head of the stairs. It was a cramped space furnished in a way to suggest a quite different use than was our intent, but it was large enough for the six of us there, with the conspirators perched on the edge of a filthy bed, their heads bowed like penitents waiting a good shrift.

Fawkes told our captives that if they tried to leave, we would denounce them as the thieves they were and raise the hue and cry against them.

The threat did its intended work most wondrously. The three men were tractable now, even the brutish Flynt who before was all thunder and lightning. Looking at their downcast faces and their timorousness, I wondered why I had ever feared them. Yet I knew I owed their surrender, and therefore my salvation, to Gabriel and Fawkes and certainly as well to Doctor Forman, whose advice was the beginning of my rescue. But for their love of me I would have needed to deal with my enemies on my own.

"You have stolen my play, lied to my face, and threatened my life," I said, looking at each man, adopting as stern a visage as I could. "Even now you would have killed me in the street had not my friends prevented it."

None of the men answered my accusation, but held their heads down and kept silent, as at trial when all evidence has been heard and the jury's verdict is a foregone conclusion.

It was just as well, I thought. The time of disputation was past. I was ready to pass sentence, not to hear a defence of their villainy. Meanwhile, Fawkes watched the men with wary eye, as though he expected them to rise up and attack us.

Then Nicholas Morgan spoke, but it was a confession not a defence.

"It is all true what you say, Master Shakespeare. I stole your words, copying them from the pages I had found in Gabriel's room, and then selling them to John Flynt here. The three of us intended to sell them to another company of actors in the city and make profit thereby."

"Our threats against your person, Master Shakespeare, were made in haste, in surprise at your finding us out," Gilbert said. The youth seemed near tears. "We meant you no real harm."

"No enmity!" I exclaimed. "What of your letters to me, the threats upon my life?"

"They were in jest," Flynt muttered.

"A jest, you say. Threats to kill? Threats to dismember and scatter my bones?" I was near speechless with anger.

"Shall we haul them to the magistrate, Will?" Gabriel asked. "Certainly, somewhere in their deeds is a hanging offence. They can make their apologies afore they swing. At the very least their thumbs might be cut off to teach them better manners."

"I think we can spare the trouble, which will be as much ours as theirs, I fear. They are hardly worth the trouble, none of them," I said.

"Well, then," said Fawkes, "it is you they have offended, Master Shakespeare. What is to be done with them, since they are not worth a rope to hang them?"

"They are worth hanging," I said. "But not by me. I will have my play returned, for one."

All three offenders spoke at once, a confusion of voices.

"We shall return it and forthwith," Morgan said. And with that he reached inside his jerkin and pulled therefrom a sheaf of papers. He thrust it toward me as though it was hot to his touch and he could not wait to be rid of it.

I perused a few of the leaves, recognized the first act of my play despite the wretched hand that copied it, and nodded to Fawkes, who although he had been in my service but for a handful of hours now seemed to have taken over as my chief lieutenant.

"Second," I said, "you must swear an oath."

The three men nodded their agreement before hearing what it was they were to swear to.

I said, "Your oath must be that you forever swear to respect my work and make no effort to represent it as your own or any other person than myself. More, that you swear you will here and forever, never so much as threaten to do me hurt again, or any of my family, or any of my company of players."

"How shall they swear, Master Shakespeare?" Gabriel asked, obviously enjoying the humiliation of my enemies as much as I.

"In blood?" Fawkes suggested.

Gabriel said, "I mean upon what authority—on Christ's blood, to the Virgin, or to God and the heavenly hosts? You cannot let them swear upon their heads, their mothers, or their honour, since they have here demonstrated that they have none." Gabriel fixed Nicholas Morgan with a stare that would have been as deadly as Fawkes' rapier had it like power.

"Well, they do have mothers I believe, and heads, at least for the time being, but that they lack any honour I agree," I answered. "Let their oath be to God simply. Thereby can a man of any faith be bound, be he a Christian, Jew, a Mohametan or other pagan. For all have gods to whom they owe obedience and whom they fear should they break an oath."

My three enemies took the oath even as I prescribed it, standing, their hands raised to the square. None hesitated, but professed his repentance wordlessly, a solemn admission of guilt and remorse worthy of the most pious supplicant.

Or so I thought.

All this pleased me well. It seemed then a fitting conclusion to an unpleasant episode wherein I had been made afraid and thereafter seen my enemies helpless before me.

I thanked God no blood had been shed, although later I was to learn that Gabriel had suffered a broken bone in his foot in his stumbling. I was much relieved that my play was secure from villainous profiteers, and I from would-be murderers. For this I was grateful to Gabriel and to Guido Fawkes, and especially to the latter, who had acted with courage and resolve and, by his hardihood, driven the three miscreants to their knees.

Fawkes glared at the men and said, "Now go. Get you away. If I see any of you again, I will think you have broken your oath. By Christ, I will take vengeance upon you before the god you have forsworn does."

We watched the men go from the room, then followed them downstairs and through the tavern.

Our passing drew no curious stares from other patrons of this sad place. The drama was done. My three enemies disappeared into the night.

Downcast, chastened, forewarned.

Yet why did I believe that this episode of my life was over?

Something within me told me it was not.

16

We rode forth from London on a Monday in June of that same year, a most convenient month for the journey we intended. The weather was fair, and we set our course for York, where we had sometimes played before. That city had, it is true, its own theatres and two or three companies of players, yet far inferior to our own in repertory and skill. We drew multitudes when we appeared, but not the throng we enjoyed in our beloved Globe, where an audience might well exceed several thousand souls on a good afternoon.

York is not London. Compared to the latter, York is infinitely smaller and less varied in its populace, which is to say there are many fewer displaced country folk and foreigners, idle students, defrocked priests, and prodigal sons, whores and their punks, not to mention the army of courtiers, secretaries, servants and the guards and soldiers that grease the wheels of the royal court.

There were but five of us in our bare-bones troupe besides me: Dick Burbage, Robert Armin, Gabriel Catesby, and two apprentice boys to play the women's parts. The names of the boys I have forgotten. Neither fulfilled his promise when his beard grew in, so we wished them well in other trades. We had two plays to offer that month, *Romeo and Juliet* and a pleasant comedy titled *As You Like It.*

Since we were few, we would each play two roles, and sometimes three or four, and trim the script to a dozen or so scenes. All this was our custom. We had done it many times before. Rarely had an audience complained of it or been aware of it.

We stopped in several manor houses along the road to fatten our purse for the month. The lords of the manors paid actors well, and they housed and fed us well. Such was our due, for we were famous tragedians from London, not mere bumpkins to strut upon some rude platform and provoke laughter and the hurling of rotten fruit at our perceived ineptitude.

We played also in several inns where we received a mixed response from unruly audiences, most were farmers and their sons, with big eyes for physical clowning but quite deaf to verse. They laughed and cried, cheered and jeered. Often in the wrong places. Sometimes we could hardly hear ourselves think, much less speak our lines. Once a fight broke out whilst our Romeo soliloquized, and Bob Armin was stabbed nearly unto death by a drunken tailor who thought he winked at the tailor's winsome wife.

I think Bob did, but hardly deserved to die for the offence.

After a fortnight of journeying, we heard word that York would be closed to us, that there like unto London the plague had struck and the mayor and his council forbade public assemblies.

We were at an inn in Sheffield, a place called the Bear and the Ox, when we heard about York. We made plans then to return to London wherefore our hearts failed at the thought of a week or more of unprofitable travel, even in good weather. But then Gabriel said, "I have a thought, Will, if you and the rest will entertain it."

"Speak," I said. "Given that we are entertainers, we must perforce entertain all thoughts."

"I know of a manor in Staffordshire whose lord will welcome us and pay us well for our services."

"Do you?" I answered. "And who might that be and how would you know of it?"

Gabriel said, "Through my cousin, Robert Catesby, whom you will remember from our youth, though he was but a young lad then. Now he is a man full grown, a man of means and some reputation. His good friend is Stephen Lyttleton, and it is his manor house I speak of: Holbeche House. It is newly built and well-appointed with a great hall that would suit us well for our business."

"Staffordshire is out of the way," I said doubtfully. "I would not want us to trouble ourselves with the journey unless we were assured a welcome and ample reward."

"I could ride on ahead," Gabriel said. "Holbeche House is no more than a day from here. I promise I shall return the day following. I will commend us to Master Lyttleton, but in all truth he already knows of us. He has seen us perform at the Globe, and if he does not bid us come to him straightway, I am no man at all. Besides which, he is a great friend of my cousin Robert."

This cousin's name I remembered, and the little boy who bore it, though it had been years since my visit to the Catesby manor house. I envisioned Robert Catesby sitting in the garden with his noxious tutor, pouring over a book. Yes, he too would be a man now, and doubtless someone of substance in his county given his lineage.

Later, the rest of us discussed Gabriel's proposition and except for Burbage, who was eager to return to his family, we all agreed that Gabriel should set forth as our agent plenipotentiary. I prayed Gabriel's optimism was justified. The income would hardly match what we would have earned in York. Still Staffordshire was only a little out of the way, and I was determined that we should profit all we could and not return to London with so little to show for it.

By the time Gabriel returned to us with the news that we would be more than welcome at Holbeche House, Burbage had come about to our way of thinking. We determined to set out the next morning, which would have kept Gabriel on horseback for three days straight, yet he bravely volunteered, undaunted by the tedious ride. He thereby rose in my esteem, and indeed I had been on better terms with him since his heroic act against Flynt and his friends.

"As to the play, what is his lordship's pleasure?"

"He is no lord."

"A knight then?"

"A country squire only, but well-heeled and admirably wived. The lady is young and a great beauty. You shall see for yourself, and not contest my estimation of Mistress Lyttleton's charms."

I asked again about Lyttleton's preference.

Gabriel shrugged. "He said nothing about that. Only that he was overjoyed at the prospect of our coming. I suppose we may perform what we will."

"Then so we shall," I said. "*As You Like It* will surely suit. It is a pleasant comedy set in a French forest. That is an appropriate setting for a country gentlemen's household."

I was confident in my choice, for it was common for the manor houses to prefer the comedies, perhaps because we oft performed while they ate and laughter was better sauce for a good supper than tragedy or tears. Still, I was resolved that we should give Lyttleton and his comely young wife all they desired by way of our performance. Were we appearing before the king, we would have done no more.

Do you know Staffordshire? It is a most delightsome part of England, reminding me of my own Warwickshire, which indeed is but a good day's ride to the south. On our way we met rolling hills of green and I know not how many pretty vales and streams. We were weary of travel yet the lay of the land delighted our eyes and lightened our hearts.

We talked familiarly along the road, laughing and sometimes singing with Burbage's strong tenor for he was an excellent singer and knew many a ballad both from London and other parts. We thought that if England could ever be thus, even Adam would be consoled for the loss of Eden, for truly it was a paradise we rode through on our way to Holbeche House.

Toward evening of that day, a Wednesday I remember, having begun our journey well before dawn, we drew nigh to our destination. Presently we came upon a stately manor, which Gabriel said was the very place we sought. Glad we were to find it as Gabriel had said, a promising venue for our labours, for we were all weary of our ride and hopeful of Master Lyttleton's hospitality.

For all its newness, the surrounds of Holbeche were most well-groomed and orderly as though the manor had enjoyed its seat for a hundred years or more. There was a fine large garden and an orchard that seemed to cover several acres and be the very symbol of Flora's abundance.

We noticed in a pasture nearby, a dozen or more horses of good stock and, in the midst of them, as many sheep grazing. So different was this scene from the city and its crowded environs that it was like unto a different world, and I wondered if I might be mad to prefer London to such a rural paradise.

Gabriel led us around to the rear of the house, for as actors we were still regarded as servants, our royal patronage notwithstanding, and we knocked upon the postern door. It opened to us and we were immediately welcomed not by some major-domo or butler, which we might have expected, but by the master and mistress of the house themselves, easily recognized by their garb, for I do know the finery of the rich when I see it, as who does not?

Stephen Lyttleton was of middle height with reddish, short-cropped hair and a neatly trimmed beard of the same colour, a broad forehead and lips so thin that there seemed to be no lips at all. His good wife was shorter than he, much younger, slender, beauteous as Gabriel had claimed, dressed in a fine gown that I imagine was the work of a French seamstress so delicate were its stitchery and adornments. Both smiled radiantly.

Before I could speak, they embraced Burbage and me who were at the front of our little troupe and commenced to praise us—for our plays, several titles of which they named, our skills, and our use of language, which they said had no rivals. Gabriel had not deceived us. The Lyttletons proved themselves to be true lovers of our work. Rarely had we been welcomed so, and therefore we were all well pleased with Gabriel, but for whom we would not have had such good fortune as to come to this place.

I introduced each of us to our host and his lady, and Master Lyttleton took each by the hand and shook it as though we were prodigal sons come home again. "You must be hungry, the lot of you," he said loudly as though there were some servant in the recesses of the house who needed to be alerted. "Come. We have been awaiting you all the day. You shall eat your fill and drink to your heart's content. Afterwards, we shall talk of plays and things."

For me, I was more weary from the day's ride than hungry, but my companions pushed their way into the house following an old servant who had suddenly appeared to escort us.

We went into a long corridor that ended in what was clearly the great hall of the house, a commodious, darkly panelled chamber that I immediately conceived as a theatre space although there was no stage and a long trencher table and chairs took up much of the room. On each side, tall windows looked out into the garden, presenting to us a floral abundance quite remarkable for its rich variety of blooms. The servant, a thin old man with a dour countenance, ushered us to our chairs. We stood until our hosts were in place.

At once two other servants, young boys, brought in plates heaped with a variety of meats and fowl; there was also fresh fruit, and a steaming pudding. The old servant, I took him to be the butler, filled our glasses with a sweet wine our host told us was from Spain. I have forgotten from which region of that sunny land, although that is of little importance now.

The Lyttletons indeed lived up to Gabriel's promise. They conversed freely with each of us and spoke knowledgeably of our work. It seemed they spent as much time in London as in Staffordshire, and it appeared they used Holbeche as a summer house, returning to the city in winter where they said they had a house on the Strand.

At meal's end, Master Lyttleton asked to speak to me privately. We withdrew to an adjoining chamber very well appointed with ornate wall hangings and portraits of what I took to be stern-faced ancestors of Lyttleton and his wife. Lights had been fetched. There was a desk in one corner of the room behind which was a bookcase with a collection I would have fain examined under other circumstances.

"Please be seated, Master Shakespeare. We have much to talk of."

I sat down as I was bidden and looked at Lyttleton. He had the solemn expression of a magistrate, yet there was naught in his voice that instilled awe or fear in me, but comfort rather. I thought him a kindly man, well disposed toward us players, treating us almost as equals. This was a rare instance indeed, for with us, the English I mean, the first thing a man must know about himself is who is above him and who below, that he may act rightly—with due reverence or disdain.

He said, "Tomorrow my guests arrive. I expect them early. There will be Master Robert Catesby and his friend a Master Peters and several other gentlemen and their wives."

"Very good, sir," I said, wishing to seem as agreeable as I might.

After naming these persons, he was alert to my reaction as though he expected I might know them and appreciate the quality of his guests. Gabriel's cousin I knew of and said so, though I mentioned nothing of having met him in the flesh when I was a boy and he even younger.

"Robert Catesby is a cousin of Gabriel Catesby, an actor in our company. It was he who came to you to discover whether you wished us to entertain your household and then rode all the day to bring us word we would be welcome. He has often spoken of him, his cousin I mean. The other gentlemen I do not know personally or by reputation." None was of title or public note. I assumed they belonged to the landed gentry who dwelt in manor houses, kept horses, and for pleasure chased the hapless hare or deer. It was not a world I was part of, nor one I envied, content with my own state.

"They are here for a hunt, which will occupy their time during the day," Lyttleton said. "The evening will be yours to entertain us, which I trust you will be pleased to do."

"And so we shall, sir," I said. "That is our business, Master Lyttleton, entertainment. We shall not fail to please you."

Lyttleton nodded agreeably, then continued.

"Oh, by the way, Master Shakespeare. This Catesby of yours, Gabriel by name."

"Yes, sir?"

"You called him Robert Catesby's cousin," said Lyttleton. "I suppose you could call him that."

Lyttleton smiled when he said this. I remember it was a curious smile; his thin lips pursed as though he were on the verge of a revelation of some gravity. And so he was.

"I knew him as a youth, sir," I said. "I once went to the house where he was partly reared. I met his mother and her sisters. I also met his young cousin."

Lyttleton said, "Ah, they are more than cousins, Master Shakespeare. They share the same father, you know."

"But not the same mother," I said, remembering that Gabriel's mother had once been a serving maid in the Catesby house. I saw then the picture his words had painted and wondered that I had not seen it before.

Lyttleton said, "Robert Catesby is an honourable man. His father was an honourable man as well and a devoted Catholic, but, alas, Christ and the Holy Mother alone are without sin. For the rest of us mortals, well, I do not need to tell you, sir, how we all labour against the temptations of the flesh."

I needed no country gentleman to tell me this. Perhaps Lyttleton thought that as an actor I was steeped in sin, as all we actors were supposed to be and in truth most of us were. Still, I knew the temptations well and God knew I had succumbed to them more than once in my life to my regret and shame. As for Gabriel's account of himself as cousin rather than half-brother, I found little fault in his lie, if that is what it was. Perhaps Gabriel was ashamed to admit the truth, to make public his bastardy, to submit himself to ridicule and scorn. If so, he would not be the first man to obscure a parent's disgrace and safeguard his own name from obloquy by hiding the truth of his parentage.

More, what cared I that Gabriel was a bastard? I suppose I had always suspected the same, despite all his talk of kinship. But a man was what he was, I believed. The legitimacy of his birth was a legal quibble. Though a sin, what Sir William did with his maidservant was common as mice in the cellar or a bee amidst flowers. So reasoned I.

"I say not that it is a fault in him," Lyttleton said. "But Gabriel usurps the Catesby name. He presumes upon his tie to an ancient house. He asks from the true heir not merely civility but the bond of brotherhood. Robert Catesby is loath to acknowledge that bond. And pray why should he acknowledge it? Is it a singular honour to have a bastard for a brother?"

He paused, waiting my answer.

"I think not, sir."

"You shall see for yourself how mutual is their love, Master Shakespeare," Lyttleton said, seemingly encouraged by my response, "how Robert Catesby keeps his brother at arm's length, although Gabriel ever yelps at his heels for attention and declares before all the world that he would serve his cousin to the death. It is pathetic to observe such obsequiousness in a man, be he bastard or no."

"Well, this is nothing strange," I said. "Oft it is that not even full brothers in blood regard their fraternity as anything more than an accident of birth. It is no surprise that half-brothers, divided by a father's adultery, should not warm to each other."

"True indeed," Lyttleton said, "yet I advise you while you are here to say naught of their consanguinity. It is enough for you to know that it is a bleeding sore with Robert Catesby, who regards his would-be cousin as a nuisance at best, a plague upon his reputation at worst."

"I will follow your advice, sir, and watch my words," I said. "I do promise you, Master Robert Catesby will have no cause for offence from me, though what Gabriel says to his half-brother whilst my back is turned, I cannot govern."

"I understand," Lyttleton said, smiling pleasantly. "I do not expect you to be his governor, perhaps only his advisor. But now we must plan the evening's events. I thought the great hall might be well suited for your needs and ours. The table, the chairs, can be moved. A stage of sorts can be constructed."

"We are a small number of players, yet I believe we can perform to your satisfaction."

"Excellent, Master Shakespeare. In which case, nothing remains but that we should establish your fee."

He paused, his hands folded. He looked at me inquiringly. His speaking plainly about money at once pleased me. I always preferred that our hosts understood that we did not do our work gratis, that our skills merited more than applause and a half-dozen free meals.

I paused to reckon the cost of our travel. I also considered how much Lyttleton might be able to pay, for we actors, though no tradesmen, were no novices in bargaining. Augustine Phillips had been the best of us at it. I knew that Lyttleton with his London house and his country manor could probably afford to be generous. I named a sum. It doubled what I might elsewhere have charged.

"Fair enough, Master Shakespeare," Lyttleton said. "You shall have your money upon your departure along with my thanks, which I now offer you in advance. I know your play will please my guests and my wife and me as well."

"We will need some convenient place to rehearse," I said.

"You shall have that too, good Master Shakespeare. And a good night's sleep after your arduous journey."

I stood, thinking our business was done, but I was wrong. The most important aspect of it was yet to be decided.

"There is one thing more," Lyttleton said. He bade me sit down again.

"Sir?"

"The play?"

"I thought *As You Like It*, sir. It is a pleasant piece."

"I know it," he said, but his face showed no delight in the prospect.

"We also have a tragedy, *Romeo* by name."

Lyttleton knew the play well, he said. "I would prefer something other than your *Romeo*, which for my company might be too dark in its sad conclusion. As for the comedy, while it may display wit and provoke laughter, yet it wants something I do think in gravity and insight."

For this response I was not prepared. To this moment Lyttleton had been the soul of courtesy. Suddenly, he was a critic.

"Insight?" I said, bristling a little, for I held that comedy was no trifling stuff wanting insight or wisdom, but like tragedy, an imitation of life from which a man could learn social graces, love's rewards, wit's true nature, the virtues and duties of kings, and I know not how many other things pertaining to God and man. This was true of my *As You Like It* which dealt as much with equity, honour, and filial regard as it did with the verbal wit of Jacques or the clowning of Aries.

"Do you mean you want a weightier theme?" I asked. "Something deep, difficult? Something that must be teased out or it makes no sense?"

Lyttleton laughed. "In truth, I was thinking of something with a classical flavour, an old Greek setting, or a Roman."

Here he paused, placing his finger to his forehead as though he were running over in his mind the repertory of my work and knew it all as well as I. "*Julius Caesar*. His murder in the senate. The heroism, the patriotism of Brutus. Yes, that would please me well and our guests too. All are interested in politics, affairs of state, you see, and your Julius Caesar is a political play, is it not?"

"It's a play about an assassination," I said, trying to choose my words carefully. "About treason and its consequences. Yes, that would be political enough, but perhaps inflammatory. I have had some experience offending the powers that be with plays touching upon the murder of an anointed king."

"But Caesar was no king," Lyttleton protested.

"He would have made himself so," I returned. "It is a distinction without difference. At least in this case. The essence is not in the title. It is in the function, the role. Kings, emperors, dukes, earls—it is all one if they are in lawful authority and those beneath are restive under their rule, rebel, murder him duly appointed."

"Yet your audience, sir, consists of gentlemen and their ladies, not the common rout who are subject to the inflammation of which you speak. Surely, you do not expect them to insurrect like a mob or conspire in back alleys to undermine the State."

He laughed, though I thought my argument sound enough.

"To be sure," I said, not wanting to be disagreeable to so congenial a host or impugn the loyalty of his guests. "Caesar's tragedy is an old play for us. We have not performed it in a half-dozen years. Playing it will burden my colleagues who must perform from memory. I have not the playbook with me, and so we may be able to perform the work but in part. Dick Burbage, who has played Caesar more times than great Caesar himself, has an excellent memory, but, alas, he is only human."

Lyttleton said, "If it were no more than the scene of Caesar's murder, and yet Brutus and Mark Antony's famous speech thereafter it would delight and instruct us all. I pray you, Master Shakespeare, I would consider its performance to be a most singular honour to me and my guests."

I saw that, though inconvenient for us, there would be no denying his request. I said, "We will do what we can do and put new wine into an old bottle."

118

"Oh, sir, I will make your task the easier."

"How so?" I asked.

"I have a part of your script. Not your script, but say, a copy made by one who wished to peruse the play, not merely see it performed, one who, say, desired to reflect the very essence of your genius."

Was this false praise ringing in my ears, or the declaration of an honest appreciation? I could not tell from Lyttleton's expression. At once I thought of Nicholas Morgan, who had purloined Gabriel's copy of *Othello*, but before I could imagine his career of script snatching reaching back so far into the past, Lyttleton added, "It was done, this transcription, by my servant at my behest, so impressed was I by certain scenes in the play."

He reached into the drawer of his desk and pulled from it several sheets of paper. He perused the writing thereon and then handed the pages to me.

"There are not many scenes here," I said, having quickly read through the same pages. "It is but a part of my play. Much is left out."

"True, Master Shakespeare, but important scenes are included, ones that show the true dignity of Caesar's tragedy. Also, the eloquence of your invention."

The eloquence of my invention. It was a phrase that pleased me well. I bowed my head at the compliment. I could do no less, yet I could not help thinking on how difficult it was to keep one's work his own. Was there a way to prevent audience members from bringing pen and paper with them to the theatre? And what of those with so excellent a memory that they could recall whole passages without effort?

Perhaps it was hopeless. Still, I could hardly reprimand my host for possessing that which I would prefer he not. I had been through that with John Flynt. I would have less success with a lord of the manor.

He rang a bell sitting on his desk before him. At once the dour butler appeared at the door.

"Your comrades have already been shown to their chambers and may already be asleep for all I know," Lyttleton said.

"Well deserved their slumber," I said. "We set out before cockcrow. It was a long, hard ride."

"Then, sir, is your rest well earned. Templeton," Lyttleton said to his servant, "show Master Shakespeare where he shall lodge during his stay with us. And see to it that all his needs are met."

The butler said, "All has been prepared for Master Shakespeare. He shall want for naught."

Lyttleton turned to me and fixed me with a contemplative gaze. He was not smiling now, but clearly distracted by some idea. I could not fathom it but was at that moment too weary to care. He said, "I wish you a good night then, sir, and pleasant dreams. Consider this house as your own."

What host who tells a guest the house is his has ever meant it? I know not, yet I was grateful to my particular host for his many courtesies and went bedward with that gratitude warming my heart. I was led up the stairs and down a passage with a row of bedchambers on each side, the butler, who I now knew as Templeton, tottering before me, his candle trembling as he walked, creating strange shadows on the walls. Presently, I was shown into a chamber with a huge bed with four posts like tree trunks and a tall ornately carved wardrobe. It was a handsome room, one designed for a person surely greater in station than I, though I made no objection to my assigned place of repose for all that.

A brace of candles burned steadily by the bed. A fire had been laid on the hearth, for though it was summer, the house was cold. There was also a basin of water and soap and towel at hand. This I much appreciated. The day's long ride had left me covered with dust and sticky with sweat.

Templeton gone, I sat me down upon the bed with a groan and began removing my clothes. My buttocks were sore from the saddle. My head ached a little as it sometimes did after I had spent a whole day in the sun. I washed myself with the sweet-smelling soap. It was scented with lavender, ever a delightsome aroma to me.

I fell asleep at once. If I dreamed, I do not remember it.

It has been, after all, many years past.

17

Come morning I roused myself with some trouble from a sleep that had so enveloped me that when I first moved, my limbs were slow to answer to the helm of my will, and I lay there in the soft morning light like a man sapped of strength, old before his time.

In truth, I am no hot-blooded youth, still not so old as that.

Next came a resolute knocking at my door. "Come," I said. And then appeared not the dour butler I expected but a young maid of perhaps twelve or thirteen years, very winsome but downcast as though she bore the weight of the world on her thin shoulders.

She was, as I say, a pretty maid, a vision of youthful innocence if such exists in this fallen world. She bid me good morrow and then said in a sweet, lilting voice that quite enchanted me, "Your companions already are at table, sir, and feed as though it were their last meal. They asked me to wake you. They said they want your counsel, or so they told me."

"My counsel? They said that, did they? Then they shall have it and in good supply," I said. I looked at her sad countenance again and wondered whatever should inflict such sorrow.

"What is your name, child, and what is the matter? Why so

despairing when you have youth and beauty as well to commend you?"

She did not answer my question as to the cause of her sadness. Nor did she blush at my feeble flattery of her charms. She did tell me her name. "Alice," she said. "Alice Simpkins."

Her lips were little rose buds. Her eyes were clear and blue as robin's egg.

"Have you been a servant here long?" I asked, thinking it impossible that she should be as young as she seemed.

"A month this Friday."

"Are you treated well by your master and mistress?" I asked, thinking that ill use might be the cause of her sorrow.

"Oh yes, sir, very well. I eat two meals a day and have a dry bed, which is far more than I had at my father's house. And here I am not beaten."

"I am happy for you," I said, wondering that a parental hand should ever be raised against such an angel child, or what silly offence might provoke it.

"Well God save you and bring you good fortune," I said.

I gave her a coin from my pocket. On second thought, I gave her another. I was sorry for her, and in my ignorance of her troubles I felt helpless to do more. I sent her off to inform my friends that I was not dead but much alive and prepared for the new day, which, when I looked from my window, was one of supernal loveliness, the perfect complement to our good fortune, and augury, I believed, of more good fortune to come.

Below in the courtyard I saw certain gentlemen and ladies descending from their mounts. Lyttleton's guests, I supposed, one of whom would surely be Gabriel's brotherly cousin, Robert Catesby. And with that I remembered Lyttleton's admonition that I say nothing of what I had learned about them, not to Gabriel Catesby, not to Robert Catesby.

It would be, I thought, an easy promise to keep. My lips were sealed. Why should they not be? The two kinsmen's relationship and its complexities were no business of mine.

Below stairs, I found my friends at table amid the remains of a generous breakfast. Again, we had been served in the dining room rather than the kitchen, where we were by custom hosted when performing at a country house. I had heard my friends before I saw them, for they were engaged in lively talk about some bear the dogs had subdued, on which vulgar occasion Burbage had lost a goodly sum in a foolish wager. My friends argued the merits of the bear, not the dogs. Burbage complained that for a big, hairy fellow, the bear was a right coward and should be ashamed of himself for losing the contest.

I greeted all, cut a sliver of cheese to slack my appetite, and began to explain what I had discussed with Lyttleton the night before.

"*Julius Caesar*!" Burbage exclaimed. "Good God, I don't think I remember the lines."

"You shall refresh your memory with a script, which Master Lyttleton gave unto me last night," I said.

"A script, you say? But how did he—?" Burbage began before I interrupted him.

"How he came by it is a tale for another time, good Dick. When I learn it myself. As for now, you and all, wipe you mouths and let us to work. We are not here to gourmandize, but to perform our craft and confirm again that of all the players in England we are foremost. Come now, by Master Lyttleton's bounty we have a place to rehearse, the promise of a handsome fee for our services, and but a few hours to perfect ourselves."

They rose from the table, Gabriel with the most exuberance, for he was obviously eager to show his competence in a new part. Templeton had entered to convey us to where we should rehearse the "Roman play" as he called it. We followed him down a corridor and then turned into a long, pleasant gallery, well-furnished like the rest of the house.

We seated ourselves.

"Wherefore should we not present the play as a whole?" Burbage asked. "If the man likes the play, why should he wish it shorter?"

Burbage's complaints were echoed by Armin, who had also performed in the play five years before.

"It is a mockery if this is all there is," Armin protested. "This performance will be all about Caesar and his sins. Save for delivering the final blow, Brutus has little to declaim, less to do. And there is no third and fourth act, so his repentance of his deed and self-condemnation go unexpressed. He shall never fall upon a sword in this version. He shall have no cause. There is, in a word, no tragedy of Brutus, only Caesar's fall."

I agreed. "The death of a man condemned for his ambition."

"Well, it is a far different play than we staged," Burbage grumbled.

"By heaven, it is a different play than I wrote," I returned that he should know we did not differ on that point either. "My words, yet not my plot. Still Lyttleton is paying for our service and that is no small matter. Wherefore I have committed us to Master Lyttleton's script, mockery though it may be."

There was some more talk among us about this. No surprise there. Though I was a principal sharer in the company yet was I no dictator. What we did together we did by mutual consent, consent sometimes achieved with difficulty since our mutual love did not erase our differences of opinion, which were not a few and touched almost every aspect of our work.

"All who favour our going forward?" I asked.

All hands raised.

I was much relieved.

"Then let us decide who shall play which part," I said.

"I hope to be Caesar since I am seasoned in his toga," Burbage declared.

"You have never worn a toga, Dick," I said. "Your hose and jerkin have ever served you well enough. Besides, garb is not the essence of history, or tragedy, which are so often the same."

"True," Burbage said. "Who cares what old Romans wore in ancient times, and in a climate that would permit it? I would look unseemly in a toga."

We all laughed.

"Very well," I said. "Dick will play Caesar, as he prefers."

"May I be Brutus, then?" Gabriel asked.

I said, "Methinks I will save that role for myself if you please. I do in large part remember the lines. For you, Gabriel, you must start from the beginning. Play Cassius's part, Cassius the seducer without whom Brutus might never have joined the conspiracy. The part will remind you more than a little of Iago. I swear it is no piece of fluff. It will challenge your talent for duplicity, or at least its likeness. Are you for it?"

"Duplicity is against my nature, Will, but I am an actor."

"And, therefore, your particular nature is immaterial to performance. Is that not true?"

"I have so been schooled," Gabriel said, making a little bow.

"Then do you be Cassius and hold back nothing in duplicity and most subtle malice."

"They are yours, with all my heart," Gabriel said with a crisp bow.

Gabriel Catesby could charm when he put his mind to it.

"We shall require some citizens of Rome, an angry mob to cheer and jeer," Armin said.

"Two or three will have to do," I answered.

Our boy players were following our talk with great interest. "The true version of the play has women's parts," I said. "Portia, the wife of Brutus, and the wife of Caesar, Pompeia. Sadly, Master Lyttleton has not included their scenes in his version. You two must represent the Roman spectators to Caesar's fall."

"Shall we have lines, Master Shakespeare?" one of the boys asked.

"No," I said. "But you must cheer when signalled. You may use what words you wish to express your joy at Caesar's demise. Master Lyttleton can supply a gardener and a cook to swell the scene."

"That's still a small Roman crowd," Burbage observed.

"Small but sufficient," I answered, growing impatient with Burbage's cynicism, even though in part I shared it. "Imagination that must furnish the antiquities of Rome on a naked stage can also make of a half-dozen citizens the larger assembly they represent. When in the history of our craft has imagination not accomplished its worthy end? It is the very essence of our work."

"So then," Burbage said, "your tragedy of Caesar is reduced to the temptation of Brutus and the assassination of Caesar."

"Also Brutus's speech of extenuation," Armin said.

"In the full play refuted by Marc Antony's famous lines," Burbage noted, unnecessarily since all of us knew the play well, save for Gabriel and our two apprentice boys who admitted they had never seen it. One of the boys said he had never so much as heard of Caesar, Julius or otherwise, and that he understood Rome to be somewhere in Wales.

We all laughed at this, even the boy who had confessed his ignorance. No great shame there since we were actors, not geographers.

"Oh, it is capital drama," Burbage said, laughing more loudly than us all. "If it takes us more than a quarter of an hour to do this version of your play, good Will, it will be because one of us has forgotten his lines and must go fetch a prompter from the next town over. We shall not give our audience time to blink afore the action's done and we stand before them to receive their applause, should there be any."

More laughter followed.

"*Friends, Romans, and countrymen, lend me your ears,*" Burbage intoned with all the gestures as though he were on stage and not seated in a chair, as were we all in this pleasant chamber. "*I come to bury Caesar, not to praise him.*"

I joined in. "*The evil that men do lives after them. The good is oft buried with their bones.*"

"As true a statement as ever made," Burbage said. "And the word you wrote is *interred*, Will, not *buried*, though I grant they mean the same. Besides which, the good is almost always interred with one's bones. Supposing there be any good to inter."

"Aye, that is the question," Armin said.

We all laughed.

"Our audience will receive no more than that," I said. "Lyttleton assures me that will be enough. Besides, we might offend him if we do more, since we would be contradicting his express instructions. Let's be at peace with this. Let's resolve to do our best."

"You are scrupulous to accommodate our host," Burbage said, regarding me suspiciously.

"I am," I said. "He pays us well, more than double what we might have expected save the king's in residence. You shall see. And he has friends who can do us good. I am only being practical, Dick."

Burbage snorted, a noise I knew expressed his doubt.

18

For the next several hours all practised his parts, alone or with another with whom he should converse in the play. When we stopped it was past noon by the clock. We were far from perfect, but when was it otherwise? A rehearsal could be free of error, yet the performance go awry. I had seen it happen many a time. It would happen again. We had all suffered such outcomes and lived to tell the tale.

"Let us take a rest from these labours," I said to them all. "And then meet again at two o'clock. Let each go his own way and do whatever he wills. Sleep or talk, whatever. Let the words of your roles settle in until you and your role are one and the same soul."

It was counsel I had given many a time. It was counsel I gave unto myself whenever I took the stage to play a part.

My role as Brutus was easy enough. I had played him often and the script did naught more than nudge my memory and bring all back in a flood. Burbage had little need of the script. He had a prodigious memory. I might forget lines I had written, but Burbage never forgot lines he had uttered. He was quite wonderful that way. We all envied him.

I passed my time out in the garden, making myself into a Roman senator, the noble Brutus, yet too easily seduced by Cassius to his friend Caesar's hurt and his own, for like a good Roman he takes his own life in the end.

We were not to show that, however. Lyttleton had forbade it.

I recited what I had written five years before. It was difficult not to wish to change a word or phrase, to clarify the sense, to tweak a metaphor or simile, or just to massage the metre to my ear's liking. It is the bane of authors that at some point in time their words are fixed beyond repentance, which words at an earlier point that author presided over like unto a god, adding and subtracting at will.

I was about to return to the house when I heard my name called and looked up to see the mistress of the house advancing toward me.

This gentlewoman was, as I have written, a personage of some beauty. That day she wore a plumb-coloured gown adorned with ornate lace and a bonnet displaying the same skill. Yellow locks rained upon her shoulders, framing the face of a goddess. Her lips were full and rosy and her cheeks perfect damask as though neither wind nor sun had ever abused them, nor would dare to do so. I reckoned her to be twenty or twenty-two, considerably younger than her husband, who must have been near unto my age, perhaps a little older.

"Master Shakespeare, we are well met," she said. "I have found you in good time."

Attempting gallantry, I answered. "What time would not be good for you to seek me or any man, dear lady?"

She laughed a little at this clumsy flattery, for that was what it was, and her countenance became all the more radiant.

She took my arm and guided me along the path as though I were some tottering elderly fellow who needed steadying. It would have offended had she not been so fair a creature.

"My husband is much pleased by your visit," she said. "He has heard so well of you from his city friends. How you and your company are the best of players of the world. That you and your troupe should visit us here at Holbeche House is an honour we never contemplated should be ours."

"Your praising words do me more honour than I deserve, my lady."

She said a few more things that pleased me greatly, praise of my plays, praise of my acting. I lapped it up like a starving dog. Condemn me not. Who, pray tell, is not pleased by the compliments of a beautiful woman?

I am but a man.

When I become a god, upon oath, I shall resist flattery.

Then her expression darkened. "This is an awkward thing I have to say to you," she began.

"Let it not be so, Mistress Lyttleton. Nothing is awkward if it be graciously intended and received in the same spirit. Speak, I pray you. Fear nothing of me."

She paused and stared at the ground nervously, but most charmingly. "You have among you a Gabriel—"

"Catesby," I said, providing the name she had yet to utter.

She paused for a moment and then continued:

"He is a proper man, this Gabriel Catesby, your friend, your colleague. I mean with handsome features, and he is well-spoken."

"I suppose that can be said of him," I said.

"And most alluring to women," she said. "To some women, at least."

I am no simpleton who must be kicked in the behind to catch her drift. I spied the port she sailed for. I began to sweat. My collar tightened. I could not defend Gabriel, not at this minute until I knew whereof he was blamed, yet it took no prophet to foretell the offence complained of. Gabriel, for all his professed religiosity, was besotted with women. He had proved it often since we had renewed

131

our acquaintance but, as it was naught to me what he did in his private hours, I had said nothing. It was his business, but at that moment I feared it was about to become mine as well.

"He flirts with our maids, uses fine words to seduce them," she said. "Especially one named Alice Simpkins, who is but twelve years and the youngest of our housemaids. Our housekeeper caught the two of them in a dark corner doing that which is not to be done save within the bonds of matrimony, and not to one of so tender an age as she."

"When did this happen?"

"Yesternight, near eleven o'clock."

"He forced himself upon her?" I asked, holding my breath and at once remembering Alice Simpkins' dejected countenance.

I saw it pained her, this virtuous lady, to even give the deed a name. And I did agree it was beyond the pale of decency, beyond question a rape, given Alice's age and the great unlikelihood that she consented to the act with a strange older man.

"And you have no doubt it was Gabriel who accosted her?"

"None," she said. "Our housekeeper saw the act, saw his face. She is an honest woman. She would rather die than bear false witness."

What could I say to this? I could not fly to Gabriel's defence. The housekeeper's account was too plausible.

"I will rebuke him," I said. "I promise you there will be no more trouble of this kind. And he will be punished, punished according to his deserts."

I declared this confidently, but in truth did not know who should administer such punishment. The law? Ourselves? Or should we wait upon God's judgement to strike the miscreant down? The rape of a serving girl was a crime in law, but if such offences were ever prosecuted, I knew naught of it. Not when the perpetrator was a gentleman, or anything like unto it. I was full of doubts as to what should be done.

"I have not told my husband of this," Mistress Lyttleton whispered confidentially, touching my shoulder. "I know he would send this actor of yours from the house and thus defeat his desire to hear your play. I too would be disappointed."

"I thank you, lady, for your discretion," I said. "Trust me. Gabriel Catesby will not offend again, not while I am here to prevent it."

"Thank you, Master Shakespeare. I am in your debt."

"No, dear lady. The debt is mine."

Another much practised bow, more restrained than the first but to my mind sufficiently solemn.

The lady smiled wanly and bid me good day, assuring me that she was as thrilled about our upcoming performance as was her husband. Yet she looked worried.

I feared my brave assurances had erased the doubts of neither of us.

19

I was still thinking about Gabriel and poor Alice Simpkins when I heard my name called again.

"Master Shakespeare?"

Stephen Lyttleton walked toward me, not a minute beyond his wife's departure.

"A word, Master Shakespeare, if you please."

Lyttleton was not alone. The garden which I had envisioned as a peaceful retreat had become a thoroughfare. Was I now to receive yet another account of Gabriel's lechery? Or perhaps some even more distressing report?

Thankfully, it was otherwise. Lyttleton's broad smile assured me of that even before his next words.

"I desire you to meet my guest, Master Shakespeare. May I present Master Robert Catesby. He is from your own part of England and much wishes to make your acquaintance."

I made a quick bow and took Lyttleton's guest in. This Catesby I had met when he was but a young boy at his tutor's side, shy and largely indifferent to his older cousin's friend. Would he remember me? It had been more than a score of years gone. If he did, he made no sign, but gave me a long, penetrating stare, as though he would know not only me, but my heart of hearts. I was struck at once by his resemblance to Gabriel. Had I not learned that they were half-brothers I might have supposed them to be so, merely on their likeness, which I now realized Gabriel had cultivated. The colour and cut of their beards were alike as though they shaved at the same glass. Their eyes were the same eyes, their brows arched alike, the tone of their flesh equally radiant with health. I imagined how the younger brother must have bridled at the older's copying him, the conscious imitation another stain upon his honour and affront to the family name. At least as Lyttleton recounted it.

Granted, Robert Catesby was the better dressed for he was well to do, legitimate and schooled in the manners of the court. I remember he wore a grey cape and a doublet with silver buttons. Some bird had sacrificed colourful feathers for his hat. He had a neat white collar, then in fashion among London gentlemen, and boots that were shined to glass as though their soles touched only upon Turkish carpets or tread the streets of Heaven. In sum, he was an imposing gentleman, and even before he spoke, he expressed a kind of confidence and superiority even in the way he carried himself.

I took note of the silver crucifix he wore about his neck. It was a handsome piece, worth more than twenty crowns I supposed. It was a bold declaration of his faith in a time when such boldness was perilous, yet he was on friendly ground at Holbeche, the Lyttletons being Catholic.

I waited for him to speak to see if the voices were as alike as their general appearance. They were not. Robert Catesby's voice was the deeper, his speech more clipped and full of authority; a man used to command; a man conscious of his station, of his heritage, of the fact his ancestors were named in Holinshed's history as counsellors to kings.

"I have heard oft of you, Master Shakespeare," Catesby said with the slightest of nods toward me.

"Good things, I pray," I answered, bowing politely at the compliment.

"Wondrous things, in fact."

"Well, sir, I am but a poor player."

"And maker of plays," Catesby added. "But excellent on both counts, or so I have heard."

I bowed a third time. A little deeper now, and with a flourish of my hand. It was my afternoon to be praised, I decided, and timely too, for I was much depressed by what Mistress Lyttleton had told me about Gabriel and already I was preoccupied with what was to be done with him.

"Let us go indoors," Lyttleton said. "The sun is hot. I trust we may pull you away from your meditations for a brief hour."

I was about to explain that I was rehearsing, not just thinking, but then decided against it. He was, after all, my host. What could I do but comply?

We three went indoors to Lyttleton's study. Templeton brought wine, I remember, a different wine than we had had the night before, but equal in quality, fruity with a pleasant aftertaste. I resolved not to drink too much of it. I prefer to remain in control of my tongue, and wine is a great liberator of that oft-troublesome organ.

"I have told Master Catesby of the play you intend this evening. He is most eager to see it."

"I am indeed," Catesby said, smiling in a way to make me suspect his warmth was false. "I understand it treats of Caesar's assassination."

"That is the gist of it," I said. "Though the full play addresses more. It shows Brutus first being led by Cassius to betray his friend. It does show how he becomes betimes a part of a conspiracy and the operation thereof. It—"

"The part in the script I gave unto you is that part which interests Master Catesby the most," Lyttleton interrupted in such a tone of voice, it was clear that he should not be persuaded otherwise.

"We shall perform as you directed, sir," I said, turning to my host. "No more nor less."

"Very good," Lyttleton said.

Then Catesby said, "You know, Master Shakespeare, you and I have met before though it has been many years. I was a small boy then in the company of my tutor. You came to our house in Lapham with a present for my father. It was a handsome pair of gloves. Do you not remember?"

"I do remember," I said.

"My father who, like your own, now receives heaven's honours, treasured those gloves all of his life. He gave in return I believe a certain document to your father, or saw that he received it.

"He did," I said, wondering that such an august gentleman should have troubled himself to take note of my father's death.

"Do you still have it?"

"My father hid it away," I answered.

I saw no reason to lie. I trusted Catesby was no agent for the government seeking those who might have loyalties to Rome, which I suspect my father did, although he did not press his religious opinions upon his wife and children.

"Fathers and sons often share the same devotion," Catesby said.

"So they do," I answered. "Yet my father's beliefs were his own. I have not been persuaded in that direction."

"Not persuaded, Master Shakespeare? I do not understand you," Catesby said.

"I mean his faith was deeply rooted in his childhood. My father and I were of different generations for all the blood that ties us. Our Stratford church bore no images of the Old Faith, which images had been erased from its walls. Our priests married. We honoured the Virgin but did not equate her with God or Christ. We prayed in the queen's English, not in Latin."

Catesby pursed his lips, smiled indulgently, and said, "Some of these differences are but outward trappings, nothing of the essence. And does it make so great a difference in what language prayer is uttered? Does not God speak every human tongue, so that no man can say he does not pray because God does not comprehend his language?"

I followed these gentlemen into the house and into Lyttleton's study. I was invited to sit, and almost immediately a knock came at the door. Lyttleton said, "Come." A man appeared who was presented to me as John Peters.

This Peters, unlike Lyttleton and Catesby, was more soberly and plainly dressed in dark hose and doublet devoid of ornament. He looked about thirty or perhaps somewhat more. He wore no hat, bore no sword or other weapon, and his black curly hair was tight upon his scalp. Of complexion he was swarthy, like an Italian or some Frenchmen. He had a hawk-like nose, thick, sensuous lips, and a kind of lisp when he spoke. He smiled a good deal, a trait that some admire and some despise. I know not where I stand on the question, yet I thought him inoffensive enough, despite a penetrating gaze that I am sure would have intimidated the devil had it been fixed upon him.

Peters held a small book in his hand which I recognized as a prayer book, not the Book of Common Prayer which we used at home, but a Roman missal. By this sign I inferred he was a priest, probably a Jesuit missionary, although he had not been introduced as such and he wore no crucifix about his neck as Robert Catesby did.

"Come in and sit with us, Master Peters. We were just talking about religion."

"Were you indeed," Peters said, smiling broadly at me as though he could not wait to hear my views on the subject. He spoke with an accent of sorts. I did not recognize it. Some part of England I did not know. "Pray do not let me interrupt. I will sit and prepare myself to be edified."

"This is Master William Shakespeare, the London playwright," Lyttleton said, nodding toward where I sat.

"Who has not heard of Master Shakespeare?" Peters said, making a perfunctory bow and then taking a chair opposite mine.

"A good many, I would think," I said.

"I beg to differ," Peters said. "Everywhere your plays are spoken of. You are a man of considerable influence, you know."

"What Master Peters says is true," Lyttleton said. "Influence for good, for a proper understanding of things."

"Take, for instance, the England that now is," Catesby said, leaning toward me. "Everywhere there is confusion."

I did not know what he meant, which uncertainty must have shown in my face.

He continued. "Confusion about what is true and what is not, what is right and what is wrong. These are the fundamentals of morality, are they not?"

Catesby looked to me for an answer to this question.

"I do believe they are, sir," I said.

"Of course they are," Peters declared triumphantly as though someone amongst us had suggested otherwise.

"Master Shakespeare's father was a good Catholic, though forced to hide his faith," Catesby said, turning to Peters.

"A great shame." Peters shook his head and looked at me with sad eyes.

Though these sentiments were doubtless intended to console me, they did otherwise. I bristled with annoyance.

"My father, John Shakespeare, was a worthy man," I said. "A sound Christian. He was no Papist. I grant you he was not unsympathetic to the plight of some Catholics, the oppression I do mean, yet he attended our Holy Trinity faithfully. Our whole family did. He was never accused of neglecting the duty that the law requires."

Catesby said, "I am sure that is true, yet did he not cross himself daily on one occasion or another? Did he not venerate the Virgin Mother and pray to her in the quiet sessions of the night?"

"I know nothing of my father's private prayers," I said, much annoyed by this prying. For was that not what it was, a rude intrusion upon my father's deepest thoughts? Why should these men inquire as to what my father affirmed or denied in the way of faith? Was not this the most personal of matters, to be offered to another voluntarily, not by compulsion?

I continued. "And if he ever mentioned the Pope's name, I never heard it. He was honoured in our town, granted a coat of arms, which arms I secured for him with much effort. He held public office. None of these would have come his way were he Papist, not in Stratford."

My ire was rising. These men had presumed over much upon my free and open nature, and I was almost ready to declare my service in the house at an end. What if we lost the generous fee Lyttleton

140

promised? There were other manors in England, other lords and ladies hungry for our work.

Peters must have seen my agitation. He raised a hand to silence the others.

"I fear we have offended you, Master Shakespeare. For that I am heartily sorry. Such was never our intent, but only to commend your father for his faithfulness and at most remind you of your heritage."

"I need not be reminded of my heritage, sir," I returned sharply. "My heritage is my father's decency, his honest effort. His loyalty to his country and to his queen. That is my heritage from my father."

"Granted, sir. He was like unto your Brutus, an honourable man," Peters said.

I didn't know how to take this remark. Was it an insult to my father, or merely a slip of memory about my play, since Mark Antony's description of Brutus, dripping with irony, was far from being a genuine compliment? I decided to give Peters the benefit of the doubt.

"Your own religious sensibilities notwithstanding, Master Shakespeare," Catesby said, "I do hope you share your honest father's sympathies for what we suffer under the present king."

"With all due respect to you gentlemen, I may not hear the king spoken ill of," I said, interrupting what I feared might become a long recital of the king's wrongs and ready to stand in protest to these impertinent suggestions. "I am His Majesty's servant. I wear his livery. Should I speak ill of him, I would be both ungrateful and treasonous."

"I understand you, Master Shakespeare," Catesby said in what I took as an attempt to calm me. He laughed. "No one speaks of treason here. Why, sir, perish the thought and be assured that we are all true Englishmen, loyal to a fault. But you see everywhere we Catholics are persecuted, fined, imprisoned, and yes, sometimes slain, for doing nothing more than desiring our own way of worship. I myself was imprisoned for a time, and fines still weigh heavily upon my house because we were in league with my Lord of Essex."

"Essex was a traitor and justly executed," I said. "Besides which, he was no Catholic."

"Nor was he a Puritan, or a persecutor of our cause," Catesby said. "Had he prevailed in his contest with the queen, we should have been free to worship as we pleased. We would have enjoyed liberty in our own country and not been persecuted for our faith."

"Think on this, Master Shakespeare," Peters said, picking up the thread of his companion's argument. "As I have said, you are a man of influence. Thousands see your plays and learn from them the ways of honest government and righteous rule. They see, for example, the mighty brought down by vain ambition or greed. They see the rewards of virtue, the consequences of vice. They see the true depiction of royal greatness and tyranny's cruel fist. They see what follows from mob rule. Wherefore I say again, you, sir, are a greater teacher than all the professors of our universities who, with their tedious lectures, dull the ear, whereas you incite the imagination to deeds of valour and civic virtue."

Peters stopped and looked intently at me. He was breathing hard, full of passionate conviction. His forehead shined with sweat.

I felt it was my turn to speak again and yet I had naught to say to this fulsome flattery, which I knew it to be, having practised the flatterer's art myself more than once.

I sat quietly for a while as did they. Finally, Lyttleton said, "I think we have stayed you too long, Master Shakespeare. We look forward to seeing Caesar slain this night. In the meantime, we ask only that you consider our words. In the near future things may change in our country. The state of Catholics may improve and all and sundry enjoy the liberty of conscience. How might this come about, you ask? I answer that God will bring it about, for He is mighty to save. It would please us if you were a part of this great change."

My host smiled and even laughed a little as though to make light of the prophecy he had uttered. "Who knows what may happen in the fullness of time."

"I do hope we can talk more of this," Catesby said, taking my hand in his. It was not an ungracious gesture, but I felt uncomfortable with it. Indeed, I felt uncomfortable with them all. I had talked religion with Ben Jonson more than once. He was Catholic to the bone though I do not think this was known by many. Nevertheless, we talked, he to learn my thinking, I to understand his. Neither tried to persuade the other or coerce. It was not like unto the conversing that I had just experienced where I was besieged by three gentlemen more knowledgeable and zealous than I, each bent on beating me into submission with his learned arguments and talk of God, the persecution of their sect, and disorder in the state.

It may not have been treason I heard, but did these men not totter wildly upon its verge?

20

In the long and elegant gallery, Armin and Burbage went through their lines. I was thankful Gabriel was not with them. I needed to speak to my friends alone. "We must talk about Gabriel," I said.

"What of him?" Burbage asked, looking up from the script.

"He has accosted a young serving girl of the house," I said.

"This is news?" Burbage asked, with something between a laugh and a snort. "Surely, Will, bees are less drawn to honey than he to a sweet wench's breast or thigh."

"The wench is Alice Simpkins," I said. "One of the maids of this house. She is but twelve or thirteen. His act is an indecency not to be endured or tolerated by us."

"I think I know the deflowered virgin of whom you speak," Armin said. "A fair piece, with very good features and a body that belies her age."

"The very one," I said.

"Pray tell, did they do the deed of darkness?" Burbage asked. "Or did he only grope her?"

"I don't know the details of the offence," I said. "And does it make a difference, since the assault was upon a mere child and certainly unwanted? I heard this from Mistress Lyttleton herself, and she from the housekeeper, an honest woman in whom her mistress has implicit faith as a witness to the assault."

"In nine months it may make a great difference," Burbage said. "And in the meantime too, when her belly begins to swell and questions are asked. How came you by this? This housekeeper saw them at it, you say?"

"Saw him at her," I said.

"Did Mistress Lyttleton tell her husband what happened?" Armin asked.

"She told only me," I answered. "She wants our play to go forward for her husband and her guests' sake and believes that if her husband knew he would dismiss us all and goodbye to our fee. A wasted two days."

"Very likely he would," Burbage said.

"Gabriel has assaulted a simple girl, a child. We talk of rape here. There is no other way to say it," I said. "And it touches upon our honour as well, since he is one of us. What he has done cannot be ignored or mitigated."

"So what's to be done with the ravisher?" Burbage asked. "Shall we hang him to a tree, or deprive him of his manhood, haul him before the sheriff, or bind him till he die of hunger or thirst?"

"Something less severe, I think, for we are neither executioners nor jailors, and I would not match his outrage with one of our own. Rather, I say though he is my friend and we have a long history, let him find other business for himself and stain not our honour nor our reputation, which we all have nurtured most carefully. We are King's Men, not ravishers of children. Should this be bruited about the court, our theatre would be in grave jeopardy."

The more I gave voice to those thoughts, the worse it was with me. I nearly choked with anger. Yet my friends were not so eager to pounce upon our fellow actor. I could see the hesitation in their faces.

145

Neither spoke. There was a long silence. I imagined the cause of their reluctance before they expressed it.

Then Burbage spoke, but calmly in contrast to my indignation, for he was ever calm in disputation. "You're right, of course. We shall tell Gabriel that he is no longer one of us. Tell him that he presents too great a risk, for what he has done in this house he will surely do in others, exposing us to shame and lawful retribution."

Armin agreed.

Burbage continued. "Say to him that when we leave a great house, we look for thanks and gold, not to see ourselves pursued by outraged masters, husbands, or fathers seeking righteous vengeance. Say to him that if he must satisfy his lust, let him do it upon a full-grown woman who consents to his advances, not on children. Yet—"

And when Burbage uttered that short word, I knew he was ready to present the other side, for that was ever his way. He was nothing if not circumspect in all matters.

"Let us not be hasty in execution of our judgement, dear Will. But stay your wrath to consider this, that without Gabriel we cannot do the play tonight. We are in a dilemma, Will, if I may say so, though your old friend has put us there."

"What are you suggesting?" I asked.

Burbage went on. "Simply that we not act against our own interests in pursuing a swift justice."

"Our own interests?"

"May we not wait until our performance is complete and Master Lyttleton satisfied, and then and only then inform our wayward colleague of our displeasure and his fate?"

I considered this, then said, "Such mitigation does not set well with me. It means we keep silent about his wrong to our own advantage. Are we not thereby complicit in the deed? I don't like it."

Burbage said, "Nor I, Will. I agree absolutely he must go. But the timing…"

"Timing?"

"Well, of his dismissal."

"What matters time? He is either justly dismissed or not."

"But stay you, Will," Burbage said. "Think on this."

"Think on what?" I asked. "Some excuse for his villainy?"

"I pray you consider the lady, I mean the beauteous Mistress Lyttleton, who also does not disclose his crime to her husband that the play might go forward. Were we to denounce Gabriel at this instant, we would defy her wishes, injure her in her husband's eyes. He would no doubt demand to know why she had not informed him earlier."

I felt myself yielding to this argument. I liked not the thought of betraying the lady who had been most gracious to us.

"Very well," I said. "We shall wait until our work here is done. But then I am finished with him."

"Even though he twice saved your life?" Burbage asked, not quite convinced, I suspect, of my resolve.

"I will tell him plainly to his face. We are done with him."

I thought then that we should be even, Gabriel and me. He had saved my life. I would save his neck. It seemed an even trade.

Yet there was one thing I was resolved to do, and that was to keep my promise to Mistress Lyttleton that Gabriel should offend no more. That meant that while his dismissal might be delayed, I must in the meantime warn him against further assaults.

It was a conversation it pained me to think of.

Before we performed the few scenes requested of us, we dined generously, for the Lyttletons employed a most excellent cook, a moon-faced

Irish woman with crooked teeth. I spare you the details of our repast for fear that you would not believe it to be had in a country house so far from court.

Supper done, I drew Gabriel aside. It was now nearly seven o'clock. We were to begin our scenes an hour beyond. As for Gabriel, I was willing to keep my promise to my friends not to dismiss him for the outrage until after our performance, but I worried that he would in the meantime offend again, either with Alice Simpkins or another of the maids. There were at least a half-dozen girls in the house that I had seen—young, vulnerable, available, perhaps more than willing to couple with a handsome actor from the city. Or perhaps not.

Mistress Lyttleton had shown restraint in her complaint. She had not told her husband. I could not trust that she would keep silent should Gabriel offend a second time, or perhaps a third. Lechery, as all the world knows, has a sharp nose and nimble feet. Once is never enough.

Besides, I had given the lady my promise to prevent another offence. In that regard, my honour was at stake, as was our fee.

"What think you of Holbeche House?" I asked Gabriel, as though my intent were no more than to pass the time of day before we should perform.

"Oh, 'tis a goodly house," he said, cheerfully. "We are well supplied. I have not eaten as well ever in my life, and Master Lyttleton has been more than accommodating."

"Master Lyttleton has indeed showed us many courtesies. But what think you of his lady wife?"

"Why, she too," Gabriel said, grinning. "She is a most gracious lady, as well as being a woman of singular parts."

He paused, meditating I suppose on those very delights that I myself had contemplated at my leisure. Suddenly, he looked at me

148

suspiciously, aware I think that my intent was to do more than pass the time until our play was to begin. He fixed me with a suspicious eye, as though prepared to defend himself from some accusation.

But I made no accusation. Instead, I put my hand on his arm in a fraternal way and patted it reassuringly, playing the part of a jolly uncle to conceal my disdain for him, for that is what I felt.

I said, "I pray you stand clear of the women of the house. These maids, I mean. Some might tempt a saint. But it would be well to let them be while we are here. You get my meaning, do you not?"

"You mean I should take a vow of chastity, like unto a monk?" He smirked.

"Not a monk," I said. "Not so austere. Only keep arm's length from any trouble."

"What trouble?"

"You know, I think. Entanglements that might embarrass us before our hosts. We are guests in his house. We must behave as such."

He answered nothing to this pronouncement, which to my own ears rang pompous and insincere. Had I suddenly become the Polonius of my *Hamlet*, a purveyor of conventional morality, a tedious spoilsport while doubtless even an offender myself?

He kept his eyes fixed on me, waiting. Those eyes, suddenly, were the eyes of a stranger. I confess I was a little afraid of him, for now he seemed a different man than I had known who, before, around me was more likely to be obsequious than defiant.

"Gabriel, neither of us is a child," I said. "We are not unaccustomed to temptations, to which we may succumb or resist according to our wills. If either of us were to yield to those temptations, say kiss, or fondle some person of the household, or even go farther, it would end badly for us all."

When he again made no answer, I went on.

"Consider, Gabriel, how it might be detrimental to the whole enterprise. I do mean our company and its purpose. In sum, we are the King's Men, not the King's Ravishers. And our duty to His Majesty, who is scrupulous in matters as all the world knows, behoves us to restrain ourselves. In seeking pleasures."

"Of the flesh, you mean?"

"Yes."

"Oh, Will," he said. "Think you not but that the king himself has his vices though he be most royal? I mean of pleasure-seeking, his power being such that few can refuse His Majesty? Why, 'tis no more than the perquisites of his high office."

I did not answer, thinking it was not my place to defend the king's morals. I determined not to be distracted.

"Little we do in this house goes unobserved, Gabriel. Trust me, I mean only to protect your reputation as well as our own whilst we are beneath Master Lyttleton's roof."

He spoke as though my concerns had naught to do with him. Finally, he said, "I do see, of course, the need for what you call appropriate behaviour whilst we are here."

But he gave me that stranger's look again. His lips were pressed tightly together. He nodded and was silent, which I interpreted as consent, not so much because I believed it was so, as that I was eager to put a period to my conversing with him.

21

Conversing with Gabriel relieved my burden somewhat. That he should miss the implication of my warning, I could not conceive. I had admonished him. I had spoken plainly. Such was my duty and my promise to my host's lady. Should Gabriel ignore that warning now, defy me, all would be upon his head. There would be no question that we should be rid of him.

I went into the great hall to find all prepared for us. Lyttleton's servants had done it. Well and good. I had not looked forward to a sweaty wrestle with heavy furniture as a prelude to our performance. Lamps had been fetched and set along the edge of a platform that had been brought from some other part of the house.

This was to be our stage. Our audience was yet to appear.

All we actors had now assembled. We had before established where each of us was to stand and what gestures to use. We had also tried the chamber itself to determine how our voices carried. We were ready, although Burbage still grumbled about the truncated script. A travesty, he called it. I agreed, but then in an hour our performance would be done. We could forget about it.

A few moments later the door of the dining room opened and

151

Master and Mistress Lyttleton appeared. Robert Catesby and his disguised priest, Master Peters, followed. Peters had changed his garments to somewhat lighter colours and fit in better with the company. His face wore a less severe expression. He seemed more amicable, less reserved. He laughed and conversed pleasantly, especially with the women. Several of the party I had yet to meet, but they were accompanied by women I assumed to be their wives. After them the servants filed in and took places against the wall. They would stand during our performance while the gentlemen and their ladies took chairs. The servants stood as solemn as in church, but the gentlemen and ladies talked and laughed as though they thought little of what they were about to see, as though we actors were not there at all.

Alice had come into the chamber along with the matronly house-keeper, who seemed her protectoress. The woman gave Gabriel a hard stare. I would have expected no less. As for Alice, she stood shamefaced and I think trembled a little. I turned to see if Gabriel, standing by my side, noticed her or cared how she might respond to him, her ravisher.

If he did, he made no sign.

That, too, I expected.

We actors waited for a signal to commence, but Lyttleton seemed involved in a deep conversation with Robert Catesby. I feared to disturb him. Had he too forgotten why we were here, or that we were here at all?

After nearly a quarter of an hour he pulled away, looked up at us as though he was surprised to see us there, and waved a hand I took as a signal we should begin.

I had composed a preface to our much-curtailed *Caesar*, which I myself was to present. I took the centre of our makeshift stage. The wood creaked and felt soft and yielding beneath me, a sensation I disliked, but what was to be done but press on?

"*Gentles all,*" I said, taking on an orator's voice. "*We lay our scene in Ancient Rome, where the noble senate waits the triumphant Caesar, fresh come from the wars.*"

I paused here, pleased that all eyes fixed upon me, all ears bent upon my words. I pitched my voice higher, and with my arm pointed to a place closer to the edge of the stage, I declared:

"*Give heed, gentles all, and you shall hear anon the noble Brutus, Roman senator and Caesar's friend, converse in such a way that Brutus will presently his loyalty discard, and think upon betrayal and murder foul. But no more of this prologue, gentlemen and ladies too. You have not come to hear a stumbling Prologue speak. I pray you see the deed itself. I do myself play Brutus.*"

Was there applause at that? It should have followed. I do not remember. I pressed on.

"*Presently, you shall overhear my conversation with Crassius, another senator, who shall lead him carefully into his way of thought. Behold the act itself.*"

I bowed and took centre stage, my legs braced as though I stood upon a ship's rolling deck and feared to fall headlong into a tumultuous sea.

Our several scenes passed into the night as quickly as Burbage had foretold. I slowed my speech, expressed myself with greater deliberation as though each word struggled to be born from my lips. Gabriel, our Crassius, matched me therein.

To be fair, I allow Gabriel played his part well enough. He spoke clearly, his voice richly veined with treachery. I supposed it came naturally to him, despite his protestations otherwise. Burbage was as good as Caesar as ever he had been, so good that when he looked up at me to utter his final reproach for stabbing him, I nearly wept for the pity of it.

And, thus, it was done, the shortest of my tragedies at that time, made shorter by our host's command.

So be it, I thought. Lyttleton was paying us double for our pains. If that is all of *Caesar* he wanted, who was I to complain?

At our scenes' conclusion, we stood together, even the boys who had played the Roman multitude, to receive our reward in clapping hands and cries to gratify our pride. This passed to Burbage, whose excellence as a singer we all had long recognized, filled out the hour with a half-dozen merry tunes, some of his own composing.

It was all very lovely, the music, and Lyttleton and his guests appeared to take much delight in it, as did I, for good music, like charity, never faileth.

But it was now nearly ten o'clock and our plan was to depart early the next day, for Lyttleton had told us but one evening was all his guests desired. Then I remembered. It was now time to fulfil my promise to my fellow sharers, Burbage and Armin, to send Gabriel packing.

But this I was hesitant to do, not because his violation of innocence seemed to me any less dastardly than when I first learned of it, but because I dreaded the bitter quarrel that would ensue. Surely, already, from my earlier conversation, he had an inkling of what was to come. He knew what he had done and knew that I knew. Already I could hear Gabriel's protests that he was much traduced, a victim of malicious gossip, and that I had betrayed our friendship in taking another's word over his own. I saw it coming, his passionate and mendacious rebuttal.

I steeled myself against it.

I looked back into the room and at first saw no sign of Gabriel. I looked again. He was in the back corner where the servants had placed themselves. He and his half-brother stood talking, congenially, their faces as close as two lovers'.

This I did not look for. Lyttleton had been most insistent that Robert Catesby detested his bastard brother. Yet here the two were conversing as though there had never been a breach betwixt them. I was amazed. Curious, too. What miracle or act of God had brought about this sea change? Had Lyttleton lied to me about how the Catesbys got along?

If so, for what purpose?

The conversation continued until we three were all that remained. I felt awkward standing there like a post, and when Robert Catesby saw me waiting, he frowned, which I took to mean he liked not my observing them.

I could do nothing but bow politely and leave the two men to their private communications, whatever they might concern.

I climbed the stairs to my chamber, much perplexed by what I had seen. I went in and shut the door. It was now hard toward midnight and I was bone-weary, yet my mind was excited with anticipation of the confrontation to come. I paced back and forth. I contemplated. I invented phrases and anticipated Gabriel's answers, assuming there were to be any, although knowing Gabriel I knew there would be. I had already had a taste of his resistance to my admonitions. The aftertaste was still bitter in my mouth.

To all this broil, I foresaw no escape, no amicable parting of the ways with my old school friend.

22

Sometime later, feeling surely that Gabriel would by now have gone to bed, I took a candle and slipped down the long corridor. I knew which chamber he had been given. I knocked. When no answer came from within, I entered. There I found him who shared Gabriel's room, one of our two boy actors, snoring softly. The other side of the bed, where I assumed Gabriel lay, was empty.

Mystified, I returned to my chamber. I thought perhaps Gabriel was still conversing with his brother. But at this late hour? Was it some reconciliation that might erase Robert's distaste for Gabriel? Or some contest of wills that should divide them the further in each other's love?

I decided to retire to my bed, believing that tomorrow when we were all prepared to leave the house might be soon enough to present Gabriel with his well-deserved fate. Surely now it was past midnight. The whole house would be asleep. Except for my erstwhile friend, Gabriel.

I know not what inspiration—from heaven or from hell— brought me from my bed and to the window, which looked down upon the front of the house to the broad expanse of lawn and then beyond to the woods' edge. A three-quarter moon illuminated this expanse, and as I stood there, suddenly I saw a shape moving from the house toward the woods.

I thought at first it was a deer, or some other creature, but it was no woodland beast.

This man's back was to me, but I could tell by his halting motion that it was Gabriel, for it was just such a way he walked like none other, his foot never having been properly set by the surgeon after his fight with Flynt. But where was he bound at such an hour?

It crossed my mind that it was some assignation I witnessed. Another of the household servants seduced into a nocturnal encounter. Perhaps even it was the hapless Alice, for now I trusted Gabriel not at all and worried my admonition to restrain himself might provoke him to greater wrong, if only to defy me.

As I thought this, I grew angry again.

I resolved to dress myself and follow Gabriel, interrupt his meeting, and keep my oath to Mistress Lyttleton. I was determined that Gabriel should be gone before sunrise, out of my life forever with my debt to him writ paid at last.

I hurried down the stairs into the central hall and through the main door into the courtyard. Ahead I could no longer see Gabriel but, guessing at which point his course might have taken him, I advanced with determination and within several minutes found myself at some distance from the house in a tangle of brush and trees so thickly grown that my passage through it was almost impossible.

It was only then that I considered what a dangerous course I had set. Here I stood in a gloomy wilderness, alone and undefended, uncertain of my surroundings, and unknowing of my fate.

Still, I went on.

It was but a dozen more steps until I came to a little clearing where the moon, freed from the thickness of the trees, now illuminated not a single figure but two.

Fearing how my intrusion might be received, I crouched, concealing my face with a leafy branch for fear the moonlight would expose my pallor amidst the leaves.

I could not hear their voices, but I could see by their gestures that the two men were deep in conversation. I was surprised that this new figure was not a woman. Had it been a woman, Gabriel's purpose would have been plain enough and at this point I might have seen him in *flagrante delicto*, as our lawyers do say when giving a gentler and more obscure name to unhallowed copulation.

But why, I wondered, should Gabriel be meeting another man secretly in the woods? He was not given to that way of love. I knew him well enough for that. Yet here he was. Was it his brother he conversed with?

I quickly concluded it could not be Robert Catesby.

Then it was that both men turned to where I hid and seemed to look directly upon me, concealed as I was. My heart pounded. I swear I had not moved from my concealment, had made no noise of which I was aware.

I held my breath, waiting for them to come at me, demand what I meant by invading their privacy, and doubtless seize me by the throat or do worse.

But neither moved from where he stood.

Now I could see both faces clearly. It was indeed Gabriel as I supposed from his limping gait. The other man I had never seen before. He was short and thick, whereby I should never have supposed he was the noble cousin who was very much the height and girth of Gabriel, sharing as they did the same father. This stranger was full bearded, wore a cap rather than a hat, and the simple drab and modest clothing of a townsman.

Gabriel conversing with a townsman? What might it mean?

The two turned back to face each other. I watched as they shook each other's hand. No, not the way two men might do at parting, where they do wish each other Godspeed casually, but as though some agreement had been struck betwixt them, and the handshake was like an oath or covenant.

Was I making too much of what I saw?

I thought not then. Looking back, I think not now.

The stranger started to walk away from Gabriel, back the way I reckoned he had come. In a moment, he disappeared into the shadowy thicket of trees and branches. As for Gabriel, he turned toward me, almost as if he knew I was there watching him. He began to move. I do not think he saw me, but then how was I to know?

I held my breath and turned to stone. A mindless statue was no more still than I in that desolate wood.

Then Fortune favoured me. Gabriel passed me by. I prayed that he would do so and he did. If he ever saw me lurking then or before when I supposed myself discovered, he made no sign. He did not break his limping stride but moved in haste toward the house as confident as though his meeting with the stranger had some honest purpose.

It may have had. Yet innocence seemed the wrong name for what I saw. The stealth of it, the unhallowed hour, the obscure place—all incriminated like the bloody stain upon a murderer's hands.

I did not soon move from my hiding place. When I did, I moved slowly, like a hunter, careful where I stepped that no cracking twig or rustling leaves betray me. I thought by now Gabriel would have returned to the house, but I could not be sure, and I dreaded the long walk across the grass until I should come to the door. There would I be exposed to any curious eye peering down into the night.

And how should I explain my being astir and lurking at such an hour? Should I say that, restless, I had undertaken to walk about in fearful solitude? Or that I was an itinerant somnambulist who knew not where he went or why?

I could not remain where I was the whole night. Even in the day I would have to explain myself if I were seen. I breathed deeply and ran, fearing at each step to hear a voice of alarm or at least a query as to who I was and why I ran, why I was not asleep in my appointed chamber. And were there dogs that might harass me, rip at my thighs and shake me by the neck until dead? I had seen none in the house, but that did not mean there were none secreted in some covert kennel, just waiting a hapless victim of their suspicion and wrath.

When I reached the door by which I had left the house I found it bolted against me.

I had not anticipated this, more fool I, but of course Gabriel, re-entering, would have secured the door behind him, having no more interest than I in anyone's knowing that he walked abroad at midnight on some secret errand.

I cursed my luck, uselessly. The mistake had been made, and I could not conceive how to undo it.

23

It would do no good to pound on the doors for admittance to Holbeche House, front or back. I might wake all within and embarrass myself at best, be beaten or killed as an intruder at worst. I passed the night fitfully in a gardener's shed, one of a number of outbuildings not far from the manor. It reeked of mould and horse dung. I woke before dawn, unsure of whether I had slept or merely dreamed of sleep.

Alice Simpkins was the first I saw emerge from the house. From my hiding place, I watched as she approached me with a pail in each hand, a heavy load for one so young and tender. From the stench, I knew it was night soil she carried. With so many guests in the house it would be a heavy and odiferous load, back and forth to the midden heap that lay a prudent distance from the house.

I hailed the girl, wishing her good morning. She emitted a little cry of surprise and nearly dropped one of the pails. "Master Shakespeare," she said. "You are risen betimes, sir."

I was indeed. Only now was the sky lightening in the east.

I told her I thought to take a walk in the early morning. For my health's sake, I said and because I loved the quiet of the early hours and what I called birdsong's sweet commencement. It was a pretty phrase I think wasted on her, and at once I felt foolish for having uttered it. She was a simple country girl, and such practices must have seemed strange to her, this rising before dawn only because one wanted to and not out of need to perform some useful task, comply with some master's order.

I offered to help her with her burden. She declined. She seemed almost afraid of me. After what she had suffered from Gabriel, her refusal and wariness did not surprise me.

"The postern door is unbolted?" I asked, unnecessarily because it would be if she had just left the house that way.

"Why, yes sir, it is. The cook's just up and stirring."

"Well and good," I said, saluting her with a wave. "I wish you joy of the new day, Alice Simpkins."

Her lips curled into a smile, the first I had seen on her face since coming to the house.

Whilst ensconced in the shed, I had resolved to travel alone to Stratford, being as I was so close to my own county and to leave later in the day after my companions set out for Oxford and then on to London. We had agreed to meet at the end of the week wherefore my visit home would be brief. I looked forward to seeing my wife and my two daughters, and they undoubtedly looked toward my coming since much of my share in our excursion's profits would be theirs to spend on my household with some moiety left, I trusted, for those baubles that please women.

But my first charge of that morning was to dismiss Gabriel. It occurred to me too that I might inquire just what business he had in the woods the night before and with whom he conversed. But I was loath to reveal that I had spied upon his secret meeting. Eavesdropping seemed to me unworthy of the gentleman I aspired to be. Besides which, I decided perhaps the question was moot, since our friendship was a closed chapter, the laboured sentences of which I had no interest in rereading. Truth was that he now disgusted me. Truth was I disgusted myself, for having welcomed him into the circle of my friends, for having been so credulous.

I found him in his bedchamber still asleep. I woke both him and the boy, sent the lad off to convey my plans for travel to Burbage and Armin, and sat down upon his bed. Gabriel seemed half asleep still. I decided that might be all the better, supposing he might be less surly when I announced his fate.

"I have a thing to say to you, Gabriel. I pray you will not take it badly, or misinterpret that which I intend. We must think of the good of the company."

My words alarmed him. I could see that plainly. He stared at me as if already he knew what was to come from my lips. He raised himself on his elbow. I could see he wore no shirt. The smooth flesh of his bare arms and shoulders was shiny with sweat as though he had run a long distance or fretted over some difficulty. I thought it unlikely that his encounter with Alice caused this. I could not envision him with a nagging conscience.

He said, "What is it, Will? I see some heaviness in your heart that you are loath to express. I pray you speak honestly to me as you ever have since we were boys together."

"Very well," I said. "I will speak plainly. Our hosts in these great houses put confidence in us. Our business is to perform, not to assault serving girls."

"We have already spoken of that, Will," Gabriel said. He sighed heavily. "And I agreed that we should be scrupulous in our dealings with the servants. I have not been otherwise."

"But you were not so with Alice, the young maid that saw to our

163

needs while we have been here," I said. "She's a young girl. By her lady's account, but twelve years. Yet you did rape her—"

That said, Gabriel came fully awake. He leapt from the bed to face me. "Rape, you say? On my honour, I never did such a thing, nor would I. He who says otherwise lies."

Gabriel looked around him, glaring, searching it seemed for his accusers.

"Mistress Lyttleton says otherwise," I said. "And I have seen the girl's crestfallen face. It speaks of her misery. I heard a voice of pain and suffering."

"Look then to another to have committed this," Gabriel said. "I am not the sole man of the house. There are menservants here aplenty. A lecherous brood if you ask me. Or one of our host's high-born guests. Blame them, not your friend, which I have ever been since saving you twice from death."

I ignored his appeal, which I had fully expected. I had steeled myself against it.

"You were seen, Gabriel."

"Doing what? Talking, flirting, planting a kiss upon her cheek, such innocent dalliance that our courtiers do daily without protest or reproach. More, the women are happy for the attention."

"I speak of a rape, Gabriel, not a dalliance."

"Never."

"You were spied in the very act."

Gabriel looked to his feet. His expression darkened. His lips twisted into a cruel grimace. "What appears to be is not always what is," he said. "Truth is that she seduced me, Will. She wanted me to love her, to take her. For all her precious youth you celebrate, I swear she's no virgin. I gave her no new joy of her body, or her brain. If she says otherwise, then she is naught but a lying whore."

I raised a hand to strike him. Something held me back, I know not what. Perhaps the strong grip of prudence, or perhaps mere cowardice.

"Do not shame her, Gabriel," I said, my anger now matching his own. "God knows she is an innocent child you assaulted because you could. Which thing is a crime, no mere indiscretion. And it is a grievous sin in your religion which you frequently have professed to me, so that I truly mark you as a hypocrite. You have betrayed me, betrayed us all. It was our good fortune that Mistress Lyttleton said nothing about it to her husband or we should all have been sent forth in disgrace."

For a moment he made no response. The silence was heavy between us. Then he spoke again.

"So this is how I am to be used after all that I have done for you?" Gabriel asked, eyeing me with disdain I had never before seen in his face. "My God, Will, she was naught but a slut. Is it worth it all—this division betwixt us?"

"It is," I said. "Trust is all betwixt us. We cannot work together otherwise."

Sighing, he picked up his shirt and jerkin where they lay on the bed. He dressed himself, slowly. I watched without saying anything more. Finally, he said, "In fact, Master Shakespeare, my dismissal from the company comes at a happy moment."

I asked him how this was so.

"You see I have decided to leave the King's Men in any case," he said. "My cousin, Master Robert Catesby, has offered to employ me as a secretary. I will miss the stage, Master Shakespeare, for I do think I am gifted therein. But my cousin will pay me well, and so I am satisfied enough with what fortune has given me."

With that he turned away from me, walked to the window of his room, and looked out. It was as though of a sudden he had put me from his mind, as if I were no longer there.

I did not bid Gabriel goodbye. We were well past such civilities.

Then I heard Gabriel call my name. "Master Shakespeare?" For he no longer addressed me familiarly by my Christian name, but more formally, marking thereby the breach betwixt us. "What of my money?"

"Your money?"

"I mean my share. My private life may not have met with your approval, Master Shakespeare, but I have played my part in many of your plays and I do think I deserve what is my due."

He stood before me, audacious and impudent, holding his open palm, waiting for his reward. I hated him more at that moment than ever I did before, or since.

I had left my purse in my chamber and without a word went to fetch it. Returning, I placed a half-dozen coins in Gabriel's hand, which I thought fair enough, but he looked at it as though it were a pittance. He scoffed. "A pitiful sum for a fortnight of hard travel and memory work."

"You undertook the journey of your own free will," I answered. "You prevailed upon me to come with us. You understood the terms of your service and have therefore little cause to complain."

"Oh, I have cause, Shakespeare. Ingratitude is always a good cause to complain of."

I knew he would come to that, my great debt to him. And he had.

"Now we are done, I do think," I said. "There's nothing left to speak of."

Gabriel gave me a blank stare. Again, it was the stare of a stranger, mixed with a kind of malice that was in itself threatening. He said, "You mean our long friendship is at an end, and over a simple whore of a maid who could not wait to spread her legs at the first invitation? What is it, Shakespeare, do you want the girl for yourself? Is that the true cause for all this moral umbrage which I must confess I find passing strange, coming as it does from one such as yourself."

"An actor, you mean?"

"Well, yes. Your sort are not known for purity of act or thought."

"All beside the point, Catesby," I said.

"We were friends."

"Some friendships are too costly," I said.

I turned away from him. He said something to my back but I could not make sense of it, and I was not about to ask him to repeat it, thinking it was probably some curse. His mother had been a witch.

24

I do not know when Gabriel Catesby left the house, or indeed whether he had, but I saw him no more that day. The truth was I did not want to think of him anymore, what he had done to Alice Simpkins, or how he had twice put himself in harm's way for my life's sake.

As it happened, my plans to set out for Stratford changed along with the weather. A sudden summer storm came up and the Lyttletons prevailed upon me to delay my departure another day.

I was well pleased with their invitation. I never liked riding while drenched or navigating muddy roads. What sane man did?

My friends gone, and Gabriel too, I spent much of the afternoon in Lyttleton's library. It had a fine collection of books for a country manor house. Predictable classics occupied their solemn places on his shelf, and then a large number of pious tomes of the Church Fathers in Latin or Greek. I read Latin with some ease. Greek was a different story.

Among these worthy books, I found with delight a copy of Edmund Spenser's *Faerie Queene*. I read a dozen stanzas with great pleasure and potential profit, since I am ever alert for new plots for my plays, and judicious theft is always to be preferred to the sweat and uncertain outcome of fresh invention.

I supped that night with my hosts and with John Peters and Robert Catesby, both of whom, like me, had taken refuge from ill weather. The conversation was dominated by Catesby, who discoursed at length on the war in France, and London fashions and seemed conversant on a wide variety of subjects, for he had been to university and was well educated. But never did he touch upon religion or the king's faults, for which I was grateful.

There was no further entertainment after dinner, which I thought odd, since in most country houses the guests might drink into the night, or play at cards, or wile away the time before sleep in other pleasantries. My host and his other guests, having some business to discuss which did not concern me, I politely withdrew, bidding each of these gentlemen goodnight and making my way up the stairs.

I found Alice there preparing my bed. When I entered, she looked up, startled, but then seemed uneasy, as though she feared someone else might find her there.

She started to leave but I urged her to stay, grasping her thin arm. She shrunk at my touch. I well understood why and released her. "Do not go, not yet."

"Your friends have left?" she said, staring at her feet.

"You know they have," I said. "You must have seen them riding off."

"Even the gentlemen that is Master Catesby's cousin?"

"He too."

I wondered who had disclosed Gabriel's relationship to her. But then as suddenly as I asked myself the question, I knew its answer. Who else but Gabriel himself? Perhaps to make himself more attractive to her, a simple housemaid easily impressed by rank and station? He had, after all, boasted of his family ties to everyone else, even when a boy. Why not to her?

She breathed a sigh of relief and her small face, stricken with fear before, now resumed its wide-eyed innocence and trust.

"See, now, you have no more to fear from him," I said, in what I hoped was a confident voice. "He will not return here. I have sent him away forever in disgrace."

She sighed again. "You have been most kind to me, sir, kinder than other guests of my master. Kinder than my own father and mother. God bless you for it."

I had rarely been so sweetly blessed, and I had been blessed by priests and bishops, persons whose station might be thought as more efficacious in securing heavenly aid than a simple servant girl.

"Here," I said, "keep this for yourself."

I reached into my purse, found a few coins, and gave them to her. It was not compensation for the wrong done to her. Money would not erase that injustice, or salve that wound. Yet I had given to beggars a greater sum, who were less needy, and this girl deserved it for what she had suffered and for what she continued to suffer in the house from whence she had fled.

"Tell no one that you have it, or any other thing I may give you. Swear to me you will not give it to your father."

She promised she would not, the affirmation slipping from her lips like a little explosion of air.

"You come from London, they tell," she said, hiding the coins in the folds of her apron. "Cook told me that in the kitchen. You and the other players. She said you are a famous playwright as well as an actor, and in the city everyone knows of you and speaks well of the plays you make."

"I don't know if that's true," I said. "Yet I do wish it to be so. Every man desires to be spoken well of."

"I would like to see a play, like unto the one performed yester-night," she said.

"Then you must needs come to London," I said. "For there are many theatres in the city, though the best and grandest of them is my own. We call it the Globe."

"The Globe, but why, sir?"

"Because it is the whole earth in miniature and encompasses all this world offers. That is why."

"Should I come there someday may I see you there, Master Shakespeare?" she asked.

"God willing, you may indeed, my child."

"I would so like to be a player on your stage," she said.

I had not looked for this in her, nor would have done so in any maid. Her silly notion was preposterous on its face, and yet who could condemn the imagination of a child as she was? Much of her innocence I knew was ignorance of men and things. I could hardly blame her for her wish.

"Women cannot be players," I said.

"Is it not lawful?" she asked.

"Well, it is against custom, which does inform law. The women's parts are played by boys, like unto the two that we had with us. "

"Oh, sir, I know that," she said. "Yet I do think there may be a time to come when it is otherwise. I mean someday women may play themselves. God created them so to do, do you not agree?"

I could not deny it. In her simple theology there was too much logic. Yet I might have told her that logic rarely masters custom, a lesson learned in maturity not in the sunny days of youth when so much in the world seems possible. I might have said that men do what they have always done, and to move against tradition's tide is to war against the very sea itself. I might have given historical incidents, even.

But I did not. They would have meant nothing to her, being as she was without learning and experience in the world beyond her village.

"Oh, we shall see what unfolds in the fullness of time," I said.

She smiled and blessed me again.

"Gramercy," I said. "I am in much need of blessing these days, as is any man."

"You shall have another then," she answered. She reached up and kissed me on the cheek. It was a chaste kiss, of the sort one might have bestowed upon a kindly uncle, or a father, even.

That night a fever and sweat possessed me, the consequence I suppose of having passed the night before out of doors. My head ached and my throat was raw. There was no water that I had not washed in, wherefore about an hour after I bid goodnight to Alice, I ventured forth to find something to slack my thirst. I went downstairs toward the kitchen and as I passed the door to the library, I heard hushed voices from within, an intoning more than words, like wind through trees, but softer yet.

Curious, I paused, listened. It was John Peters.

I know voices and can discern one from another even though I may not have seen its possessor in years. It is because of my long time in the theatre, which is, after all, largely about voices. Therefore, I was confident it was he and none other.

I also heard that it was Latin he spoke, nay, chanted, not English, and I knew what he spoke for I heard it often enough in Stratford where there were a dozen or more recusant families that had hidden priests and covert sacraments.

My host and the others had left the door ajar. I looked in, careful not to be seen. The library had been transformed into a chapel. On Lyttleton's desk was a large cross of silver. I had seen it before, this scene. It was the mysterious sacrament in which the wine is turned to Christ's blood and the wafer into Christ's flesh.

Our communion in Holy Trinity was not unlike, yet we believed differently about the sacred elements: they represented, not transformed, and the Eucharist was spoke in the king's English so that everyone could understand, not just the priests and the learned.

Peters stood garbed in priestly vestments and held a chalice high above his head. Before him knelt the Lyttletons, husband and wife, their heads bowed. Robert Catesby was there too, and the old butler, Templeton, was also there, kneeling with them. One or two more I recognized as other household servants.

But I did not see Alice there. Nor did I see Gabriel Catesby, who might indeed have stayed if his new appointment as his cousin's secretary was not a lie to save face.

I drew away, fearful of being observed or perhaps heard. I had played the spy long enough in Holbeche House.

I passed into the kitchen where there was an urn of fresh water. I found a cup, drank deeply. The water tasted earthy, but it satisfied my thirst and eased the soreness of my throat. I discovered an empty bottle, filled it with more water and skulked back to my room.

I paused at the library door. It was shut now. I heard no voices within. Silence only. Had I seen what I thought I had seen, or was it only another dream or vision?

Whichever it was, the mass had ended.

Before I yielded a second time into the softness of my bed, I walked to the window and looked out into the night. It had stopped raining and the moon was now a great swollen sphere, illuminating the space between the house and the woods, a lovely array of light.

I thought I saw a figure making his way toward that leafy retreat, but then decided I had only imagined it. I was in that state of mind. Seeing things that were not.

Gabriel Catesby was truly gone, gone forever from my life.

But I have said that before, have I not?

25

Some years before this most unhappy time when the old queen still lived, I met a man in a Southwark tavern, who said his name was Nicholas Owen. We talked affably, Owen and I, as one might do with a stranger in such a place, not thinking our acquaintance might last beyond the night and not caring if it did or no. He asked me how I earned my keep. "A writer," I said, "a writer of plays." I sought to know the same of him. He said he was a builder.

"A builder, are you? And, pray sir, what do you build?" I asked, thinking he meant he was a carpenter, a turner, or a joiner, or of some other reputable calling concerned with the erecting of houses or barns or even churches.

But he leaned toward me and whispered as though his vocation were a dark secret to be shared only with a few and I should be privileged to be one to whom his mystery was revealed.

"In truth, sir, I build hiding places in rich men's houses—the best priest's holes in the world," he said, laughing, glassy-eyed, beads of liquor on his beard. He winked at me knowingly as though we were now partners in his enterprise.

Did I say he was thoroughly besotted when he made this confession, this boast?

Had he been sober, he would have known to keep silent about his curious and dangerous business. In that part of London, half the patrons of the tavern were spies for this lord or that bishop. The other half would become spies in due course. So it was back in that time, when the queen was in her dotage and fear more than faith ruled the world. The Jesuits had sent their priests throughout England to keep alive the Old Religion and proselytize among the theologically infirm and confused. I could name a dozen Church of England friends who had been converted, as they were pleased to call it, and now doffed their hats to the Bishop of Rome, either in public or in private.

Later I discovered that Nicholas Owen's claim was no idle boast but true as God's word. I heard rumours about him from persons I trusted. I had been in houses where his handiwork was whispered of and marvelled at. I had heard stories of Jesuit priests travelling about the countryside, concealing themselves from magistrates and constables in closets, attics, chimneys, hay barns, rabbit warrens, pig sties. Sometimes in spaces where there was hardly room for a grown man to breathe, much less to stretch limbs. Sometimes in places where their concealment was so narrow and obscure that those places proved, at last, to be their very graves.

Owen, it was said, would come into some Catholic house, inspect all its chambers and outbuildings, and then devise a hidden compartment, some nook or cranny, some tunnel or attic retreat, where a priest might hide to avoid capture, he and all his Papist paraphernalia, altars, priestly vestments, prayer books, papers, images, relics or whichever other thing might be used in his forbidden rites. Owen would construct this hideaway so that its door or opening was invisible to the eye, save the master of the house knew where it was and how to gain access to it.

To those who knew of Owen's work, his labours seemed more art than craft, more magic than simple manufacture. It was said of him that never had one of his concealments been discovered, nor any of their occupants taken.

His services did not come cheap, it was said. It was also said that he was a devout Catholic and performed his works for the greater glory of God and the return of a Catholic king.

One might say it was his contribution to the cause, given that he himself was no priest or missionary.

You may ask why I digress from my story to memorialize this worthy man, for he was in truth worthy in his own light and in the light of his friends and fellow Papists.

Patience, I pray you. You shall know anon and be content.

Sick and weary, I might have slept long past dawn to my health's restoring, but it was otherwise. I had set my mind on leaving Holbeche that day, after breakfast God willing, hale or ill. I had had enough of the Lyttletons and their manor and the sinister happenings within the house and without.

It was Alice Simpkins who awakened me. I had not bolted my door. I had no fear of thieves or interlopers.

"Good Master Shakespeare, Master Shakespeare," she cried. "Awake in God's name, awake. Save yourself!"

Drowsy, heavy-lidded, I asked, "What is it, child? Is it fire?"

I asked this, even as I smelled no smoke, saw no flame, heard no clanging bells to sound alarm. Truth was that I had great fear of fire, of dying in flames, and oft imagined myself buried in the ashes of a burning house, so that my body should be cremated such as I heard was the fate of Indians and other pagans when they were dead.

But that proved not to be the danger I faced.

"Many men, sir, a mighty company. They have surrounded the house and demand to be let in. Cook is terrified and told me to wake you."

I sat upright, wondering if this were true, or some girlish dream or fantasy that, should I take it for fact, I would prove myself a gullible fool, my alarm an object of well-deserved derision.

But I knew her warning was well-founded. I could not see the girl jesting that way, although I could well imagine a dream that seemed real enough to her upon waking that she might act upon it as though it were true. I had had such dreams. Who has not?

I was half dressed, having succumbed to sleep before my weary body touched the bed. I ran to the window to look out.

What I saw then struck me with a terrible fear. Alice had not lied, nor been deluded. If there were less than a hundred mounted men before the manor, arrayed as though prepared to advance upon walls and doorways bearing weapons to force their entry there was not a one.

They were not the king's troops I quickly gathered by their dress and demeanour, but local citizens, a *posse comitatus*, no doubt gathered at the behest of the county's sheriff.

"They be all about the house, sir, front and rear," Alice gasped from behind me.

"What do they want?"

"I know not, sir. My master and his lady have gone forth to discover it."

It occurred to me to ask her if this had happened before, this raid upon a gentleman's home. Perhaps such raids were routine in this part of God's world, like a periodic visit of a rat catcher or a season of plague.

"Indeed, Master Shakespeare. It has happened thrice since I am come to the house. They look for priests. My master and his lady are Papists, you see. It is no secret what they believe and who they pray unto, for I have seen them at it. Many times."

I told her I knew this. Had I not seen the mass celebrated in the library with my own eyes, I might still have discerned that this was a Catholic house. The Lyttletons had made no effort to hide it.

"Have any priests ever been found here?"

I thought of John Peters who I now knew to be a priest, whether a Jesuit, for which the government had particular suspicion and hatred, or some less offensive order I did not know. I was not sure Alice knew about Peters. I saw no cause to tell her. In matters such as this, ignorance conferred a measure of safety.

"Nay, sir, not a one, ever since I am in the house, but my father says that priests come and go. They come and go, he says. He says he can smell them. He says that the place is crawling with them, priests. Devil's disciples, he calls them.

"I perceive your father is no Papist," I said.

"Why, he hates Papists, sir, hates them more than sin itself."

"I wonder then that he suffers you to serve in such a house, inhabited as it is by devils."

"Ah, sir, he hates losing the pittance I earn the more."

She begged me again to flee the house. Her eyes were wide with fear and her voice trembled.

"Why?" I asked. "I have naught to do with your master's guests."

"But the men will think otherwise," she said.

I looked into her face with its agonized concern. I knew she was right. It would not be true, my complicity with the priest, yet certainly it would be believed so. Defending myself against treason was a vexation I did not need, for I wanted nothing more than to be about my own business, not answering the questions of a meddlesome sheriff or constable relishing the catching of such a fish as I in his net.

"Come," Alice said, seizing my hand as though I were a wayward child resisting a mother's direction. "I know a place where you will be safe."

She led me from the chamber down a back staircase used by the servants, and toward the front of the house and the hall where Caesar had died and Burbage had sung so sweetly. Tables and chairs were as before. The room was empty.

She drew me toward a panelled wall. She reached out and touched a piece of dark moulding around the artfully crafted mantelpiece, twisted her wrist, and the panel slid open without a sound.

Within, I could see a dark recess, and then the top rung of a ladder leading down into a still deeper and more formidable darkness.

It was then I thought of Nicholas Owen. Surely this was his handiwork, and now perhaps my salvation. I turned to look at Alice. She nodded in the direction of the ladder. "Oh, pray make haste, sir," she said. "I hear voices even now at the door."

"But where does it go, the ladder?" I asked, not certain I wanted to trust my life to some darksome hole in the earth. Perhaps it would be better to face the sheriff and his men. I was, after all, innocent of wrongdoing. I was no Papist. I conceived of no plots against the State. But then, I considered, I had conversed and debated with John Peters. I had been in his company, talked with him of religion. Templeton and other servants might testify against me, if only to clear themselves from blame or curry favour with my persecutors.

"Will I be able to find my way out?" I asked Alice, staring down into the darkness.

"I swear it. Have faith. Hurry, Master Shakespeare, or we both are lost."

None of this I liked, but I took her counsel. For both our sakes, as she said.

26

The panel door slipped shut, as smoothly and silently as it had opened. I was left in darkness absolute. Breathless, I groped for the top rung of the ladder, seized upon it, and began slowly to descend. As I did, I could hear voices beyond the wall, from the room I had just left. They were loud voices, angry voices. My escape had been timely. I remember it all as if it were yesterday and not so many years past.

I heard Stephen Lyttleton. His was the voice of protest, of outraged innocence, of contempt for the sheriff's authority.

Lyttleton was lying about being innocent, and his performance was execrable, but I allowed that he could do no less. It was his house, and he was as vulnerable to arrest and punishment as was the priest he concealed. Through the wall I could hear his wife's voice too. It was shrill and plaintive at the same time. Not the voice I remembered from the garden, when in dulcet tones she urged me to restrain Gabriel Catesby's lechery.

Her protests struck me as more convincing, although she was equally culpable. She did have her beauty to argue her cause, and perhaps her tears, but I could see nothing of the latter, save in my imagination where her clear eyes swelled with water, making them the more lustrous.

Then I could hear no more for my right foot, then my left, felt a hard surface and I saw a light ahead. It was enough to illuminate the passage which I now saw was bricked above as well as below and on each side. I understood now that my refuge was no mere hole in the earth but a structure of some height and breadth, the work of a cunning artificer well advised as to how such a passage might be needful, for concealment or escape.

I walked a dozen paces or more until the passage widened into a kind of chamber. It was not untenanted. There before me, sitting upon a bench and looking up at me with a wry smile was John Peters, the Lyttletons' priestly guest.

He did not seem surprised to see me sharing his dismal retreat.

"Well, Master Shakespeare," he said. "We are well met, which neither of us had good cause to expect this morning."

I saw he was cradling a rosary in his hand, at the end of which hung a silver crucifix. I had interrupted his prayers, no doubt.

"You are sought for, Master Peters."

"I fear so," he answered calmly. "You are quite correct about that. But then someone is always seeking after me, seeking after us, these days. It is my duty not to be found. You see, I perform an essential service, Master Shakespeare. I supply God's word and His grace to souls thirsty for true religion. It is for that reason that Master Lyttleton prepared this place for me—and also for my predecessors, who found safety where otherwise they would have been taken, tried, and presently quit of this life. With God's help, I hope to avoid that fate."

He said this with so little emotion that he might have been speaking of a common thing, not the horrific death of himself and other of his fellows in faith.

"Please be seated then," Peters said, motioning for me to join him. "And by the way, sir, since we are to be companions in this place, at least for now, you might as well know my true name. I am John Gerard. I serve God as one of his true priests. The name Peters I use from time to time, for reasons you can well imagine."

I sat down alongside him. I told him I had supposed he was a priest but said nothing of having witnessed him performing the mass with the Lyttletons and Robert Catesby as communicants. He nodded in approval. He said, "We can return to the house but not soon. The sheriff's men are very patient. They know they have a priest at bay. They salivate with anticipation like hungry hounds. Yet they know not what tree he has scaled. Wherefore they will stay in Holbeche until they find me."

We sat together conversing thus, like old acquaintances, which we were surely not, yet neither were we enemies. It seemed strange to me to find myself in these dire circumstances, calmly conversing as if no danger threatened either of us, but of course it did.

"I could go out, surrender myself," I said, as much to see his response as to suggest an alternative to patient endurance.

"And betray me? Betray whoever showed you to this haven?"

"Not to betray you, nor any other man, but to liberate myself from this tomb," I said, thinking also of Alice Simpkins. Of course, the constable's men would want to know who had revealed the hiding place to me. Someone would be incriminated by my action. I was resolved that it should not be Alice, who had suffered quite enough from her association with me and my friends.

"It's all one," he said. "Your intention does not matter, Master Shakespeare, though it be innocent. Only the consequences of your action signify. Reveal yourself and they will find me. Reveal yourself and they will demand to know who led you here, who showed you this place. Reveal yourself and they must discover why you consort with a notorious priest."

"Notorious? Are you that, sir?"

"I fear so."

"You seem calm enough, sir."

"I am in God's hands. If He wills it, I shall be taken. If not, I shall live to serve Him."

"You reason coldly, like a Jesuit," I said.

"It comes naturally to me, Master Shakespeare. I am of that order."

He confessed this without shame, but triumph rather. He knew I would not surrender. His confidence of that was plain on his face.

"Who did show you the way?" the priest I now knew as John Gerard asked. "Was it Master Lyttleton, or his lady wife?"

"Neither."

"Templeton, then?"

"No." I could not conceive of the dour butler being so obliging.

"Another of the household servants?"

I shook my head.

He saw I would not reveal my guide. He smiled and nodded. "Well, no matter who it was, he is protected as am I by your keeping me company for the next few hours at the least. Fear not, sir. Master Lyttleton has provided us with provisions for a longer stay."

He pointed to a basket sitting at the foot of the bench. I had taken no note of it before.

"Very well," I said, and seeing there was no help for it I joined John Gerard on his bench.

27

What thoughts and words did we two share during those solitary hours, the priest and the playwright, being as we were such strange bedfellows?

I discovered quickly that this man had little interest in the theatre, despite his expressions of pleasure at our performance. His mind, instead, was fixed upon religion, as I might have expected given his vocation, and also upon politics, as I might also have expected given his particular sect. He was on good terms with a number of prominent gentlemen, officers of the court and even friends of the king, most of whom I knew to be Catholics or sympathizers therewith, and others whom I suspected to be such.

Gerard admitted that he performed many a mass and exorcism for Papist families. He acknowledged himself to be their confessor too, their spiritual counsellor and guide. He had a dozen or more stories to tell about each.

But in all of these tales—and I assure you he was a most excellent anecdotalist—his religion was part.

This hardly surprised me, nor did I object. Religion was his business. And, in truth, there was no little entertainment in the wiles by which he and his companions in faith evaded the law. What would we have done otherwise to pass the tedious hours?

In due course, I asked, "How shall we know when we are safe to leave this place? Is there another way out than the way we have come?"

"Oh, good Master Shakespeare, there is always another way out."

I did not know whether he meant this literally, or whether it was some figurative meaning he intended. With Father Gerard, it was difficult to tell, for I soon learned he was given to cryptic pronouncements, which he did seem to utter as much for his own entertainment as his listener's edification.

I surprised myself in not having asked him this before, the question about our escape. But then how long could the passage be? I thought of that expanse of long grass between the house and the woods. I knew not the passage's extent or its course, but I assumed it proceeded toward the woods beyond where, God willing, there would be a ready exit.

"As to who will give us notice that it is safe to leave, that will be Master Lyttleton," Gerard said before I could ask.

At this I thought, but did not speak aloud: And what if Lyttleton is arrested or, worse, slain? What if his pretty wife is likewise? What if Templeton is taken? What if beyond this subterranean passage there is naught but an empty house, forsaken by all, or an even deeper hole in the earth?

Was my imagination running wild? Were these fears unfounded?

I thought not. I imagined a soft knock on the wall. I imagined I heard the panel sliding, even as silently as it had moved erstwhile, and then looked up to see Alice Simpkins' angelic countenance beckoning me. But perhaps she had been seized upon too? Would she be hanged as a Catholic sympathizer? Children even younger had not been spared the rope or rack.

"You are beset with unreasonable terrors, Master Shakespeare," Gerard said, when I had disclosed my worst fears. "You are conceiving a plot only that it might terrify yourself. Matters will not fall out as you suppose. Be of good cheer. Should they not find me, our friends will be in no danger. The raid will be another embarrassment for the heretics, who have raided Holbeche at least three times this year alone in the vain effort to discover a hidden priest. I confess I relish their embarrassment. Do you think that uncharitable of me?"

"Not particularly uncharitable," I answered, "or if so, a venal sin."

The priest laughed pleasantly.

After a while we left our little chamber and returned to the foot of the ladder. He said, "I once passed a week in a priest's hole. It was a miserable business. Food was gone the second day, water the third. After that I fasted."

"Like Christ in the wilderness," I said.

"But not for forty days, thanks be to God," Gerard said, smiling. "And the Devil did not come to tempt me, only the constable's men who took my host's house half apart to discover where I lay. And I did lie, Master Shakespeare, not stand. You must know that there was no room for standing. The temptation was to give up, to surrender, to plead for a quick death. I resisted. Like unto Paul, I fought the good fight. I finished the race. When I was told all was clear, I could barely walk. I was plagued by aching joints and shin splints. It was a full week before I was myself again."

He stopped talking and listened. We both listened. He shook his head. I had the feeling he had told this story of personal suffering before, along with its Biblical enhancements. It had that practiced sound that as an actor I knew well enough.

He said, "Too soon, I think. If you leave your hide too soon, all is wasted. I would be arrested. You as well. You will be taken for an accomplice in my escape."

He had uttered this warning before. He must have thought it worth repeating should my resolve fail.

And so we waited. Gerard told me several more stories, these having to do with his near escapes from capture. He had led an exciting life. He had suffered much for his faith. I admired him for that, although some of his exploits seemed foolhardy, flirting with danger, inviting capture. Yet he had succeeded in evading his enemies.

He climbed to the top of the ladder a second time with the same result as before. Silence beyond the wall.

"Well," Gerard said sometime later, "A week in a hide is an experience I like not to repeat, if I can avoid it. Come, Master Shakespeare, this tunnel must needs go somewhere. Shall we discover where and perhaps find our long-delayed freedom?"

I followed Gerard down to where we had first encountered each other and then beyond, taking two of the candles with us for light.

The air was foul here, the passage narrower. My discomfort at this perilous course was at its height when, after what seemed several dozen yards, I saw a light ahead. It was a small light at first, but as we advanced it grew larger and more welcoming. It was not the light of candle or fire, but of day.

Our salvation seemed at hand.

I soon found myself and my priestly companion in the very woods I had envisioned. The passage's entrance had been concealed beneath a growth of bracken, thick enough to obscure the small opening, but sparse enough to let light penetrate. We crawled on our knees like supplicants before the cross or some other monument worthy of worship, clawing at the branches that seemed intent to prevent our escape.

Gerard was in due course able to stand. He surveyed the scene with more daring than I could muster, still fearful of discovery as I was. Then he looked down at me with a kind of amused expression as though this whole episode had been a jest. He smiled grimly and said, "I must be gone, Master Shakespeare. I have enjoyed our conversation, forced upon us as it was by circumstances beyond our control. Perhaps we shall meet again. Even in this life. You understand the urgency of my leave taking, I am sure."

He nodded toward the house. I could see that the raiders had not yet departed. Several dozen of the men stood about in the courtyard with their horses. I crouched low as I had done the night I had observed the mysterious meeting between Gabriel Catesby and the stranger. Then I heard a breaking of twigs, turned to look up at Gerard, only to find the priest had vanished into the wood while I had looked away.

For the rest of that day, I watched the house, the zealous searching of the sheriff's men, household servants about their duties and, once, a scowling and indignant Master Lyttleton standing with arms folded outside the main entrance. I was a mere observer, you understand, reluctant to move a muscle or cause a twig of my hiding place to crack and thus betray me. It was only at sunset that the sheriff's men gave over their search. I later learned they had looked in every chamber, probed every chimney, sounded each floor and wall for a hallow within or beneath. The whole of the day they had laboured and apparently found nothing to incriminate, for had they done so, surely the Lyttletons would have been in their custody.

Though no partisan in these religious wars, I rejoiced nonetheless in the sheriff's failed effort. As a youth, I had been contemptuous of the constabulary. I had believed them addled or corrupt men who could not find honest work otherwise, or brutes who behaved with gratuitous violence under cover of law. I thought little better of them now. In my plays I had mocked them as ignoramuses, dupes, and villains. Yet the real ground of my joy was this, that their failure had been my salvation.

My intent now was to collect my few things, find my horse, and leave Holbeche House without further ado. I knew courtesy dictated that I should thank and bid farewell to my host. But I was weary of Lyttleton and his pretty wife, even more weary of the constant disputation about religion, which thing was never to my liking. For now, my sole destination was Stratford and then beyond to London and my life there, my true life.

I watched as the men formed a single column. They rode at their leisure no more than a dozen yards from where I hid. I saw their faces. Some were disappointed—undoubtedly, they hoped to have a priest or two as a trophy of their search. Perhaps a dead priest or two, that their efforts might seem the more valorous to their fellows and their enemy the more malevolent and devious.

Then I saw three men leave the house, mount, and ride forward to take the head of the column. One of these, by his dress and a stern, authoritative countenance, I took to be the sheriff and leader of the raid. A gentleman, clearly, used to command. He sat upon his mount as though it were a part of himself. By his side was a thickset older man, who rode awkwardly as though he had never ridden a horse before and was resolved that this should be his last time. He, too, reeked of officialdom, but of a lesser order.

I recognized him. Not his name, but his face and thick-set body.

It was the very man Gabriel had met in the woods. My oath upon it.

Had Gabriel met there to tell this officer that a priest was in residence? Would Gabriel have so betrayed his friend, the priest and his much-admired cousin?

28

When all were gone, I shifted from my hiding place and went straightway to my chamber. I gathered my things. I would have been out the door and looking for my stabled horse but was prevented by the sudden appearance of my host.

Lyttleton rushed toward me, breathless. I thought he would embrace me so happy did he appear at seeing me.

"Master Shakespeare, you were well absent this day, or you would have been embarrassed at least by our incompetent sheriff who would find priests behind every door and hedgerow. I thank God for your escape."

He looked at me curiously. I knew he wanted to know how I had done it, the escape I mean. But I resolved not to say, not to let him know that the secret passage had been revealed to me, nor that I had spent so much time with Father Gerard. The less said about that, I decided, the better.

Lyttleton told me more about the search, which he had witnessed first-hand. He said it would take a week to put the house aright. The sheriff's men had been deliberately rough with the furniture. His wife's wardrobe had been ransacked. Several of her gowns were missing. He was sure he had lost personal things as well. Thieves and brigands all, Lyttleton said in talking about the perpetrators of the raid.

I expressed my sympathy for him and his wife and inquired how she did, thinking that if Lyttleton was upset by the day's events, his lady wife must be the worse. And she was.

"She has retired to her bed and laments the loss of her gowns, for which I paid a goodly sum. The devils took particular delight in casting all her garments to the wind."

Then he handed me an embroidered silk purse. I knew at once what it was. Our fee. I had almost forgotten it, but it was to Lyttleton's credit that he had not. I thanked him with all my heart. Then I said, "Before I leave, I have a question, Master Lyttleton, if you will be so good as to answer it."

He seemed more pleased than annoyed at the request.

"Pray, who was the portly gentleman that rode with the sheriff? I do think I know him, and would be sure, or the question will buzz in my brain all the way to Stratford."

"Ah," Lyttleton said, grimacing. "That would be Edmund Daniels. He is the secretary of Sir Arthur Thomas, high sheriff of the county. He is a man of some circumstance but of no particular religion and fewer morals, yet would he persecute those of us who have the true faith. What think you of that, Master Shakespeare? Is that right? Is that just?"

"If he lacks religion or morals, what would be his motive?" I could not help but ask. "Surely, he can find better to do with his time, save he is a great fool."

"A great fool he is, Master Shakespeare. As to his motive, it is as plain as the nose on your face. Filthy lucre, sir. It's money, pure and simple. He captures and kills for money. Do you not know that on every priest's head there is a bounty?"

Lyttleton made a little sigh of disgust.

193

"So did the false apostle betray Christ," I murmured.

"Indeed," Lyttleton said. "That is very true, Master Shakespeare. And so were my house and I betrayed by one who told Daniels that I had a priest here. Would that I knew who it was that told him that. But I do swear I will find him out and when I do it will go very badly with him."

Strange, it occurred to me then that the betrayer might well have been Gabriel, but I said nothing. I was, after all, the only witness to the nocturnal meeting. It would be my word against his.

"You might bring an action for slander against the betrayer," I said.

Lyttleton laughed. "I hold little by lawsuits, Master Shakespeare. They usually enrich no one but the lawyer. I prefer a simpler way to achieve justice."

He made a motion suggesting the slitting of a throat. It was chilling to see it, for Lyttleton seemed a pleasant, congenial man before. This was a darker side of him, a fearsome side.

I made no further comment about remedies for his betrayal.

"By the way, do you indeed know the man, Daniels I mean?"

I shrugged. "No, sir. I think not. He resembles a friend, a friend of my youth, but I cannot reconcile his present hypocrisy and avarice with the man I knew."

"Men change in time," Lyttleton said, bitterly. "The virtues of youth give way to the vices of age."

For a few moments, he waxed philosophical on this theme, but I was impatient to be off now that my curiosity was satisfied. "Yet I think they be two different men," I said. "I was wrong to think otherwise."

"Then I bid you a safe journey to… where was it you were bound?" Lyttleton asked, shaking my hand warmly and patting me on the shoulder as though we were old acquaintants.

194

"To Stratford-upon-Avon," I said. "Where I was born and my family live."

"Then, Master Shakespeare, may God keep you on your way."

I bowed low and mumbled some words of gratitude to the gentleman. I remember not what they were.

"Commend me to your good lady," I said.

"So I shall," Lyttleton said. "So I shall."

Then a groom whom I had not seen before brought my horse around.

Astride, I looked back once to see Lyttleton watching me curiously. He waved once, a gesture I returned.

But even then I somehow knew that I would not see Holbeche House again, nor its master and mistress.

29

Let it not be said by any prattling diarist or gossip, now or here-after, that Ben Jonson and I were ever enemies. Let not Rumour's tongue nor historian's pen besmirch a kinship by which we both benefitted so richly. For though we were rivals for applause, and divided by religion, yet were we united in our dedication to our muse. He a bricklayer's son, I a glover's, yet both feared God and honoured the king. I performed a dozen times in works of his making, playing only a few years before and in our Globe the noble Tiberius in Jonson's play *Sejanus*, a well-intentioned Roman tragedy made more tragic by its wooden dialogue, flat characters, and snail's pace.

I offer the above as proof of our brotherhood. I respected Jonson's invention and his great learning. Still, I did not always approve of his matter or his style.

He likewise of me. He thought me poorly schooled in Latin, an ignoramus in Greek, a stumbling neophyte in the classical world, my head full of names and stories I knew second-hand whereas he had read the originals and knew the whole classical pantheon as if they were his next-door neighbours.

About all that he was right. What is important is this. No one ever took one of Jonson's plays for mine, nor mine for his. Thus, does art mimic the very creation of the world in its diversity of forms and operations.

That said, I will explain how Jonson figured in my story, for his involvement was strange and perilous as was mine, and my excursion into the world of spies and treasonous plots is not fully disclosed save his part is included therein.

Now it is August 1605.

Returned to London, I went one evening to Blackfriars to see Jonson's new play. This ancient site, at first a habitation for monks as its name suggests, came at last, in the years of our King Henry VIII, to be a theatre where I had more than once performed, but in present time served as home of the Children of The Queen's Revels, a company of boy actors whose work was sometimes excellent, sometimes execrable.

All depended on the players, which is ever the case.

How might it be otherwise? A boy comes to maturity as an actor at, say, fourteen or fifteen years. He blooms, then wilts. Overnight it sometimes seems. The player's art in him hardly waxes before it wanes.

That season the Children were blessed. The players were well schooled in their lines, ably directed, equipped with excellent memories with which the young are gifted, inexplicably since they have the least to remember. The boys were convincing as older men, which is the great difficulty in such plays. It is no great thing for the thin piping voice of a lad to imitate a woman's, but the resonance of a mature man is another matter. Voice is the very beginning of character, as I have oft observed. If it be the wrong voice, nothing remedies the fault.

The play was called *Eastward Ho!* Of its authors, Jonson was principal, but also John Marston and George Chapman, both of whom I counted amongst my friends and considered competent playwrights.

My mere presence at Blackfriars that night marked paid to three social debts. If I expected my friends to come to the Globe to see my work, I could hardly refuse to see theirs.

Fortunately, all three men were present to see me occupy a chair close to the stage where I could observe all and hear all, give good estimate of the acting and follow the jests and puns of which I assure you there was an abundance. It was a city setting, not the pastoral idyll I favoured in my comedies, and the authors were excellent in capturing the language of the streets and byways of London, the lower sorts of humanity which Jonson knew well and loved, I think beyond reason.

This play was satirical, farcical, an interlude of hilarity and shrewd caricature, yet given the time and the place a reckless enterprise. I wondered that Jonson, who had been imprisoned and examined by the authorities more than once before, would risk his liberty and reputation yet another time.

But, alas, he did.

The play I had seen in draft, and I discouraged Jonson from staging it. You shall hear presently my concern, which I do swear was aimed at saving him trouble, not jealousy that his play secured more laughter than my last comedy on the best of its afternoons. As I have said, Jonson had been in trouble a few years before with the authorities, who ever monitored our work for seditious matter, as they were pleased to call it. They supposed that what the spectators saw demonstrated upon the stage, they would do, as children mimic the doings of their parents. What they heard said, they would repeat. What ideas expressed, they would adopt and advocate mindlessly like puppets on our strings.

That our audiences were so helpless in our hands, so malleable,

I could hardly credit. The very thought made me laugh. For the multitude might be unwashed and unruly, unlettered and sometimes mean-spirited, but I never supposed them to be stupid.

Jonson ignored my advice, pressured by George Chapman I suspect. Chapman was ever reckless in such matters. I remember Chapman made light of my fears, laughing it all off.

But as to the plot. For those who have not had the pleasure of seeing the work, I provide this précis:

The play features a Sir Petronel Flash, who having spent much of his fortune to obtain a knighthood, which he does deserve by no other measure than he is a Scot, undertakes with his new bride a voyage to Virginia in the Americas, where he hopes to recoup his losses and become rich beyond his dreams. So far, so good. Who does not admire such ambition in a worthy man regardless of his nation? Unhappily, his ship is wrecked, and he is cast upon the Isle of Dogs which, as all the world knows, is but a few miles down the Thames opposite the royal palace of Greenwich, where our gracious king is wont to pass many a pleasant hour.

Improbably, I must say, Sir Petronel believes he has landed in France, but is told otherwise by a passing stranger who, by his heavy Scots accent, we are to believe is none but King James himself. The king had a palace at Greenwich, and his Scots accent was almost impenetrable at times. In London it was a standing joke.

Did my friends intend that this be the likeness of the king? Were they holding up his royal highness to ridicule and scorn?

Ask me not what Jonson or the others meant. To know I must needs be a party to their private thoughts. Which I am not. Upon oath, they never shared such thoughts with me.

Yet I do know how the scene was received. I was there. I heard the laughter, the howls, the ribald jokes about Scots, the ridicule of the king himself. Some jokes were good-humoured. Many were bitter and mean-spirited. But I remember the passing stranger's phrase: "I ken him weel," speaking of Sir Petronel. "He is one of my thirty-pound knights."

Who else intended but His Majesty?

No surprise to me, there were spies, intelligencers, in the audience that night. The audience might laugh, but the authorities were not amused. Jonson and the others had not sought permission that the play should be performed, which licence was required of them. That lapse made his fault the greater.

It all fell out as I had feared. For their mockery of the king and his Scots knights and even Scotland itself, the play's authors were imprisoned. They were threatened with losing their fingers and their thumbs and other such mutilations, as part of the executioner's repertoire.

Whether it is true or false what they suffered, I cannot say. Yet such punishments were not uncommon.

I am told that Jonson wrote letters to certain noblemen beseeching their help in his release. I heard that he had got it.

By October he was on the street again, no worse for wear, his fingers and thumbs intact, his disposition unchanged by his confinement.

30

I met Ben Jonson one day at St Paul's where, on the steps of that noble edifice, he was holding forth against some itinerant preacher so ragged in dress and hairy that he might have been John the Baptist come alive again. A crowd had gathered round the disputants. Jonson was having the best of his antagonist. He was an avid reader, and I do think he knew the Testaments as though he had written them himself.

The ranting Puritan had no chance against him. He fled the scene, abased and mocked.

Jonson turned upon seeing me observing his triumph and beckoned me to come to him.

I had not seen my friend since the night at Blackfriars when his offence against the king was committed. I was resolved not to remind him of my warning, though I was sore tempted.

I remember it was bracing weather for the month, the city grey and dirty with smoke, yet Jonson was in good spirits. He said he had been free of his imprisonment for a week and had passed all his time since banqueting his friends in celebration of his release.

He looked much the same for his ordeal. He was never a good dresser, wearing plain muslin shirts rather than doublets, often wine-stained from his nightly revels of which he was overly fond. He made money as a playwright, but it went through his fingers as fast as he made it and he was ever in debt. He owed me some ten pounds or so, enough to feed and house a family of four or five for a year or more. But I had little hope of repayment. I had stopped pestering him about it. What was the use? It was the cost of his friendship, which to me was worth more than the debt.

As to Jonson's appearance, he was a short, stocky man with a square pocky face, a bulbous nose, and thick lips, which were often chapped from his licking of them. He was younger than I. About thirty-one or two I should judge. But he had had a hard life, fighting in the Dutch wars, fighting even more in London taverns. It must be said, if truth matters at all, that he was a brawler by nature, a lover of controversy and disputation. All this showed on his face, in his eyes, and oft in his plays.

"Banqueting, was it? Marry, sir, you have not banqueted me," I said, feigning offence.

In truth I could never keep up with his banqueting or his late nights and do my work, which required solitude and a generous measure of sobriety.

He laughed. His was a jovial laugh, sometimes mischievous. "Will, good friend, that is because I have saved the best for last. Remember what the Gospel says—the first shall be last and the last shall be first. I will presently prove how that verse is fulfilled in you, my dear friend."

"Many thanks for the sermon," I said. "I am sure you will prove the truth of your text to any man's satisfaction."

We walked arm in arm for a hundred paces till we came to a tavern I knew well. We entered and found a table near the door. We ordered drink. Brown ale, I think, but who cares now? I do despise men's journals that must detail diet as well as acts and thoughts, as though otherwise the menu is lost to posterity.

In any case, Jonson regaled me for an hour with stories about his imprisonment, which he took to be more lark than disgrace. "I never feared," he said, "never for a minute. The other prisoners thought I was a very good fellow. They liked my humour, I think. The food, when we were fed, was an abomination before God and His angels. The warder was a brute, but when he saw I had friends in high places he became gentle as a lamb. At least with me. One of my fellow prisoners was a poor knight."

"A Scotsman, I wager."

Jonson laughed and said, "Nay, no Scot he, but poor nonetheless and a decent fellow his knighthood notwithstanding. He had spent his fortune on women and drink, cards, and bear-baiting. He was addicted to tennis and played whenever he could but had few opportunities whilst in prison. I think he had turned pick-purse to meet his needs. What think you, Will? Poor gentleman, he might well have remained at court and practiced his new craft there, for where does one find a better field to harvest fat purses than at court?"

I laughed. As I have said, prison had done nothing to change Jonson. Satire was in his very blood, and I had to admit I liked him the better for it. He was a man who said what he thought at the moment he thought it. A man whose tongue was witty, but thereby also dangerous.

"Come to supper, will you?" he asked.

"Tonight?"

"Yes."

"At your house?"

He made some excuse. Something about his wife being indisposed.

Jonson's wife I knew, though not well. She was a plain woman and a shrew, and Jonson had been unfaithful to her more than once.

I know this for a fact, for his paramours I also knew, a blousy wench in Southwark named Lydia and another from the Bankside, named Margaret or Morag, I think, and a good half-dozen others that shall remain nameless.

I had it on his authority that she was not a very good cook, his wife I mean. Thus, I was not surprised when he gave an excuse not to invite me to his house. I was surprised he was even abiding at home, as he called it, for I understood at that time he was living with one of his wealthy patrons. Jonson had a knack for securing such benefits.

"I know a good place," I said.

He patted my arm affectionately. "I am sure you know an excellent place, but now I do remember it, I myself am a guest of certain gentlemen this evening."

"Certain gentlemen?"

I waited for him to give me names as he might commonly do, if only to impress me with his acquaintances, for he had a great many in London, both in the city and at court. He ever loved to drop their names in the midst of a conversation, perhaps because his own origins were mean and he was sensitive to them. But he kept these names to himself.

"Tomorrow night, then?"

"I am called away. Some business of my wife's family. I am sorry, Will."

I made a sad face. Do not forget that an actor's craft is useful in places beyond the theatre. My mournful countenance worked as I had hoped. I wanted to talk to him about what happened at Holbeche House. I thought perhaps he could give me answers. He was a shrewder man than I, more steeped in skullduggery and mischief.

We had come to the end of the street where we were to part ways, he to the north of the city and I to my lodgings with the Frenchman and his wife.

He turned suddenly as though seized by a sudden thought, which turned out to be the case. "Will, now perhaps you might enjoy coming with me tonight. Some gentlemen have invited me to sup with them and now that I think upon it, they said I might bring a friend."

"A friend? You mean a woman, surely," I said.

"Nay, I think not," Jonson said, holding up his hands in protest. "Upon oath, another man was what was asked for. These are goodly gentlemen who love learning and have a liking for what we do. The theatre I mean. They would rather see a play than play at cards or go a-whoring any day of the week, and I swear you will not find them standing but sitting in the gallery or upon the stage, in the best of chairs, to see as well as be seen. I will not be paying the host's bill, but I suppose as it does not fall to you, you do not object to being my guest."

"I am not sure," I said. "Who are these gentlemen you commend so lavishly?"

"Ah, you shall see," he said. "Let it be a surprise that I assure you will not disappoint or arouse your disdain at the company. Trust me, Will. Your welcome there is by patent. You are famous in the city, after all. Who would not want you at table to boast that they dined with the great William Shakespeare?"

"More than a dozen now that I think upon it," I said.

"That is a dozen more than I can think of, and I know everyone you know."

"Very well," I said. "Where shall we meet?"

"At a hostelry on the Strand. The Irish Boy."

"I think I know it. William Patrick is host, is he not?"

"The very man. And a fine fellow too."

I knew Patrick. He had often come to the Globe and more than once offered me a free supper should I bring all my friends around.

"At what hour?"

"Nine o'clock."

"That's late for supper, is it not?"

"Some of the guests could not come earlier," Jonson said. "And we are as likely to drink our supper as choke on too much meat."

"Nine o'clock it is," I said.

I went home to find the Mountjoy house in an uproar. Husband was berating wife for some alleged infidelity. I could hear their loud voices even after I withdrew to my chamber. I heard Doctor Forman's name mentioned more than once. I could hear Mountjoy's wife cry out in protest, something about her innocence. All this was in French, you understand, but I could make out the French words for whore and slut and concluded thereby that Madame had submitted to Doctor Forman's advances and Monsieur had discovered it.

Or supposed he had, though to a man possessed of jealousy, it's all one. Cuckolds rarely lack proof of infidelity. For them it is in the very air they breathe. If it's proof that's wanted, they shall find it.

It was nearly an hour before all was quiet below stairs. I wondered how the dispute had been resolved. Had the husband beaten the wife, thrown her out of doors, or had she managed to convince the hot-blooded Frenchman that it was not true, the alleged adultery?

I thought about this for a while and then picked up my pen and began to write. I was working at that time on a new play, a play about a Scottish king. It was in the spirit of the times, and I believed if the subject pleased no one else it might please the king, who, as all know who know him in the slightest, is besotted with his own race and lineage.

I had a dry-as-dust history of Scotland before me, which I had of an antiquary friend more steeped in the past than the present. I had read it and made notes to myself and had decided my play would be a tragedy of a king named Macbeth. He was a famous king but, driven by monstrous ambition, he became in due course a tyrant who murdered without pity.

In the play I had given him a wife, whom I made his equal in evil, if not his superior. He was succeeded by His Majesty's ancestor, which I thought would be even a greater appeal to our Scottish king. But after working upon the script for an hour or more I grew weary of the enterprise and fell asleep in my chair.

I dreamed, and in my dream I was back in Holbeche House. Again, I was in the priest's hole but not with Father Gerard. My companion, rather, was Guido Fawkes, who was railing at me for my disloyalty to Gabriel, his friend. He reminded me of all that he and Gabriel had done on my behalf and asked me again and again why I had breached my vows of friendship.

In the dream I protested, I think. I do not remember what I said. My words made no sense to me and when I endeavoured to write them down with my pen, I could not read what I had written, for it was all gibberish, like unto a foreign tongue I had no knowledge of. In truth, all my senses failed, save sight.

I was as mute as an infant, as deaf as stone.

Then I woke weeping like a child, hot tears on my face, striking out at Fawkes' image, which somehow remained before my eyes even when the dream had faded quite away.

31

I came to the Irish Boy before the hour appointed, thinking that since all the guests might be unknown to me, I should be prompt, so as not to make much of my being the only stranger amongst them. Despite Jonson's assurances that I would be welcome, even celebrated, I felt uneasy. The truth is that I am not at my best amongst strangers. It is an old flaw, past remedy, which I live with quite happily, for I am daily surrounded by friends who pay me due respect and honour. He who has an abundance should not complain of a lack.

Arrived, I saw William Patrick standing near the door and went to ask him where I might find Ben Jonson. He pointed upstairs where I knew there were private rooms. Patrick's best had been set aside for him who would pay for the evening's entertainment.

"And who might that be?" I asked, thinking that I deserved at least to know whom I should thank for my supper.

"That would be Master Catesby," he said.

I started at the name. I thought he might mean Gabriel, whom I had not seen since I had dismissed him from our company, but who I had heard was still in London employed by his cousin. Then I realized it was more likely Robert Catesby he meant, for I doubted Gabriel would have a sufficient purse to host a gathering of the number and quality Jonson had claimed this to be.

"Master Robert Catesby resides at the Irish Boy while he is in London," William Patrick said, as though he wanted me to know of the quality of his guests.

He led me up a flight of stairs to the room I sought. He opened the door with a flourish, the way a magician reveals to his audience some wonder or spectacle.

I walked into a spacious chamber in which a long table had been set. About a half-dozen gentlemen were present. At the head of the table sat Robert Catesby, who, looking up at my entry, smiled warmly. "Ah, Master William Shakespeare in the flesh. You are most welcome, sir."

He did not seem surprised to see me. I wondered if Jonson had told him I was coming. I bowed at his acknowledgements and looked around at the other men present. I recognized none. Jonson had yet to appear. This was awkward indeed, and I felt my face flush with embarrassment. Save for Robert Catesby, I was alone with strangers, an outsider whose very presence at this gathering was undoubtedly a mystery to them all. I was as one who uninvited, pretends he is, that he may eat for free. I know such men well. Who does not?

Robert Catesby made the introductions.

To this day, I remember the names of each person at table and the order in which I was presented to them. I remember their faces, their dress, their voices. I remember their curious stares upon my entering, which a Moor or some German burgomeister might have deserved more than I. If anything, I was dressed with sober modesty and was remarkable in no way that I was aware of, either in face or other feature.

"This is Master Francis Tresham," Catesby said, nodding toward one of the gentlemen. "And to his left is my good friend, Thomas Wintour. Neigh to him is his brother-in-law, John Ashfield."

Then he drew his attention to the other side of the table, gesturing to each gentleman with a little bow of regard. "Master Thomas Percy and Lord Mordaunt."

This Lord Mordaunt I had heard of although I had no memory of our ever having met. He was Henry Mordaunt, I believe, and a baron of the realm, which title served him well later when he was taken and for a while imprisoned. He was a man of sober countenance, conscious ever of his rank and title, but I do think a little of the prattling fool. He seemed to glory in his association with those present, especially Robert Catesby, who I now recognized as one of those men who drew others to him effortlessly, though often to their peril.

For a while, there was idle talk at table, without any one person's discourse dominating. I maintained a dignified silence, picking at what was offered, drinking a little, laughing when it seemed appropriate, regretting that I had come, for I am jealous of my writing time and would rather have been home, pen in hand.

Then a little over a half an hour beyond my arrival, Jonson appeared, his craggy face all abloom with smiles and his mouth full of apologies for being late, which he often was to such occasions. It was not deliberate, I think. He had no sense of time, that was all.

He was not unaccompanied, however, and this is where I was surprised indeed, for with him came none other than my erstwhile bodyguard, Guido Fawkes, who had disappeared from my life upon the vanquishing of John Flynt and his crew.

"I do not need to be introduced to these men," I said, shaking Jonson's hand and then Fawkes'.

But here I found yet another mystery. The gentlemen at table were all friends, apparently of long standing. But why was Fawkes here? And why was I?

Then suddenly it appeared to me that I had mistaken Jonson's invitation as a spontaneous gesture. Now it seemed deliberate, as though all along he desired me to attend, perhaps even before meeting me at St Paul's. Was this a supper with friends, or a meeting with some sinister agenda of which only I was unaware?

I sat between Jonson and Fawkes, close together like men in a small boat with no elbow room at all. The chamber was very warm and grew warmer so that I began to sweat beneath my collar. There was but a single window, but no one had thought to open it.

Catesby began telling stories about various Scots who, newly knighted, had shown themselves unfit for polite society, as he pleased to call it. Everyone found these stories amusing and there began a general exchange of anecdotes all on the same theme. There was much laughter at these stories. I glanced at Jonson, who had been imprisoned for his mockery of Scots. He joined in with the others, and even told a few stories of his own to the end that the Scots were an ignorant race, bull-headed and dull-brained. These slanders surprised me, for Jonson had once told me he was of Scottish blood himself.

Thereafter, conversation took a different turn. Our attention was all upon Guido Fawkes, who spoke of a journey to Spain, from which, evidently, he had just returned. I noticed the others at table listened to him intently, respectfully. He spoke of the journey, which he said was arduous, giving various amusing accounts of his sufferings. He spoke Spanish, he said, but noted that the tongue was different from province to province, so different that one village could hardly understand the next.

He talked nothing of pilgrimages, which he had when I first met him. Rather, he described his purpose as having had a more secular and sinister intent. He said he had obtained an audience with a certain count who was a close confident of the Spanish king. He had given a report on the state of Catholics in England to this count, a report he trusted would be forwarded to the Spanish king for his consideration, since everyone knew of King Philip's interest in English affairs. The count had been sympathetic but had not offered help of a kind that Fawkes deemed to be useful.

"Does he want money, the count?" I remember Catesby asking.

"Alas, he is afraid, I think," Fawkes said. "The Spanish are a timid people. They are aggressive only when they are confident of victory. We English are different. We will fight a losing battle any day, and in so doing snatch a victory that was never dreamed of."

All the others agreed that this was true of the English character. The Spaniard was a different, and lesser creature. Timid, as Fawkes had declared, and deficient in valour and imagination.

On this subject, I added nothing. I watched. I listened.

My silence was noted by Catesby, perhaps thinking that it was deliberate, my supposed reluctance to join in. I remained sensitive to criticism of the king in my presence and, having heard both Catesby and Fawkes speak on the subject aforetime, I sensed the talk was drifting in that direction again. How might Spain help England, but in its religious wars? And who was the cause of this dissension other than the present king of England who, having promised toleration for the Catholic minority, now oppressed them?

To all this disputation and controversy, Catesby tried to draw me in. He presently succeeded.

"Master Shakespeare, you have placed many a Spaniard on the stage. What have you observed about his character?"

I answered, as I remember, "I have presented characters who were Spaniards, but I bow to Master Fawkes' authority on that question. He has travelled in Spain. He has fought, I believe, both against the

Spaniard and for him. I have done neither of these but know men largely through books and travellers' tales."

"Ah, come now, Master Shakespeare," Fawkes said, grinning broadly. "You are much too modest. Even if my knowledge is superior by experience, doubtless you have an opinion, which I pray you do share freely. All are friends here. None of us is a Spaniard, nor are we married to one that we should rush to the defence of her breed."

"Thank God for that," someone said. I do not remember who. All the men laughed at this. I confess I joined in, but only for civility's sake. The quip was not that amusing, and I had heard it before.

"Therefore, how can anything you say give offence?" Fawkes continued, as though there had been no interruption.

There was general agreement at the table that this was true, and all encouraged me to speak my mind, especially Jonson, who chided me for being evasive in refusing to render an opinion. He said that I was in truth a shrewd judge of men, and that I needed only to know one Spaniard to know all.

"Very well," I said. "As to the resolve of Spain and the strength of its army, I submit the event in living memory of us all, the great Armada of 1588, wherein had God and bad weather not presented themselves on England's behalf, we should now have doubtless a king who is Catholic indeed, and who might be busy suppressing heretics, not Rome's faithful. Spanish mettle was not tested in that encounter. But I am persuaded that had the ships landed they would have put up a great fight, one which our English army might not have survived."

I had offered this same argument before, to Father Gerard, but thought it worth making again on this occasion.

"And would a Catholic king be so bad?" Robert Catesby asked, levelling a cold eye in my direction.

"It would have been bad for the hundred thousand Englishmen who had defended the country against invasion, regardless of the invader's intent. And who had died for the freedom now lost to them."

My words, which were more than I wanted to say about Spaniards or their works, went over badly with the present company, I think. I could see it in their shifting eyes, their pursed lips of disapproval. Only Jonson, sitting beside me, came to my defence though, as I have said, he was a good Catholic at that time, and had told me more than once that he would have been pleased had King James converted.

"Master Shakespeare has a point to his argument I think," Jonson said. "When we speak of war, even civil war, most who die are not combatants. They are but ordinary folk, who lose without ever having aught to gain. My friend is concerned for the suffering innocent."

Catesby said, "Sometimes many must suffer that a greater good prevail."

"If those who suffer are innocent," I asked, "what then? How can slaughter be justified?"

"Who is truly innocent?" Fawkes interjected. "Since Adam's fall all have sinned."

I could not let this specious argument go unanswered. I said hotly, "From that it follows that were you to kill me, say, or Master Catesby here, the fault would be ours? We should be deserving of it since we are sinful creatures and you, I assume, would be blameless since you would be acting as God's instrument against the wicked, His scourge, so to speak."

I was growing impatient with this Jesuitical arguing, but it was clear it was not over. Catesby would not let the matter rest.

"This is an interesting philosophical discussion, Master Shakespeare, which makes me right glad that you have joined us. There may be a time in the near future where all these issues are resolved, and you come happily to a different opinion."

"Issues?" I asked.

"Questions of the morality of warfare in the cause of religious truth," Catesby said. "My friends here and I have been talking about this frequently in past days. You and I discussed this during you visit to Holbeche House last summer. As for resolution, I do mean some action that might tip the scales, so to speak, give those of us who adhere to Rome's dictates better advantage in the kingdom, if only to relieve us of onerous laws and fines enacted by a parliament dominated by Puritans and zealots."

Then, suddenly, Catesby set a new course. It was a deft move. It took me quite aback. He commenced to praise both Jonson and me for our important role in the kingdom. It was a theme he had struck in our past conversations, how we playwrights had the ear of the populace. How the plays we wrote might influence opinion of the great and the humble, the knight and the pauper.

"I would venture, Masters Shakespeare and Jonson, that you have more influence than our clergy with their weekly sermons, and the Puritans with their tedious tirades against what they choose to call the immorality of the age. That is why we—I do mean my friends and I—would so much wish the both of you to be on our side rather than to stand apart."

"Apart?"

"Uncommitted to either side," Catesby said.

"And what specifically would you have us do?" I asked, wondering that Jonson had not asked the same question. "Take up arms against Parliament? Force the king from his throne?"

Catesby laughed. "Oh, perish the thought, Master Shakespeare. I speak not about arms, but about the spreading of ideas, and perhaps even the intensifying of public dissatisfaction. There are many adherents to the Old Faith in England this day. There are even more who are sympathetic to our downtrodden state. Some of these might convert through the persuasions of our missionary priests. I mean those who are not Catholic now, but may become so. This is a swelling group. We are—though it may not be known by the powers that be—the future. With the right plays presented for their entertainment, they might benefit from instruction. Think of the power of the righteous example. Think of the power of the negative one."

I told him I was still uncertain what he supposed we do, we makers of plays.

"Say, Master Shakespeare, you put upon the stage a play in which there is a priest. The audience recognizes that he is no heretic priest, no Puritan ranter or Lutheran pontificator, but a holy man of the Church as it was and still is, world without end. In brief, he is a Catholic. Let this same priest be a good man, a servant of God, no fool or lecherous hypocrite. Let those who adhere to his counsel be judicious men and women too, admirable in the audience's eyes, so that they applaud the priest's actions, his compassion, the holy doctrine that is the root of his righteousness. All this thereby encouraging them to revere the priest's sacred vocation."

"You mean they are Catholics, not Protestants?" I said.

"Not explicitly, no. It would not be necessary that they should so be identified. It is the respect I am after. The image of a godly man."

"You mean you do not wish that my priests be figures of fun, satirical caricatures. That I do not play my audience for laughter?" I asked.

"Exactly, sir. Mock not sacred things or teach others to do likewise. In sum, both you and Master Jonson here are able to present moral instruction of such a sort that the public may look upon our cause with favour."

And rise against our present king and parliament with fervour, I thought to myself but had the good sense not to speak it, not in this company. I was right sorry now that I had accepted Jonson's invitation. A free supper was it, paid for by a generous host? When was such a supper free, if ever it was?

I said, "I do not present characters in my plays that disparage the righteous, regardless of the sect. But the truth is, Master Catesby, that unlike you I do not see my craft as a vocation sacred or divine. I am not a priest of any church. Nor a missionary of any sect. I do not see myself as a teacher, which thing you have called me at our first meeting. Though I grant lessons might be learned from the behaviour of the characters, their motives, actions and their fate, just as in life we learn from observing the virtues and follies of others. Is this not universally acknowledged? My aim is to entertain first, to arouse interest and sustain it with some two hours traffic upon the stage. Nothing more nor less. To instil laughter, provoke tears, create awe and terror at the denouement of tragedy. To paint the figures of justice and injustice. To show the foibles of human nature in comedy. Those are my aims, Master Catesby, simple and perhaps self-indulgent as they may sound."

I paused to take a breath, suddenly realizing that all attention was upon me and that I was being given looks that did not seem to favour my sentiments. Despite this, and recklessly perhaps, I soldiered on, blind to any consequences my fervour might have.

"I do not seek to change the order of the kingdom, or even to insulate a portion of its population from the unrighteous dominion of the government, if that indeed is what it is, unrighteous I mean. In sum, Master Catesby, I do not choose to be a partisan of any cause, at the same time allowing that the cause might be just in the eyes of man or God."

I had spoken with passion, and far more than I intended when my first words were uttered. And my tongue expressed thoughts I did not know I had, strange as that might seem. For though thought be the father of words, oft words beget new thought as well. As I think they did in my case.

When I finished this rant, the men were silent and staring. Their disapproval of my words was palpable. I saw that I had said the wrong thing to this company, who wanted more from me than philosophizing about my craft. This was not, in their minds, about the theatre or about playwrights and their visions. It was about the state of England and a war between sects that claimed allegiance to the same Divine Master, but nonetheless might take up arms and cut each other's throats.

Catesby levelled his gaze at Jonson. "And how say you, Master Jonson? Are you of Master Shakespeare's mind in this?"

I do not remember Jonson's answer. His own religious views prevented him from being so critical of what had been put toward both of us, that we should make our art an instrument of Papist policy. Is that not what was being asked of me?

But I do remember that he was less strident in his denial, more open to the suggestion that his presentations be softened so that the religion of Rome might have a good image in his art. I think he said something about the Puritans providing enough matter for ridicule that he had no need to mock God's true priests and their holy works.

32

It was near midnight when supper was done at the Irish Boy. Nearly all present were drowsy with drink, of which there had been a prodigious amount. For me, I had had but two glasses of the wine and eaten little of the food, for fear of dyspepsia, with which I am often cursed.

Besides which, the nature of the discourse had stirred me up as controversy ever did, making it a spoiler of any pleasure in the food. As I grow older, I see indigestion as a potent enemy of my spirit. Like any wise man, I watch what I eat. I watch too what I discourse upon. I try to sleep more for my health's sake and avoid silly quarrels.

But I am but a slackard in all these resolves, I do confess it.

Jonson and I left together, the others remaining behind, perhaps for more talk about Papistry and public opinion. As I had been told by William Patrick, Catesby resided at the Irish Boy whilst in London. I think perhaps others did as well. But on the way out, who should we encounter but Gabriel Catesby, a man whose face I hoped never again to see.

I was surprised that he had not joined us all for supper. Had Father

Gerard been there as well, it would have been a reunion of sorts. We might have talked of high times at Holbeche House and our happy hours in a miserable priest's hole.

At first Gabriel did not seem to recognize me, but then perhaps that was because Jonson was talking animatedly and that drew his attention. That was the way Jonson was, never a man for quiet corners although that night he had been more reserved than ever before I had seen him. I had marked his self-effacement and found it suspicious. It was a suspicion I was soon to confirm.

"Oh, it is Master Shakespeare himself, the great playwright." Gabriel said this with a derisive grin, loudly so it might be heard even upstairs where his so-called cousin remained at table finishing the last of the wine or plotting some mischief to the State.

I nodded, but coldly, and when he extended his hand in fellow-ship, I refused it.

I stared him down until he looked away.

Jonson observed my response to Catesby and commented on it later. That was after Gabriel passed me by with a sneer and declared he was on his cousin's business. It was important business, he said. He could not stay for a pleasant conversation about the old days in Stratford, although he heartily desired so to do.

It was another jab at my alleged ingratitude.

"You snubbed that fellow, which you are not wont to do. Pray, what was his offence?" Jonson asked, when we were in the street, which was now quiet and very dark, making me wish we had a torch to guide the way, although the way was so familiar to us both we could probably navigate it safely.

"Yes," I said. "A great offence."

"Then he is your enemy?"

"An old friend, a new enemy," I said. "He was once one of us, a King's Man, for a season, then revealed his true colours."

"Ah," Jonson said. "Say no more. I have more than a few enemies like that myself."

I thanked him for the supper. He said he noticed how little I ate, how little wine I had taken. Then I said, "It was always intended that I should be present at table tonight, is that not so, Ben? Tell me true, for your faith's and our friendship's sake. Your invitation was by design, was it not?"

"What do you mean, Will?"

"I mean it was always intended that I accompany you there. It was no afterthought, your inviting me to join you because I had missed all the earlier celebration of your release from prison."

Jonson stood silent for a moment, his large bricklayer's hands limp against his thighs. I could read the language of his body well enough. His silence gave consent.

He paused, then said, "Robert Catesby helped me when I was in prison. He gave me a certain sum of money. The exact amount I do not remember. It was not really a gift, more a loan. To help with, well, certain other debts of mine. He asked me to invite you to supper by any means necessary. He said he had met you a few months past, was impressed by you. He said he loved your plays. I knew you walked at Paul's at noonday. I waited for you, biding my time taking on that idiot Puritan. I am sorry I lied about that, Will. I owed Robert Catesby, you see. He said he would forgive the debt. When he asked me for help, I could not say no."

"Did you know why he wanted me there?"

"I did."

"Did you think that I would agree to subvert my plays to his politics?"

Jonson shrugged. "I thought you might. I knew your father had been a Catholic."

"Not a Catholic."

"Well, inclined in that direction."

"Yes," I said. "Inclined, not practicing."

"Whereby I thought perhaps you were drifting in that direction yourself. Many of our friends are but do keep their devotions hidden."

"Which they are well advised to do," I said. "But did you really imagine me a convert, even after our talks about religion? Whatever did I say that implied I was turning to Rome? What saint did I invoke or crucifix cradle? When did I count beads or hail Mary to my soul's salvation? Pray tell me."

Jonson said, "I am a Catholic. I believe in free will. A man can change his mind, convert suddenly through some spiritual experience or revelation. Like unto Paul on the road to Damascus."

"I have not been honoured with such an epiphany, Ben, nor look to be. Besides which, this is London, not Damascus."

Again, Jonson said he was sorry. His face fell. He did seem truly penitent, a posture I had rarely seen him adopt. I looked at him and considered the case. He was, after all, my friend. His betrayal, such as it was, was a lesser order of offence in the great hierarchy of offences.

"Oh, forgiven," I said at last.

Ben laughed, shook my hand warmly. "Still friends, I pray. Despite the deception, which I do swear had no malice in it."

"Friends still," I said. "No harm done. I have told your Master Catesby what I think, having now discovered it for myself. He should expect nothing of me except perhaps general good will and stage priests who are not monsters of inequity preying on children and virgins, but merely men with the usual range of foibles."

Jonson said, "And I am of the same mind, about what you said, and about caution."

"Caution?"

"With regard to my new friends," Jonson said. "And more especially Robert Catesby. I fear he and the others have some plot they lay the groundwork for. If so, I want no part of it."

"A wise resolve," I said. "Such plotting is good neither for your art or for your health."

"Shall we walk?" Jonson said.

"We shall," I replied. I took his arm.

I did not see Ben Jonson again until November, not until after all that was to happen happened, all of England seemed turned upside down, and I learned what mischief really was afoot that night at the Irish Boy.

I do affirm what I have related here to be the truth, whatsoever might be later claimed, either by friend or foe.

All happened on the ninth day of October, anno 1605.

As God is my witness.

33

Before dawn I was ripped from sleep by an intemperate pounding at my door. It was an awful summons, a din that stilled the heart and filled the imagination with the worst of fears.

At first, I thought it Alice Simpkins come again to tell me the house was besieged by the sheriff's men and I must flee for my life. Then I remembered all that was months behind and in a different place. Here was London now, not Staffordshire. And my own cluttered chamber in Monsieur Mountjoy's house.

As I write this, all comes to mind—the alarm, the imperative fist, the yet to be discovered catastrophe.

I staggered to the door to ask who it was who had so rudely awakened me before dawn, for I could see no light out the window, nor understand why anyone would have business with me at such an unholy hour.

"It's Ben Jonson, Will. In Christ's name, open the door."

I recognized his voice, which ever seemed afflicted with a hoarse cough even though his thick body might be as fit as any man's. Whereby I knew it was no imposter without. I thought my friend might be drunk, have mistaken my lodging for his, or have some other dubious motive for disrupting my sleep.

Or perhaps it was a prank. Jonson was given to such foolery, despite his vaunted erudition. He was, after all, a bricklayer's son, and he retained the rough manners of his humble origins, save when he was at court when he could put on the gentleman quite well, bowing and scraping like the rest of us.

I rose, unbolted the door, and was about to demand to know his purpose when he rushed in and shoved me backward with such force that I fell back upon the bed, gasping for breath.

"Something has happened," he cried. "At the House of Parliament."

"What?" I asked, still half asleep. "Let me guess. Ah, I know, brevity has been instituted in the Lords, or honesty made requisite in the Commons."

Jonson seized the collar of my nightshirt with his big hands and with such excitement I had rarely seen in him. "Nay, Will, this is no time for quips. Get you dressed. And for Christ's sake let's have some light in here. This room is as cold and damp as a tomb. How can you bear it?"

I had a brace of candles by my bed. I set all alight and for the first time I could see Jonson's face. His eyes were wide and fearful, his ruined cheeks flushed and oily, his mouth fixed in a grim lock. Something indeed had happened, or perhaps he was simply losing his mind.

"Very well," I said. "Tell me what has happened and why I must stir at this hour."

I began to dress slowly, thinking I might well return to bed if this alarm proved a hoax, or Jonson had exaggerated the event beyond reason.

"You won't believe it!"

"Prove me," I said.

He spoke rapidly. "Why, 'tis naught less than an attempt to murder the king, his counsellors, and members of the Parliament."

I believed not a word of this. "When was this enormity supposed to happen?"

"Only a few hours or more ago," Jonson said. "This very night. He who would ignite the blast was found there and is in custody as we speak. The king was to open Parliament today. The blast would have killed him, the queen, the Earl of Salisbury, and I know not how many of the lords. The entire government would have been murdered in as cruel a slaughter as can be conceived."

"But this would-be assassin has been taken, you say?"

"Even now he is before the Council. I have heard he boasts of his intended deed as though it were a work of corporeal mercy, not a heinous act of mass murder. But for the warning letter to one of the lords, the act would not have been discovered."

"What letter?"

"Why, one urging the recipient, a certain Lord Monteagle, member of Parliament himself, to keep at home. Monteagle conveyed it straightway to the king. It was His Majesty who ferreted out its intent and who thereafter ordered the Parliament building searched."

"It is a miracle then, this warning you speak of?"

"Call it what you will."

"Very good," I said, sighing with relief. "Then the danger's past."

"No one is sure if it be past," Jonson said. "More violence may be yet to come."

"More assaults, do you mean?"

"Or worse, murders in the street, the downfall of princes, the end of the very world."

Jonson was not given to dire prognostications, at least in conversation, so this image of the Apocalypse caused me to grow serious myself.

"Who was the man, this would-be igniter of gunpowder?" I asked.

"He has given his name as Johnson. John Johnson."

"A name nondescript enough. I wager it is no more his name than it is mine."

"No doubt," said Jonson. "Yet that is the name he gave."

"Surely this is the work of a madman," I said. "I warrant you he has just escaped from Bedlam hospital."

"I think not," Jonson said. "He has confessed his intent in plain language and with no signs of madness in him."

"Which intent was?"

"Why, to kill the king, his counsellors, and as many of the lords as he might."

"For what reason?"

"Ah, here's the thing, Will. He affirms he has done it because he is a Catholic and wishes the country returned to the Roman faith. He is very blunt about his purpose and fears nothing—not torture, not death, not any man's threats. Even the king has spoken of the man's fortitude."

"The king has spoken well of his would-be assassin?" I asked incredulously.

"So it is reported," Jonson said.

"I do think this fellow is a lunatic, if he fears not death nor torture, nor hell itself, for where else may be his destination for such an act but the fires of hell?"

"Come, Will, see for yourself. News of his arrest is already in the streets. By dawn all London will be up in arms. Did you plan to go to the Globe today?"

He raised a hand to silence me before I could respond.

"Don't answer, Will, I know you were. I know your habits like my own. Tell me, though, are your landlord and wife Catholics?"

"No, Huguenots, French Protestants. Not pious," I said, thinking of last night's marital uproar and the mutual charges of adultery that were a staple of their domestic discourse.

"Still, they should take care," Jonson said. "I would not be a Spaniard or a Frenchman in London right now. All are thought Catholics, regardless of what faith they profess. All are suspect. This is but one man that is taken at the very scene of the crime, but it would be a wonder if the authorities do not conclude he is part of a Papist conspiracy."

"I am no Papist, as you know well," I said. "Why should I be afraid?"

I was now fully dressed.

"You are not, but I am," Jonson said. "And you are my friend, and you have friends who are Catholics."

"Granted," I said, "still…"

"Will you go to the Globe today?" he asked, even though he had already told me he knew I was.

"I have a rehearsal," I said. "Before noon, a performance after. *Othello*. We expect a full house."

"You will never make it there save you leave now. By dawn all of London will be in an uproar. And if they do not close the theatres, I will be much surprised."

"Where did you learn of this wicked plot?" I asked, still not convinced any of what my friend said was true. It sounded improbable. Powder enough to blow up Parliament? Surely it was a figment of some madman's dream.

"I was at this tavern not far from Westminster Palace. The Prince's Pride."

"I know it."

"I am there with a few friends when suddenly in comes a captain of the guard and a half dozen of his men, all big, vile fellows with angry, self-important faces eager to find some innocent to beat upon. You know how they are. They demanded that we tell them if we knew a John Johnson, or anyone of that family name. None admitted knowing such a man, and wisely. It was obvious what they intended. He who admitted knowing Johnson would be put down as an accomplice. When they asked me my name and I said 'Jonson,' I was seized upon, for they thought I might be the man's brother."

"You spell your names differently," I said, not sure that they did but offering the suggestion as a gesture of support.

"True," Jonson said. "But why do you imagine this scurrilous fellow knew how to spell, or even read? We are not talking about Cambridge scholars here, but the worst sort of villains dragooned into the king's service. The names sounded the same. That was enough to arouse the man's suspicions."

"Why are you here now then? Why did they let you go?"

"Ah, because one of their number, wiser than his companions, said I looked nothing like unto him who was taken. He said if this Johnson and I were brothers, then we indeed had different fathers and mothers both. By their account, Johnson is a tall, broad-shouldered man with a narrow waist and close-set eyes. If he has more than a quarter inch of fat on his belly, I am no man at all."

"Well, you might have been cousins," I said. "Or still be brothers of a sort." I was thinking of the relationship of the Catesbys.

He gave me an impatient glare. "The point is, Will, that they let me go, by reason or by God's grace I care not a fart now that I am free to quibble with you here and am not languishing in some filthy prison cell, waiting to be racked for what I might know of this treason. I have had my fill of prisons for the month."

"They did not ask your religion?"

"I would have lied had they asked, and never felt an iota of guilt," Jonson said. "For a man has the right to save his life. It comes before his duty to truth, at least in my book. Come, Will, let's set out. I will accompany you as far as the bridge, and perhaps beyond."

"Why?" I asked.

"Because I think I may be safer on the other side of the river. If we be stopped along the way, we each can affirm the name and innocence of the other."

"You think the city will be that riotous?"

"I do think it, as sure as the sun will rise. The king may not be that loved by the multitude, yet he is an anointed king, God's vicar on the earth and all that rot. Besides which, we English do not like the blowing up of persons, which this Johnson fellow intended. It savours too much of Italian deviltry, Machiavelli and his ilk. Nor do they like Jesuits. Good God, Will, I don't myself like the Jesuits and I count myself a good Catholic."

"What have the Jesuits to do with it?" I asked as we descended the stairs. I saw a light in the kitchen, heard the clatter of pans and pots. That would be Mountjoy's cook. Unlike her master, the cook would not inquire what we were about at such an hour.

"Johnson has confessed this to be a Catholic plot," my friend said. "It will be universally supposed the Jesuits had a hand in it, for they are regarded here as the right arm of the Antichrist. If you think priests are hunted down now, they will be the more so come tomorrow. Mark me well, the Puritans in Parliament will bemoan publicly this would-be assassination but in private rejoice that something has happened that will finally turn the country against Rome forever."

About what would happen in the streets, Jonson was right. It was not seven o'clock of the new day but to walk toward the river was to push against a sweaty tide of angry and confused flesh, half-dressed householders and merchants, apprentice boys who ever take delight in public disorder, sundry housewives and girls, barking dogs, assorted Puritan babblers declaring the powder plot as the beginning of the end.

Shopkeepers, fearful of riot and vandals, had shuttered their windows. Torch-bearing crowds had already formed at each corner, and as we passed, we could hear from all sides the cries against the Papists. We also heard rumours that the city had also been implanted with gunpowder and that it was only a matter of time, perhaps only a few hours, before blasts would be heard, along with the screams of the injured and dying.

Some I overheard claimed the plot was designed to usher in a Spanish invasion, a somewhat lesser catastrophe, I thought, than the Apocalypse.

When we came to the bridge it was clear there was no crossing it. Pikemen and their officers had been stationed at the entrance and were letting no one through. Now it was light and we could see the full extent of the terror. Everyone seemed to be abroad. I would have crossed the river in one of the boats but there were none to be had. Regular work had been suspended. I now realized that there would be no rehearsal that morning, no performance that afternoon. All had been turned upside down in the city—and in all the world for all I knew.

Suddenly, behind us we heard loud voices demanding that we make way, that we stand aside. I turned to look expecting to see officers of the sort Jonson had described in the tavern. Instead I saw a band of brutish men armed with staves and clubs heading in our direction. These were not officers of the law, nor guards from the palace, but an unruly mob without a head and without any purpose other than to rise up and threaten all whom they encountered.

I knew the manner of men they were. Men who would find in any occasion an incitement to riot, pillage, and even murder. Jonson and I backed up against a wall to let them pass.

"If anyone stops us, tell them your father is a priest or bishop," I whispered to my friend. "And you plan to take Holy Orders in the English Church come Christmastide. Quote some Latin to them, whereby they may know you have studied for that ministry."

"Latin forfend!" Jonson exclaimed, throwing up his hands in frustration. "Should I quote Latin they will suspect I am some Jesuit. Rather, let it be Bible verses from Master Coverdale's good English text. It will be the more convincing. For your part, tell them you are Shakespeare, the writer of plays. They may have heard of you. Give them the name of some titles. Surely someone in that mob will have seen one play or the other."

"If so, I pray God they have liked what they saw, or it may go bad for me."

By good fortune, this unruly crew passed us by being blind with rage as though they themselves had been assaulted, but within a quarter of an hour, struggling to make our way back to my lodgings, we encountered three other such bands in the streets, going door to door seeking, as they proclaimed, Papist spies, for they were prepared to condemn all for the actions of one, be they guilty or not.

I swear I did see one youth, not more than eleven or twelve I should think, fall into their hands and suffer abuse for that he had a crucifix upon his breast or some bauble resembling one. They put a rope around his neck with all who witnessed it crying that he should be hanged until dead and the same for all adherents of the Pope.

By noon I had had my fill of the public calamity. Jonson was winded and footsore from walking. By the grace of God we had avoided an assault although there was nothing on our person that would have invited it, save that we might be thought to have full purses, dressed as we were.

I agreed with Jonson that we would meet the next day at noon.

"The Mitre or the Mermaid?" Jonson asked.

"Let it be the Mermaid," I said. I knew Jonson liked it best. "It matters not to me."

34

I returned to my lodgings to find the Mountjoys, father, mother, and daughter, much alarmed by the news. They had heard about the attempt to kill the king and were as appalled as anyone in the city.

They also feared for their own safety, even as Jonson had forewarned. They were not Catholics. They were not particularly religious, as I have said. They attended the French Church, where a congregation of Huguenots assembled on Sundays to sing hymns and endure long Calvinist sermons.

Yet I knew it was more for form's sake than out of any particular devotion. They worried that being clearly French by their speech, they would be suspected of being Papists. That they were foreign born made it worse.

Their thoughts as to what had happened differed from my own. This did not surprise me. Rumour had exaggerated the intended crime until the Mountjoys supposed a band of Jesuits had schemed not only to blow up Parliament, but to murder as many citizens as they might before being killed or killing themselves. The Mountjoys believed such a danger still existed.

I said to Marie Mountjoy, who was the most terrified of the

family, "Rest easy, Madame, your fear surpasses reason."

She wept and trembled. Her husband put his arms around her shoulder in a rare show of affection.

I said, "It is less than you fear, Madame. These men were not Jesuits, and only one man has been arrested. He confessed his aim was to blow up Parliament, the House of Lords, killing the king, the queen, the Earl of Salisbury, and many of the lords, temporal and spiritual. It is an awful thing this man contemplated, but there is no evidence he desired to harm the general citizenry. I do not think you or your family are in any danger."

I said this but thought otherwise. One man? And that enormous load of gunpowder? Surely, this was the work of more than a single devil. More were needed if only to transport the powder.

"The people, they think we are Catholic," she said in her heavy accent.

"Stay indoors for the next day or two, I beseech you for your safety's sake," I said. "The furore will subside, I promise you. Already the city is full of the king's troops. The riots will be suppressed. Order will be restored. Presently we will know if this arrested man—his name is John Johnson—had accomplices in this enormity or acted alone. The guilty will be discovered and punished."

"But wherefore should this Johnson want to do so wicked a thing?" their daughter asked. "To kill the king and all these people. God will surely punish him."

I was not sure the family was aware of how we English punished traitors. There had been public executions since their arrival in London, I knew that. Public executions were wildly popular, even more than bear-baitings. More popular than my own plays. Still some thought them cruel and barbarous, even for traitors, and refused to attend such gruesome exhibitions.

235

The daughter's name was Mary, after her mother, Marie. She was at that time eighteen or nineteen I think and was married to Mountjoy's apprentice, Stephen Belott, also a Huguenot who had taken refuge in England. The Mountjoys had hoped, I believe, that being winsome she might marry above her station, to their advantage as well as their daughter's, but she had given her heart to Stephen.

I liked the young couple, who seemed wholesome and truly devoted to each other. I had been of some help in arranging the marriage, at her father's request, whereby he owed me thanks.

Monsieur Mountjoy frowned and spat. "The English, they are ignorant. They think all we French are Catholic. They cannot conceive that some of us hate those who bow to the Pope, and it is for this we have fled our country and come here. My family, my father, my mother, two of my brothers, were killed in the great massacre of St Bartholomew in Paris, when Catholic murdered Huguenot. The Catholic, they showed no mercy. There was blood in the streets. I remember it still, though I was but a child at the time."

"Do not fear, Monsieur. There will be no such massacre here," I said. "The king will not permit it. The king is a good man, a good Christian."

"But this Johnson you speak of tried to kill him," Mountjoy said. "Will the king not seek revenge?"

"He will seek justice," I said. "Johnson will be tried for his crime, and when he is proved guilty, then and only then will the king have his revenge. All will happen according to the law. Trust me, it will be so."

Monsieur Mountjoy still looked worried. His wife continued to weep softly. Only Mary seemed satisfied with my explanation.

I allow it was a weak argument I had made, a desperate bid for peace in a troubled house. Fate might bring about the very calamities my friends feared. Still, I had done my best as a consoler of the distraught. I could have done worse.

* * *

The Mountjoys followed my counsel about staying indoors. They shuttered the windows of the ground floor of the house and bolted the door. Someone came knocking there whilst I was still with them. Mountjoy shouted that the shop was closed. He said there was disease within, not naming it the plague, but neither refuting the implication.

They invited me to eat with them and I accepted. I was weak after my ordeal in the streets and Mistress Mountjoy's cook was more than competent. That night, however, she was too distraught to cook. She had in her larder some salted pork, a portion of a carrot pie, and several apples. Such was our simple repast. Along with a good French wine. It was Lenten fare, not French finery. But good enough. None of us at table, I think, had much appetite.

About eight o'clock I went up to bed and happened to look from my window into the street. Across the city I could see fires, a dozen or so of them and from different neighbourhoods. At first, I thought London was ablaze. I was alarmed. I imagined a larger conflagration in which the city and my theatre would end up ashes. Perhaps the Puritans were right. This was the end of the world, the long-prophesied Apocalypse. The powder plot was only the beginning.

But then I saw that these were bonfires, deliberately set, and knew I was witness to a celebration, not a riot.

I called down into the street to a passer-by. He carried a torch in one hand, a bundle of faggots in the other.

"Hello, you in the street! What fires are these abroad in the city?"

"They celebrate the king's deliverance from the Catholic treason," came the reply. "Come rejoice with us, sir. The more, the merrier."

I waved him on encouragingly, but I was ready for bed and what I hoped would be a dreamless sleep.

This was the fifth day of November, 1605.

Sufficient to the day is the evil thereof, as Christ says somewhere in the Gospels.

I do not recall chapter and verse.

35

On the day after the terrible event, life had not returned to what it was before the powder plot's discovery. While it was easier to pass through the streets, to buy or sell, or find easy fellowship in a tavern or inn, still outrage prevailed at what had nearly befallen us all, and new rumours of Catholic conspiracies, some of which seemed the ravings of madmen but nonetheless were being credited by many, as theories of conspiracy ever are, were a staple of conversation everywhere.

In such times as these, reason falls victim to panic. So say the ancients. They had seen it all before our time. We now living have likewise observed the truth of it.

I saw many men with pikes and halberds patrolling the streets and was given to understand that I would still be unable to cross the river to the Globe. The house of the Spanish ambassador, a personage never liked by the English in the best of times, was surrounded by guards for his protection and the protection of his household. The bridge was guarded by troops of the king, and the wherries that took passengers from one bank of the river to its opposite had been confined to shore for a time, to the great distress of the wherrymen. The ports were closed as well.

That the theatres should be shut down under such circumstances was inevitable.

As I promised Ben Jonson, I made my way to the Mermaid tavern, which was located east of St Paul's Church at the corner of Friday Street and Bread Street. I did not patronize this tavern often, preferring the Mitre, a more quiet and worthy establishment not far distant, but I knew the Mermaid was much favoured by Jonson and other literary gentlemen of the city, who met once a month to commend or disparage each other's work and enjoy mine host's wine cellar that a lord might have envied. It was all a good fellowship, to which I had often been invited, but as often declined as accepted.

Walking in, I found Jonson possessed of his favourite chair in a corner and by the looks of him well liquored. His head drooped upon his chest. "Asleep, or at prayer?" I asked, approaching him. "Your slouch admits to either interpretation."

Jonson looked up startled, as though he had forgotten our appointment. "Neither asleep or at prayer, Will. I was contemplating the state of the world and God's judgement to come upon it, if you must know. Be seated, you saucy rogue."

"So I shall."

"Rest your skinny buttocks and enlarge your mind with my company."

"Glad I am to do both," I said, beckoning a server, for I knew conversation would not be enough for Jonson. He would want more drink and possibly food, which would allow him more drink.

It was noon and the Mermaid was more crowded than usual. Had it been a ship it would have sunk beneath the load. Many faces I recognized and with most of those persons I exchanged greetings, but briefly. Everyone wanted to talk about the powder plot, to know my mind, my fears. I waved them away, claiming to have pressing business.

Which was, for the most part, true. I had awakened that morning earlier than usual, my belly rumbling. Madame Mountjoy's salted pork, I suspected. But during an hour of wakefulness, I thought about all that had happened since Gabriel Catesby had come back into my life. It had been but a year, but his presence seemed to have stirred the water of my otherwise placid existence as no other acquaintance had, leading it down strange and dangerous courses. It was a concatenation of events of which I suddenly realized the powder plot was the climax. But what common thread bound these events? Were Gabriel and his Papist coterie a part of it all? Or were they but incidental to some other monstrous event yet to be revealed?

I knew that of all my friends in London, Ben Jonson was the one who could help. He was master of theories of conspiracy and deception and could talk of them at great length with detachment and a Jesuit's hard logic, thereby separating wheat from chaff. I badly needed the benefit of his counsel, for somewhere in the back of my mind I was developing a conspiracy theory of my own, and I wanted him to tell me how I was wrong in thinking it.

Jonson said he would take no drink nor food. I was astonished. "Are you sick, then?" I asked. "Or fasting?"

"Not fasting. Not sick. At least not in the way you mean."

The host came and asked what we wanted. "Some private hour with my good friend," I said, nodding toward Jonson. "Nothing more."

And so we were left to our business.

I began at the beginning of things, without which nothing that follows would make sense. I told Jonson how I came to know Gabriel. I told him how as a callow youth he had saved me from a watery tomb.

I told him how, coming lately to London, Gabriel had joined our company and then had introduced me to Guido Fawkes and how the both of them had given me aid when I was threatened by John Flynt and the other thieves of my *Othello*.

"Cursed be they who steal another man's labour, which labour is our plays," Jonson stormed and commenced to rail eloquently upon the villainy of script plagiary and copying, to which he too had fallen victim. It was an annoyance all of us suffered, we playwrights, and I was content to allow my friend to vent his spleen for a quarter of an hour on the subject until, winded by his own rage, he calmed himself and looked at me, bidding me to continue my story. This was, after all, the reason for our meeting and had little to do, finally, with filched scripts. Or so I believed then.

"It was Gabriel Catesby through whom I met Guy Fawkes, or Guido, as he liked to call himself, because it sounded different, fashionably foreign."

"I prefer good solid English names like Ben and Will," Jonson said with a snort. "Guido sounds Italian, and therefore disgusting."

I continued, knowing that I would be interrupted from time to time in my narrative by Jonson's comments. He was a good writer, but a poor listener. He had too many opinions for that, and because he believed he was always right, that he should speak his mind whenever it pleased him seemed reasonable and apt.

"I thought it was my good fortune in meeting Fawkes," I said. "He was there in my time of need. He was a soldier in Flanders, or had been. He and Gabriel discovered where the thieves lay and captured them before they could do me hurt, although the principal thief, a man named Flynt, threatened my life, and I think would have killed me and drunk my blood had he opportunity. At least that is what I thought then."

"In what manner did he save you, this Fawkes?" Jonson asked. "For he struck me at supper as a braggart with all his haughty opinions of Spaniards. Did he have a strong right arm? Could he wield a sword, aim truly, and, ah yes, did he have a brain? A brain is what is needed at last, even for a soldier."

"Ah, Ben, you shall see what brain he had, and has. He near killed the man that would have killed me. That is how he ran my enemy off. Off the very earth."

I spared no details of the account. It is no more nor less than what I related earlier in this secret history. But Fawkes' bravery did not impress Jonson as much as it had impressed me when I secured his service, for Jonson at heart was a brawler himself. He had fought duels and engaged in I know not how many less serious altercations in his life. He had been imprisoned more than once for battery and assault, an experience I never had or hoped to have.

"That these enemies of yours surrendered with such wondrous alacrity amazes me," Jonson said. "It does not often fall out that way, you know. I mean in conflicts such as yours."

I said, "Now that I think upon it, it seems all too convenient, Fawkes' sudden appearance. I am wondering if I have misunderstood all. Taken events at face value, as a fool does who believes any man's word or sees in any offer of help naught but a good intention."

"How do you mean?" Jonson said.

"Not every Good Samaritan is good. He may not even be a Samaritan. But let me present my case."

I leaned toward him as though I were about to share a secret, which I suppose I was.

"This morning when I could not fall back asleep, an impression came to me."

"A dream?"

"Not a dream. I am content that it should be called an impression, nothing more. Hear me out, Ben, before you speak again, or I fear I may lose my thought. This Gabriel Catesby, this childhood friend and saviour of my person, desires to nurture my friendship because he needs employment in London and acting seems something that he can do. He comes to me to reclaim a debt, the saving of my life. Did I ever confirm that he had the experience he claimed, as an actor I mean?"

"My guess is that you did not," Jonson said.

"No, I did not. I had taken him at his word and when he showed some modicum of skill there was no need to question how he came upon it."

"I see," said Jonson, nodding his head sagely. "So let me speculate the further.

This Catesby prizes his association with you and makes use of old loyalties as a lever to gain his end. You owe him, he thinks, and so think you."

"I did so think," I said, suddenly feeling like a gullible fool for having succumbed to a false tale without putting it to the test. I knew why I had done so. Gratitude, loyalty, they had their claims upon my heart, yet that made me no less the fool for having let these prevail over caution, or even cynicism, well allowed to be a potent nostrum against deceit.

"My script is stolen," I said, continuing my theory. "From Gabriel Catesby evidently, or so he claims. His neighbour in the room next, also an actor, breaks in, steals the script given to Gabriel to practise his part, and then copies it, delivering the copy to Flynt. Flynt and friends talk it up at various taverns my friends are known to patronize, until such a friend of mine overhears and betrays them to me. Later, all this made known to me and having confronted the thieves and incurred their wrath, he and Fawkes offer to hunt the men down before the villains kill me, as they have threatened. The men left me messages, threatening to maim or kill me. You know whereof I speak. It is common bullying."

"Yes, go on," Jonson said, quite caught up now. He told me once he had received death threats himself. He didn't say from whom. Doubtless from some outraged husband or creditor, but he did not say that.

"Thereafter I am led to where the thieves congregate, so that they can threaten my body's health and instil deep fear in me. It is by chance, or so Gabriel would have me think, that this unemployed soldier, Guido Fawkes, fleeing the curse of idleness, is eager to be of service in my hour of need. Catesby and Fawkes become my rescuers again, subduing the thieves, wherefore my obligation to them is tenfold."

"And the threatening Flynt and his friends?"

"Bought and paid for by Gabriel Catesby and Fawkes, I now suspect. A fraud, a piece of theatre I did not recognize as such. Thus, the ease with which my supposed enemies surrender. They have completed their work, played their parts. I see them no more."

"Who were these others, these two you mention who were Flynt's companions?"

I named names.

He knew neither.

I went on. "I had come to trust Gabriel. Besides, there were no more threatening messages. I suppose if I had world enough and time I could find Flynt, sitting in some tavern, drinking up the proceeds of the fraud and probably laughing at the great William Shakespeare, gulled like some country simpleton."

"All this to compel your loyalty and gratitude," Jonson mused, shaking his head.

245

"Is my theory preposterous?" I asked. "Tell me wherein I err in thinking it not."

Jonson mulled over my question before answering. "Not beyond belief, not in this wicked world. Yet you say gratitude is what this Catesby wanted. Was there nothing beyond that?"

"He wanted my help," I said.

Which led me to recount what befell me at Holbeche House.

I told him about our poor truncated tragedy, which had left so much out of my play that it became a travesty. I told him about the secret meeting with Gabriel's cousin, Robert Catesby, and the priest, Father Gerard. I told him about the sheriff's raid on the house and my escape through the tunnel.

"Your poor truncated tragedy? What play was that?"

"*Julius Caesar*," I said.

"Truncated how?"

"Master Lyttleton, whose house it was, wanted us to play only the scene of Caesar's murder by Brutus. And something of the conspiracy before."

"Only those?"

"No more."

Jonson thought for a moment, pursing his lips. "Then you have it," he said, pounding the table with his fist. "They would make you a tool in rebellion, as Essex and his men did when you ran afoul of the authorities for your performance of *Richard II*. These treasonous devils, these purveyors of wicked insurrection and deceit."

I said, "They praised me as a great teacher of men, as an influence greater than the preacher in his pulpit or the professor at his lectern. You heard Robert Catesby at the Irish Boy. It was the same siren song. Yet I was deaf to it."

"And wisely deaf," Jonson said. "Like me, you must have sensed then that a conspiracy was afoot, though neither what it was or what its magnitude, and that you, and I too, were being invited to take part therein."

I said, "I think I did, but knew not what it was, some Catholic stratagem, only that I wanted to stand clear of it, as a man who walks into the wood senses some peril and flees, never knowing of the danger but certain that he was wise to free himself from the trees."

Jonson paused again. Then he looked hard at me. It was the kind of penetrating look whereby Jonson claimed to detect a lie, but also a look he used when he wished to make some point in debate. He said, slowly and deliberately, "I am a Catholic. Not a good Catholic, but a son of the Church nonetheless. I sin and then confess with monotonous regularity. So much so that my confessor prescribes my penance before I open my mouth!" We both laughed at this, knowing that it was true.

"Then go I forward in my life, hoping to be saved in the end as does any Christian. But you must know that never would I countenance revolt against an anointed king. James may be a Scot and drool and ramble in his beard, yet he wears England's crown. Therefore, will I sustain him in his royal appointment. If he is attacked, I will defend him, with word if possible, with sword if driven to it."

Jonson had risen to his feet for this patriotic declaration. He looked around him now, as though anticipating challengers in the crowded room. But it was clear no one else was paying attention to us. Seeing his utterance had gone unnoticed, he sat back down and wiped his sweating brow with his shirtsleeve.

I said, "Ben, your loyalty to king and country I doubt not. Now tell me true. Think you the plotting that was going on in Holbeche House is part of this powder plot just uncovered? Hold nothing back in this. I must know the truth."

247

"Time will prove the depth and breadth of this mischief," Jonson said. "But this I can say. The events you have recounted, the fortuitous meetings, the deceptions—they have not the look or feel of accidental events, but rather evidence of a sinister purpose into which you are unwittingly made complicit. Even your friend Samuel's report, his fortuitous coming upon the thieves whilst they referred to your play, smells to high heaven of treachery."

I had not thought of Samuel as part of the conspiracy against me, and in so doing felt the pain of yet another betrayal. But his collusion with the thieves now seemed more likely than not. I looked at my friend, Ben Jonson, across the table and remembered even though I had forgiven him for it, he had lied to me. For all my achievements since coming to London, was I a tool so easily manipulated by false friends with their own secret plots and designs?

36

Our conversation done, our path now took us close by to Whitehall Palace where the greater number of the king's guards gave us more hope that we should escape hanging or some other violence directed against us. At one of the gates thereof, a large assembly had gathered. There I met a friend who told me that the perpetrator of the deed was presently to be taken from thence and led to the Tower, either for interrogation or torture, although these generally were much the same. Jonson and I stayed by him, this friend, and it was not but a few minutes until a company emerged, in the centre of which was a single man who, by his demeanour and his shackles, was evidently the John Johnson who had been found with the gunpowder and confessed his heinous purpose.

He was a tall, sturdy man, somewhat bent over as though walking were painful, which was not surprising since I thought he had probably been racked and prodded well enough already. It was the way such things were done. The law decreed that it should be so, that truth might be known, that the man's accomplices, should there be any, might be discovered and likewise punished.

This abject prisoner wore neither hat nor cloak, which I assumed had been taken from him that he should exhibit no shred of dignity in his apparel but stand naked and exposed to the world. As he drew nearer a great roar of rage and disdain came from all those watching, and everywhere were cries that the prisoner should be executed straightway, hanged and drawn and quartered in this very place, for such was the penalty for treason, which this surely was and to which this man had already confessed, or so it had been reported.

I would have joined the cry for his death myself when the prisoner came within a dozen feet of me, had I not then a more severe shock to my senses.

To that moment, the prisoner had walked with his head down, as was the practice of men conveyed to their death or lesser punishment, either as a sign of penitence or a wish to avoid the hostile gaze of an angry crowd. Sometimes they prayed. Sometimes they thought upon their crimes. But on this instance, this Johnson raised his chin and looked ahead of him, as though he were proud of what he had done and felt no remorse at all for the horror he had intended, which would certainly have meant the death of many an innocent soul of whom he had no knowledge at all.

When he was abreast of me, the prisoner turned suddenly to look in my direction. Our eyes met for an instant and his lips curled in a smile of recognition as though even in this abject condition, he was proud of his work and inviting me to commend him for it.

I must tell you then I knew this wretch. Indeed, I knew him well. John Johnson he might have called himself when taken amidst his barrels of gunpowder. I knew the man by yet another name, his true name I believe, for when I once called him friend and saviour, he would have had no need for alias or pseudonym.

This same prisoner, John Johnson, I recognized as Guy or Guido Fawkes.

* * *

Jonson had not seen Fawkes, or not recognized him, for the prisoner was battered and bruised. Besides which, Jonson knew him less well than I.

The company passed with their prisoner. I watched until the group disappeared. The crowd of witnesses now dispersed. Jonson looked at me and asked, "What is it, Will? You look sick of a sudden. As though you just ate bad fish or someone tread upon your grave. Pray, what's the matter?"

My friend, an actor from another company, had already left us. Jonson and I were alone in the street. I said to him, pointing in the direction that Fawkes had been taken, "I do know that man."

"Which man mean you?" Jonson said, looking about him. "The street abounds in such creatures as men."

"The prisoner, he who would have sent the king to hell in bits and pieces."

"This John Johnson fellow?"

"Yes," I said, "but that's not his real name. The prisoner is Guido Fawkes."

Jonson started. Then looked at me as though I were mad.

"Good Christ, you mean the man at the supper, at the Irish Boy," Jonson exclaimed, a fearful expression on his marred face as though I were about to reveal my own part in the conspiracy and he dreaded to hear of it.

I read that in his eyes, his fearful thoughts. Did he think me mad? Or at least verging thereon?

"I am not mad, Ben. I swear what I saw is true. It was Guido Fawkes. I do swear upon my mother's head and my father's too. Did you not see him? He looked directly at me and gave me a knowing look that chilled me to the bone. It was as though he were mocking me."

"I did not see the man's face that well," Jonson said. "But now that you speak of it, I think it was Fawkes. The man at the Irish Boy. The soldier who had travelled to Spain. Your friend and protector. I was too deep in my cups to note his face in all details. But a traitor, a regicide?"

"The question now is whether he acted alone or with accomplices," I said.

"And whether the accomplices are numbered among our friends," Jonson added, his face showing growing alarm. "My God, Will, we broke bread with Fawkes. We drank with Fawkes. There are those who can, and perhaps will, place us there at the very damnable moment in which the conspiracy might have been hatched for all we know. By Christ's bones, Will, I am heartily sorry I ever accepted Robert Catesby's invitation, pocketed his damned money, and thereby got you mired in this treasonous business."

"It is beyond help now," I said. "Our complicity will be taken for granted. Pray God, none reveals our presence at the Irish Boy so that we too appear before my Lords of the Council to answer to treason."

"Which we never committed nor would," Jonson said.

"No, yet appearance is often enough to bring a man to judgement. That, and mere association with them who are truly guilty."

Jonson looked down at his big hands and said nothing, but I knew his fear was mine as well.

37

Within a few days of his capture, John Johnson, all boast and bluster for a while, had given up the names of his fellows in the powder plot. He had also revealed his true name, Guy or Guido Fawkes, and become thereby a hiss and a byword throughout England.

Three of the men he named had been present with him at our supper at the Irish Boy—Thomas Percy, Thomas Wintour, and Robert Catesby, who Fawkes claimed was the conspirator-in-chief. Percy had been arrested in London before he could flee the city. Catesby and the Wintour brothers had been more fortunate, at least for the time being. They had escaped to Staffordshire, back to Holbeche House.

Word had come that Catesby and several others had taken refuge there, and when it was clear their capture was certain, they determined to fight to the death.

I was told Robert Catesby and Thomas Wintour had been killed by the same ball. Whether this be true or not I cannot say. One hears so many things. How many can be taken for truth and not mere supposition or wishful thinking?

I learned Catesby's body had been buried somewhere on the property, but then by order of the Privy Council it had been exhumed and decapitated. It would presently be on display somewhere in the city as a remonstrance to other persons tempted to take up arms against the king.

Some of this was now generally known. Some I had from a friend employed in some lesser office with the Earl of Salisbury. I did not know then the details of Catesby's final hour, which turned out to be every bit as mysterious as the rest of this pernicious plot. In due course I would learn them from one who had been present and whose account of these matters I was prepared to believe without question.

I write it here and after, that a fuller history of Robert Catesby's life and death might be known.

It was a week or more beyond the day of the plot's discovery. The city had returned to its usual business, though there was still talk of the powder treason. How could it be otherwise? The event had shocked all, from lord to commoner, with its audacity and evil intent. It was said that even in foreign parts the assault upon royal persons was deemed an outrage in the eyes of man and God. But now the ports were open again. Fawkes and some of his companions remained in the Tower awaiting their trial, and they were much abused in common conversation, even by Catholics.

The playhouses had been opened again too, and I was spending every afternoon at the Globe, where despite the coming of winter we remained, although it would not be long before our beloved theatre would close for the season. Meanwhile, we played *Othello* to throngs and much applause, for our audience loved to rail at the wicked Iago, played most confidently by Burbage, and wept copiously at the deaths of Desdemona and Othello, though he were a fool for ever being taken in by Iago, whose treachery was plain to all save the Moor. It was a gratifying response to me, for it was my belief that one coming to the theatre should feel deeply as well as see and hear, else what was its purpose? They might as well watch bears maul dogs, or gawk at magicians on street corners.

Behold me then at our Globe, standing outside the main door watching the file of persons coming in, and I see beyond, on a far corner of the street, a young girl, alone, watching. Watching me, I think. I am sure of it.

Hearing someone call my name, I look away. I exchange a greeting, then return my gaze to the girl.

I see all this clearly in my mind's eye, though it is years past.

She stands there still and watches me. She knows me, I think. There is something about her that seems familiar. Then I recognize her. Although it has been months since I last saw her, it is the misfortunate Alice Simpkins from Holbeche House. Though neatly dressed before, she now seems bedraggled and wretched as though she has walked a great distance.

I went to where she stood watching and greeted her.

"Alice," I said. "You have come to London after all, even as you said you might. To see a play?"

She didn't answer me, but began to tremble and to weep softly, tears making little rivulets down her cheeks, which were scratched and torn. I drew near to her and took her small shivering body in my arms to comfort her. I led her down the street until we came to a small shop where food was served. We went in and took a table in a quiet corner where we might talk privately.

A server appeared from the kitchen. Had Alice walked all the way from Holbeche House? That she could have done so was unthinkable. It was a good two or three day's ride on horseback. It would have been a week or more on foot, even if one as young and tender as she could have made the journey unattended. I asked her about that, how she had come to London.

She confirmed my worst fears. "I was helped aboard a farmer's cart, and then another. I have been ten days upon the road."

"To see a play?" I asked. "Or perhaps to see the sights of London's Tower, the lion and the tiger, the creature they call the giraffe with the longest neck in the world?"

When she declared she had come for my sake, to see me and none other, my levity shamed me.

"Why me? What of your father, your mother?"

"They cast me out, Master Shakespeare. When I began to show my burden."

I looked at her again. Beneath her filthy smock I could see her swollen belly.

So Gabriel Catesby's seed had been planted. It was as I had feared. What sin does not bear bitter fruit or reveal itself in the fullness of time?

"When he saw I was with child, my father threatened to kill me. He called me slut and whore and other things I cannot repeat without shame."

"And your mother, did she not help you?"

"She fears my father. She would do nothing. He beat her too. He beat the both of us, to our great hurt and many tears."

She wept again, and I came near to weeping with her, for her case was indeed a sad one, to have a brute for a father, and now, to be burdened with the child of another man who had abused her.

In part to distract her from her grief, in part to satisfy my own curiosity, I asked her, "Were you at the manor when the sheriff's men came?"

"I was there through it all," she said. "I mean through most, I think. I suppose I am what they call a witness."

She was no longer weeping. She wiped away her tears with the back of her hand. I saw it was better that she speak of things other than herself and her brutal father and bastard child.

"Were you there when Robert Catesby was taken, he and his confederates? I am told they took refuge in the manor."

"They did, sir. My master and my mistress were away when the sheriff's men came this last time. It was the same as before, I first thought, looking for a priest or two, but it was different. I did not know about the treason then. It was night when they came, Master Catesby and four or five other men. They had weapons and a cart loaded with barrels, which I found out after were filled with gunpowder. Our butler told them the master and mistress were away, but they said they cared not who was in the house. They ordered the cook to prepare supper, for they were very hungry they said. They were all at sixes and sevens, running about the house, spying from windows. Some were very frightened and weeping, but Master Catesby seemed calmer than the rest. I knew something dreadful had happened, or was about to happen, and I was very frightened, more frightened than I had ever been before."

"And you saw all this?"

"I did, Master Shakespeare. I swear I did."

The server brought bread and cheese and a good strong ale. I paid him for the food and sent him away.

I watched the girl as she ate. She wolfed her food as though she had not eaten in a week, taking short breaths between each mouthful.

When nothing was left on her plate, she continued her story.

"I hid where they could not see me, because I was afraid of what they might do to me and to Cook."

"Where was the cook?"

"She laid food for them in the master's study, then ran out the back door and across the fields. I do not know where she went from there. The other servants in the house had run off as well. We were all confused and much afraid of the men, for we did not know them or what they wanted. They were heavily armed. We could not stand against them."

"No, you could not. Did you see their faces, these men with Catesby?"

"I saw only Master Catesby. And one other gentleman I had never seen before. I remember he was telling Master Catesby that they should surrender themselves, and that they were undone, since all the world now knew who they were and what they did. It was useless to run, the man said."

"How did Catesby answer?"

"He declared he would not surrender but die first. He said that everything he had done was for the Holy Church and the Virgin and the Pope and the liberty of true believers. Yet one of the men to whom he spoke said the Pope had forbade what they had done, and he—I do mean the man who spoke—was most grieved for it now."

"Grieved, was he?"

"That is what he said, sir, but Master Catesby said he himself regretted naught that he did. He said he was only sorry that their plot had been discovered."

"You are sure that is what was said by these men?"

"Every word, sir. I do swear it. The men talked for a long time. They never said what they did, but talked about what might happen because they did it. Then a terrible thing happened."

"A terrible thing?" I asked. "What thing?"

Her voice fell to a husky whisper. We were ourselves like unto conspirators. "The men had brought these barrels into the room with them. It was gunpowder, I think. I heard the men say that the powder had become damp and it would be useless save it were made dry again. They laid a fire in the great room and had spread the powder out on the stones before it. I watched this and then, whilst all the men were gathered about the fire talking of whether they should surrender or flee, there was a great explosion in the room."

"Explosion?"

"Ay, sir, a great deafening blast. The whole house shook. It quite knocked me down. I suppose a spark from the fire had struck the powder. Or maybe it was God that did it to them."

"God?"

"Striking them down for the evil that they had done. Flames from Heaven. A destroying angel."

It was Alice Simpkins' manner of speech, the way she thought. Earth was a sliver between heaven and hell, and all things therein were reflections of one or the other. The punishment of sin did not wait until the Judgement Day, but befell the sinner almost upon the transgression itself. It was her theology, her very Gospel. Yet I had seen the sinner prosper enough times to know that it was not mine. Sin would be punished indeed, but not always in this world, perhaps rarely so.

"What then?" I asked.

"The room was filled with smoke and stench. One of the men staggered toward my hiding place. It was the time I was most afraid, for I asked myself what he would do if he saw me spying on them. What he would believe, being as they were desperate men and I but a simple maid."

"Did he see you?"

"I think not. It would have been impossible for him. He was blinded in the explosion. 'Oh Jesu, I am blind,' he cried. 'Precious Saviour, I am blind.' I remember that was what he cried out. His screams were terrible, Master Shakespeare. My blood ran cold on hearing them. When I shut my eyes and think on it, I can still hear him screaming."

She fell silent for a while. I watched her across the table. Her face was drained of colour. Her eyes were tight shut as if to erase the vision in her memory. I reached out and laid my hand upon hers. I asked, "What of the others, of Robert Catesby?"

She thought about it. Then she said, "He was hurt too. His face was all black, scorched. Yet he could talk and move and see, I think. Another man had died, they said. And then there were two others who were not hurt at all.

"After that I got me upstairs, leaving all them in the great room below. There was more gunfire from the courtyard. I found a place in the attic room to hide, but they never came for me, though I worried that they might do so all the night. Oh, Master Shakespeare, I prayed so hard that they would not find me, for I knew now not what they had done to be in flight, but that it had been for a good reason that they were being sought. In the morning when I awoke, it was all quiet in the house. I thought maybe the men below had escaped and I was alone. I waited all the morning. I watched out the windows of the attic that looked down into the courtyard. It was then that I saw the other men."

"The other men?"

"The sheriff and those with him. This time there were even more in his company. I could not count them all. They set themselves all about the house, before and behind and on each side, so that none could pass save they were aware. I could see their swords and their halberds and their muskets. It was just as before."

"Before?"

"When you were here and the sheriff came and the house was turned upside down looking for the priest."

"Save now they were not seeking a simple priest," I said.

"From a window, I saw two of the men run out into the courtyard. They had drawn their swords. Then I heard more gunfire, loud reports and saw one of the men fall. He with him lifted the wounded in his arms and they came back into the house."

"Which man was it? Was it Catesby?" I asked.

"I don't know. I saw only his back. There was more firing, puffs of smoke from the column of men. Then the sheriff's band advanced in a line. They were firing their muskets. Everywhere there was smoke. I thought the house would catch fire. I imagined myself burned alive in my hiding place. I ran down the stairs thinking I would rather have a ball in my heart than to have my body burned as was the man when the gunpowder exploded. There was no one in the great hall, but outside the firing went on. I ran into the dining room where you did the play for us. It was there I saw a man, all bloody, lying on the floor. His arms and legs were splayed. His face was burned black. O God, it was a terrible sight. I remember he had a gold crucifix in his hand and beside him was a little picture. The man was Master Catesby."

"How did you know?" I asked.

"Because of the picture."

"A picture of what?"

"Why of Our Lady, the Virgin. Other men might have held a picture of their wives, but not Master Catesby. My mistress told me his wife had died. She said that the love he had had for her he now devoted wholly to the Virgin. I had seen it before. It was Master Catesby's as was the crucifix, for I had seen him wear the cross and possess the picture I had seen in his chamber. He was a very devout Catholic, you see."

"Yes, very devout," I agreed.

"There was blood on his coat. He had been shot. There was

another body too. He had also been struck dead. Or at least I thought he was dead."

"What did you do when the sheriff's men came into the house?"

Her eyes grew wide at the question. "Oh, sir, I did not wait. I was afraid they would think me one of those they hunted and, though I was but a maid without any part in what they did or planned, they might kill me too. So I ran away."

"Out the postern door, like unto the cook?"

She smiled thinly. It was the first time I had seen her smile during our talking. And it was the last.

"I knew where the priest's hole was, as you know well. I went to the panel and pressed the lever, even as I had shown you. The door opened. I shut it behind me and went down the ladder. There was no light in the passage below, in which I had never been. Yet I knew it was the way you had taken, to escape the house, I mean. I trusted in God that I might do the same."

She stopped here, as though reliving what she had done. I urged her on, suspecting that there was more to be revealed.

"I felt along the wall and kept moving even when the tunnel seemed to grow narrower. All the way I prayed that I might not be discovered, that I might not be taken away and imprisoned and tortured, as I hear is often done in such cases. You see, sir, I knew then already that I was with child, and though I hated the man who had fathered it, yet I loved the child within me. I escaped for the two of us, not only for myself."

"You were a very brave girl," I said. "Even with light, that passage is a fearsome place. I remember it well."

"It was fearsome for sure, sir. Yet I moved forward, praying all the way that I should get out again and not die in so horrible a place. Once, I thought I did see light ahead of me. Like a candle flickering.

I thought it might be an answer to my prayers. I followed the light, though at a distance. It was a miracle, I think. Like those the Scriptures speak of. Do you believe, Master Shakespeare, that there are miracles in these last days?"

"Miracles? Do you mean like those Christ and his apostles did?"

"I mean the ones that befall common folk, when a good thing happens that needs to happen, and no human hand has wrought it, but angels of heaven."

I said, "I don't know about angels, Alice. But if this light you speak of helped you through the passage, then it was a miracle indeed. Who is to say your prayers were not answered? It seems a simple enough thing for God to provide a small light in the darkness that an innocent might escape from those who are not so."

She seemed encouraged by my words. She spoke more confidently now. "After a while I came to the end of the passage. There was a large bush covering the opening. It was hard to find my way through it, yet I did, though my arms and my face bled from the scratches."

"I know," I said. "You are right. You helped me escape Holbeche House by the same means."

She went on, undaunted by any fear that I should not believe her story.

"I went home then. My father was away, God be thanked. In the village, I think. I told my mother what had happened at the manor. She told me that, in the village, word had come that treason was afoot in London, that the king and all the lords had been killed and that the men at the manor were Catholic traitors who had done it and deserved to die and to burn in hell. She told me my father was returning soon and I should leave. He would be drunk, she said, and he would be angry. Go where? I asked her. Just go, she told me. God would protect me, she said.

"I kissed her and she kissed me. I took some food and a change of clothes and rolled them into a bundle and left. The first day I walked until I could walk no longer and came only to the village next to our own. The rest of the way I walked or rode upon carts as I have already told you."

The girl looked at me with sad, tearful eyes. I well understood her state. She had seen terrible things; she had seen violent death. It was a vision that would be imprinted on her memory until the end of her time on earth. I knew that. Above this, she was to become a mother, a mother of yet another bastard, even as her baby's father was.

I prayed that her son, or daughter, whichever it was fated to be, would not be as wicked a person as its father.

"The king and the lords live still," I said. "The rumour otherwise is not true. The man prepared to ignite the powder was seized before he could do the wicked deed. Robert Catesby, your master's guest, it was he that conceived the plot."

She thought about this for a while. I said nothing. Then she spoke again.

"And were my master and mistress also with him in his plotting?" she asked hesitantly, as though fearing my answer.

I decided to give them both the benefit of my own doubts. I said, "I don't know. Time will tell. But I will say this. I knew nothing of the plot, nor did any of my fellows. Perhaps your master and his lady were also ignorant of what their guest planned."

She accepted this with a wan smile, yet I knew my answer had not satisfied her. Why should it? The plot had already tainted the lives of hundreds, nay thousands, that had no knowledge of it. Her fears were more than reasonable.

* * *

I knew Alice would be homeless in London. She had neither money, nor friends. She told me she had come to the city that very morning, entered from the north by the Oxford Road and had been overwhelmed by the size of the houses, the multitude of people, the noise of the streets, the absence of a familiar landscape. She had nearly fainted, both from surprise and also from hunger and exhaustion. I knew if I were to abandon her, she would end up a beggar in the streets or, worse, one of the Bankside whores, of which, God knew, there was already a sufficient supply. She would be dead of disease and abuse before she was sixteen. Her baby would not live.

"Come," I said, standing and beckoning her to follow. "Come with me."

"To your house, sir?" she asked.

"It's not my house. It's the house of a friend, my landlord. His name is Christopher Mountjoy, but you must call him Monsieur, for he is a Frenchman."

"And what manner of man would that be?" she asked. "Frenchman." She pronounced the word in a way I had never heard. I was charmed. I would not correct her.

"A species of mankind, the Frenchman," I said. "Neither better nor worse than the rest of us. You shall straightway see for yourself. Monsieur Mountjoy is a man like other men but born and bred far off, in a pleasant land called France. They speak a different language there. He speaks English now. After a fashion, that is."

She looked at me doubtfully, but said nothing. I pressed on.

"I have a room in his house, and I have done his family some few favours, for which my reward is past due. He may be able to find a place for you and honest employment as well. You will not want in London, I promise you. I promise more, that the troubles of this time will pass, as all troubles do."

"Oh, I pray that it will be so," she said, clasping her hands together. "I have too much to remember."

"Which of us does not?" I said.

Then she said, "I am sorry I missed your play. I thought of it all the way to London."

"*Othello,* do you mean?"

"Why, any play, sir. I would have delighted in seeing any play, most especially if it was you that wrote it."

"There will be other performances. And perhaps a play you would like better than *Othello,* which though I conceived it, I confess it is grim business with an ending that may not please one of your years."

We passed out into the street. Behind me coming from the theatre I could hear clamour, cheers and howls. All was coming from the Globe. I had no doubt of its cause. It was Iago's fall, the promise of his punishment. Our audiences loved it.

Nothing satisfies like seeing justice triumph in a wicked world. Yet, somehow, I found no solace in that hope. I looked at the girl beside me. Her state was wretched, her fate uncertain. How might justice ever be served in her case? Even the death of her abuser would not put things right.

"Have you ever been aboard a boat?" I asked as we walked toward the broad, slow-moving river called the Thames since Roman times and before.

"Never," she said.

I shepherded her along towards the Bankside. The play concluded. The crowd would spew forth into the street, seeking some new thing to interest them. I did not want us to be seen, questions asked, gossip or slander engendered by the spectacle of me walking beside a young girl with child.

"Then this is a day to remember. Like unto a Saint's Day," I said. "Come, child. We shall cross the river by wherry."

"A wherry?"

"A sort of boat. Have no fear, the wherrymen are skilled mariners. I promise you, you shall not drown. Upon my oath, you shall not even get your feet wet."

I took her arm and looked into her sad face. There were bread-crumbs on her lips. She leaned toward me as a daughter might have done with her father.

She smelled of earth and tears.

38

On the ninth day of November of that fateful year, His Majesty addressed the Parliament, both the lords and the commons. It was by all accounts a noble speech, the king's Scots brogue notwithstanding. I suspect the text was the Earl of Salisbury's work, so crafty and politic it was. I learned from friends who had been privileged to hear it.

The speech aimed to assuage the widespread fear of more explosions and murders by assuring the country that the conspiracy had been limited to a small band of fanatics unappreciative of the king's bounty.

To the disappointment of the Puritans, no Jesuits or other priests were numbered among the accused. There was an annoying lack of evidence of their complicity. Yet the inquiry continued. Both Salisbury and Sir Thomas Coke, the two men at the head of the prosecution, hated the Jesuits. They barely tolerated the Catholic laity.

As for the accused themselves, there was Robert Catesby, he who was named the grand deviser of the plot and Guy or Guido Fawkes, the would-be igniter of the powder. These were men I knew relatively well, well enough to have it thought I might be sympathetic with their aims, if not a party to their treachery. There was also Thomas Percy, whom I knew but not well, the Wintour brothers, and Thomas Bates,

Robert Catesby's servant, whom I had seen at Holbeche House although with him I had never exchanged a single word; also, Sir Everard Digby, whom I did not know at all but like another member of the conspiracy, John Grant, had houses in Warwickshire, my native county.

In all this uproar, I set about to finish my *Macbeth*, a tragedy upon which I had pinned much of my hope for further royal bounty.

I proceeded haltingly. Always at the back of my mind I feared my association with the plotters would somehow implicate me. In that dark vision I imagined myself dragged before the lords of the Privy Council, interrogated, tortured ruthlessly, and finally meeting the horrific end that all traitors must endure, to be drawn and quartered, my head and other body parts set upon pikes as exempla to other malefactors.

I imagined my wife and daughters learning of their husband and father's disgrace thereafter. They too would be ruined, left to beg for their bread, the Shakespeare name a burden, nay curse, to my progeny.

My plays would not be remembered, only my treason.

It was well that my father was in his grave. His Catholic sympathies mattered not. He would have repudiated a son who would so offend heaven by taking up arms against an anointed king.

Such was my state during that cruel month. Not in my sleep only came the dreams of crime and punishment. My waking life was likewise tormented by these visions.

In all this tumult of spirit, I tried to write, but sat often in a stupor of thought, my senses dulled. Alone in my chamber, desolate, fearful, distracted, caught up in the most lurid imaginings, I considered that I might as well be guilty of the false charges I feared for all my conscience was racked and my future blighted by fears of imminent arrest.

I did not go to the theatre. I did not see Ben Jonson. I did not talk to the Mountjoys although, less fearful now for their own safety, they tried to engage me in the joys and tempests of their lives. I began to write a letter to my wife, but gave that up as well, although it had been long since I had written her.

Oddly, there was some little thing I did with my Scottish play, which was to add some few scenes of witches. These I thought might give Macbeth's rise to power some needed otherworldly gravitas and please the king as well, whose interest in witchcraft was well known. But, as fate would have it, the witches I devised were the very creatures I had met years ago when Gabriel Catesby took me to the hovel of his mother and her sisters.

Is that not a strange provenance for a play's characters? Perhaps not, for if old and mouldy tomes can deliver to the imagination fresh voices to speak to us now, should not experience, the lord of life, likewise provision us, perhaps even more richly?

Then the thing I most feared came to pass.

Mark this well, you who believe Fate rules the world. I talk not about dreams and vain imaginings now, but events actual, events temporal, the things that happen to a man in the quotidian when he is full awake and all his faculties alive and well and he thinks but of what there is to do and when, and not the ultimate cause of things, either on earth or in heaven.

Mid-month, I think on the sixteenth or seventeenth, though which makes little difference now, I was in my chamber, still labouring over the Scottish play when three men appeared at my door.

Of these I recognized an undersecretary of the Earl of Salisbury, one of his lordship's minor functionaries, a drab, self-important little man named Thomas Wilson. The other two men by their breastplates and halberds were officers of the Privy Council. Such men are ever to be distinguished from the normal man of the city. If not by their garb and weaponry, then by their severe expressions of public duty, their squinty eyes, their penchant for sudden violence when crossed in their purposes.

"Master Shakespeare, is it?"

"You know it is, Master Wilson. We've met before."

"We have indeed, sir, but on happier occasion, I warrant."

"I do pray this occasion is not unhappy," I answered.

I looked at Wilson's companions. Their stern countenance made it clear they were on the king's business. My heart began pounding as it had done too much of late. Was this not like unto my waking dreams—officers at my door, the cold claw of authority. When I spoke again, I sounded not like myself but some croaking ancient, gasping his last breath.

"You have some business with me, sir?"

"Official business," Wilson said. "I am come to summon you."

"Summon me? To what?"

"Why to the Council, sir."

"I am under arrest?" I asked, my voice even raspier. "Am I charged or indicted? And if so, what is the charge against me? I am allowed to inquire that far into what your official business may be, am I not?"

Wilson said, "Nay, sir, neither charged, nor arrested. Only summoned. And as to its purpose, that is not my place to reveal, but at a later hour you shall know."

He managed a smile, but it was a thin, poor excuse of one. I did not believe for a minute that it expressed any good will toward me but delight rather that I should presently find myself in his power.

I was about to ask if there was some distinction of which I was unaware in the two words, *arrested* and *summoned*. Doubtless lawyers bothered themselves with such quibbles. But I held my tongue. In the face of officialdom, it is never wise to be facetious, or to be thought so.

Wilson had in his hand a scrolled parchment. It was a manner of

271

document I had seen many times in the grip of officers of the courts. The sight of it sickened me, for I knew what it signified. He offered it to me for my inspection. I tried to read the single page but my eyes, already weary from my work, could make little out but my name. No matter, I thought. I knew its intent. The rest would be the convoluted language of the law, which I disdained even when my vision was clear and my brain not muddled by panic.

Wilson's companions did not manacle me, for which I was grateful. I desired not to be a spectacle in the street, much less downstairs where my piteous state would surely alarm my landlord and his family and incite a flurry of questions as to what heinous deed I had committed to be so forcibly and ignominiously conveyed.

I walked out with the two guards, one on each side of me. Thomas Wilson walked before. Strutted, I should say. I much resented the pride in his step, his raised chin, his quite intolerable sense of satisfaction that he had William Shakespeare in tow and could convey him where he willed.

We had not walked the half mile to Whitehall before it began to rain, softly at first and then with a will. By the time we reached the gatehouse and passed within, I was soaked to the skin.

It was only then that I wondered why we had come to Whitehall and not to Westminster where more commonly the Council did its business. Beyond the gatehouse was a street entrance and from there we passed up stone stairs into the floor above. I had been here before. The ornate, high-ceilinged corridor was filled with petitioners and other persons, probably lawyers, looking at me with a mixture of envy and dislike since, evidently, I was privileged to see the great man before them, the great man being, as Wilson had disclosed in a reverent whisper, Robert Cecil, the Earl of Salisbury himself.

On this occasion, it was a privilege I would gladly have surrendered to any of these envious onlookers.

Wilson steered me toward a closed door. My guards fell back, evidently no longer fearful that I should escape their custody.

"You may go through there, Master Shakespeare," Wilson said. "Knock three times."

I did what I was told, wishing the signal would have told me why I had been summoned. To my fear was now added a great physical discomfort because of my wet clothing, which hung upon me like a shroud.

A voice I knew bid me wait.

I stood there shuddering.

Then, in another minute, the same voice bid me enter.

39

All the world knows that the most powerful of men is the king, for he reigns by divine appointment and sufferance and is God's viceroy on earth. But he who is second to him is not his queen, should he be wed, but rather his chief counsellor. The queen shares the king's bed, bears the king's children, but the counsellor is the sharer of his thoughts and, often, the very creator of them, for it is not always the duty, or ability, of the king to think for himself. This august personage, this counsellor, may have not a drop of royal blood, but wields power by his learning and political cunning. Yet even more by his office, which though he may not deserve it by a wise man's judgement, yet he has it. Nothing else matters.

Such a personage stood before me. He had risen to welcome me to his private chamber, a singular honour for one such as I without rank or title to commend me. The room was panelled in dark oak and dominated by a large table or desk. Scattered about was an abundance of books and papers, official documents, letters I am sure from important persons of the kingdom and beyond, for Cecil had business with every nation. Such was his office, his high commission.

At the far end of the room a curtain had been drawn, which I

imagined concealed an even more intimate
man, this room would have served well to p
women of the court who cared little for thei
tion. That, however, was not the Earl's vice.

The figure of Robert Cecil, Earl of Salisbur
men in the street who have only heard of the c
to see higher than their feet and the common earth beneath have
heard of him, know his name and conceive of his image when he is
spoken of. Since he has been described many times by sundry authors,
I shall be brief in drawing him.

To wit, he is some forty years of age or more. His face is manly
and not unhandsome, with a high, broad forehead, dark penetrating
eyes, and a neatly barbered beard brought to a fine point.

But herein, too, I must take note of the faults of his body, which
were pronounced and infamous. For that noble head sat upon a diminished torso with spindly legs and a crooked back, so that although
he was feared for the power he wielded, yet was he also mocked for
his deformity, which deformity is ever regarded by the common
herd as a sign of some untoward and malignant disposition of the
soul. He was the son of the Great Lord Burghley, Queen Elizabeth's
principal secretary, succeeding to his father's office upon that worthy
man's death. He had been an instrument in the king's succession to
the English throne, choosing his side shrewdly so that his place was
assured in the new monarchy.

What more could be said of him? The king trusted him implicitly.
I doubt few others at court did. To speak truth, he was not well loved
by any but his own household. He had many enemies, both at court
and beyond. My encounters with him had been few but cordial. He
was a learned man, no Philistine, whatever other faults he had, but
after the king himself, he was arguably the most powerful man in

around such as he, one must ever tread circumspectly.

, fear the worst.

ʋur lordship," I said, making a graceful bow I had made on the
ʋtage a thousand times or more.

"Master Shakespeare. You are very good to come, sir."

"I was summoned, my lord," I said. "Or so I was informed by
Master Wilson, and the document he bore with him."

Cecil said, "Quite so. I knew my invitation would not be refused.
On the other hand, I have a matter to discuss with you that is of some
gravity. I am afraid it could not be delayed."

As said, I had met Cecil before. Our conversations had been brief
but not unpleasant. I think he liked me but his power was too great
for me not to quake before him, especially in these circumstances.
When we performed at court, which we did now increasingly, I had
noticed him in the audience, yet his pleasure in my plays seemed
somewhat restrained, as though he took even the comic moments
too seriously, as though there was something sinister in them that he
feared he might miss to the detriment of the State.

"Sit you down, Master Shakespeare," Cecil said. "You are not on
stage now. I shall not ask you to play a part but be only yourself and
speak forthrightly."

"That, my good lord, I will gladly do," I said. "I do delight in
plainness of speech."

"I share your delight," he said, smiling.

A chair sat opposite the desk. This I took and sat down carefully
as though I was unsure it would hold my weight.

"You will naturally wonder why I sent for you," Cecil said. "Let
me say first that it has naught to do with your theatrical work."

"I am at your disposal, my lord." I bowed my head in saying this,
wishing at the same time that my presence was indeed caused by

Cecil's interest in my plays. I feared the worst. That it was the powder treason we would speak of.

I straightway learned my fears were well grounded.

Cecil said, "On the fifth day of this month, a small group of disaffected Catholics plotted to blow up Parliament House, the king, the queen, their sons and me with it. The destruction would have gone farther. You are aware of all this, I trust?"

"It is a fact universally known and wondered at, my lord. In the streets of the city there is talk of little else."

"You are aware of the names of the men who undertook this enormity?"

"I am, my lord."

My heart was beating now more rapidly than I thought possible. Surely, I feared, Cecil must hear it pound and know of my guilt before I uttered another word.

"I will not mince words, with you, Master Shakespeare. We are both busy men, and my prosecutorial duties give me little leisure. I am told, on very good authority, that you know many of these traitors. That you kept company with them at the home of one Stephen Lyttleton, at his manor, Holbeche House, at which time and place you also consorted with one John Gerard, a Jesuit priest."

I was about to answer this charge, but Cecil went on as if he were quoting an indictment he had written out before and committed to memory. I feared to interrupt.

"And that you also were present at a meeting, at a tavern called the Irish Boy, wherein those in attendance included Robert Catesby, the ringleader, Robert Wintour, and also Guy Fawkes."

Now my heart stopped. I started to speak, but before I could, Cecil continued.

"Let me advise you, Master Shakespeare, to tell me the whole truth, withholding nothing. For if you were to lie, say, not because you shared their devilish plot, but only because you wanted to free yourself from blame, I should know it. I should know it, sir, for that is my business, to know such things. And that lie, Master Shakespeare, regardless of how well intended to preserve yourself, would in and of itself be a treasonous act. You would be obstructing the course of justice, at the very least. Do you understand me, sir?"

I said I did.

"It's well that you do."

At this moment, I confess I sent a wordless appeal heavenward that I might be delivered from my present circumstances, which were as perilous as any I had ever suffered. That a merciful deity would snatch me up and put me in a safer place, or that I should die and at once be at peace.

But there was no such deliverance. Cecil eyed me coldly, waiting my response. And I knew that he was right. If he knew this much about my recent associations, he surely knew more. Someone had told him. Who?

I breathed deeply and commenced my confession, fearing that in so doing I was sealing my fate.

"I deny nothing of what you have said, my lord. I and my players were bid come to Holbeche House by Master Lyttleton, whose manor house it is and whom I had not met until then and with whom I have had no business or association since. Whilst there, I was introduced to other gentlemen, guests of Master Lyttleton. One of these was Robert Catesby."

"And Father Gerard?"

I stirred uncomfortably in my chair, tried to discipline my breathing lest it betray my fear and turn my truths to lies in his eyes. "Yes, my lord. He too was a guest in the house, Master Lyttleton's guest. I

278

knew not at first that he was a priest. He gave a false name, calling himself John Peters."

"An alias he has used more than once in his travels," Cecil said. "How came you to learn that he was a priest?"

"I inferred it from his manner, his conversation."

"You surmised this?" He regarded me sceptically.

"Later, he did not deny it, that is, who he was, what he was. He confessed it unto me."

I did not say that I had seen Gerard in his priestly vestments, administering Christ's body and blood to his fellow religionists. I feared that might imply that I too partook. It was a lie I reasoned was safe enough, the suppression of this evidence, a sin of omission rather than commission and therefore less culpable. At least to my way of thinking.

"The house was raided and the priest escaped. How?"

I told him about the priest's hole, the secret passage, describing it in detail.

"No surprise there," Cecil said with the beginning of a smile. "Such retreats are as common as chimneys in Staffordshire. But how did you know where it was?"

I paused, wondering if I had spoken more than needful to satisfy my interrogator, but then thought, what was the use? I was already in more trouble than I imagined in my nightmares. How could I make matters worse?

"I used it myself to escape the house."

"You were afraid of being arrested yourself?" he asked, his eyes widening in surprise. "Why, if you were guilty of nothing?"

"My lord, I know my own innocence as I know my own face," I said. "Yet another man may read me differently and judge me guilty on mere circumstances of time and place and association. I do swear, my lord, that I am no conspirator and have had neither hand in this plot, nor knowledge of it. I am not a Catholic. Yet were I one, I would have denounced these men out of loyalty to king and country."

Cecil made no answer to my defence. At least not at once. He sat very still and looked at me as though it were my soul he searched, not my eyes. I knew what he did. He was weighing my words, my loyalty. The Papist priest Cecil so much detested could not have scrutinized me with more severity. Did he believe my profession of innocence? I could not tell. Then he went on, as though I had made no response at all.

"You say you escaped through a passage, a sort of tunnel?"

"So I did, my Lord. It was behind the panelling, well concealed. A serving girl knew of it and showed it to me. It led down to a tunnel of sorts, below the floor. When I descended, I saw a light and presently came upon another occupant who had taken refuge there."

"Father Gerard?"

"The very man, my lord. It was there he revealed to me his true name and confirmed my suspicions that he was a priest."

Cecil looked at me thoughtfully. He sat silent, trying, I think, to read my mind, search out my guilt. Finally, he spoke again:

"You also consorted with Robert Catesby in London at a certain tavern?"

"The Irish Boy. I was invited to supper by a friend. I would not call it a consorting."

"What would you call it, Master Shakespeare, being as you are a man who chooses his words carefully?"

"Robert Catesby was one of several guests at Holbeche House. I was a guest at the Irish Boy. That was the extent of our association. I do not count him a friend. I am sure he does not consider me one."

"He who invited you was Ben Jonson, the poet and playwright,"

Cecil said, smiling grimly. "You see, Master Shakespeare, I am become expert in your most recent history. I know more about your comings and goings than your wife in Stratford or Master Burbage your colleague. And, by the way, if I might ask, what would you call your breaking bread with a traitor other than a consorting? Do you not like the word?"

"In truth, not very much, my lord, at least as it is commonly used in talking of plots and conspiracies. I went there for no treasonous purpose. The plot to kill the King's Majesty and your lordship was not talked of at table."

"What was talked of?"

I said, "The character of the Spaniard as opposed to the English for one."

"I trust we English came out on top in the debate."

"We surely did, my lord. On that point all at table agreed."

"But no talk of gunpowder or other explosives, cellars and under-crofts, or when the Parliament was to commence its labours?"

"On my honour, my lord. Nothing like that was spoken of."

"Have you seen Catesby since?"

"No, my lord."

Cecil nodded, but whether in agreement or in weariness of my denials I could not know.

"Robert Catesby spoke of what at table?"

"He much lamented the sad state of his co-religionists. He lamented what he called the oppression of the sect. There was something said of the need to do something."

"I see," Cecil said, "But not what."

"I swear, my lord, the conversation never reached so far."

Another silence followed. Did I say how dark the room was, although it was midday without? There was a tall window, but it was curtained. Two candles burned on Cecil's desktop. Once as we conversed, I thought I heard a rustle behind the curtain at the end of the room, and then what sounded like a cough. I thought it would be like Cecil to have a spy concealed there, a recorder of my every word. The raw stuff of my prosecution to come when my feeble defence would be thrown back into my face and I condemned like the rest of the conspirators.

"So you are, in sum, innocent of any wrongdoing?" Cecil asked.

"I do swear it, my Lord. I swear upon any Bible your lordship may choose. Any one. I swear upon the head of my father, upon the head of my mother. Upon the heads of my children."

"Ah, Master Shakespeare," Cecil said, "you do protest too much, if I may borrow a line from your *Hamlet*."

"I mean only to insist, my lord that I am guilty of no treason." I was standing now, although Cecil remained seated behind his desk. His hands were in front of him, the fingertips meeting.

It seemed a long time before he spoke. Then he said, "Rest easy, Master Shakespeare. I do believe you. Pray sit down again."

I let out a breath of air that seemed to have been trapped within my chest since I entered this fearful place and sat me down.

"It was necessary that I subject you to these interrogatories, for your good as well as the king's. Your presence at these places, your meetings with these men, all were reported. It was my duty to verify all."

I had to ask. "Your lordship, may I inquire who reported these things?"

I hoped it was not my friend, Ben Jonson. I hoped it was the dour butler at Holbeche, whom I did not trust and who I had reason to believe disliked me. But Cecil's answer surprised me.

"I have my spies, Master Shakespeare. It is part of my duty to my king and to my country. You ask who reported you?"

Cecil paused, for effect I think. His lips formed a thin smile.

"I would know my accuser, my lord. It seems only right that I should know him."

Cecil paused again, as though he were deciding whether I should have an answer or no. Then he said, "Very well, then, Master Shakespeare. It was your old and faithful friend Gabriel, Gabriel Catesby."

I could not hide my wonder or my disgust, for both responses warred within me at that revelation. Gabriel Catesby a spy for Cecil? It seemed unthinkable. But then I remembered Gabriel's nocturnal meeting with the sheriff's man, the raid that followed, my suspicion that it had been he who had reported Father Gerard's presence at Holbeche.

Cecil laughed. "You are surprised that a cousin or half-brother, whatever he is, could betray a brother? Or that an old friend could betray your trust? If so, you are little acquainted with the sea I swim in. Conspiracy runs in families, as this current plot proves. Moreover, remember that Christ himself was betrayed not by the Jews who hated him, but by the disciple who professed his love. It is the oldest and dreariest story of the world."

Cecil laughed again, not heartily now, but wearily, as though he had made a poor joke and felt apologetic for it. "Does that surprise you, Master Shakespeare, that this Catesby, not the younger brother but the bastard, should have been in my employ? Or that he should desire to be so employed?"

"He was an actor in our company," I said. "We were boys together. In Stratford-upon-Avon. He once saved my life."

Cecil nodded. "I am acquainted with that chapter of your history, Master Shakespeare. Gabriel Catesby told me, in rich and self-congratulatory detail. But you must also know that he accused you of being a principal in the plot."

"Did he?" I said, anger now dispelling fear. "He is a damnable liar

283

then," I protested. "Oh, your lordship, I could tell you other things he did that would make you detest him, though he be your servant."

"I did not employ him because of his virtues," Cecil said, "but because of his vices. And he is not my servant. He is my spy, to put a finer point upon it. Now I must take my turn to quibble about words."

"And lecherous," I said.

"Doubtless," Cecil said. "Few spies are chaste. The truth is that he wants his legitimate brother's inheritance. That is to be his reward. His fondest desire is to see his younger brother brought low, after which happy event Gabriel Catesby rises in his brother's place. We have been watching Robert Catesby for some time. He and the Wintour brothers as well. We suspected they might be plotting some revolt, but we had no idea what form their treachery might take. Thanks be to God that we discovered it in time, or the whole kingdom might have been undone."

"Why did not Gabriel Catesby warn you of their intent, he being your spy?"

"He claims he did not know of it. The details, I mean."

"And you believed him, my lord?"

"I did. He had too much to gain by revealing those details had he known them—the time, the place, the means of the plot. He would have had everything he wanted and been proclaimed saviour of the nation as well. No, Master Shakespeare, Catesby's knowledge did not extend that far."

The cough came again. I saw the curtain move.

"May I be bold to ask another question, my lord?"

"Be bold, Master Shakespeare."

"I perceive, my lord, that there is someone hidden behind yonder curtain."

Cecil laughed. "A spy, you mean?"

"Well, yes, my lord. Do forgive me if my curiosity offends. I mean no disrespect."

"No offence to me, Master Shakespeare. I have saved the best for last."

With that Cecil stood and walked over to the curtain. He drew it aside with a flourish, his lips curling in a subtle smile.

40

I did suppose I might see Thomas Wilson standing there, equipped with his pen and paper, taking down my every word to be used in evidence. Or now that Cecil had told me of Gabriel Catesby's spying, Gabriel's evil visage, in which case I already imagined how I would stuff the false accusation he had made against me down his throat.

But it was not Wilson. Nor Gabriel Catesby.

I fell to my knees. I bowed my head. "Your Majesty."

The king said, "Rise, Master William Shakespeare. Your honesty and loyalty to me have been put to the test. You have been weighed in the balance and found innocent of any traitorous act or intent. Fear not, you shall not be presented before the Council."

The king's Scots accent was so strong that I was at some pains to grasp his words, yet I caught the gist and was as glad as ever I was, for it now seemed I had escaped the worst, that I should be accused of treason and my pleasant and prosperous life be changed forever.

"I do thank you with all my heart, Your Majesty. I am your true servant."

"And I am right glad that you are so, Master Shakespeare," said the king. "For I would be sorry to lose the delights you and your fellows provide me. Very sorry, indeed. They who wear the king's livery must, like Caesar's wife, be above reproach."

The king had made the same allusion to Caesar's wife when we were first blessed with his patronage. It was an allusion of which he was especially fond, although it only served to remind me of our performance at Holbeche House and what followed thereafter.

After some few more words that I no longer remember, I was dismissed, with Cecil admonishing me that I should go home at once and change into dry clothes, for having observed my sodden state, he feared for my health.

In the corridor without, Thomas Wilson met me to usher me from the building. I assured him that I needed no guide. I could find my way out well enough and with a glad heart.

I had not reached the gatehouse before I heard my name called from behind. I turned to see Cecil himself advancing toward me. He walked like a man in pain, which I suppose he was. I had heard he suffered mightily from various ailments, made worse by his deformity.

"Master Shakespeare, stay a moment, I pray you."

"My lord?" We stood face to face, I looking down upon him. For though not tall myself, yet was I taller than he, I felt almost compelled to lower myself that I should not offend him with my modest stature.

"I trust you will not suppose our conversation to be a complete exoneration," Cecil said.

"Exoneration, my lord?"

"Understand that I am satisfied of your innocence. As is the king, as you have heard His Majesty declare. All well and good for you, Master Shakespeare, but then there is Sir Edward."

"Sir Edward?"

"Sir Edward Coke, who will sit with me in judgement on the

conspirators. You know him. He is rightly accounted a hard man. Where he sees a Catholic, he sees a traitor. He also received intelligence from Gabriel Catesby, so your association with these plotters is known to him. You must hereafter do nothing, nor have any association, that might cast doubt on your loyalty to the king or to his religion. Were I you, I would attend the trials of the conspirators. Also their executions, where it would be well were you to be seen celebrating their deaths, not grieving their loss or joining them in prayer, which condemned men are ever wont to do. Pray, that is."

"I do understand and will do all you advise, my good lord, to be quit of any suspicion of me."

"I know you are right thinking on the king's business, Master Shakespeare. I merely desire that you appear to be so as well. In these matters appearances are important. Sometimes they are everything."

"I do understand you, my lord."

He reached toward me and took my arm. "And one last thing. This play the king has asked for, *Macbeth* is it?"

"My Lord, it is. Though it is not yet ready for performance."

"Make haste then to finish it. It treats the history of the king's own progenitors, the old kings of Scotland, does it not?"

I said it did, although with some elaborations of my own invention.

"Excellent. Then use it to ingratiate yourself in His Majesty's love."

"I will, my lord."

"And be you sure there is no cause of offence, to him or to his race. His Majesty is sensitive to any belittling of Scottish blood or name."

I gave my solemn word. As though I had choice in the matter.

41

Alice Simpkins lived but two days with the Mountjoys before Madame found a home and employment for the girl at the house of another French family whom the Mountjoys knew well, the Duprees.

The Mountjoys' daughter, Mary, told me Alice's youth and beauty were too much temptation for her father, even though the tyre-maker denied it, which of course he would. He said that he never looked at Alice beyond the time I had introduced her to the family and urged them to harbour her. Well, as I have said, my landlady was a jealous woman despite her own amorous trysts.

I think it was a better match, Alice and Monsieur Dupree. He was a baker on Simon Street with a good reputation and a large family. Eight children, I think, beneath a single roof like rabbits in a warren.

Alice was to help take care of the younger children. It would be good practice for her own motherhood, Madame Dupree said.

Before I presented Alice to the Mountjoys, I had advised her to tell them she was a young widow. This I believed would invite her employers' sympathy, and make it more likely that Alice could find, in God's good time, a decent husband. Alice, her face flushed with embarrassment, hesitated. She did not like lying, she said. A lie was a sin, she said.

"Surely God will forgive so small and innocent a deception," I answered. "Your intent is not to deceive but to protect yourself. Yourself and the child, who would be at a great disadvantage were the truth known."

Alice thought about this for a moment, then said, "What if I am asked by what means my husband died? What if they ask me his name?"

"Tell them his name was John," I said. "That's a common enough name. Every second man has it. It was my own father's name. As for his death, say that he was kicked in the head by a horse. An honourable death, is it not, for an honest husbandman?"

I did not say this to incite her laughter, but her laughter that followed was a good sign. She was beginning to heal. It assured me too that she was right likely to have a good life in time, or at least a better one than she had with her brutish father or in service in a manor house.

At length, she agreed to this harmless subterfuge. I think it served her well. She told me she had been well-received in the baker's household and, having said she was a widow, none there had sought to question her burgeoning belly or assail her virtue. For though she was not at fault in her deflowering, some might blame her still. It was the way people were.

All this I learned because Alice had come by the theatre twice since arriving in London. I had told her that she could always enter when she willed, without charge. It was then she told me something strange. It was something that should not have surprised me at all, yet did.

"I am sure I have seen Master Catesby," she said.

"Do you mean Gabriel Catesby?" I asked.

But since the brother was dead, I had to know she meant our mutual enemy, save she had seen a ghost. I knew Robert Catesby was dead.

The girl herself had been present at his end, had seen his body. The traitor's head was now fixed upon a pole near the very building the conspirators had sought to destroy. I myself had walked by it twice and stared up at the hideous thing. A placard below told inquirers whose head it was, should there be any in the city who did not know already. Yet although I knew the man, I could not have sworn it was his visage rather than that of some other hapless soul. The countenance bore the agony of his wounds, first the explosion of powder, then the ball that by report had pierced his breast.

"You have seen the man?" I asked again.

"Yes, Master Shakespeare, or so I think."

"Where and when?"

"In the street between here and your theatre."

"On which side of the river?"

"North," she said.

"What was he doing?"

"Standing on a corner of the street. He was talking to another man, whose face I did not see."

"Did he see you?"

She shrugged. "I do not think he did. When I saw him, I ran."

"Wisely done," I said. "Avoid him at all costs. He is a wicked man."

I asked her more about this strange sighting, all the time thinking that it was not so strange, really. Cecil had disclosed Gabriel's covert role as a spy. The master had spoken ill of the servant. He had not said the man was no longer in his employ. I presumed that remained his function, spying on enemies of the State, spying on Catholics, spying even on his friends. Who among us all had he not betrayed in the pursuit of his ambition?

This concerned me, not just this innocent girl, who might believe the father of her child was stalking her. My concern was that even if

Gabriel Catesby learned both the king and Cecil dismissed his report of me, that might not keep him from finding more sinister ways to befoul my name at court. The man's enmity was deeply rooted. It would not die until he did, and although Cecil had said he had not seen Catesby lately, that did not mean he was not still lurking about, thirsting more than ever for revenge upon my person because he believed I had betrayed him.

On the other hand, perhaps she had just taken a stranger for him she feared. It was not beyond crediting, for many a man has another who might well be his twin.

I reached out and took Alice by the shoulders, bringing my face close to hers. "You must let me know if you see him again, and most especially if he accosts you or even if he threatens to do so."

She looked at me doubtfully, as though she supposed me incapable of protecting her. Perhaps she was right. If it was truly Gabriel she had seen, Gabriel was a larger man than I. He was a mean and brutal man, prone to violence, hardened in warfare. I was soft and yielding, an avoider of trouble, with feeble knees and poor eyesight.

"I have friends who can protect you," I said.

She gave me no answer. I urged her to speak. She looked up fearfully, her stare stark and cold as if I, not Gabriel Catesby, were her enemy.

"But Master Shakespeare. I fear he will kill me—and his child I carry."

"If it was indeed Catesby you saw, it is more likely he stalks me than you."

"Why, sir, how could that be?"

"It is a long story. And it has naught to do with you. Remember, if you see him again, tell me. And do not let him see you by any means."

Alice reported to me no more sightings of her tormentor. Which did not mean that he was not still at large in London. Thereafter I kept watch for him myself, alert to his familiar features and finding occasional resemblances that proved false, to my relief. I wanted Gabriel Catesby out of my life as much as out of hers.

Meanwhile, his brother's head continued its inexorable decay. English weather is not good for the unburied dead. The persistent damp hastens the rot.

Already Robert Catesby's severed remains were almost unrecognizable as human.

42

Come January, I followed Cecil's advice and secured permission from Thomas Wilson to attend the trial of the gunpowder plotters. It was held in the great hall at Winchester and on the day thereof, it was the twenty-seventh day of the month I recall, the room filled with such a multitude that I was hard pressed to find a place to stand since all the seats were filled with almost every other person of name and note in the kingdom.

Herein I must admit to a kind of shameful jealousy. It is certain that none of my plays had ever drawn such a throng. Nor would they. Yet why should they do so? My plays were figments of my imagination. They were works of craft, not the stuff of life, nor events to topple kingdoms.

It is always wise to keep these things in perspective.

At the head of the great hall sat the august members of His Majesty's Privy Council including my lord of Salisbury and certain dukes of the realm, sufficiently well known so I have no need to mention them. The prosecutor was, I already knew, Sir Edward Coke, looking very stern and confident, for although this was a trial and English law decreed that the defendants therein were innocent until their guilt be proved, the verdict, all agreed, was a foregone conclusion. For one, the defendants had confessed. For another, so great was the hatred for these men among the populace that even a tolerant jury moved by compassion for their deluded souls would have not dared to find their guilt anything but certain.

I marked the king's absence from these proceedings and marvelled at it. Surely, he would desire to see for himself how the State prosecuted his would-be murderers. But I suspected he was listening somewhere in a nearby chamber, much as he did when I conversed with Cecil and His Majesty eavesdropped behind the curtain. The king was like that. He ever wanted to see, but not always to be seen.

Once I caught Cecil's eye and was pleased that he noted me there. Had he not urged my attendance, I might have stayed at home revising an old play or commencing a new. In truth, I was working on a new play. It had filled my brain since I first conceived it, excited my imagination. New plays always did, even when they reworked old Italian or French novels or mouldy English histories. I hoped my compliance with his wishes would strengthen his belief in my innocence. I continued to feel vulnerable, for there was still evidence against me should anyone want to charge me with complicity in these dire events.

I knew the conspirators had been brought from the Tower that morning. They had come up the river by barge. Now when they were led into the hall there was a great roar from the observers mixed with jeers, howls of rage and contempt. It was deafening. I had planned to join any such display, again as Cecil had advised. Instead I stood silent. What, after all, would my single voice do to enhance such clamour, such rage?

Then was the assembly called to silence. The defendants took their place on a dais. I had been to trials before. I had seen defendants quake before the majesty of the law, the terror of punishment. But these men stood firmly, their heads raised, as though an honour were about to be conferred upon them, not a sentence of death.

Or in their special case, sainthood perhaps.

I can see their calm, resigned faces even now, years beyond the event. There was John and Christopher Wright, Robert Keyes, Thomas Bates, Robert and Thomas Wintour, John Grant, Ambrose Rookwood, Francis Tresham, Sir Everard Digby, and of course Guido Fawkes.

Beyond that auspicious opening, notwithstanding that next to the coronation of His Majesty there had been no other public assembly of equal pith and moment in my lifetime, I remember little. Do you not think that strange? Memory is a mystery, fragile like a flower. Perhaps God made it so that man should not suffer overmuch his sins by recalling them with too much exactness. Therein is oblivion one of life's blessings, though much disparaged by the thoughtless. Methinks our clergy should do more to propagate this doctrine. It would do more good than haranguing against the wicked, who do not harken to sermons and who often feel their condemnation by the righteous, a challenge to do even worse in their lives, to the great hurt of their souls and the good order of the commonwealth.

The defendants seemed to have been as much resigned to their fate as was the jury, in this case the Lords of the Council, who were to be their ultimate judges. Yet when they were asked how they pled to the charges, each pled not guilty.

Their response surprised most in the hall I think, since each had earlier confessed to his part in the conspiracy. Yet it was the added accusations of three Jesuits as equally culpable for knowing of the plot that stirred most controversy. One of these, I remember, was my companion in the priest's hole, Father John Gerard. The other two I did not know. One was later to be drawn and quartered. I know not whether he was guilty as charged or accused merely because he was so intensely hated by the prosecution.

I do remember the testimony of Guido Fawkes because, of the defendants, it was he I knew best. He had come limping into the great chamber, his back bent, his face pale and contorted with pain. I remembered when he was a bold soldier, a commanding presence. Not so now. He had been tortured. The torture had ruined his body, and perhaps his mind. This I had from one of the warders in the Tower sometime after Fawkes' death, the facts of which I will presently relate.

There was, as I have said, little remorse shown among the defendants, and most especially Fawkes himself, who seemed more to take pride in his part than rue the events that had led him to his own tragedy. I suppose his faith, which he had tried to press on me, bore him up in his extremity.

I do remember he surprised those in the assembly when he pled not guilty to the indictment after having confessed earlier his part. When asked by Cecil about this inconsistency, he explained that there was a part of the indictment he did not understand and for that reason was reluctant to admit guilt to all, if unsure of his guilt for part.

It seemed to me a lawyer's quibble, this reservation. Yet such was Fawkes' mind. He was a soldier, no lawyer, but he sometimes thought like the latter.

Some of the accused gentlemen took their moment in court to plead for their families. Thomas Bates, Catesby's manservant, pleaded so. He was the only one of the accused who was not a gentleman but a common person who he protested was drawn into the conspiracy out of loyalty to his master. Otherwise, he declared, it would never have occurred to him to take arms against his sovereign king.

He pled for his wife and children, who he claimed knew nothing of his part in the plot, nor could they have conceived of such an act.

Of the accused conspirators, Sir Everard Digby earned perhaps the most sympathy. Well known in the city, he was a handsome man, tall and well formed. As he spoke of his faith, I looked about me, wondering how many of those assembled and prepared to condemn the acts of the accused shared the same devotion. I could not count the secret hearts, yet I knew there must be many there who had taken the forbidden communion within the week and now sat in judgement on their fellow believers, who laid claim to having no other motive than to return true religion to a benighted land.

It was not a long trial, as trials go. I had endured lengthier ones of much less import. I had enjoyed trials that were as suspenseful as any play I ever wrote. More so, I do confess it.

This was not one of those. For the defendants said nothing they had not previously declared and been reported widely to the public ear. The questions and responses of Cecil and Coke were equally predictable, at least by this time. There was some effort of the prosecutors to implicate the Jesuits as a group in the plot. But this effort came to nothing, for each defendant, when asked, swore before God that no priest knew aught of it.

Indeed, the conspirators claimed to have gone out of their ways to make sure the priests would not know of it. This was because the Pope had expressly forbidden them from revolt and they had defied that instruction. How could they not be culpable unless one lived in a country whose laws made no objection to the murder of a king? All defendants had confessed their treachery. What was left but to pass sentence?

In time, the Privy Councillors, robed in their splendour and authority, retired from the chamber to deliberate.

They returned straightway, as though they had some pressing appointment later in the afternoon.

They judged every man before them guilty.

How could it have been otherwise?

I marked well the faces of the accused as they received judgement. I confess admiration for their stoicism. Each man knew his fate. Each acknowledged his guilt. Yet none quaked or wept. Only Thomas Bates, Catesby's servant, looked as if he might. He had lost his beloved master. Now he would lose his life in his master's cause.

I heard afterward that his family was spared, even as he had begged the court to do. The families of other of the conspirators were not so fortunate.

Later, I walked from Winchester to Mountjoy's house with a heavy heart. I tried humming one of Burbage's merry tunes to lift my spirits. Music does, I believe, have that power. Yet in this case, it did nothing for me. I felt the dreariness of the day heavy upon me like a cloak of despair. True, it was very cold in London and there was a thin layer of snow on the cobbles. But I suffered from a greater melancholy. Perhaps the danger I had suffered from the conspirators, now removed I then supposed, had been but a blessed distraction from some deeper ache and loss within me.

I tried to think of our recent performance of *Macbeth* before the king, who had taken great delight in the play and most particularly in the depiction of the three witches.

I did not tell His Majesty that without the Catesbys I might never have conceived of these otherworldly creatures. There was nothing of witches in the history I drew upon. But there were days I cared little for such records. My plays were never about history, truth be told, but more about the men who made it, their ruthless ambition, their torments of conscience, and, often, even in their heroic aspirations and commendable civic virtues.

299

43

By now the plot was becoming old news. Still, the country waited the execution of the conspirators. That, too, I would witness. I continued to follow Cecil's advice. I liked not executions as a spectacle any more than bear-baitings pleased me. It was not the blood I abhorred. Enough of it ran through my veins. Wherefore should I object to another's? Nor was it the lolling tongues of the hanged, or the excised bowels and genitalia, which the hooded hangman so delighted in exposing to public view. It was, I protest, the response of those who looked upon the event, their unwholesome fascination with the brutality of punishment, their greedy joy in another's pain.

Or perhaps it was only relief that the pain was not theirs.

Whatever it was, it was not a response I desired to share, nor to observe, nor to fix in my memory to disturb the innocence of sleep.

Yet the truth was, there was one execution that I did long to see with my own eyes, which was the execution of Guido Fawkes.

Like Gabriel Catesby, Fawkes had made himself my bitter enemy, for reasons I had never fully understood. No matter my lack of understanding, the great thing in life is to know one's enemy. The wherefore of his enmity is sometimes unknown even to him.

I arrived at my lodgings to find a letter beneath my door. It was from Madame Dupree, Alice's employer. It beseeched me to come at once to the baker's house. Since it did not say why I should, seeing no compelling need to respond and being weary in body and mind, I went straightway to bed and fell at once asleep, intending to rise early to write, hopeful to finish my play.

But come morning, four or five of the clock, I forgot about the letter. I wrote all the morning until my poor eyes burned, then got me to the theatre at Blackfriars where we often performed in the winter, our exposed Globe now becoming too cold and wet for comfort. One of the players in the company had fallen ill. I was to take up his role. Which role? I cannot remember everything, but it was no great part, some minor character needed to advance a scene or bring news upon the stage. Not more than a dozen or more lines. Per act. A child could have committed them to memory in a minute. A child could have played the part as well as I.

Later that night, our play done and the audience departed, I looked across the room to see a woman advancing toward me with an expression that left little doubt that I was the object of her visit. I did not know her, but I could tell by her garments that she was neither beggar nor lady but something in between, perhaps a merchant's wife come with some bill to be paid, or an anxious mother wanting a place for her young son, who she avowed had talent to become a player like unto us. To such pleadings I was inured.

But it was otherwise than I feared. When the woman had come to where I stood, she told me she was Juliette Dupree, the baker's wife who had taken Alice in.

It was then I remembered the letter beneath my door. I started to ask her pardon for my fault in failing to respond to it, but her own speech prevented it.

"Monsieur Shakespierre, Monsieur Shakespierre!" she exclaimed, her face ruddy with excitement. "Alice has given birth to her child. It came upon her *toute suite*."

"Given birth!" I exclaimed. But before I could inquire after the mother's health and whether the child was man or maid, I detected tears in the woman's eyes.

"The baby came before Alice was aware. She said she had no pain at all, and thought at first it was a miracle, giving birth so and feeling not a twinge."

"But wherefore was it no miracle? Surely to give birth without pain is quite beyond the natural course," I said, remembering my poor wife's suffering.

"The baby was born alive," she said, "but within the hour it was dead."

Hearing this, my heart ached. What if the child were the fruit of violence, I thought, still it was a child, the child of a child, innocent. The father's sin did not make against that.

"*Oui*, and he seemed as healthy as any of my children bursting from my womb. I put the baby to suck upon Alice's breast, but it would not. I left the room where she lay for but a minute to fetch some water, for Alice complained of being thirsty. When I returned, the baby, he was dead."

We stood silent for a while, then I asked, "Did she give her son a name?"

"Oh *oui*, Monsieur," Madame Dupree answered, smiling through her tears.

"And the name given him?"

"Thomas."

"Not John, after its father?" I said, remembering the fiction I had pressed Alice to convey.

"Nay, sir, Thomas. It was, she said, her own father's name."

Madame began to weep. Great tears streamed down her cheeks as though the dead infant had been her own flesh and blood. She looked upward as though appealing to God for mercy, on herself as well as the dead child and her poor mother.

I said, "Tell me, Madame Dupree, how does Alice?"

"Oh, she does well, Monsieur. She even smiled a bit when I told her the baby was dead. Is not that strange, Monsieur, that she smiled? I asked her, how is it with you, dear girl? And she answered, 'Oh, Madame, I am well enough off, and now my baby is where he ought to be.'"

"In heaven?" I asked.

"So I believe," she said. "The Catholics believe that a baby dying without baptism has no hope of heaven, but what say you, Monsieur Shakespierre, being as you are a philosopher, or so I am told by Madame Mountjoy?"

I sighed heavily. "No philosopher, Madame. I write plays. Sometimes I act in them."

I was no philosopher. Nor was I a priest, I might also have said. I was wont to leave the mysteries of God to the learned and pious. But then I said to her, since her question demanded an answer if only that she be consoled, "I do think the power of God is ample to save the innocent even if they are not baptized. And to condemn the wicked even if they are."

She thought about my answer. It seemed sufficient for her, though I was unsure myself if it were true, about baptism I mean and innocent children. I hoped it might be true. It seemed just and right, even if it might be wrong in God's eyes.

Then she said, "Will you come to my house, Monsieur, straightway? Alice desires to see you. She is ever prattling on

303

about you. She says Monsieur Shakespierre is the best of men she has known."

"Even better than her husband, John, of beloved memory?" I asked.

"Oh, ever so much better, sir. Ever so much the better."

44

I followed Juliette Dupree to her house on Fleet Street, though I was little inclined to it. I did not look forward to witnessing Alice's anguish at the death of her child. Madame Dupree had said the girl appeared cold and distracted, a thing to me more wondrous than that she should have given birth without pain. Surely, Alice must have felt pain, I thought. Now as surely, she must grieve. What mother would not? In my Scottish play I had made Macbeth's lady wife a monster for her callous motherhood in that she declared she would rip her babe from her dugs. But Lady Macbeth was an unnatural thing, a hellish hag, which her descent into madness did well prove.

Alice was no Lady Macbeth.

Yet, herein for me was the sticking place. I am not comfortable with the grief of others, though I have suffered my own losses. I am helpless before their sorrow, their broken hearts and stricken countenances, their agonies of conscience and terrors of divine retribution. I lack the healer's touch, a gift of God I think it be.

Alas, I confess it is no gift of mine.

When we arrived at the Duprees' shop, it appeared the young children of the household had been put to bed. At least they were not to be seen. Nor was Monsieur Dupree, the baker. Madame Dupree led me upstairs to where the family lived and then to a door at which she gave two sharp raps.

From within I heard a thin familiar voice say come, and I walked into a tiny room with a narrow bed and a candle burning by the bedside table. There was no hearth, no fire, no comforting warmth. A cheerless, coffin-like closet, well suited for reflection on life's brevity and death's certitude.

On this bed lay Alice, looking very pale and wan. She was covered by a ragged quilt, a cast off doubtless of her new mistress. Her eyes I could see even in the candlelight were large and glassy. Strange to say, I was relieved. I liked not the picture of the girl painted by the Frenchwoman of stony indifference to a dead child of her own body. The child's father might be a villainous ravisher of innocence, but Alice was a mother. Mothers grieve. Alice must needs grieve. I could not conceive otherwise.

The girl's lips parted in a timid smile when she saw me.

"Oh, Master Shakespeare, you've come."

She spoke my name with a tenderness that surprised me. Like unto a whispered prayer. Before she was respectful. Now she was almost worshipful.

"Alice," I whispered, "how goes it with you?"

It was a foolish question, as I recognized as soon as my mouth uttered it. How did I suppose she was, given that her child was dead?

She lay there shuddering, half alive herself.

But she did answer and, with an alacrity that surprised me, she raised herself up on her elbows as she spoke. Her threadbare gown parted, exposing a swollen white breast that might have given suck had her child lived.

"I am well. I do mean I am as well as I can be, having come so near death myself that God snatched my babe up and took him to Himself."

I looked at Madame Dupree standing behind me, remembering how she had made so much of the ease with which the child was delivered into this life. A miraculous birth, she had called it. Painless, the delivery, Alice being almost unawares of the moment of the birthing, the child slipping into the world on cat's feet.

"You nearly died?" I asked, hardly believing that I had heard her rightly.

"Not from pain," she said in a whisper and with an indulgent smile. "I was asleep. I had a dream, or vision. I was taken up, into heaven I think. But then was sent back to the world and this sad life. And when I awoke, the baby was between my legs, whimpering. It was then I screamed for Madame. And, praise be God, she came to help me."

Madam Dupree said, "I cut the cord and went for water to wash the babe. When I returned the child lay still. It did not move. It did not breathe."

He. The child Alice had named Thomas. Thomas, after her own father. She nodded to a small mound in the quilt beside her. I walked over and lifted it. The infant was motionless and still, bloody from the birth.

I pulled the blanket up over the small dead face.

I noticed that since my entrance, Alice had not looked at her babe, not even when I exposed it. For her, it was as if the child's body were already gone with its spirit. Perhaps to the same heaven Alice had dreamed of.

Madame Dupree said, "There is a small graveyard near the French Church, where we Huguenots worship. Our pastor is a good man. He will see that the baby is buried there."

"Yes," I said. "It would be good of you to see to that."

Madam Dupree continued. "Alice must remain in bed. As you can see, Master Shakespierre, she needs her rest. Her body is worn down from the birth, but with God's help she will be well again."

"I am truly sorry, child," I said to Alice who had closed her eyes and perhaps even fallen asleep. "God keep you and your child. I will return in a few days to see how you do."

I bent over and kissed her forehead, which was damp beneath my lips and tasted of salt. Had I been Papist, I would have made the sign of the cross. Since I was not, I merely laid my hand on hers, as I oft comforted my daughters when they were children and lay sick abed.

Did she hear this promise? I could not tell. Had she felt the touch of my lips or my hand upon hers? Beneath the quilt her chest was rising and falling as it does when one has fallen asleep, a sweet expulsion of air and then drawn again.

Madame picked up the babe's corpse. I followed her out of the room. We made a solemn progression of mourners down the narrow stairs where the Frenchwoman found fresh water and washed the tiny body. She used a rag and cleaned with smooth strokes the arms and legs, the chest, the tiny thing like a bright button.

"He would have been a fine son," she said, looking at me. "See, Master Shakespierre, do you not think he would have made a beautiful boy and then, after, a handsome man?"

"Yes," I said. "He would have made a handsome man."

In truth, I had no knowledge of what manner of man Alice's child might become. Gabriel Catesby had no doubt been a beautiful child, yet as a man he became a liar, ravisher, and traitor, deceiving his friends and abusing the innocent. How little the beginning of things foreshadowed their end. This was a truth to be endured, not denied.

When she had finished washing the body, Madam Dupree wrapped it in her apron. She said, "I will take the child to the Church tomorrow.

I will let the pastor know what has happened. Surely there is a place in some corner of the graveyard for this infant. The child will have a decent Christian burial."

"Why should he not, since his mother is a Christian?" I asked.

She looked up at me with a severe glance. "Some pastors will not suffer a bastard child to be buried in sacred ground."

"Bastard!" I exclaimed, taken aback by the word. "No bastard this babe. Alice is a widow. Her husband was killed. The babe was born in wedlock."

The lies slipped easily from my lips, but Madame Dupree shook her head. She looked at me doubtfully, smiling grimly. "I think not, Monsieur. Alice told me that story. I believed not a word of it. I may be French and a poor baker's wife, yet no fool. The girl, she is not a good liar. Besides, she is too young for marriage. She is twelve years, a child herself, no? Who would marry one so young? What father or mother would permit it? What minister or priest true to his faith would perform the rites? No, sir, she is not married, nor was she ever. Her child is a bastard. But if that were known, its resting place would be by the side of the road. It would be a disgrace in men's eyes and in God's."

I shook my head. The woman was right, of course. If the child's origin were known, the body would not be welcome in sacred precincts, Catholic or Anglican. An obscure roadside grave would be the fate of Alice's little son.

There was no point in maintaining the fiction I had invented. "You will not tell your pastor the truth?"

"Him?" she snorted in disgust. "Why should I? The infant deserves a decent burial. He has not sinned, but his parents."

"It was not as you suppose," I said. "Alice did nothing wrong. She was before a chambermaid in a rich man's house. She was a virtuous girl attacked by one of my actors, more's the pity and to my shame since I had brought him to the manor house."

When I said this, she looked up at me with surprise. I had surprised myself, for it was the first time I had admitted that the blame was in part mine as well as Gabriel's. But for me, the girl would be a virgin still.

"You are not the father then, Monsieur?" she asked, a touch of incredulity in her voice.

Now was I the more amazed. Had this woman thought Alice's child was my own from the beginning? Or was it that I had kissed and blessed Alice before her eyes, showing an affection otherwise inexplicable, save the dead child were my own and I Alice's lover?

"Upon oath, I am not the father," I protested. "I have never touched her in that way. I have never regarded her as anything but a young friend. I have a wife and two grown daughters in Stratford."

"Ah, Monsieur, to many men such accoutrements as wives and children mean nothing. They are no bar to a man's will."

She was right about that too. And the truth was that I had not always been faithful to my own wedding vows. I confess I am a man, no saint. Still, I was innocent with Alice Simpkins. A father to her I had been, neither wooer nor lover.

I said, "She is also very young. Hardly more than a child. I am almost thirty years older than she."

My defence fell on deaf ears. I could tell that well enough. I started to say something else in support of my innocence, but then saw that all defence was futile, as such defences so often are. Her mind was set. An angel come from heaven could not have convinced her otherwise.

I decided to let the brutal accusation go without further denials. The baby was dead. Gone to heaven, as Alice had said. And I should presently be gone from the baker's house, not to return.

A thought came to me then, like an arrow piercing my heart. It was a question, a disturbing one. How did the babe, born alive, die so soon thereafter? While Madame Dupree had withdrawn from the room. To fetch water, she had said. Had Alice done something? Had she stifled the baby's breath, because although it was the fruit of her body it was also her ravisher's son? Had she murdered her own child and thereby expunged her shame. Had she revenged herself upon Gabriel?

Such things had been done before. It was a sin not without reason. Yet I shuddered to think on it. Not only because it was done, but that Alice, sweet, innocent Alice, had done it.

Or perhaps not.

As I pondered this, Madame Dupree's certainty that I had fathered Alice's baby seemed the least disturbing of the questions before me. What cared I that the Frenchwoman thought of me as an old satyr having his wicked ways with children? Were actors not often thought to be immoral? Were not our theatres routinely condemned as school-houses of iniquity and vice? Ask any Puritan on the street what he thought of our damnable breed. Ask the good bishops of the English Church what they thought of the theatres. Corruptors of youth, seducers of foolish women, fomenters of discontent and disorder, enemies of the State.

As actor, I had little reputation to lose. What cared I what the Frenchwoman supposed?

Yet I did.

Monsieur Dupree returned. I waited while his wife told him of the baby's fate. Heavy and loutish, the baker grunted a reply, some consolatory phrases in French. The whole conversation had been in that tongue, yet was I able to get the gist. The baker seemed to take the child's death philosophically. It was God's will, he said. *La volonte de Dieu.* These things happen. Death was all around. It was the common fate. He wanted to know when Alice would be able to continue her

311

work in the house. At least, I think that is what he asked. Perhaps it was something else he said. As I have confessed, I know but a little French, enough to buy bread or say good morrow or declare my love.

But now was I sore weary of all of this, the grief or lack thereof, the dispute about the child's true father. Then, of a sudden, I had an even blacker thought.

Alice's baby was full-developed, perfect in his parts. It had been but eight months at most since the assault at Holbeche House. Catesby had sworn the girl was no virgin, that another had had her before. I supposed, then, that Gabriel had lied. It was, after all, his nature. Yet Alice had named her child not after the husband I had created for her, but the cruel father she had fled. Had Thomas Simpkins violated his own child?

It was all too tortured and repellent to contemplate. How was one to know the truth?

I thanked Madame Dupree for helping Alice, and gave her some money for her pains, which money her loutish husband immediately snatched from his wife's hand as though it were his, by marital right, which the Frenchman undoubtedly believed it to be.

I stepped out into the night. The cobbles glistened. Above me, the stars shone on this mystery with blank stares, bereft of tongues to speak the truth I sought.

Tomorrow the executions of the traitors would take place. Yet I did fear the first execution had already been done upon Alice's poor babe.

45

For posterity's sake, I am perforce turned a writer of history, for history is part of my story. Bear with me, I pray you. Upon oath I swear it. The end of all is in sight.

On Thursday of the week, the thirtieth day of January, four of the conspirators were conveyed from the Tower to the square before St Paul's Cathedral, a felicitous public place for the judgement to come, being that it is so stately a structure and godly in its purpose.

Their conveyance had been upon wagons, their bodies bent over so that their faces were toward the ground, their very posture only the beginning of their public mortification. This solemn prelude to punishment had caused a great stir as the wagons rattled through the streets.

I confess I did not witness this dreary procession, not directly. I heard after that the prisoners passed their time praying along the way and crossing themselves as Papists do, even as curses and garbage flew from the windows of houses as they passed. Londoners have learned well how to express their feelings, be they ones of celebration or disdain.

In the square, a tall scaffold had been erected along with a gallows tree fixed in its centre like a ship's stout mast. It had been built several days before the trial, and it had stood unused until this moment in happy and certain anticipation of its ultimate purpose.

Along with the scaffold were other benches and platforms constructed that the nobles and gentlemen and their lady wives might view the scene above the common herd who would soon fill the square to overflowing. It was, so it came to me then, a theatre of its own, built for a single performance that each of the principal actors might play their parts, either well or ill.

I said there were four of the condemned in this company. They included Robert Wintour, John Grant, Thomas Bates, and finally Sir Everard Digby. Why these four at this time and place and not all of the traitors? I know not. I did not inquire of Cecil, or any other person who might have been privy to the king's mind.

And it would have been the king's mind that governed, none other's. The true master of ceremonies, he wanted perhaps to instil the greater horror in those whose execution would be delayed a day. Or perhaps he divided the company of the condemned to prolong the ceremony, the way a play is divided into acts, a book into chapters, a life into the ages of man.

The square was full of onlookers and was, like all public executions, a little world mimicking the greater. Persons of every rank and condition stood elbow to elbow, striving to get a look at the prisoners, or to hear their speeches were they to make any, to see and be seen by the courtiers in their midst. It was, as I have said, a form of public entertainment, featuring torture, oratory, and spectacle as its solemn burden.

Did I forget justice?

Yes, sometimes even that.

My place in the assembly was not far from the scaffold itself, not ten yards I should judge, a position I achieved by arriving before light when the square, already filling with spectators, was illuminated by torches placed all around, giving off in the dawn a timorous yellow light.

It was bitterly cold, being as it was the very bottom of winter.

I was continually jostled by those standing next to me, which looked by their dress and demeanour like a flutter of lawyers from the Inns of Court. While they waited, they spoke of laws and suits and other matters that bedevil lawyers' brains. They made jokes, complained about the cold. I recognized none amongst them.

I looked around for members of the Privy Council, but although I saw them collectively at an advantageous place in the square, I could not see Cecil. I saw no face I knew, heard no familiar voice. I might have been in another city far away, yet in truth it was London and a neighbourhood I knew well. Cecil would have to take my word that I had followed his advice to make myself a spectator of these grim proceedings.

Then it began, almost without prologue, save for a sustained blasting of trumpets and beating of drums, as if all the king's regiments had been called to muster.

It was now fully day. Everything could be seen and heard.

The ceremony of death, the great parable of justice, had indeed begun in earnest.

Of the condemned, Sir Everard Digby was the first to mount the scaffold. I watched him stand there on the platform, his eyes shut, his hand working to cross himself, but trembling so that the motions seemed stilted and forced, as though he were controlled by a power outside himself. His prayers caused the assembly to fall silent, or at least grow less boisterous. Perhaps out of respect, for Digby's part in the treason was widely regretted. I remember he declined the offer of several Church of England ministers clustered on the platform like crows that they should pray for his soul. He refused them. He called upon any Catholics in the assembly to join him in prayer. Thereby was the old sectarian divide made part of the spectacle.

When Digby was asked if he had words of contrition to offer, he said he did and proceeded to speak with great dignity that impressed all who heard his voice. He confessed his part in the conspiracy but denied that it was wrong what he did. He acted, he said, not for personal gain or power, but for the glory of God and that the true Church might be restored to the land.

I believe many in the crowd would have said amen to Digby's wish had they dared so to do. Yet I heard no voices raised in support of him. Digby granted that he had defied the King's Majesty but insisted that God's law should take precedence over those of mere men, even if they wore crowns and wielded sceptres.

I do not recall much else he said, or his exact words. I give you the gist only, as God gives me to remember.

Digby was a very brave gentleman, I think. Even to the end of his life, which many people said, but for his treason, was a model of gentility and honour. His end came quickly. He mounted the ladder that led up to the hangman's tree. The noose was placed about his neck, his collar having been removed before. In a blink of an eye, he was dropped through the hole in the platform on which he stood and then as quickly cut down so that he stood again, the noose still around his neck.

Digby had struck his head falling through the trap door and now reeled as though dazed. In truth, I think he was. It was as though the executioner desired that he know the pain of strangulation without its fatal consequence, an act not meant to cause death but to tease with its proximity.

But then as suddenly his body was seized upon, his flimsy

garments were slashed, his genitals exposed and in almost the same instant excised from his body.

In all this horror, Digby made no cry, no utterance, despite what must have been excruciating pain.

Disembowelment followed, and these hitherto private organs, along with his still beating heart, were burned in a fire before his eyes.

In the still morning cold, you could smell the stench of burning entrails.

Digby must have seen what was happening to him for I saw his eyelids flutter.

Then he was dead.

I prayed he was dead. For I deemed his punishment more than any soul, no matter how wicked, should endure.

The executioner now threw the body to the platform and with his great axe hacked off first Digby's head, then quartered him.

The executioner lifted the severed head to the multitude as a sign that law had been imposed.

The crowd roared with approval.

I turned away, sick at heart.

46

In this account of what I witnessed, I may seem indeed too squeamish in my response, too womanish in my distaste for violence, the impulse toward which being often considered the very essence of manhood.

If so, then that is what I am. Think of Will Shakespeare what you will. But those of you who have never observed such a spectacle judge me not too harshly. When you have stood as did I to observe a man's ordeal you may well join me in my tenderness of heart, my womanishness.

Of Digby I have said that his public reputation and physical presence were such as to create some sympathy in the hearts and minds of those who witnessed his cruel death. I saw tears stream down faces as he died. I heard whispered prayers on his behalf. These I had marked at his trial. These I had marked on that cold January morning when Digby gave up the ghost.

With each step in his execution the clamour lessened, until at the end when he was no more than body parts and his soul had flown upward to the God who gave him life, silence followed. Whether at relief that the traitor was dispatched, or horror at the means of dispatching him, or respect for Digby's courage and faith, each must answer for himself.

318

All this I saw, and faithfully report.

The deaths of Masters Wintour and Grant followed in the same grue-some manner although these gentlemen were allowed to hang longer so as to be but half-conscious during the remainder of their ordeal.

Wintour said little before his execution. He spent most of his time praying, which one can readily understand since a man under such circumstances might expect to meet his God straightway.

John Grant spoke at some length, which pleased the multitude for whom oratory, especially by the condemned, was expected and often a cause of delight as well as moral instruction. The wretched man had regained some of his sight during the weeks following the explosion at Holbeche House but still used his hand to help guide him. I marked he had trouble climbing the ladder to where the noose hung, though now that I think upon it, why should any man have hastened to such a fate?

Thomas Bates came last, perhaps because in the scheme of things he was the lowest born, a mere servant. In his statements, which were few, he admitted he had been guilty before God and had been a traitor but claimed he was induced to participate out of love for his master, Robert Catesby.

I know not how much sympathy this plea earned him. I thought even a servant might exercise as much free will as a duke or an earl or even as a king and protest to his lord and master: nay, sir, I love you well, yet will I not do that thing that is wrong in God's eyes and the king's.

Bates was soon dead, along with his betters.

The next day, Friday, the place of execution was changed. Again, do not ask me why. This new venue was next to the Parliament House.

There was on this day a greater assembly than that of the day before. Perhaps word of the execution had spread, and those who had missed the edifying spectacle on Thursday were now more than determined that they should not be deprived on Friday. Throughout the city there was talk of little else.

On this day it was my good fortune or not, depending on how one looks upon such matters, to be better situated. Thomas Wilson, Cecil's secretary, had marked my presence in the crowd, standing over against a wall where I could see little but the backs of heads and the large, wide brimmed hats that were then in fashion with our gallants.

Wilson beckoned me to follow him. I did, and soon found myself on a raised platform sitting next to Cecil himself. I was not unappreciative of this singular honour, or how it might be a sign to Cecil of my compliance, my being on what he called the right side of things.

He greeted me with great courtesy, asked how I did, and inquired had I been to the previous day's executions.

"I saw all, my good lord," I said.

"Those Papists will make long speeches before they die, do you not think, Master Shakespeare?"

"It seems the people are aggrieved if they do not."

"Each of the traitors seemed committed to exculpating the damnable Jesuits," Cecil murmured. "Even more than begging for mercy from the king."

"I marked that well, my lord."

"And what think you, Master Shakespeare. Do you not think that the Jesuits in particular and the Papists in general are at the bottom of all of this mischief in that they allow, nay, promote, the murder of an anointed king if he defies their perverted doctrines?"

I was careful in my response to this, even as a man is careful when he steps upon stones to cross a rushing river. I had no firm knowledge

320

that the Jesuits were a party to the powder treason, that they planned it or even knew of its progress, but I knew well that Cecil expected me to affirm his belief that they were. Should I have done so, I might have given credence to the thought that I knew more than I should have known of the Jesuits and their machinations. Therefore, I thought well before I spoke, a good practice for any man to learn who hopes for a long life in a troubled time.

"My lord, I leave such matters to those who know best the workings of these persons, such as the king and your honourable self. I know little of Catholic doctrine, less of Catholic politics."

I opened my palms to suggest helplessness before these great mysteries.

Cecil smiled and nodded. He said, "A politic response, Master Shakespeare. Yet I cannot fault you for your discretion, which I believe in one of your plays you honour as the better part of valour. Granted the man who utters it, your John Falstaff, is wont to play the fool. Yet even a fool sometimes utters wisdom. You are right, sir. The times do call for discretion. But as to deathbed oratory, we shall hear what we shall hear. It will doubtless be more exculpation of Jesuits I fear."

At that, the Earl turned his attention to the centre of the square. The traitors had come with their company of guards and their pious faces and gestures.

The prisoners on this day were Thomas Wintour, the younger brother of him dispatched the day before, Ambrose Rookwood, Robert Keyes, and Guy Fawkes. These first three men I hardly knew and might not have recognized them on the street were they to be at large and I pass them by.

It was Fawkes I fixed my eyes upon. This tall and sturdy former soldier seemed even more enfeebled than before when I last saw him in the street. Although I think I hated him—both for his crimes against the State and for his betrayal of my friendship—it was painful to watch his stumbling gait, even more to see him struggle up the gallows tree, which he did with unexpected results I will presently relate.

But first I must speak of the other three, who deserve attention even as they deserved their punishment.

They met their end with the same stoic dignity as their fellow religionists the day before. They prayed devoutly, made the sign of the cross as many times as they could, so as to leave themselves breathless from the exertion and, as Cecil had prophesied, made speeches about the innocence of Jesuits. These comments did not please many assembled, who made noises of disapproval at anything that might commend the much-hated order, for of the warring parties they were loved least.

Ambrose Rookwood begged mercy for his wife and children, a most pathetic appeal that moved many present to tears. I remember Keyes did the same. I wondered that these men should not have thought about the fate of their families before undertaking so dangerous an enterprise.

Still, they proclaimed themselves good Catholics, true to their faith and despising of heretics, a view that condemned me, like so many of my countrymen, to the fires of hell.

Guido Fawkes came last, signifying his ignoble role as the one who would have struck the match and commenced the conflagration, bringing the kingdom to its knees.

I said he was much changed and he indeed was a different man, not in his voice or appearance so much as in his body, which seemed a poor likeness of its former self. As I have said, he could barely walk and needed help in ascending the platform. There he too was asked if he had words for those assembled.

I expected a long speech from his lips, but there was none. Like his friends, he proclaimed himself a Catholic who had acted to benefit his fellows. He had no family to beg for, at least not one he was prepared to acknowledge. He did not ask for mercy himself. He was a hard, cold man as I had known him, a zealot with a zealot's indifference to mortal concerns. He cared not a fig for life. He declared he would lie down in darkness with a cheerful countenance, trusting in the salvation of God.

It was hard not to admire him for that, given what he faced.

When he was silent and it was clear there was nothing left to do but cut him off, something happened that no one could have foreseen, not even the Earl of Salisbury. In climbing the ladder to where he should be hanged, Fawkes either lost his footing on the rungs or cast himself off of his own free will.

In either case, I watched as he turned and plunged headfirst to the platform below him.

His healthier self might have survived the fall, or might have averted it. There was a rush of officers to get to his broken body, as though this were no accident but an escape attempt that needed to be prevented. But the officers might have taken their time. Fawkes was dead. All could see it. His neck lolled upon his shoulder when he was lifted up by the executioner. The head, presently to be severed, was a useless appendage now to a body already ruined by torture.

Fawkes' unforeseen demise provided no respite from judgement. The throng would not be deprived. His lifeless body was stripped naked, castrated, disembowelled, quartered. His head was struck off with a quick, deft blow that won the applause of the gaping multitude who ever prized efficiency over mercy. Do I sound too much the cynic? What man of reason does not sound so?

All this was done to Guido Fawkes, but by then he was in quite a different world. Howling in hell, I devoutly wished.

47

Fawkes' fall from the ladder, intended or accidental, was a great disappointment to the multitude of observers, who cried out in protest and were not pacified by his being hacked to pieces thereafter. It was, thereby, what we call in the theatre, an anti-climax. The planners of the event had saved Fawkes for last, only to find his performance sadly wanting.

I had seen that happen in the theatre many times. Performance is always a risky business with failure as likely as success.

Cecil bade me stay briefly as the throng disbanded, the detritus of death was removed, and the scaffold was being dismantled. I could hardly deny him, though I had had more violence for the week than I could comfortably stomach. I felt a great need to return to my work, which was something quite different from recording for posterity the details of executions. Of death, savagery, and torture, I might write, but to observe them in life was another matter altogether. Life. My craft. To confuse the two was madness.

And I was not mad, either then or now.

"I have been thinking, Master Shakespeare, of our recent conversation. I mean when you came to the palace and we spoke at length."

"Yes, my lord, as have I. I am most grateful for your concern for me."

He responded with a graceful wave of his hand. "What I wanted to say to you is that Robert Catesby was right."

"Right my lord?"

"Yes, Master Shakespeare, right indeed."

He paused. I was astonished. I waited breathlessly for what Cecil might say, for in our previous exchanges he had nothing good to observe of any of the conspirators, much less of him who conceived of all.

"Catesby told you that yours was an important voice in the kingdom. That your plays had power to influence men for good, or for evil, should you have taken them there. That is, to an evil place."

"True, he did say that, my lord," I answered. "He flattered me outrageously. Yet I did not believe half of what he said, about that or any other matter of which we spoke."

"As I say, he was right about that," Cecil said. "Catesby may have intended to flatter you, to win you to the Papist cause. Still, his intent notwithstanding, he spoke truth to you in regard to yourself. You know not what you are to this kingdom. You are a rare treasure."

I looked at Cecil's face, to see if he was jesting. I concluded he was not. "Oh, I must protest, my good lord. You do me too much honour and teach me to be proud, which I would not be for heaven's sake."

"Nay, sir, His Majesty agrees. You have no title, no significant land. You are not wealthy, though you keep company often with them who are so. Yet the public that comes to your plays, Master Shakespeare, the lords and ladies of the court who see you perform there, all these feel the effect of your words, your thoughts."

I thanked him for this praise, which I confess made my face burn. But I offered no further protest. What could I say? Was it true, this influence he claimed I had on the public? It seemed wrong, exaggerated, but I was not about to contradict the king's chief minister in his convictions. Whatever good my acts had done me in Cecil's mind, I was not about to undo them. I record all this in deepest humility. I do affirm I never wrote but to please myself as well as my audience. If it all amounted to more than that, I have left for others wiser than I to say, and time, the ultimate judge, to prove.

"This is why it is so important that you keep on the right side of things," Cecil continued. "I do mean true religion, obedience to the laws and to the king."

"I study nothing more than to have a loyal heart," I said. "I admire nothing more. God bless King James. I am the king's good servant, and yours too, my lord."

Cecil said, "Catesby would have you serve the cause of Rome, or at least advocate a simple tolerance, which is at the end only another way of supporting the cause and is the very doorway to oppression. With tolerance, Papistry will increase. With its increase the public danger as manifested by this plot will increase. The persecuted will become the persecutor."

Cecil paused. He looked at me as though assessing my agreement to his hard, cold logic. I did not know whether I agreed or no and made some ambiguous nod of my head. He continued.

"It is very simple, you see, Master Shakespeare. We are living in dangerous times. That danger proceeds not only from our native Papists but from abroad. I do mean Spain, who never yet has made peace with regard to our religious right to determine doctrine for ourselves. Wherefore I do beseech you to stay true to the king's cause. Let him have no reason to suspect your loyalty. This I cannot emphasize overmuch. Do you understand me, Master Shakespeare? You have seen this day and yesterday the bitter fruit of treason. How shall I put it? You have smelled the blood on the cobbles."

"I have, my lord."

And I did mean what I said, for I believed my understanding of his words was perfect in that it omitted no implication of his argument. Still, I was unhappy with the promise he had extracted from me. In truth, I have no heart for treason. Left to myself, I am as loyal as an old dog who sits beside his master's chair for all his life and understands well by whom his life is sustained. Yet as a man, when I am compelled to believe, to act, to promise, it is ever a cause of revolt in me. I am too much a lover of freedom to brook a slavish compliance. I hate being coerced. Am I alone in this dislike? I think not.

Still, I knew how to keep my rebellion in check. I am nothing if not an actor. Which is to say, I know how to play a part foreign to my nature. At least Gabriel Catesby and I had that in common.

I had the honour of conversing with Cecil yet another time that month. It was a casual meeting at one of my plays at which he was in attendance. I asked him then about Gabriel Catesby, whether the man still was employed by him to search out Papist conspiracies in the country, or if he might have fled abroad.

"Why would you ask, Master Shakespeare? Why would you care? Do you have aught else against him, some suit at law perhaps?"

"Not so, my lord," I answered, taken aback by his curt response. "I pray you forgive an idle curiosity on my part. Since he and I were old friends before we became enemies, I would gladly know how he does and where in the world he might be."

Cecil answered directly, but with a note of irritation in his voice. "Master Shakespeare, I no longer employ your former friend. I have not seen him since he falsely reported your complicity in the powder treason. He proved a poor spy at last, as faithless to me as to yourself, or to the wretched Guy Fawkes whom he used for his own fell purposes. He had too many hidden agendas to be truly loyal to any man. I know not whether he be alive or dead. I could not care less."

It was unwise to press Cecil further. I saw he was reluctant to speak of Catesby. So be it, I thought. I was myself reluctant to think about him, to remember his works, or even utter his name.

48

Throughout that hard winter my pen burned hot in my hand. I wrote as in a fever, my head full of strange images, my ears full of even stranger voices. My eyes often grew bleary, and I would hold the page close to read for I liked not spectacles for vanity's sake. If there were a playwright in London who worked harder at his craft, I knew him not. As for the King's Men, we plied our trade, sometimes at Whitehall before the king and his friends, sometimes at Blackfriars, to all and sundry. Our dear Globe, open to the sky and winter's cruel fist, was still out of the question in that dark season of the year.

As the King's Men, we stood ready whenever His Majesty should command and, because he loved us, he commanded often. We performed old plays, sometimes new. Most were mine, but not all. It was indeed a marvellous season in which I strove to put behind me the gunpowder plot and its dangers to me and mine.

Thus, did our state and condition improve in all ways. We were much sought after, and for myself I was left alone to do my work. In my few direct communications with the king there was no more talk of the plot. Still, I had an uneasy feeling that the event that had so undone the nation was not yet over. For one thing, Parliament, upon whose acts the Puritan faction had a strong grip, passed more laws to oppress the recusant Catholics. Cecil and Coke, the champions of Protestantism, still railed against the Papists, whom they considered the root of all civil discord and a continuing threat to our happy land, such happiness as we enjoyed. Jesuits were ever being hunted and their protectors prosecuted. Beside which, not all the suspects in the conspiracy had yet been run to ground.

One of these was my host at Holbeche House, Stephen Lyttleton.

Lyttleton had been away when Catesby and the others made his manor house their refuge. Alice Simpkins had affirmed that in her account to me, and many others had done so since. But Lyttleton had consorted with the principals in the plot and that in and of itself was sufficient to incriminate him, as it had been to pull me into the shadow of suspicion.

From that unhappy hour, Lyttleton had been a fugitive, hiding in barns and sheds and dovecots. Finally, he hid himself in his uncle Humphrey's manor, where the master's cook, observing the greater quantity of food requested by his employer, surmised that there were more stomachs to feed than could easily be accounted for. He grew suspicious, cheerfully betrayed his master whom he heartily disliked, and told his tale to the local magistrate. The house was raided, and uncle and nephew were both taken, along with Thomas Wintour, cousin of the Robert Wintour who had been executed before.

Come March, both met their end in Stafford, not far from Holbeche. Their deaths were according to the prescribed manner. I forbear to rehearse the details, for it offends my sensibilities, as I have said.

I heard report of this several weeks after it happened and found myself surprisingly grieved. It was not for Lyttleton, though I held naught against him. He had shown me and my fellows great kindness, and I believed his professed love for my plays was sincere. It was rather sympathy for his young widow, the delightsome mistress of Holbeche, whose charms I had more than once contemplated since my conversation with her.

That winsome lady had been in London visiting her family when the assault upon her husband's Staffordshire manor house occurred. I believe she was ignorant of the conspiracy, or whatever her husband's part might have been. Nor had others charged her. Women often fall victim to their husband's devices, which in their seeming wisdom men keep from their wives lest they raise reasonable objections, as I believe Mistress Lyttleton might well have done. She was, to my thinking, an intelligent woman with a tender heart, whom I would have fain known better. I remembered her kindness to Alice.

Her beauty, too, I remembered, which beauty might have been the subject of a sonnet had I not given over that species of composition for the season. I lamented her dismal future as the widow of a much-despised traitor. What would befall her in after years but the lingering echo of ignominy? At least that is my thought. In truth, I have heard naught of her for the past ten years or more. Perhaps she fled the country, or has died of shame and grief, or married another and, taking his name, obscured thereby her disgrace.

Come June, I planned to return to Stratford to see my long-neglected wife and daughters. At that time, I was in the midst of purchasing more property in my native place, to which I thought to return when I should finally retire from the theatre and its troubles and delights.

Before I left London, however, I resolved to see how Alice Simpkins did in her new abode.

Hearing from Madame Mountjoy that Alice was still living with the Duprees and being courted by the Duprees' eldest son, I undertook to visit her to ascertain her condition for myself. A new life was in store for her by all accounts, and for me this was good news, for I no longer harboured fears that she had murdered her own babe. It had been a wicked thought, that suspicion, harmful to believe, even if it had been true. Which I am convinced, in a less melancholy humour, it was not.

I chose a Sunday afternoon for my visit, when the bakery was closed and the family was at rest. I was greeted amicably by Monsieur Dupree and his wife, and warmly by Alice, who seemed less a child than I remembered her, though she would now be perhaps thirteen or fourteen. Her face had changed. Her eyes now seemed the wiser for her suffering, her cheeks less full. Her demeanour was different too, perhaps because she had fallen in love with a man of eighteen or nineteen and she was rising to his expectations. The wedding was planned for the summer. It was to be held in the French Church, where the Duprees worshipped before a stark altar devoid of Roman embellishment and heard the Gospel in the French of the Parisian streets.

All of us talked, in my tongue and in theirs, over excellent port supplied by Madame Dupree. Afterwards, pleading the need to return to my lodgings to complete some work, I drew Alice aside to speak to her privately, for the younger Dupree children were a raucous brood, forever pulling on Alice's skirts for attention.

"How is it with you, Alice?" I asked.

"Oh very well, sir," she answered brightly and then began to sing the praises of her intended to the degree I imagined him a paragon of every virtue. I had seen the boy, a callow youth with pimples and a low brow. Yet such was young love. I could not fault it with a cynical aside or cautionary tale. How married love would prove she would straightway discover for herself. As do we all.

"Still, I am afraid," she said.

"Afraid of what?"

"Gabriel Catesby."

I might have expected this, yet acted surprised.

"Don't tell me you've seen him again?"

"Only in dreams, sir."

"Ah, dreams. The theatre of our worst fears," I said. "I believe Gabriel Catesby has left the country."

I hoped to comfort her with this assurance, although I had no knowledge that what I said was true. Cecil had allowed simply that Catesby had disappeared. That he was no longer in his employ. A failed spy of the worst sort, Catesby, Cecil had declared. A purveyor of self-interested intelligence and lies.

Still, none of this meant he was not still lurking about somewhere in the city, hatching some new plot against someone, somewhere. Yet I thought it was likely true, his disappearance, and because I could see no reason Catesby would threaten her, it did my conscience no hurt to say what I said.

"Don't worry. He's gone. And if he is wise, he will not return should he be so inclined. His affinity to his cousin, Robert Catesby, will surely damn him in the eyes of the king." I said nothing of my discovery that Gabriel had been a spy. It would only have complicated matters and confused the girl.

I gave her some money, five shillings I think I remember, which I counted out into her soft white palm. "Consider it a wedding present," I said.

She thanked me and said, "We will not be married until midsummer."

"You may use the money when you choose," I said. "And I may return to the city by then, in which case I do pray I may wish you and your husband well on your wedding day."

"We are to be married in the French Church," she said.

"So I have heard."

"It is at the end of the street, next to the grocer's."

"I know exactly where it is," I said. "I have walked by many a day."

I had kissed her soft cheek at my last leave taking. This time I kissed her hand after the French fashion.

The gesture seemed to delight her. She said she was learning French. I wished her luck in that too. It is no easy tongue for an English mouth.

49

The day thereafter I set out for Stratford, riding as always along the road toward Oxford where I was wont to spend the night on my journeys home. I had planned a fortnight's absence from London, which would give me sufficient time to make the near one-hundred- mile ride and have a handful of days in my native place before returning to the city.

The weather was dry for June. I made excellent time along the way and found good lodgings with clean beds and decent food and arrived in Stratford a whole day before I had thought to.

I had written my wife, Anne, of my coming but had received no letter from her acknowledging my intended visit, whether it was welcome or no, convenient or no. Granted she did not write often, or very well. Yet could she scribble some words. She could make her mark. It vexed me that she had not answered.

When I arrived at my Stratford house on Chapel Lane, it was late in the afternoon. It eased my heart to find I was expected. The lack of a response from my wife had awakened fears that something untoward might have happened in my absence, but meeting me at the door and running forward to embrace me even before my horse was secured, my wife said, "Well, husband, we did not think you would be here until Friday at the least, but now it is midweek. Expect no feast for your homecoming, at least not this night of our Lord. It will be simple fare at best. Left over soup, some mouldy bread spared by the rats. A few morsels of cheese. We do live most humbly in your lordship's absence."

She laughed. It was a full, mocking laugh. I knew it well. It had won my heart when we had courted so many years before.

I told my wife that simple fare would do, knowing that I would be fed enough if not royally. Beside which, I was more weary from the journey than hungry.

"You did not answer my letter," I said, trying not to sound reproving.

"No I did not, husband," she snapped. "I am not such as some who are at leisure to brood over a book or scribble upon fine vellum. I have a house to run in my celebrated husband's absence."

I said no more about the missing letter. She berated me no more about my being absent from home. It was a welcome truce. My long London sojourn was ever a tribulation to her. Even in her silence, rebuke ever nestled like a snake.

We had passed into the kitchen of my house and sat at a long table where we ate our meals when only family were present. My wife said, "Good husband, get you washed. You stink of the road and the horse you rode in on. I will break no bread with you in such a state as you are in."

I rose from the table to do as she bade me do. I might be a person of name in London who mingled with kings and earls and other quality, but at New Place I was but a mere husband whose wife, on most occasions, ruled her roost and issued orders freely.

I went obediently to wash myself, though I do think after I still stank of horse at the very least, if not my own acrid sweat. Four or five days on the back of a horse are good for neither beast, nor rider, nor sweetness of air.

The next few days were a pleasant idyll, even as I had hoped. I visited friends and neighbours in the town, who then returned the favour and visited me. I enjoyed my garden, conducted some business about the property I intended to purchase, made love at least six times with my wife to our mutual satisfaction I believe, contended with her as many more on this issue or that, most too trivial to record, and renewed my acquaintance with my daughters, Judith and Susanna, who, like all their age, changed so much it seemed from month to month as to be almost different persons than before.

I visited the graves of my father, and son, Hamnet, and mourned afresh my son's loss. Had the boy lived, he would now have been twenty. Resembling me? Eager for adventure, as I had been? Of a literary turn? Who could know? All love is mixed with sadness, and joy and grief are bound together like an old married couple.

And that's the truth of it.

50

I was well fed before I left Stratford, a homecoming celebration of sorts, or perhaps a leave taking for I love not home and hearth so much as not to miss my city life. I begged my wife to be practical, not invite half the town. She agreed. "You have too many friends here. We cannot fit all at table. Your family may have secured a coat of arms, but it is yet to win a palace that we may entertain royally."

Anne had invited guests to join us, including Stratford's only physician, Doctor John Hall. In a year's time, he would become my eldest daughter's husband. Then, he was a mere family acquaintance and a frequent visitor. Whether my daughter, Susanna, had already set her cap for him I cannot say. At table both seemed shy and diffident. Neither spoke to the other or exchanged long, amorous looks as lovers are wont to do. Besides this, my long residence in London did not promote a close relationship between my daughter and me. Susanna respected me as her father, I believe. But that she loved me for the same reason I cannot prove by aught she ever said or did. Was the fault mine, or hers? Her mother thought it mine. My self-imposed exile from home and hearth, the cause. Perhaps she was right. Yet what father, even though he stays at home always, knows his daughter's deepest heart?

On this occasion, the good doctor was invited to eat, not to heal, although Anne gave me to understand that she had consulted him several instances since his first arrival in Stratford, which was around five years before this time. Since then, his practice had flourished. He had patients both in Stratford and in neighbouring towns and villages and even saw to the needs of the landed gentry in the county, having travelled as far as Manchester to practice his healing art.

At that time, John Hall was a man of about thirty years I should judge, of middle height, thin as a rail, and blessed with a pleasant, kindly disposition that earned him friends as well as patients. He was learned too, no fraud with nostrums, having studied at Cambridge University and received there both a bachelor's and master's degree. He had studied medicine in France. He was well travelled. I loved him well from the first time I met him, and naught he ever did thereafter belied that first impression.

Not every man can say that of his son-in-law. I could not, in all honesty, say it of him my other daughter, Judith, was in time to marry. But let that pass.

With Doctor Hall, Anne had invited to celebrate my homecoming, my good friends Hamnet and Judith Sadler, after whom I had named my twin children. Hamnet Sadler was a baker by trade and a shrewd man of business. He knew all the gossip of Warwickshire and was an excellent player at cards, at which we would sometimes wile away the hours when I was home. He was also a good companion who never held my London years against me, not supposing me, as some did in Stratford, one with superior airs or dissolute from the city's stains.

So then, we were seven at table including of course my younger daughter, Judith, who at that time was about twenty-one and much reminded me of her mother in features and manner, whereas Susanna, alas, took more after me, poor soul.

Judith was, to my knowledge, a virgin, for I had had no ill report of her, nor had her mother. Of Susanna, the same might be said. I hoped it was so.

I should say now that, since I have done so well in London, the servants at New Place have swollen in number. Ten years earlier we had a chambermaid and a cook. Now we have a cook and a scullery maid, a serving man for odd jobs, three chambermaids and a gardener who came thrice a week in growing season and in winter fetched wood indoors for our fires. We paid none of these very much for their labour, but then who in Stratford did?

I have long forgot what was set before us that evening, what we ate or drank. I do remember the talk was all the business of the town. At least at first. Births, deaths, marriages, inheritances, disputes betwixt one family and another. No one asked how I thrived in London or what new plays I had begun or finished. No one asked about the high and mighty with whom I consorted in the normal course of London days. Not even about the king.

I cared not. On that occasion, I wanted not to reflect on the city, but enjoy the business of the country, my beloved native place, and people whose names and histories I knew as well as the back of my hand.

We were in the middle of the second or third course when the talk at table turned to religion. I ever try to avoid that subject while I eat, since there is nothing like a quarrel over God and His Works to cause a bout of dyspepsia or turn old friendships sour. But the contentious theme did not put any of us at table at odds with the other. Surprisingly, it united.

Susanna said that she had been put on a list of persons in the town who had failed to take the Blessed Sacrament at Easter past and was thereby suspected of being a recusant, which she swore she was not. If anything, as well as I could discern, she leaned toward the Puritan side, which I understood was also the inclination of Doctor Hall, a man of religious sensibilities but no crank or zealot. When the Sadlers admitted that they were on the same list, the talk was all whether these accusations ought to cause fear. I argued that they should, mindful still of my near escape from royal condemnation.

"I think it is a fault in your daughter, Master Shakespeare, that can be easily remedied. She need only attend church again soon," Doctor Hall said. "That should pacify the concern of our vicar that she be fully committed to the Anglican communion and has no Roman sympathies nor associations."

Doctor Hall was good friends with our vicar at the time. His opinion in this matter was worth attending to.

Sadler agreed with this, saying that he and his wife had missed the Sacrament at Easter because they had travelled to Norwich that month, where one of their sons resided. They had explained this to our vicar, who straightway took steps to strike their names from the list of offenders.

"We are now counted decent Christians again," Hamnet Sadler said with a laugh. "We shall neither be fined nor defamed in the town. You need not fear we ruin your spotless reputations in Stratford with our presence."

"It would take more than your presence to taint this household," my wife declared. She pointed an accusatory finger at me. "Even my husband's presence here, bringing as he does the evils of London in his wake, is not sufficient to keep us being greeted by our vicar and the town burgesses as respected citizens."

Despite these diverse mitigations, I did not hold back. I said, "This is not a time to take being on such a list as some silly misdemeanour. Do not forget what happened in November in London. How the king and the lords of Parliament were almost murdered. In London there is still talk of the trials and the executions and fears of Spaniards, Jesuits, and even common priests who do no more than hear confessions and say mass in barns."

Sadler said, "We have not forgotten, Will. We in Stratford are not so far afield that we have not heard all this news. Who knows not how the king was spared and thanks God for so great a deliverance? We pray daily for His Majesty and his safety. But we are talking here about having missed communion on Easter, not blowing up Parliament. We are guilty of being lax in our devotion at worst perhaps, not of being embedded in treasonous thoughts and deeds."

I looked at Sadler's serious face. Fearing I had pressed my case too strongly, I said, "My worry is that a good man may be hanged for keeping bad company. Take Robert Catesby, Sir William's son, he who dwelt not that far from this house. Consider how those who befriended him and made up to him have implicated themselves in his plot. Oh, I could tell you stories—"

But the doctor prevented me from going further. He said, "I have been just this week to the house in which Robert Catesby was reared. I know it well. It is in Lapworth. His widowed mother still dwells in the manor and mourns her son and what horrors he intended against the king and the lords. She prays a thousand times a day for his soul and has worn out her rosary beads in her incessant petitions."

The doctor's revelation amazed me. "She is your patient?" I asked.

"Why yes, sir," Hall answered readily. "She and her nephew."

"Nephew?"

I sat forward in my chair and quite forgot about the pudding we had been offered as final testimony to cook's skill.

342

"Yes, Mistress Catesby suffers from a chronic digestive condition," Hall said. "I would give you the symptoms but they are disgusting and might spoil your dinner, Master Shakespeare, which I am loath to do since it is your homecoming we honour."

I assured him my dinner would not suffer from his candour. He named a few symptoms. They were indeed revolting. I told him he need say no more.

We ate the pudding. It was indeed excellent but all I could think of was what Hall had just said about Lady Catesby's so-called nephew.

The servants came to clear the table. The Sadlers bid us all good-night, for they were famous in the town for their early bedtimes, which they claimed promoted health and kept melancholy at bay. When my wife and daughters were out of earshot, I turned my attention again to Hall.

"Tell me, Doctor. You speak of a nephew of Lady Catesby?"

"Ah," Hall said. "That would be Gabriel Catesby. He lives not in the manor but in a cottage in the woods. He and his companion. It is a tumble-down affair, this cottage, unfit for neither man nor beast. And it is deeply concealed. It was the devil to find it, even after Lady Catesby explained how I should come to it, which was no easy task."

"And his companion?" I asked, even more interested now. "Who might that be? Are you speaking of his mother and her sisters, who also live in this same cottage, where as a boy I once was, along with this same Gabriel Catesby?"

"They are all dead these five years. Their graves are behind the cottage deep in bushes, bones now. I have seen them, peeping up in the weeds. I speak of another man, living and breathing."

"And who would that be?" I asked.

"I don't know his name. He never gave it, nor did I ask it of him."

"Gabriel Catesby's servant?"

"I think not," Hall said. "More a friend, an equal by his demeanour."

"Describe him, I pray you."

"Well, Master Shakespeare, I can make the attempt, yet I am not your match in these delineations. I am a physician, no writer."

"I beseech you to make an effort, sir," I said.

"I will, yet I do not understand why it is so important to you."

"It is only because I took him on in our company," I said. "He was destitute. He needed work. He had once saved my life, you see. Many years ago. An old debt, yet one a gentleman feels obliged to honour."

Strange too, that I called myself gentleman at that moment. I rarely did. Yet I ever aspired so to be and had for years. Perhaps that year I had achieved it, so spoke it broadly. My father had his coat of arms. I had taken pains to secure it for him. Gold on a bend sable. A single spear argent. And so forth. Oh, yes, a fancy French motto I had from somewhere: *Non sanz droit*. Not without right. I was his son and heir. William Shakespeare, Gent.

I went on. "Gabriel Catesby proved not so bad an actor, but then did a thing for which we expelled him from our company. He disappeared after the arrest of the gunpowder plotters."

"He was a part of the conspiracy, you mean?" Hall asked, interested himself now, for who is not bewitched by talk of treasons and betrayals, deaths and executions?

"Let us say he was well acquainted with the conspirators," I said. "Gabriel was not a cousin to Robert Catesby but his half-brother, but never acknowledged by the family, although I suspect all knew of it. Gabriel's mother had been a servant in the house. She attracted the eye of the master. An old story, the end of which you can readily imagine, a swollen belly, a birth cry, and another bastard comes into the world."

"Ah, yes," Hall said with a wry grin. "I understand you perfectly and the relationship you describe. But as to this Lady Catesby, twice I have visited her upon her own request and come to her bedside. She is an old woman now, nearing sixty I should think. She is Catholic like her whole family before her. You know, with Papist shrines within the house, and I know not how many prayers to the Virgin each day. I suspect she keeps a priest at hand, although one is never sure of such things. We do not talk of religion, but I am not blind to the signs. The manor house reeks of incense. I would not be surprised if she does not have a priest hidden somewhere within the walls."

"Is the old woman dying?" I asked.

Hall shrugged. "It's likely," he said. "Her health has been wretched a long time. She is world weary and prays to Heaven for release. I give her certain palliatives for her pain, yet promise her nothing in the way of cure. I cannot. I am a physician, not a magician. As for the nephew, he has a more serious malady, connected with wounds he received in the war."

"What war?" I said.

"I think the war in Holland. He fought, he said, for the Spanish. And was in a great many battles in which, according to him, he wielded his sword with such distinction as to win praise of both friend and foe."

I had no recollection of Gabriel ever boasting of his military past. Fighting for Spain? Surely this was Guido Fawkes, not Gabriel. What was the point of Gabriel's lying now? But then perhaps that was the thing about liars. They were like unto industrious spiders that must ever be spinning a web of deceit even when there was no prey in sight, or thought of gain.

"Old wounds sometimes poison the body, as in his case," Doctor

Hall observed, falling now into his professional manner, his voice low and gravelly. "His aunt, Lady Catesby, may live a dozen more years, tough old bird. She may never be well but she might just creep slowly toward death rather than plunge headlong. With Catesby it's different."

"How so?" I asked.

"Alas, poor wretch," Hall said. "Even now he may be dead. When last I saw him he could barely utter a word and was unable to rise from his bed. His aunt arranged for my attendance on his person, paid my fee, though she never came to visit him in his affliction, at least to my knowledge. Strange, do you not think, Master Shakespeare, that the woman should be so distant from her own kin?"

"Her husband's bastard. Not at all strange," I said.

"Yet she took him in, at least she allows him to dwell at the cottage."

Doctor Hall now had all my attention. So my worst enemy was at death's door. He had vanished from London and Cecil's view by returning to his ancient place, the wretched hovel in the woods, which I remembered as well as anything I remembered at that juncture of my youth. I had not forgotten the three old women. Their hideous, bearded faces. Their arcane rituals that so terrified me when I was hardly older than Alice Simpkins was now.

"Tell me of Catesby's companion," I urged again. "I pray you describe him."

"Very well," Hall said. "I put him above six feet. His face is well-shaped, with few if any blemishes. His eyes are clear and green or blue, I do not remember which. His lips are full. His beard is unkempt now, but I believe was not so in the best of his times. And, oh yes, I near forgot, he has an almost woolly hair, black as an Italian's."

346

"I see," I said. "You think too little of yourself, sir. You have a good eye for detail, an excellent quality in a physician. This man, this companion as you call him, I think I know him. He is John Gerard. A Jesuit priest. I do know the man. Though not well, well enough."

Hall expressed no surprise, nor disputed my supposition. He had already said he suspected Lady Catesby of keeping priests in her house. From there it was but a small step to believing that the desolate cottage might also be a refuge. Surely an obscure cottage, be it ever so humble, was better than a priest's hole.

"Shall you be returning to Catesby Hall any time soon?" I asked, endeavouring to suppress my excitement.

"Only if I am bidden," Hall said. "It's too far a ride to make without the assurance of my fee."

I looked at Hall. He was a kindly young man, much admired for his charity. Yet he was no fool. He had a living to make. I approved his practicality. Yet while he might have no reason to revisit the Catesbys, I did, and a compelling reason it was.

I said, "I would very much like to accompany you, Doctor Hall. And if you are concerned about the time and cost of travel, let me allay your fears. I will bear our mutual cost."

"To see Lady Catesby?" Hall asked, looking at me as though I were jesting with him.

"No, sir. To see this nephew you speak of. I have an old score to settle with him."

"You do not mean to kill him I should hope?" asked the doctor, alarmed, even though he was smiling through it.

"No," I answered. "I have not the urge or skill to seek that manner of revenge. Beside which, from what you have said, he has not long to live."

Hall thought for a moment. "Very well, Master Shakespeare. I will tell Lady Catesby that I was in the neighbourhood and stopped to see how she did. She will not question this, for I have visited her before on the same account. But what of Catesby? For that, I should think a more compelling warrant is needed."

"Be assured, sir, I have a plan," I said.

"And what might that be, Master Shakespeare?"

I spoke resolutely. "If we are asked wherefore we have come we shall answer that we are commissioned by Robert Cecil, Earl of Salisbury, to make inquiry into his former servant's health. And inform him of some generous pension his labours have deserved."

"A pension, you say?" Hall's eyes widened in disbelief.

"For certain services rendered to his lordship."

"But will Catesby believe it?"

"Oh, he shall, sir. Upon oath, he shall. If only because he may wish it to be so."

"And are we so commissioned and so empowered?" Doctor Hall asked.

"Absolutely not," I said. "Still, we will affirm we are. I promise you that Gabriel Catesby will never deny his service to the Great Earl. He will, rather, boast of it, for he is a braggart by nature. I do know that of him well enough. He will admit us straightway to his presence if only for the prospect of a handful of silver. Never fear. We shall get in and out again with no danger to ourselves."

"You think so, Master Shakespeare?"

"I know so, good doctor."

"What are you two talking of, you who conspire in corners?" my wife said, coming back into the room. She eyed me suspiciously.

"Oh, grave matters," I said.

"Oh, and what such matters might these be, husband? God's

348

judgement on the wicked I warrant, the death of kings, or the end of the world?"

"Yes, just such matters," I said.

As it turned out, my grand stratagem was never needed, yet it seemed to give the good doctor comfort. Me as well.

51

The distance from Stratford-upon-Avon to Warwick being some eight miles, and from thence to Lapworth almost as many more, weather permitting and well-mounted, we might make our journey in two hours or less.

So was my intent, at least.

As it turned out rain fell in heavy sheets as if Heaven itself admonished us to turn again home. Soon, our path became a sea of mud so that, while we left Stratford at dawn, we did not draw near Lapworth until nearly noon. Our horses were tired, and my physician companion and I were as thoroughly wet as though we had fallen into the sweet-flowing Avon.

The night before we had laid our plans with the care of conspirators, which I suppose we were in truth, for I shared nothing with my wife or daughters about the expedition, thinking the less they knew the better. Explaining my long and tortuous relationship with Gabriel Catesby to them would have been difficult, if not impossible. Besides, I feared it would subject me to my wife's censure. She surely would think me a fool for having provided Gabriel so convenient a means of undoing me. Not only me but putting my family also in peril from the strictures of the law.

The plan as I conceived it was for Hall to go directly to the manor house, present himself to whichever servant his knocking summoned and tell the man he had come at Lady Catesby's behest. Hall assured me that any of the servants had seen him often enough that none would think little untoward in his sudden appearance.

As for Lady Catesby, Hall said her memory was as fragile as her body. He thought it unlikely she would deny sending for him. He would then proceed to examine her, as though the purpose of the visit were no more than that and, in the course of so doing, discover if the cottage was still occupied by her nephew, his friend, or both men. I did hope the latter was the case. Whilst Hall did all this, I was to conceal myself in the woods nigh to the manor and wait his report.

This I did, finding a dry place beneath some trees where I could observe the front of the manor.

Whilst I waited, my thoughts were entirely on Gabriel Catesby and his companion who, I was now convinced, was Father Gerard, if Hall's description was true. I imagined the confrontation that I intended wherein I should reveal to him my conversations with Cecil and denounce Catesby as a duplicitous spy whose master had disavowed him for his incompetence more than his disloyalty.

As for Father Gerard, whom I also expected to find in the cottage, I knew him to be a fugitive from the law himself. Cecil had told me this. Fathers Telemond, Davis, and Gerard, a treasonous triumvirate, as Cecil viewed them, as guilty as the principals in the conspiracy. I had every belief that in the moral contest between us I should enjoy the higher ground.

Of Gerard, I had no fear. Whether he was as deep in the powder plot as Cecil believed and surely hoped, I was in doubt. But my time with him at Holbeche House had persuaded me he would present no physical danger to me.

As for Gabriel, his threat was considerably diminished by the decrepit state Hall had described. I imagined the conversation to come, his surprise at my sudden appearance, the confusion at how my charges might be answered. I wrote a script for each actor in my head. I revised and revised again. In truth, I laboured more on this imagined conversation to come than I had on scenes in some of my plays.

The rain stopped, but the sky remained dark and ominous. I waited some hours, ate an apple and drank port wine my wife had packed for me. After a time when Hall did not return, I grew concerned, gave over fancy's flight and began to worry about the doctor. What kept him? Had his ruse been discovered and he placed in custody as a suspicious person, a housebreaker or an interloper?

Within the hour, Hall emerged from the house, walked to where he had tied up his horse, mounted and headed toward my hiding place.

Almost at once he began his report.

"First, I was made welcome when the servant saw who I was. He did not know that his mistress had not summoned me, and allowed me in without question, keeping me at the entrance for nearly a quarter hour while he described his own aches and pains. For these he sought my counsel, which gladly I gave to make my appearance the more plausible. He seemed to think that what his mistress might pay me for my attendance upon her would also cover his own treatment."

He laughed, then grew serious. "I became a doctor to do good, not to impoverish myself with unrewarded labour."

"You did see her at last?" I asked.

"I did indeed," Hall answered. "After my talk with him the servant took me upstairs to where she lay in her own private chamber, which is in the back parts of the house and very grand for a country manor.

I found her seated by the fire, complaining of the cold, just below a portrait of her late husband, Sir William, a fine-looking gentlemen if the artist aimed at a true likeness and not mere flattery."

"He was a handsome gentleman by all accounts. I remember him spoken of in my youth. My father knew of him and once the two exchanged gifts."

I thought of the gloves my father had made for the knight. I remembered the document Sir William had given my father in return. A Catholic testament of faith, an oath of spiritual allegiance. My father had signed the oath. Now it can be said. I myself saw him do it.

Afterwards, he swore me to secrecy. The testament was somewhere hidden in New Place, or so my father had assured me sometime before his death. I resolved upon my return to find it and destroy it, for safety's sake. I believed in so doing I would not offend my father. Was he not now and these past years with the angels? He could not care more for earthly testaments of his faith, now that he stood before Heaven's throne to declare it.

"Did you ask her about her nephew and his friend?" I said.

"I did. She said her nephew had improved. She said that he was walking again, although with difficulty. I was surprised. I thought him near death on his last visit. She said my medications had helped him gain strength, but for the most part she attributed his recovery as she called it to the miraculous intervention of the Virgin Mary. She told me she prayed every hour for her nephew. She is a very pious woman."

"Then Gabriel remains at the cottage?"

"She said nothing of him having gone elsewhere, even were he able."

"His companion as well?" I asked.

"His constant companion. Lady Catesby said she herself never left the house. She did not have the strength, she said."

"Then I shall find them there," I answered, both relieved and also unnerved at the prospect. My fear must have been written plainly on my face.

"Should I not accompany you?" Hall asked.

"I think not," I said. "Get you to the village. There's an inn there where we can stay for the night. Secure a room for us and wait for me. My business here will be quickly done."

Hall looked worried, but I assured him all would be well. "I know both men," I said. "I know of what they are capable and what not. Trust me, doctor, I will be in no danger."

"Can you find your way to the cottage?"

"It lies not far from here. I believe I remember the path," I said, with more confidence in my voice than I felt, yet it was for me to confront these men, not Stratford's doctor.

I confess I felt some trepidation as I watched my companion ride away. He looked back once at me, perhaps to see if I had changed my mind about his remaining with me. Another pair of arms and hands in case of trouble. A witness to whatever was said.

I had half a mind to call him back.

But it was only half a mind, which left me little mind remaining to repent of my false courage.

By now the doctor was beyond hailing.

52

I guided my horse carefully through the underbrush, an experience that reminded me of my escape from Holbeche House some months before. In time, I came to the cottage, which was more overgrown with nature's verdure than I remembered. It had been, after all, many years since I had last seen that cursed place.

Smoke rose in a thin column from the chimney in front of which Gabriel's mother and her sisters had once performed their unhallowed rites and offered their dark prophecies. I thought of the three creatures now. Hall said they were dead, but I half expected them to emerge from the trees about me and curse me for invading their former domain. Had I been Papist, I should have cried out to some saint to protect me. Being as I was not, and ignorant of which saint protected the living from the dead, I whispered the sacred name of God's son, hoping that it would be a sufficient protection from whatever evil lay ahead of me.

I left my mount tied to a tree and was about to approach on foot when a man appeared at the door and then walked slowly into the clearing before the cottage.

It was not Father Gerard. This man was nothing like. I supposed it must be Gabriel. I drew back. Of a sudden, I was afraid. I forgot about the damp and my wet clothing, and fixed my attention on this person who was not Gabriel, although he resembled him in stature and in the shape of his face and the cut of his beard. He resembled him indeed. But he was not the man I thought to find there.

No, it was not Gabriel Catesby.

It was a ghost I saw, a revenant. Not Gabriel, but his so-called cousin, his half-brother.

Robert Catesby stood before me. Afflicted, aged before his time, pale of visage like Banquo's ghost in my Scottish play.

Still, none other than Robert Catesby, he who had conceived of the gunpowder plot and whose severed head was fixed upon a pole in London.

Or so it was thought by me and all the world.

Now was I struck beyond help, feeling my very bones and sinews weakened and all thought blasted. Surely this was a ghost, the first I had ever seen, though not the first I had created in my imagination, and as I watched the dead man limp forward then stand unsteadily in the clearing, I held my breath and drew back even further for fear he would see me, for I supposed that to be seen by such a spirit must at least be as perilous as my seeing one.

It went through my mind then that this revenant was a thing conjured up by Gabriel's mother before she died. It would have been like her to raise an evil spirit to taunt and harass the living, to do to others as she had been done by. But then I thought again. I could conclude nothing but that this was a spirit, for I had seen Catesby's body, or at least the head thereof, with my own eyes.

In the next moment a second man emerged from the door and called to the first. "Robin, for Jesu's sake, come inside. You are not well enough to go out in such weather."

It was Father Gerard. Him I recognized at once. His face and voice were the same that I had known at Holbeche House. That he had called out the name of this creature only confirmed the identity of the ghost. Robert Catesby, in the flesh.

I revealed myself of a sudden, emerging like some wild beast too long pent up, noisily, with cracked twigs and snapping branches, stumbling forth in hopeless confusion toward Catesby's ghost.

To any observer, I must have seemed deranged. And perhaps I was at that instant. Surely, I was not in possession of myself.

Ghost and his priestly counsellor looked up startled, their eyes wide with surprise.

"Master Shakespeare, is that you indeed?" the priest asked, as Catesby's ghost looked upon me with dead eyes, his pale, dead lips pressed together as though sewn shut to keep his mouth from gaping.

Struck dumb, I could not answer, but nodded my head.

A few seconds passed. Then Gerard said, "I must bring my friend indoors again. You can see he is infirm. Come in yourself, Master Shakespeare. I know not by what ill wind you have discovered us or for what purpose, but here you stand. Still, Christian charity compels me to bid you come where there is a fire to warm you. I suppose you are full of wonder, or at least curious as to what you see before you. I pray you enter, sir."

"I will," I said, capable of speech at last, despite my gasping at air.

With that, Gerard went toward the ghost, took it by the arm, and led it within the cottage.

It went through my mind then that I should flee, that the time to do so was now if I were to flee at all, but curiosity overcame my terror. I was beguiled by the manifestation before me, and therefore helpless to escape it. I followed, fearing what I might find inside the wretched hovel besides what I had already seen years before.

Within, the cottage was the same as when its denizens were the three witches of my memory. I was astonished at how little had changed there.

Until that moment, the ghost had not spoken. I wondered if it could. Perhaps that was the state of the dead, deprived of tongues to utter either blessings or curses upon the living such as I. Yet I could hear the ghost breathing, see its chest rise and fall. The sight repelled me.

We three took chairs by the fire. The same crudely wrought chairs Gabriel and I had sat in when his mother and her sisters were the occupants of the cottage. The fire's warmth did little to appease my troubled spirit or dispel my horror of this cursed place and my present company.

"Are you in God's truth Robert Catesby?" I asked, no longer able to withhold the question that burned within me. "Or are you his ghost?"

Catesby said nothing. He continued to stare at me, an unwelcome intruder in yet another hiding place.

Then Gerard answered. "This is indeed Robert Catesby, Master Shakespeare. Yes, he who is thought to be dead. He is no ghost or spirit that you should fear him, but a living soul who has come to recognize his faults and repent of them that he may stand before his God without reproach."

He nodded toward Catesby, who seemed content to let his confessor speak for him.

I tried to take this in, to understand what I was being told, unable to keep my eyes off the dead man, or the man I now understood to be alive. I asked then how that could be, that one thought to be dead was alive. At that moment, it was my only question.

Then Catesby proved himself capable of speech. He who was before dumb as stone, now proved voluble. He spoke in a low, dry voice weakened by obvious pain and long festering injury.

"I see you wonder how this all could be, Shakespeare. It's simple.

358

sir. I escaped, as you can plainly see. When the men came to arrest me, I received several wounds by their marksmen. The dead man thought to be me was in truth another, someone else. We created an illusion, you see. Somewhat as you do in your theatre. Do think of it as a performance of sorts, a kind of show, that which allows me to sit with you at this table conversing, though thought dead by all the world."

"The man thought to be you was your half-brother Gabriel," I said, the truth coming suddenly into my head as though by some divine inspiration.

For a moment Catesby did not answer. Then he nodded. His lips parted in a ghastly smile.

I knew not whether this man was more horrible alive or dead.

At that Catesby began to cough, drawing up from ruined lungs a string of phlegm. He was seized by this fit until I thought he would topple from his chair. Father Gerard, standing, supported him until the seizure passed. Catesby wiped his mouth on his sleeve. Gerard sat back down.

When Catesby spoke again, he spoke slowly as though every word he uttered was at terrible cost, or as though all were being written down by some hidden scribe for generations to come and, therefore, he must speak slowly and deliberately so as not to outpace the scribe who recorded him.

I thought of how the king had hidden behind the curtain while I spoke to Cecil. Was there a silent witness to this revelation? There was no curtain in this wretched hovel. No curious king to eavesdrop and mark my every word. No other spy to confirm this revelation of appalling deception.

"You have come a long way to find me, Shakespeare," Catesby said. "As you can see, I have escaped death at Holbeche House only to find it here, in my native place. There is no point in my not telling you all my story, if you will suffer it from my lips. Father Gerard, my good friend, has confessed me. You might as well do likewise."

"I am no priest to hear confessions," I said. "I cannot absolve you of your sins."

"True," he said weakly. "You are no priest, but you are a man. Will you give heed, sir? You are a writer of stories, are you not?"

"A writer of plays," I answered.

"Is it not much the same? In any case, I think you will consider my story worth your while."

But he had collapsed in the chair again. His eyes were shut. Had I been more charitable to the man I would have insisted he rest and not speak, for he was struggling I could tell and his pale brow was moist with sweat.

I leaned forward, my hands on my knees, and looked into that ruined face, made more repellent by its deathly pallor.

"I will hear your confession gladly, Master Catesby. But I beseech you to tell me a true story. We have dealt with fiction overmuch this past half year with I know not how many false identities and subterfuges. It is time for truth, which has been kept waiting too long in the wings to come forth."

"I will tell you the truth, sir," Catesby said. "At least I will have confessed and who knows but that it will work to put things right with my God, though I may never do so with my king."

53

This is how we conversed, the two of us, a man not dead but dying, and I, a witness to it all, a recorder of secret history.

Robert Catesby took a deep, raspy breath, then spoke with great difficulty as before.

"First, Shakespeare, I will tell you about Gabriel. He was as you know no cousin but the son of my father, Sir William. Gabriel's mother was a servant in our house. It is said she was quite beautiful when he first had her. You saw her as she was later in her life. No beauty to admire then when evil had worked upon her body as evil will."

"All this I know, Master Catesby," I said, resisting the temptation to suggest that evil had done its work on his own body well enough.

"Of course you do. You knew my bastard brother. Gabriel ingratiated himself with me just as he had with you until we both discovered the depth of his dishonesty and depravity."

"He violated a chambermaid in the Lyttleton household," I said. "She was no more than a child. He also conveyed false facts to the Earl of Salisbury implicating me in your plot, about which you yourself might testify I knew nothing."

He raised a hand to acknowledge the truth of this. "Gabriel betrayed us as well. It was he who sent a letter to Lord Monteagle, a man with whom he had had some dealings, warning him to stay away from Parliament on that day. An attempt to ingratiate himself, I think, with the great and powerful, something he always lusted after. Monteagle took it to Salisbury and from there it went to the king himself, without which our plan would have been carried out and England might even this day have been saved from heresy. When we learned of it, we treated him as he deserved."

"You murdered him?"

"How Gabriel died is nothing that would interest you, Shakespeare, and because it was not by my hand that he was killed I will not betray him who did it."

"And your own wounds?" I asked.

"By fire and musket ball," he said. "I took two balls when the sheriff's men attacked the house. My plan of escape came to me in an instant. Not as a divine revelation, you understand, but as memory. Gabriel and I did, as you know, favour our common father. We would not have been taken for twins, but brothers, yes. After he was dead—"

"Murdered, you mean?"

"Your word, Shakespeare. I prefer *executed*."

"After Gabriel was dead, you were saying."

"I took the crucifix I was wont to wear about my neck and put it on his. I laid in his hands a miniature of Our Lady that was ever in my possession and which I was well known to wear and venerate."

He paused for moment, overcome with another fit of coughing so extreme in its violence that I felt the pain of it in my very bosom, for now his unkempt beard was covered with dark spots of blood. The man was sick indeed, and probably unto death, as Doctor Hall had surmised.

"I made my escape, leaving my bastard brother in my place, which place he had always coveted."

"A clever plan worthy of admiration," I said, "this most convenient substitution, though I do not approve its purpose. You said memory was your help, not divine revelation."

He tried to laugh, but it was more a choking than laughter.

"You, sir. It was you, Shakespeare. I mean it was your very idea. I pray I do not offend in borrowing it for my own."

Here I could not stay silent. I began to protest this strange and quite unexpected accusation that I should have been somehow a part of his deception.

He raised a hand to silence me. "Patience, Shakespeare. I said I would explain all, and so I shall. You asked me once if I had ever seen your plays. I said only one. You did not ask which. I will tell you now. It was *Measure for Measure,* a play I much enjoyed and from which I learned much, without which it would indeed be my head upon the pole in London and not Gabriel's."

"I do not understand you," I said. "My play is about corruption and malfeasance in office, not treason. My characters—those who are good men, good women—are caught up in a web of lechery and unjust laws."

"And the men who are not good, Ragozine, for example?"

"What of him? He's hardly more than a name in my play. He is spoken of, that is all."

"Still," Catesby said. "I owe him much, and more to him who created him. Though you gave him no lines to speak you gave him death that I might live."

"Ragozine?"

"The notorious pirate in your play, conveniently dead of a fever."

Catesby had said enough. I saw now what he meant. What he

had done. In *Measure for Measure*, Ragozine is a fellow prisoner of Claudio, whose condemnation for getting with child his betrothed is at the play's very heart, for although the condemnation is lawful, yet it is unjust. When Ragozine dies, the duke, disguised as a priest, directs Ragozine's head to be severed and uses it to prove to the corrupt and tyrannical Angelo that his orders for Claudio's execution have been carried out.

The deception saves Claudio's life.

It is, I grant, a deception that strains belief, for some at least. But yet the play is what it is, a play, not a true history of facts and men who lived and breathed. Catesby's substitution of Gabriel for himself I must allow was much more plausible.

So it was true what Robert Catesby had claimed. For all my protests of innocence, I had unwittingly become confederate in his escape by suggesting its means. My play had become his script. He had cunningly followed it.

"I told you once, Master Shakespeare, that your influence went far beyond mere entertainment but instructed in many ways. You may have thought I meant only to flatter you. But I spoke truly. I owe you my life, sir."

We sat silently for a while, he struggling for breath, I letting the truth settle in and striving to make peace with it. Then I said, "Through the passage, the tunnel, you escaped? The one behind the panel?"

"Yes."

I remembered Alice's story. How she had seen a light in the passage. She had thought it a miracle. But it was Robert Catesby's light she had seen, not God's. Catesby had escaped before her. Had she hurried, she might have caught up with him and seen that he was a mere mortal, like unto herself.

Catesby said, "You knew about the passage then?"

"I myself used it when the sheriff made an earlier raid upon the house, finding neither me nor Father Gerard where we hid. But why were the sheriff's men so sure it was you who lay dead and not your brother?"

"Ah, the butler Templeton swore it was my body that lay dead. I gave the old man money to say so, believing that what he might not do for love of me or God, he might do for filthy lucre. His identification of the body, Gabriel's scarred and blackened face, and the crucifix and the picture of the Blessed Virgin, were tokens enough for the sheriff, who wanted more than anything to have it known he had killed the traitor."

I asked him where he went after his escape.

"I walked for miles, weakened by my wounds. I came at last to a farmer's hovel, where I gave him three shillings for his plough horse. He was glad enough for the money. He was very poor, you see. Also, he was a good Catholic, although I never told him who I was."

He paused, as though seeing again the place and moment he described. Then he continued, smiling slightly as before, proud of himself and his cleverness and his deceit.

"The farmer thought perhaps I was merely another wayfaring Christian. Or maybe a priest in flight from the king's men. In any case, to me he was the very Good Samaritan of which the Scriptures speak. God will reward him more than I ever could.

"I rode the horse for three or four days, mostly at night, until I came here. My poor mother was horrified by my wounds, especially my face."

He paused at this, reached up to touch, almost caress, the ruined flesh the powder had burned. Then he continued.

"I was weak from hunger, my pain was agonizing, and already I was sick unto death. More horrified still for she had learned of my part in the plot, which rather than raise the rebellion I had sought, brought the burden of infamy down upon my shoulders and, as she complained, disgrace to the family."

"How came you to this wretched place when you might well have enjoyed the comfort of a bed in the manor house?"

Catesby said, "Alas, my mother refused me a place in the house and sent me here instead. Still, her motherhood prevailed over moral outrage. Against my will she had a doctor from Stratford come to minister to me. Like most physicians he did little good. I was too far gone, you see. My wound had become corrupted. The doctor tried compresses and herbs. I know not what other medications. Then there was this pestilent cough, which has grown worse this past month and more of a curse than my wound. I fear, nay hope, it will be my end. I am too much a son of the Church to take my own life. Therefore, do I leave my end to God's own good time."

"Where had you planned to go?" I asked.

"To France, to Spain. I have friends on the coast. Had I strength I would be there now, enjoying the sun. Perhaps being congratulated on the very attempt to reverse the course of my country's miserable history. Not every Englishman hates me, you know. To some, I am a hero."

"You are unrepentant then, despite what Father Gerard said?"

I turned to look at the priest, who seemed determined to be a silent witness to these proceedings.

"Unrepentant?" Catesby asked. "Wherefore should I repent?"

"You committed murder."

It was the third time I had accused him of this. His eyes flared. His chin jutted in a gesture of defiance. He looked sick unto death, yet there was still spirit in him.

"I feel no guilt for my dead half-brother, if that is what you mean, Shakespeare. He took my place. Which place he had always coveted.

366

That he should have achieved his desires in his death is an irony I regret not at all. I contemplate it daily now, with more satisfaction than you can imagine." He smiled grimly.

"I was thinking of your plan to kill the king, his sons, the lords of the Parliament. You plotted the kidnapping of the Princess Elizabeth."

"All I did, all I conceived, I did so for Holy Mother Church. I wore my crucifix about my neck near all my life, Shakespeare. I never dishonoured that holy image. I never betrayed my fondest wish. If I had only succeeded, history would remember me as a hero of the faith. Perhaps even as a saint."

"You worked no miracles for sainthood," I said, more forcibly than I had intended. My sympathy for the man's suffering was declining beneath my distaste for his pride, his vanity, which in the pious is ever more contemptible than any in the common rout of men. "You seem confident, Master Catesby, that having confessed to me the truth of your recent history I will not presently convey the same to my lord of Salisbury. Were I to do so, you should be straightway arrested, sir. And you shall suffer the fate of your fellow conspirators."

Catesby made a gurgling noise at this threat that might have been laughter had he the strength for it. He had worn himself out in the telling of his strange story. Still in his pained eyes was the look of derision, even contempt.

"Oh, Shakespeare, Shakespeare. With all due respect to your vaunted authorship, you are not thinking clearly. Do you not understand me, sir? You will say nothing. What I have told you is for your ears alone, that you might be satisfied as a reward for your persistence and for your—may I say it?—modest contribution to my efforts."

I did not tell him how discovering his presence in Warwickshire was an accident and that had I not known Doctor Hall I would never have discovered his false death.

I said, "I still do not understand your confidence, Master Catesby. I may speak to whomever I will."

"It is simple, sir. Were I to be taken, I would easily say that you helped convey me here. That you have been here before, even to this wretched hovel, is a matter of record, which you will not be able to deny. I should say that you were privy to all plans and in secret sympathy with the Catholic cause. As was your dear father."

"The lie would not be believed," I said.

"Perhaps not. The Earl and his friends at court may affirm your innocence against my testimony. Or they may not. My question to you is whether you are willing to take that risk. Are you a gambling man? When you entered yon door, you came within the web of my so-called transgression. Whereby you are a partner in my crime, whether you will or no."

I stood and looked down on the man, racked by sickness and pain. He was a good ten years younger than I by my reckoning. Now he seemed much older. A wicked old man with devious thoughts overlaid with delusions of pious grandeur. His eyes were coals of hatred. The duplicity I sought to understand in his bastard brother, I now found in him. He was descended from honourable stock. What had happened to him, to his half-brother, that they should have become what they were?

"I will not wish you well, Master Catesby, wherever you are going, to Heaven or to Hell," I said. "But I will bid you adieu."

"You will not report me then, or what I have confessed to you?"

"Only if I must to protect myself, or my family."

"I will trade my silence for yours, and my safety which I now put into your hands," Catesby said.

"Do you swear it?" I asked.

"On my hope of Heaven."

"And have you, Catesby, such hope, after all you have done?"

He did not answer but stared off toward the doorway which had stood uncovered during the time of our conversing, as if he saw someone standing there, watching us whilst we conversed.

Who might it have been, this watcher? One of the men whom he had seduced into joining him in his traitorous enterprise and was now truly dead? Some servant from the manor house? Some stranger wandering in the wood as wet and cold as I?

Or perhaps, I thought, the Devil himself, for I felt all about me the noxious stench of him.

It was dark when I came to the inn where the doctor waited, an inn called the Lion and the Lark with crudely painted figures on its sign, figures that resembled neither creature.

Seeing me bedraggled and distraught, Hall was at first alarmed. Perhaps he thought I had been assaulted during my visit with his former patient or somehow infected with the disease from which the man suffered.

I assured him I was unharmed, that all was well with me.

Neither was true. I had been harmed, at least in my mind, and sickened in my soul for the discovery of Robert Catesby's perfidy and for the grand imposture that had been visited upon us all. That this malicious creature should escape his just deserts was anathema to me. That he should not avoid heaven's wrath offered me no consolation, I confess it.

Then Hall wanted to know if the old friend I had sought had indeed been the man he had strived to heal in the cottage.

"Not exactly," I said.

"He was not your friend, then?" the doctor asked. "Not Lady Catesby's nephew?"

"Neither her nephew nor my friend," I said. "It was some other in the cottage, a dying man, a poor wretch who did but resemble him, and his companion, a Papist priest named Gerard."

Hall nodded, then looked concerned. "Perhaps I should go to him."

"I doubt it will do much good," I said. "He that is dying hath no need of a physician but of a priest, which he indeed has. Besides, he is a mere ghost of a man. If he lives until morning, it will be a wonder."

Hall looked dismayed at my response. "I am surprised you do not have more compassion for the dying, Master Shakespeare."

"Not this dying," I said. "Father Gerard will administer the last rites. Let him perform his office. I am done with both these fellows."

Let the dead bury the dead, I thought.

In the morning the doctor and I rode back to Stratford. We talked little along the way, I buried in my thoughts of the man I had thought to be a ghost but was in truth only an imposter; the doctor's mind, I suspect, fixed upon my daughter, although perhaps I gave him too little credit. He was a serious man, dedicated to the sick and dying, or on his hope of heaven, being as he was of a religious turn. To another's true thoughts, we all are deaf and blind. So was I to his.

I remained in Stratford with my family for a few more days before returning to London, a little longer than I had intended. During that time, I settled my business about the purchased property to my satisfaction, and even became closer to my daughters, especially Susanna. I suspect my growing friendship with the doctor had something to do with that. She saw it and approved. Which only persuaded me the more that something was afoot betwixt them.

I told my wife what I had observed and what I predicted as the happy outcome.

She laughed. "Oh William, you are just noticing that, you who are so celebrated for your knowledge of the human heart?"

I said, "They did conceal their mutual love for a long season."

"Ha, husband, from you perhaps, but not from me."

"Well, it is a wise man who knows his own child," I sighed.

"Yes, husband, but a rare woman who does not," Anne said.

My wife must ever have the last word.

54

Returned to London, I passed my first night amid familiar surroundings, in my own untidy chamber in Monsieur Mountjoy's house, grateful for the solitude, which blessed peace I had not enjoyed for a fortnight. Before, however, I paused by the Parliament building to stare up at what all the world thought to be the severed head of Robert Catesby.

The ghastly thing was now almost all blackened by soot from the bad city air. Had some miscreant stolen it and replaced it with a wooden block, who could have told the difference?

"Gabriel Catesby," I said beneath my breath. "You envious, duplicitous fool, you fool."

Then I thought of Alice Simpkins, whom he had ravished.

Later that same day, I found her tending to the children at the Duprees' house, by all signs content with her lot. Her face grew bright as she saw me standing in the doorway, and then she looked at me as though to ask why I was there.

"I bring you good news, Alice."

Her face brightened the more. "Oh, Master Shakespeare. Pray what news might that be?"

"Tell me, do you still dream of the man who hurt you so?"

I think the directness of my question caused her heart to fail her. She shuddered. All colour left her cheeks.

"Sometimes, sir. Still when I have such dreams I pray."

"Prayer is good," I said. "But I have news that will free you forever from such dreams."

"And what would that be, Master Shakespeare? I would gladly know such news."

"You may rest easy. The man you feared is dead."

"You have heard this news?"

"Heard things, yes. More important, I have seen his body for myself, or at least what remains of it. In truth, he has been dead for some time."

"But, Master Shakespeare, I am sure I saw him in the street, that time I told you of."

"Perhaps that was his ghost, then. I swear Gabriel Catesby is dead."

I might have added that he would ravish no more children, betray no more friends, defame no more innocents.

"He is no more a danger to you, or to any woman. My oath upon it."

Nor was he a danger to me, I thought, either as living man or ghost.

I blessed her and gave her money. It was near all I had in my purse. I doubted I would see her again. Her part in my story had ended, as had my part in hers. God willing, she would have a good life, have more children, grow old with her young husband, stand clear of villains and traitors.

55

A month beyond that very day I hold a letter from John Hall, telling me Lady Catesby is dead. She had been ill a long time and, Hall wrote, her death is a blessing. He thought I should know.

He also said that the inhabitants of the cottage, whom I had visited, had vanished. The cottage stood empty, decaying, dissolving into the woods. He mentioned that fact in passing, almost apologizing for it since in his mind our journey to Lapworth had been futile, the lone occupant not being he whom I had expected to find there.

He said he was sorry for my disappointment. The fruitless journey.

I could never tell the doctor the truth, which was that the journey there was a revelation of that which few, if any, in England were aware, or would be aware.

Finally, he mentioned my daughter, Susanna, and the business which I do believe was the real burden of the letter.

It was as I had foreseen and my wife, Anne, before me, as she had been at pains to point out. A happy event in a wicked season. Hall asked for my daughter's hand in marriage.

Well, it would be a good match, I thought. Hall was a competent doctor, a decent man. He would be an able provider for my daughter and any grandchildren to come. It would be good to see Susanna settled in her own home with a good man who was no extremist in religious matters, but sane in his beliefs and practice.

I replied to his letter straightway, giving my consent and promising a generous dowry.

Later that day, passing by Parliament House, I thought of Robert Catesby again. *Vanished*, the doctor's letter had said. A curious word, all things considered, *vanished*. To the life to come or to some covert place in France or Spain, to live out his life a celebrity among the faithful? Or like a ghost, concealed in the obscurity of some monastery, under yet another false name, praying to the Virgin in blissful indifference to his monstrous plot?

Then as I stared upward at the decaying head, I heard my name called behind me. I turned to find Doctor Forman advancing upon me in great haste. His eyes were alight with interest, or perhaps amusement. He was, as I have said, a strange man of stranger manners, a human enigma. To read his expressions with any confidence was never easy.

He called to me. "My dear Master Shakespeare. I do fear I owe you an apology."

"An apology, sir?" I said, taken aback by this unexpected contrition. "If so, I know not wherein you might have offended. Remind me, I pray you, what is it you did or did not do that I should forgive you?"

"Herein is my fault," he said, catching his breath, his ugly face suddenly composed. "You asked me some time ago if I would determine the trustworthiness of this friend of yours, this Gabriel Catesby. I never answered. Not deliberately did I fail, Master Shakespeare, but negligently. I confess your charge slipped my mind entirely until yesterday when I recalled your visit to my house, October last I think it was, and my promise. Since that time, I have studied my charts, cast this Catesby's horoscope and determined thereby his fidelity."

"Have you indeed?" I asked, a little amused myself since the question of Gabriel's fidelity was now well settled in my mind. Besides which, the head of the very man we spoke of was now staring eyelessly down at us, although Forman did not know that. At the least I believe he did not, for what powers might be possessed by such as he I am not certain.

I asked, "And what is your learned opinion, your verdict upon the man?"

Forman broke into a triumphant smile. "Ah, assurance, Master Shakespeare. I bring you assurance. Very good news."

"Nothing can be more welcome. Pray tell me," I asked.

"Gabriel Catesby is indeed a man to be trusted. Your suspicions are unfounded. I pray you can make it up to him insofar as he was aware of your distrust. You may have caused offence to him and to God in bearing a false witness."

"He was aware of my distrust," I said. "But, regrettably, I cannot ask his forgiveness. He is, you see, quite dead and gone. I can ask forgiveness of God, if I misjudged the man."

"That is regrettable," Doctor Forman said, shaking his head. "But such is life, Master Shakespeare. Or death, I should say in this instance. We err in our estimation of others, and then find there is no means of seeking forgiveness for our misjudgement."

"Alas, so true, sir. So true," I said, feigning remorse and at the same time trying to stifle my laughter.

The truth is, and was, that I have never put great faith in horoscopes or prognostications. So much of it is the purest twaddle, the excretions of an idle mind. Call me a cynic, if you will. Call me an atheist even with respect to the heavenly bodies and their influence upon us mortals. For I hold man's ills are rooted in his own nature and nurtured by his choices, which becoming habit, then make the man himself, directing him up or down, towards heaven or towards hell

But I beg your pardon. I wax philosophical. Worse, perhaps, even theological, a thing for which I have no gift.

I thanked Doctor Forman for his service.

We went our separate ways.

And then I remembered Gabriel's mother and her prophecy that her son should die a malefactor's death. Her prophecy had come to pass. I felt a chill in my flesh and then a strange elation. Might her prophecy regarding me be my fate? It was a curious thing to consider, but then I decided it was too fantastical to believe—that I should achieve such greatness that she envisioned. How in this life, or in any life to come? I was no great figure in this world, only a writer of plays and even by my own estimation an actor of middling skill. A father without a son to carry on his name. My work would last no longer than the paper upon which it was printed. It would suffer the fate of all earthly things. It would become dust. Dust.

And then the wind would come.

56

I might have told our earnest Stratford vicar this whole story by way of enlightening him as to how the dead can indeed rise again even in this latter day. But wisdom sealed my lips. I share it with you only, dear reader, trusting in your discretion.

Whereby, I conclude.

But not before I offer a brief benediction, to wit:

O Catesby's ghost, with my deft pen I lay you and all your works to rest in both my waking life and in my dreams. Fare thee well, cursed shade, you cunning artificer of treasonous mischief.

Of which brother do I speak, Robert or Gabriel?

Choose whom you will, or both.

Either way, you shall choose truly.

Written by my own hand, at New Place in Stratford-upon-Avon, Year of Grace, 1615.

Wm. Shakespeare, Gent.

9 781839 012860